SNAPPING POINT

A novel by Aslı Biçen

Translated from the Turkish by Feyza Howell

Translator's Notes

Main characters, in order of appearance

Cemal *(ce-MAL)* Grocer who has been looking for his father for twenty years
Halil *(ha-LİL)* Cemal's cousin; teacher at the local lycée
Erkan *(er-KAN)* A lycée student keen on football; Jülide's irksome boyfriend
Saliha *(sa-li-HA)* Cemal's fiancée; held a good job in Izmir, but came back home after having a breakdown
Raziye *(ra-zi-YE)* 'Auntie'; the neighbourhood gossip
Saime *(sa-i-ME)* Saliha's younger sister; lycée student and Jülide's best friend
Melahat *(me-la-HAT)* Cemal's father's second wife
Cemile *(ce-mi-LE)* Melahat's daughter by Cemal's father; a bar girl
Zaim *(za-İM)* Cemile's pimp
Yasemin *(ya-seh-MİN)* Halil's wife
Kadir *(ka-DİR)* Saliha and Saime's father
Hafize *(ha-fi-ZE)* Saliha and Saime's mother
Jülide *(jü-li-DE)* An orphaned lycée student discovering her supernatural powers; Saime's best friend
Seher *(se-HER)* Jülide's maternal grandmother; venerated coffee cup reader
Muzaffer *(mu-zaf-FER)* Intrepid journalist and printer; Halil's close friend
Hakki *(hak-KI)* 'Baba'; rescues Cemal in Istanbul
Rahmi *(rah-Mİ)* Muzaffer's assistant at the printing press
Zeliha *(ze-li-HA)* Rahmi's secret lover
Abdurrahman *(ab-dur-rah-MAN)* Zeliha's husband; Commissioner of Police

Given names are accented on the final syllable as above, so *ce-MAL, sa-li-HA,* etc. Honorifics follow the first name: *bey* (sir), *hanım* (lady), *yenge* (aunt by marriage), *abi* (big brother), and *abla* (big sister), for instance.

A Brief Note on Pronunciation

Turkish is phonetic, with a single sound assigned to most letters. The consonants pronounced differently from English are:

c = j in *jack*
ç = ch in *chat*
j = French j in *jour*
s = s in *sing*
ş = sh in *ship*
ğ = 'soft g' is silent; it merely lengthens the vowel preceding it
r = r in *read*; at end of syllables closest to the Welsh, as in *mawr*
y = English y in *yellow*

The vowels are equally straightforward:
a = shorter than the English a in *father*
e = e in *bed*, never as in *me*
but ~en = an as in *ban*
ı = schwa; the second syllable in *higher*
i = i in *bin*; never as in *eye*
ö and ü = like the corresponding German umlaut sounds

1

A lacklustre glow to the right of the road heralded daybreak, rising between a pair of barren hills flung together carelessly like stunted teeth, as if somehow mislaid on the plain. Having traversed the length of the night and consumed not the miles but the hours, the coach was on its triumphant advance towards the final few minutes. The sun cast the morning from the V of the hills onto the fields nearest the road with the impatience of a catapulted stone, faster and brighter as than when setting. A nebulous wave rippled the crisp green knee-high wheat, which resembled an underwater scene in the subdued light.

With even the most resilient of the passengers having succumbed to an exhausted sleep or a groggy headache after countless hours of shuddering, the dream-heavy coach dipped into, and rose back out of, a deep pothole. Cemal, who had been asleep for hours with the ease of a seasoned long-distance traveller, banged his head on the rock-hard windowpane. His eyes opened sightlessly. The intense gold of the morning sun blended with a fresh green seeped into blank pupils. A fin seemed to rise amongst the timid shoots of wheat before a dolphin slipped back into the involuntary caress of those green leaves, vanishing as soon as Cemal's eyelids dropped, down into the soft, infinitely enveloping ultramarine with a few flicks of its tail. Cemal set off after that perfect creature, drifting effortlessly in the dolphin's wake until he sighted the powerful tail again. At long last, he caught up with the curling body, a body that descended to the shimmering white sands at the bottom of the sea and hung upside down, perfectly still.

Cemal's face felt the light eddies created by the dolphin's gentle movements. He beheld a scene to delight the senses, now that he had caught up with this quick animal, unable to survive in water without air, or in air without water. Flawless beauty tossed into a flawed exigency. Yet as he silently commended the miracle, which was millions of years in the making, he noticed a dark spot below the left flipper: man-made, a later addition, encircled by cables, it was an ominous object.

A bomb.

A primitive terror constricted his heart. Oblivious to the danger, the dolphin was raising sand clouds as it nuzzled the seabed in a likely search for food, unaware of the black full stop placed on freedom. Inimitable and serene, the dolphin continued to root through the sand, as Cemal's hand reached for the smooth, slippery skin; an unfamiliar vitality under his fingertips. *Get that black thing out, get it out, but how, where to grab?* A practically solid urgency, tangible, staunching the waters. Water that staunches the urgency. Water that weighs one down, makes one clumsy, and renders even the most skilful of fingers inept. Water that drags a couple of inches higher than needed, ever higher; water that makes you miss by a hair's breadth, water that tricks. Nimble and determined, and unlike Cemal, the dolphin was expert at this game: far too swift and lithe over the sand.

Cemal was flailing, trembling with that elemental terror peculiar to dreams. Then he spotted a black button in the white sand cloud raised by the dolphin. He knew at once that nothing would be spared once the button was pressed, and what's more, that the dolphin was trained to press the button, that it was nothing but an instrument of death. Cemal looked around to see what it was about to exterminate, but there was nothing… other than himself, that is. His heart sank as the dolphin coiled back before heading for the button…

Cemal's eyes popped open, this time really seeing, whilst his heart was still pounding and a faint ache lay on his forehead. A line of spindly pines slid past the rattling windowpanes and sliced the sunlight, which slipped away from the branches and slapped into Cemal's eyes as if reflected from water. Remembering the dolphin, his insides constricted at the fickle underwater colours of the wheat field stretching from the last tree all the way up to the hills. A perfunctory breeze had cleaved through the shoots, dividing the field like a dorsal fin cutting through water.

Still shaking, he closed his eyes and took a deep breath. All the rickety, tiny, stifling towns he passed swarmed into his mind with a strange sense of restriction. Concrete boxes, never completed beyond the ground floor for some reason, gave rise to a deep ache in a tender spot behind his eye. Places confined by rigid borders, squashed into a minute or two of the coach's movement, catching the eye and the heart in sharp focus.

Just then the coach dipped into another pothole on the crest of the final hill before their arrival and Cemal's eyes opened wide once again. The hourglass figure of sleepy Andalıç rising from the ever vigilant sea greeted him: this was the place he had once thought of as the entire world, before all the other roads, the strange places and unfamiliar people had encroached on the last two decades of his life. That playful, vivacious blue, whose name altered with every tint and shade, spread out inside him; the sea, whose absence rendered any place dead. He wondered how anyone could live without the sea, in landlocked places. He began to breathe easily once again; was there less air away from the sea?

But for that slender connection with the mainland making it a peninsula, Andalıç would have been an ordinary island. As if it had rolled down between the flat, low hills in the background, with the umbilical cord still attached.

With their night-time nets gathered, fishing vessels were returning to the small harbour to the south over the water that had yet to find its right colour. The wrinkles on the face of the old sea raced to the shore, gently swaying the still sleeping town under a blanket of morning mist.

Andalıç started at the water and rose all the way to the sky: old stone houses with tiles bleached by the seasons, cobblestone streets rising up to the hill, the odd tree squeezed into a minuscule garden, a few sad dogs, but most of all, cats. Andalıç was one of the very few towns that the morning sun would have been proud to display amongst all others flanking the country's roads like so many glum notes.

But for that eyesore that was the gigantic concrete block at the top of the hill, erected by the Council on green land, financed by doubling the costs of various services, placing collection tins everywhere and extracting donations from the residents. The Care Home. A boundary blocking the peninsula's flow from the waters up to the skies.

Cemal looked away from Andalıç towards the greyish infinity where the horizon might yet appear. The open vista shrank as the coach descended and the olive groves flanking the road spread their oddly synthetic, dusty grey over the carriageway. The sky appeared to be changing into a more familiar azure. The coach turned left over the funnel stretching towards the peninsula, down between the thinning olive trees, and then it was driving over the water. Covering the mile-long narrow isthmus in a tired wobble, it turned right immediately upon reaching Andalıç and made for the coach station to the north of the peninsula. It went through the entrance, executed a three-point turn and came to a halt with that contented metallic sigh peculiar to old coaches.

This was the final stop, the moment Cemal had been looking forward to throughout the endless journey, and his anticipation deflated at once. He may have got used to sleeping on coaches, but that did not guarantee rest. After a bleary descent, a stretch, and putting on his wrinkled jacket, he gave his eyes a little bit of time off. It was up to his feet now: they could go anywhere on this peninsula unaided.

He set off, watchful of any unexpected traps for his feet, and watching the jumble of images in his mind:

The tiny, bright green, round hill, all but a mound spotted on his way out, but failed to see again this time, despite having carved its location in memory. Unique, perfect, magical. One of those things spotted once by a single eye and lost forever.

The elderly newsagent, a scarf covering her hair, porn magazines dispersed amongst the offerings of her kiosk.

Accident victims at the side of the road, watching the coach with an idiotic smile, weepily grateful for their lucky escape.

And storks everywhere, nesting atop all manners of high objects, striding through fields and circling the skies.

Suddenly he heard a loud call from behind his back:

'Hey, Cemal!'

Turning round, he spotted Hasan, who'd drawn his taxi up by the coach station and was walking to catch up. Cemal went over, an old sense of intimacy flooding over him, an intimacy forged by scabby knees, unripe plums, Uncle Nafiz's slaps, slashed footballs, neighbourhood ladies' shrill scolding, shoes with split toes, and bleached summer hair stiff with salt.

'What's new, Hasan?'

'Same same. You're the one with the news. No luck again, hah?'

'No *abi*. He'd have been here with me if I had.'

'Not even a single word?'

'Not a thing. I'm more annoyed at myself than anything. I keep going away and returning like an idiot.'

'Why are you annoyed? Anyone else would do the same!'

'Would you? For twenty years?'

'It's your dad we're talking about. Easier said than done.'

'Stupidity, more like.'

'Don't say that!'

'I really am sick of it now. That, I guess, is something too. What if I'd left it another twenty years?'

'Are you giving up?'

'Something like that. Yes. Anyway, need to get away, I'm exhausted. I've been on the road for, what, thirty hours.'

'Well, you get to see places, right? OK, OK, don't give me that look!'

'Bye!'

'Bye!'

Cemal started walking back the way the coach had come, towards the isthmus, and turned by the olive oil factory into a hilly street beneath the looming Care Home. The only building visible at the end of nearly all Andalıç's uphill streets. Dropping his gaze, he began a slow ascent across uneven cobblestones, polished into a shiny, dark grey by years of footsteps.

The sun was right at his back, casting an even slimmer shadow of his spare figure onto the slope. The street remained ever the same for him, despite the minute changes over the years. New concrete houses erected over old gardens, an abandoned mansion that grew derelict where it stood, walls repainted to cover the dirt and the flaking paint: immutable even in the midst of all this change. The permanent façades that grant the required constancy to the mortal river flowing between their banks.

The uniformity of the vernacular architecture compounded that sense of constancy. A storeroom-like ground floor with a loo tucked into a corner, a low-ceiling mezzanine for the winter months and a top floor with high ceilings.

A youngster emerged from the ancient freckled door of one of those modest houses whose only adornment was the authenticity of stone. It was Erkan, who chased a ball for the Andalıç Council Sports Club, and who looked up with a smile from the shoes he was wrestling with:

'Good morning, Cemal Abi.'

'Good morning.'

'Where from this time?'

'From Rize.'

'Find him?'

'I wish!'

'Never mind. Sorry abi, but I'm late for training.'

'You're always on your way to training, whenever I see you. But the team always finish at the bottom. You're like me, the lot of you. All training, no result.'

'Noo, abi! Just you wait until next year. We're ready to roar our way back. Our playmaker's well up to speed now.'

'We'll see. Go on, off you go.'

'Goodbye, abi!'

From personal experience, Cemal was skilled at spotting the taint of scepticism in voices. It hung from every single question he asked in every town he had visited for years. Something matt and rusty. It was the touch of that taint that turned the geraniums in some windowsills yellow and sickly, even as others flourished. It poisoned security. It bred on doubts, lifted them higher, always visible.

His head feeling heavier than usual, Cemal passed under the mulberry tree just in leaf, staring at its tiny, prickly, green, unripe fruit. Mulberry is charitable like a countryside fountain, generous with its bounty: but this one's branches reaching out to the street had been lopped off to deter scrumpers. A few more steps took him to his grocery shop. He glanced through the window. Everything looked just as he'd left it, and immediately he heard Raziye call out from somewhere above and to the rear. She looked ready for the attack, curiosity colours nailed to her mast, not that Cemal took it personally. Her range of stares was not vast, dominated as it was by a single variety of curiosity, whether she was staring at a cat, a cloud, or the sea the size of a postage stamp in the distance.

'Are you back, Cemal?'

'I am, Auntie Raziye.'

'What'd ya do son, did you find him?'

Cemal's hopeful look caught an indistinct shadow weighing down the net curtain in another window. The inner voice chiding him since the morning stilled, everything stilled: the neighbourhood 'auntie' Raziye's curiosity, the yowls of male cats and his own voice about to reply. For just a moment, an urgent attention blanketed them all.

'No, I couldn't find him this time either.'

Raziye attributed his momentary hesitation to sorrow.

'Don't worry. Never lose hope in Allah.'

'True.'

'Are you opening the shop?'

'I'll go home first. I'll open up in half an hour or so.'

Despite the determination to keep his eyes on the street, he still hoped that the strange numbness he felt behind his head was caused by a gaze following him. Saliha's gaze, smouldering even behind the curtains.

A sudden cool descended as he turned right, towards his own street hidden by the sun and Saliha. Two decisions uppermost in his mind. The street, too narrow for two vehicles to pass side by side, suddenly widened on the right past four small terraced houses towards the steep hill downwards, the coach station surrounded by four- and five-storey apartment blocks, the isthmus, land, and olive trees.

His family home perched on a rocky shelf. A fifty- or sixty-foot rock wall to the rear and a steep descent in front, leading all the way down to the coach station. The Care Home right above was invisible from the house. Its vista instead was the fragments of sea squeezed between the land and the peninsula, and the grey-green olive-clad hills all the way up to the horizon slashed by the mountains.

His mother's portrait hanging in the sitting room greeted him as he entered the hall. Compared with the terrible yearning inside, this portrait held little capacity to evoke any feeling. All the same, Cemal was unable to stop his voice ringing like a stranger's in the empty room:

'This last one was for you, mum. No more. I couldn't find him this time either. I don't know why I've been looking for twenty years. We'd have found him if we were meant to. I'm done.'

He entered the tiny bathroom of black stone, the bathroom that looked as if a toilet pan and a washbasin had been placed over a shower tray. Removing all his clothes, he stuffed them into the laundry bag, washed with water from the instant heater, wrapped his towel around his waist and had a shave, careful not to bang his elbows on the walls. He picked a clean set of underwear, a pair of trousers and a shirt from the worm-eaten musty wardrobe in the bedroom. His mother's floral frocks caught on his hands. He thought for the nth time *I ought to give them to someone who might need them*. And as quick as the thought itself, he put his nose between the hangers and sniffed deeply. The clothes of an old woman that continue to grow old in her wake.

The wavy mirror that hung on the wall like a fairground attraction had been his favourite childhood toy. He would squat and rise, altering his face beyond recognition, now extending his nose like Pinocchio, now making his lips large and flabby. This time it was his rather unfamiliar distorted nakedness that caught his eye. Perhaps it would be seen by someone else as well in the near future. With an embarrassed dip of the head, he dressed in a hurry, and instead of taking a rest, went out and shut the door.

The scent of his mother's soap was soon wafted away by new moments, draining and unfamiliar, and a decision forced by a desperate fatigue. He reached the shop like a robot, opened the padlock and went in. A mélange of smells chafing at three days of imprisonment charged at the door, stroked him right and left, and shot out into the street. He dusted the shelves with flicks of his father's 25-year-old goose feather duster, and gave a damp wipe to the counter with a greying cloth. After placing the loaves of bread in the cupboard, laying the newspapers out on the display case, and serving the pre-breakfast rush of customers, he strode over to the small room at the rear.

Taking out a perfectly rounded, smooth, hard, yet strangely soft grey-green stone from the pocket of the jacket hanging on the large rusty nail on the wall, he placed it on the narrow shelf behind the door. He then wrote *Rize* on a price sticker, which he affixed to the underside of the stone. One of those perfectly rounded stones he'd brought back from the Black Sea coast, the stones that had conceded all their indentations and protuberances to that crazed sea, become uniform in the face of its tremendous might, and rolled hither and thither, ever smaller like melting snowballs.

There were now twenty stones of varying sizes and shapes lined up on the shelf. Snow-white oval marbles, iron-rich knobs with red veins, rough grey rocks crammed with minute sparkles, and all bearing a sticker underneath with the name of a city: Konya, Mersin, Samsun, Eskişehir, Adana, Bursa, Manisa, Izmir… The stones that were weighing him down; orbiting an old loss like small celestial objects; reminders of decisions retracted each time he heard of an alleged sighting somewhere.

He placed the Rize stone at the very end, a full stop on the right.

A loss, an absence. An absence that set him off to tramp along roads, gather stones, suffer heartbreak, one that gives him hope, makes him break his word, and transforms despair into an obsessive search. A void. A well he keeps throwing stones into, listening for the noise, a well that keeps its secrets to itself: how deep is it? Does it hold water? Stones that existed before anything else, stones inside everything, and stones that will survive everything. That know the void and nothingness and…

'Cemal!'

A soft voice. As soft as every hesitation. Damaged by cigarettes, perhaps, and perhaps other things too.

Cemal put his head round the door and greeted her with the head-to-toe smile, which was known only to Saliha.

'I'm at the back; come over.'

They sat down on the narrow sofa by the door to the tiny back garden.

Saliha's gaze wandered to the shelf of stones behind the frosted glass.

'You couldn't find him?'

'Uh-huh.'

'Perhaps now…'

'I've given up, I'm dropping it.'

'Best thing, really. Are you tired?'

'A little. Your mother not around?'

'She's gone to my aunt's. Dad's at the coffee shop.'

He watched a few strands of Saliha's dark blonde cropped hair moving gently in the faint morning breeze. He'd told her about his first decision. Now for the second. He sought strength in the showy conical calla lilies, with their huge leaves like elephants' ears.

Saliha had always been a bit of a tomboy, his closest playmate. Later, as her body filled out into a more feminine shape, their friendship had dwindled lest 'people talked'. But the idea of love had occurred to Cemal in the final year of lycée, as he felt the mutual understanding in their gazes whenever they met, however seldom, and the important things they discovered during their short conversations. Then Saliha went to Izmir for a degree, and Cemal's love contracted into an ache at the top of his nose, often felt when alone, an ache that one would freeze in the hope of numbing it. Saliha finished university, joined a bank in Izmir, was promoted, and then promoted again, intending to stay there till eternity, and Cemal, unfamiliar with other loves, forgot all about romance.

Saliha was an old friend who only came back on holidays, activating a cherished war wound that ached from time to time. But one day she came back for good. Her goods arrived next. Yes, she'd had a good job, yes, she'd had a good salary, could have had her pick of men, but whatever happened, happened, and she couldn't stand it any more, she ran away. Spoilt, it was said, just had it too good. That's what comes from too much education. She sat in one room for months, blowing through the net curtains the smoke from the endless packs of cigarettes her sister Saime fetched. For months, all that Cemal could see of her was the ghost of a languid white hand that flicked ash out of the window every now and again. 'It's nerves' was the only talk in town. Saliha waited, at the dark threshold into insanity, baulking at the abyss emerging under her feet.

What Cemal had was a heart ... and a shop window to reach out to her. That window was a dusty mess, which had remained roughly in the same arrangement his father had always used. First, he cleared it out; threw out a shedload of junk: drinks bottles placed as décor, faded boxes of a chewing gum last manufactured in the 1980s, the old, broken clock, and a plastic doll. He picked a bright red to refresh the frame and the rust-spotted iron door. When all that was done and the glass had been polished to a high shine, he stood, at a loss what to do next. What does one put in a grocery shop window? Something sufficiently eloquent eluded him, so he stretched an old white bed sheet over the space. And the first reaction came on the very same day. Saliha's right hand and a single eye to the side of the partially drawn curtain. A question: 'Are you going away?'

He was racking his brains for a suitable response as he paced on the rug when he tripped on the tassels, revealing the corner of a poster: a reproduction he'd purchased in Ankara years ago, but never found the right place for. Van Gogh's *Starry Night*. Stars like suns, and the moon. The sky in whirlpools. The golden river behind a dark cypress spread out over the night. Into the cobalt night. The cool that flows down the waterfall hills to the town below.

And so he hung the poster on the white sheet the following day. Saliha drew the curtain to see the feeble light seeping into the mind of another melancholic soul, a light seeping through a tear in *his* night. Her hair was long and messy. She'd put on a good deal of weight. Eyes shrunk and narrowed by relentless introspection. Her lips were pale, and the two lines running down to the corners of her mouth, dark. Cemal placed a stool outside the shop and began to suck a lollipop with relish. A sugary hope spread from the root of his tongue to his ears and the back of his head.

In the afternoon, he sent Saliha one of those lollipops with Saime who'd come to buy cigarettes. He was rewarded the following morning when Saime extended the bread money wound round the lollipop stick.

As the void in his mind began to fill, he removed the white sheet. The poster, now carefully rolled, went with Saime when she came for another pack of cigarettes. Into the window went a huge glass jar filled to the brim with colourful marbles to evoke their childhood games. Transparent and lustrous. He picked a large marble with yellow, green and orange waves. He played with it for an entire day, every time he stepped outside, turning it in his hand, tossing it and catching it again. The marble then found itself in Saime's pocket on her way back from school, and then, that ghost of a hand that appeared outside that window perpetually enveloped in cigarette smoke started moving that marble up and down the length of the sill. The marble magnified Cemal's joy into something infinite before withdrawing in the nook of Saliha's palm.

He ultimately succeeded in drawing Saliha's spirit outside, with tulle-finned red fishes in a globe aquarium, along with a yo-yo he'd played with all day and sent to her using the same method, chocolates, tiny rubber balls in a myriad of colours, rabbit-shaped balloons, and his own hopeful, yet brittle expectation, sitting on the wicker stool. She left the house one morning, her hair long, her face pale, her body heavy. But instead of making straight for the grocery shop, she went down the hill towards the blue of the sea. She entered the shop a few hours later, her hair cut short, and the sweet rosiness of the sun on her face. She bought twenty cigarettes, then handed him an old, faded spinning top she pulled out of her bag. It was the old top he'd given her in Year Two, his own initials still visible.

Brief chats came next, no longer than five or ten minutes. A little longer whenever he could wangle it. Letters that began as brief notes of a few lines, dictated by the shortages of the time, then grew to pages and pages. The need to understand and to explain, the need to know; that need that grows the more it's satisfied...

Saliha's voice brought him back to the present:

'You're not listening.'

'Saliha...'

How could one get ready, prepare for something like this?

'Will you marry me?'

Silence.

Cemal waited, a relentless fear growing blacker, growing larger and rising in clouds.

'We've talked of everything Cemal, but never this sort of thing. Never even said we love each other.'

For one moment, Cemal felt all sense of equality, self-confidence and courage roll down his spine on droplets of sweat. He was silent. With a kindly, curious look at his evasive eyes, Saliha cooled her turmoil by staring at the white cones of the flowers in the garden. She broke the anxious silence, her eyes vacant, in a low, deadpan voice.

'I never wanted to marry.'

Cemal gave a sad sigh.

'I mean, when I was little, all that girls ever talked about was marriage and having kids and that. And I never really cared for any of it. We've never discussed it, Cemal.' She hesitated for a moment, seemed to be reaching out for his hand, but changed her mind halfway through and held her own neck instead. 'I have had other relationships before. Now, when you say marriage, I mean, ... I don't know what your expectations are.'

So the hesitation wasn't over him! Bright sunshiny joy returned, but alongside another emotion which at first, he couldn't name. Hurt.

'What expectations could I possibly have, Saliha? If I were that keen, would I have waited until I was thirty-eight? All I want is to live with you from now on.'

'Are you sure? Are you sure the past isn't going to be a problem for you?'

Cemal gave her a reproachful look. 'Don't you know me?'

'I do, but this is different. When it comes to certain things, men…'

'I'm not a man Saliha, I'm in love with you.'

The word *love* could have held a chill, by the way Saliha wrapped her arms around her own shoulders. She looked at Cemal's excitement, whilst on her own face lay a worry too transparent to be discernible. It was the first time she'd seen him come close to losing his temper.

'Are we getting married?'

She didn't dare drag it out any longer. 'Yes.'

'I'm coming with Halil Abi to ask for your hand this evening then. Tell your parents.'

As soon as he spoke, the broad grin that looked capable of defying anything all day long vanished instantly. 'What if they refuse?'

'We'll just have to elope then, won't we? You've asked me first, in any case. And I've accepted. No getting out of it now… Cemal, *PUH*-leeze: I'm thirty-seven now; they'll probably dance with delight. My father might grouch a bit, but that would be par for the course anyway.'

'Good… good.'

That Saliha's consent wasn't the only one he'd need was a little unnerving. Then he looked into her eyes, looked and wanted to keep looking always. His self-control vanished. He touched her for the first time. Holding both her hands, he kissed the palms one by one. They hugged tight enough to hurt, as if standing before the steps of a train about to depart. Their faces came closer and closer…

'Oi, Cemal!' came a voice.

Cemal leapt to his feet, blushing with an unfamiliar sensation of guilt. An equally blushing Saliha was tidying herself up.

'We're here Halil Abi, round the back!'

'Who's we?'

'Me and Saliha.'

'Bad timing, hah?'

If he'd been more friendly with Saliha, Halil would have wound them up a bit more: but a blush was good sport. Laughter stemming from his bushy moustache rang round the tiny room. Since the only place to sit was the sofa, Saliha stood up to leave once the greetings were done.

'You sit, Saliha, I'm just going to ask Cemal about his father, and then scoot.'

'No Halil Abi; I've got to go. And Cemal's got something to tell you, in any case.'

'Expect the unexpected, I see! So, no news of your dad, but better news otherwise, hah? Well, well; let's hope for the best.'

Halil elbowed the foolishly grinning Cemal in the ribs as Saliha left.

'At long last, lad; you were going to seed.'

Cemal's tongue failed in his slackened mouth before he gathered himself:

'You made her blush, though, Halil Abi! Shame.'

'Of course she will! Standard practice. If this isn't the time to blush, what is? That's the bliss of it, enjoy it whilst it lasts. Sooo: when're we going to ask for her hand then?'

'This evening.'

'God bless: no time to lose, hah?'

'Please, abi. Who's got time to lose?'

'I guess you're right. I'd go now if you said, "Let's go." I wish my auntie was with us now...'

The sobriety that clouded Cemal's face earned him a slap on the back.

'That's life, lad, nothing for it. So, no news of our uncle then?'

'I couldn't find him this time either, abi.'

'Stop now, lad, stop. Enough. From pillar to post.'

'I'm not going any more. I'm dropping it now.'

'That's my boy. He'd have come back, the bastard, if he wanted to. And if he'd died, we'd have heard.'

Cemal's thoughts wandered briefly. Nothing could have been further from his mind than the grocery shop until his eighteenth year. True, he was disappointed when university fell through, but his mind was on big cities. Places with endless chances and opportunities. Change. Movement. But when his father left one day with nothing more than the clothes on his back, slamming the door after a row with his mother, everything he left behind fell to Cemal's lot: his mother, of course, and the shop too. And all that time of dreaming, *If I saved a little, I could do this, if I saved a little more, I could go here,* whilst squeezing only a subsistence from this antiquated shop...

'Don't be so thin-skinned, lad.' Cemal's absorption had been misinterpreted. 'I didn't really mean to call him a bastard. I was angry. I had a lot of time for my uncle, but he was as bloody-minded as a mule!'

'No, no, that wasn't it.'

'What then?'

'Nothing. You know how sometimes you don't get a choice. Like your career and stuff...'

'Yeah, and I was going to become a philosopher. Ended up as the lycée teacher. But I'm not moaning like you.'

'Yes, but at least you got out. You studied in Ankara. You saw everything.'

'What is everything?'

'I don't know; things you can't get here.'

'Just you marry Saliha, then I'll ask you about everything. Look at the state of you! You cheer me up, mate, whether I want to or not!'

Cemal laughed bashfully.

'We'll take my wife and go this evening. You go order some flowers and that. And a box of chocolates. And if they won't give the girl, we'll help you elope.'

'Why do you say that, abi? Something you know?'

Halil was really enjoying Cemal's terror.

'Just winding you up!'

Cemal pounced and the cousins scuffled like schoolboys. With ten years between them, Halil was Cemal's closest friend ever since he'd known himself; always there, his elder brother and confidant. Someone who would always be around even if the entire world came crumbling down.

A metallic sound echoed from the loudspeakers at the Council's appointed news time. The cousins calmed down a little, although routine funeral announcements rarely merited more than half an ear. They were still panting and laughing when they were stopped in their tracks by the name. The announcement was repeated as the two men stared at each other blankly:

MUHTAR UMMAN, SON TO THE DEPARTED HASAN UMMAN, HUSBAND TO MELAHAT UMMAN AND FATHER TO CEMAL UMMAN, HAS MET HIS MAKER. HIS FUNERAL WILL FOLLOW AFTERNOON PRAYERS AT WALNUT TREE MOSQUE AND THE INTERMENT WILL TAKE PLACE AT ANDALIÇ CEMETERY. FOR THE ATTENTION OF HIS KITH AND KIN.

As though waking from a shared dream, Cemal and Halil staggered outside. Gripping the windowsill wide-eyed, Saliha was looking to them for confirmation. Cemal nodded at her, sat down on the stool and covered his face with his hands.

It felt like a fine wire had been drawn out of him. Unknown towns inexplicably familiar, small, dirty hotels that compounded the sense of loss, that miserable hope that sent him down paths he secretly knew he'd return from empty-handed, unfamiliar faces that looked like they were on their way to somewhere nasty, to tend a sick person, or a death in the family in all those late night waits in coach stations, a constant sense of unease in his own home, the short, sharp breath his mother drew in like a needle each time the doorbell rang, searching for a person whose everything you've long since forgotten, searching, searching.

'Don't do that, Cemal; pull yourself together now.'

'What does this mean, Halil Abi? Was he here all this time? Under my very nose. Is it possible? For me not to have seen him once in twenty years – in a town of twenty thousand?'

'I wouldn't have thought so. Keep calm; we'll soon find out. We can find out from whoever it was that placed the announcement.'

The sweet scent of lavender that had always stirred him drew his head upright. So he'd always find her now, whenever he collapsed.

'Can you give me another day, Saliha? Would it be all right if we came tomorrow?'

'Take your time. Whenever you want. See to the funeral first.'

'I can't believe it. Can't believe it. But we've all heard it, all of us. How is it possible?'

2

Having tailed Cemal from the beginning of one night to the conclusion of the next, and skimmed the fluff of Anatolia's parched, barren wastes, the north-easterly spent the midday hours heaping heat over Andalıç. The lifeless soil, all memory of springtime rains gone, turned into dust, sneaking unseen through open windows and doors left ajar, to darken dusters and numb housewives' minds with the tedium of routine.

Invisible motes of dust settled on Cemal's eyelashes too, as he enjoyed a half hour's nap on the sofa at the rear whilst Halil minded the shop, whilst the wind slipped into Cemal's ears to uplift his sleep...

... And he finds himself in an ancient coach. Juddering and rattling interminably. Hens, legs lashed together, cluck clucking. Bags, sacks, bundles, packs falling on his head at every bend in the road, and on his shoulders if he ducks. Ancient women, hennaed dark, scrawny hands covering their mouths with muslin scarves. Yellowing, tiny old black moist eyes sunk into skins like cracked earth. Ten old women with black cloaks flung over baggy floral flannel trousers. Scraggy hennaed braids hanging over bellies and dangling over trousers. The relentless steppe in the background, always the same part of the steppe, and always that one single tree...

They're all staring at Cemal, those women. Ten antique women, all juddering in the same way, at the same time, and straightening cloaks slipping over their heads all at the same time with the hands not covering their mouths, again, all at the same time. Never taking their eyes off him, not even for a moment...

That single tree ever present, near or far on the stony horizon, as the coach rattle rattles on...

Impossible to tell when it draws to a halt, rattling increasingly louder, the relentlessly ageing coach rattles into a station. A deserted station of steppe-coloured, steppe-soil bricks, its boundaries gradually melting into the ground with each rain. All at once the coach halts, bang in the centre of the adobe walls, hollows and crevices. Cemal has to run the gauntlet of the ritualistic swaying of the old women, who are oblivious to the fact that the coach has stopped...

Another coach slowly pulls out of the station behind the women still swaying by the window panes that no longer rattle. Backing out, revealing every passenger as a passport photo, one by one. Like a life-size photo album. And then the last photo in the album, right behind the driver, is his father. Face intent. Set off on this trip just to stare at Cemal just like this, just then, just when he was about to set off, just when he was about to slip through his fingers...

Cemal scrambles to get off the coach, to catch up with him, leaping over the tripping evil stares of every single crone. An obstacle race. Never taking his eyes off his father's stare that has lassoed him by the throat. Trying to keep his feet off those evil stares. But it's too late when he reaches the rear door at long last. By the time he's down, there's no sign of the coach, or of his father...

The only coach travelling in that direction is the one he's in. Complete with the women, bundles, and hens. The stop over, the road again, the steppe again, the same tree again, yet another station identical to the previous one. Tormented between the obstacles of the women and his father's lasso again. And once again, from the top... until he wakes up with a start.

Cemal was waiting in the deep shadow of the gigantic eponymous tree in the Walnut Tree Mosque courtyard, unable to answer a single one of the endless questions of the curious crowd, who had all heard the announcement. He had just finished telling Halil about his dream when the ezan rang out. The congregation went inside. The two cousins remained by the coffin. Hands clasped in front, like footballers lined up for a free kick. Looking guilty. Hands are really tricky when you face a dead body: you can't cross them or press them to your sides. The quick are all guilty before the dead. Even if they were to accuse the dead. His desire to see his father one last time had been blocked by the bitterness fermenting inside for years. For years and years, he had been pursuing the question 'why' under that sour dough, the inexorable weight of pointless abandonment. He looked up: the dove rising over the walnut tree sounded like a wind-up toy. Its wings met in front of the breast bone and then behind its back, alternating constantly.

The answer to the question 'why' now lay lifeless inside the coffin. The question that had bleached the horizons of his mind for twenty years, at every twist of his mother's face, every time he unlocked the shop, every time he acknowledged that the futures he had designed for himself had fizzled out.

'We never knew why he left.'

Halil, who had been posing his own questions to the devotional silence settling over the courtyard, was startled.

'And that would've changed what, exactly?'

'I would've known for sure. I would not have looked for him non-stop. I would have known where he was and why he'd gone away. I wouldn't have spent every moment waiting for him to come back. I might have made a completely different life for myself.'

'Maybe. Or maybe, you'd be living just like you are now. Thought you weren't gonna let it get to you?'

'Easier said than done. There hasn't been a single corner of the land I've not been to over the past twenty years, just looking for him. And then hey, presto: here he is. Except I'm still none the wiser. He's dead.'

Afternoon prayers over, the congregation filed out in ones and twos and stood at the ready. The imam had been called to the hospital on an emergency, so an elder led the funeral prayers. Cemal and Halil shouldered the coffin from the front, and two other men took up the rear as they carried it to the hearse. It felt so light. Cemal recalled his father's rather small stature, as well as the waistcoat he wore all year round, the chain hanging from the fob pocket, and the way he hid his gappy smile behind his hand... For the first time in a long time, his father was not a missing but a real person who had actually participated in a period of his life. Then he regretted not having made any effort to see his father one last time. At the point of the customary response, 'We knew him to be good,' Cemal had not forgiven his father, but decided he would anyway, since the dead man was so light.

The hearse set off. A few relations only seen at weddings and funerals joined them in Halil's VW Beetle. The cemetery was near the western tip of the peninsula, on a hillside a little beyond the coach station. So Cemal had finally found his father on this trip, and lost him for ever. The mid-afternoon sun on his legs inflamed a new numbness inside; it was vexing, not to feel any sadness at all. Just when he had given up the effort to right the wrong he had faced, even that decision had been snatched from him; he was baffled, utterly confused. He raised a hand to shield his eyes from the dazzle of the sea, and his dry eyelashes blinked against his salty palm.

They arrived at the cemetery gate after a drive in the busy traffic of the only artery of the small town, passing between grave faces that had spotted the sad load of the vehicle in front. This feather-light man was carried to a freshly-dug grave. The coffin lid was opened to the sound of prayer. Seeking comfort in the thought of touching his father for one last time, Cemal bent down and froze, a profound shock slapping everyone present before bouncing back to him.

The coffin was empty.

A missing man. A man who managed to stay missing even in death. A man who repudiated him once again just when something definite had been attained, a man who repudiated him for all time. A missing person who mocked those thousands of kilometres that had been traversed as he reappeared at *Go*, whence he promptly evaporated. A father who denied his son even the simplest consolation at the point where all strain came to an end. Always running away, getting away, and never getting caught...

The ground liquefied under Cemal's feet. Anger slashed the long silence. In the darkening blue of the afternoon, the cypresses, woodpeckers' taps, iris petals hanging like heavy drops, shocked exclamations, laughter, Cemal's hands, his fingers growing longer into a tangle, the sweat enslaving his forehead and neck in rivulets, the sharp collar of his shirt, the familiar ache in his left shoulder blade, names filling tombstones, eyes, eyes, eyes: they all rushed over him, like an attack, like the still shocking outcome of an accident watched in slow motion. Cemal tried to walk away from time slowing down in a strange brush with the quagmire of dry reality.

His father wears a blue apron. His hand goes to his left pocket so often that the stitching in the corner is frayed. He puts his hand in the pocket. Takes out the change and extends it to the waiting hand. That's the 20-lira pocket. The tenners are in the other one. The coins are mixed in the drawer. You have to riffle through them one by one as if you were picking over rice. His rough hands, the wrinkles darkened, slice some cheese. The left index finger's nail is black; it's obviously going to fall out. He wraps the cheese in waxed paper and then in a sheet of newsprint. He wipes his hands on a greying, damp towel. Inside the front door, extending his jacket to his wife, four fingers curled like a hook. The dip between his right index finger and the middle finger is stained yellow; he rolls in thin cigarette paper the damp tobacco taken from the case. But the mouth where the cigarette goes is missing, the face is missing, the voice is missing. Empty, blank, no head, no self.

On opening his eyes, his locked jaw aching, Cemal saw the rippling sea ahead and felt Halil's concern from behind. He had yet to figure out how to escape from this ominous film. His brain, which distorted what his eyes saw into a misty blur, remained out of reach.

He saw himself entering the Council building with Halil, who consulted the girl in charge of announcements, grabbed him by the arm and led him outside. They went back to the mosque, faces on the street sticking to them like burr. Halil exchanged a few words with the elder who had led the funeral prayers, then placed Cemal back in the passenger seat of the Beetle and took him to the hospital. They found the imam. As the other two were talking, Cemal realised he was able to recognise words again. The final piece of the jigsaw puzzle settled into place and completed the picture called meaning.

His father really had been in Andalıç. He really had died in Andalıç. His funeral really had been held at Walnut Tree Mosque and he had been buried in Andalıç cemetery. But at noon, not mid-afternoon, as was incorrectly announced. Washed as his wife's… his wife's… The dressing trolley was pushed down the hospital corridor, squeaking in protest at the pain awaiting it. Washed as his wife's tears streamed. His father's wife. His still living wife. The wife that wasn't Cemal's mother.

'Cemal… get a grip, son!'

'What?'

'Stop that blank stare. Are you even listening?'

'Uh-huh.'

'So, what did I say, then?'

'Don't know.'

'There's nothing weird. Just a misunderstanding. The imam led your father's funeral prayers at noon, and your father was buried. Then the imam went to the hospital to see his ailing mother, who'd taken a turn for the worse. And the others there didn't know we were standing by an empty coffin, so they thought there was a funeral.'

'What was the coffin doing there?'

'Search me; it must have been forgotten. Now, pull yourself together.'

'Abi, did my father have a wife?'

'Yes, Cemal, he did. I've got the address. Somewhere called Martyrs Street. Seems that anyone who takes it into his head can just go and rename streets nowadays. I've lived here all my life, never heard of this street. Never mind. I'm sure we'll find it.'

'Abi, what are we gonna do now?'

'Didn't you want to know what was going on? We'll go and ask. Come on, let's go.'

'OK.'

Their footsteps echo on the afternoon-silent stairs. There was something missing in the warmth of the sunlight spilling through the windows. A horde of sorrows steamrolled over all that is wholesome in the external world.

'No, no. I'd better go on my own.'

'You don't look like you could cope.'

'Let's have a cuppa on the seafront. I'll feel better then.'

'Why don't you want me to come along?'

'She may not be able to talk as freely if you're there. Don't know. Actually, it's more like… some things, you need to do alone.'

'I'll walk you to the door, but you're on your own beyond that. Who knows, the house could suddenly vanish too!'

Halil was dragging him by the wrist. Chair, table, tea garden. The sea below wrinkling in a tail wind. The resiny smell of the stone pines to the rear of the peninsula, warmed all day long. Bitter tea catching in his throat as it goes down. He rubbed his head in one big sweep from the forehead to the neck. Kept his hand there briefly, on the cool of his sweat. His fingers were scorching.

He had always been weak before his father. Before those powerful, callous hands. Not physically, perhaps, but always weak. Weak with something that held him back, something he was taught. His father was scared of nothing. Just when Cemal was shaping up into a presence no longer daunted by those hands, his father had slammed the door one evening, leaving his son alone with rebellion and resolve for a confrontation, and did so with derisory indifference. Left without defeat. Without closing the accounts. No chance of a reckoning now. Cemal stopped thinking, alarmed at the sense of injustice bubbling up like a swamp. Watching the capricious ripples of the sea, he conjured up his customary composure. To quell, to forget, to bury.

They left the tea garden and turned into one of the countless climbs of Andalıç. They set off for the street they must have always known, but estranged by its name, asking passers-by and staring at road signs in their own hometown. Since every route to his father had sent him back empty handed, Cemal had no doubt that it did not exist. Maybe they were given the wrong address. Watched by houses jealously protecting their inhabitants behind complicit curtains drawn over someone who didn't want to be found, they were looking for an unfamiliar house where answers and explanations awaited. Cemal stared at the sign that said Martyrs Street. He would have kept staring if Halil had not exclaimed, 'Here we are!' Trying to decipher the numbers on rusty plates or written directly on the walls, they spotted the house tucked into a ramshackle dead end to the right. The old yellow paint showed through the whitewash in patches; flecks of paint clinging to the woodwork suggested they once were blue. A plastic doorbell was tacked, askew, to the door of the metal porch.

'You can go now, Halil Abi.'

'OK, if that's what you want. I want a detailed report later, though, down to the last comma. I'll die of curiosity otherwise!'

'All right.'

Watching Halil's departing back, Cemal hesitated for quite a while at the door. Then looked at the crooked doorbell like it was a dangerous object. Yet this was the only address he had come up with after all that searching. The address that would solve enigmas. A tentative finger reached out. Pressed the round plastic button, but the bell didn't ring. His bent index finger was reaching the glass pane when he heard voices. Pulling himself together, he took a couple of steps back. The door inside the porch opened, and four or five middle-aged, headscarved women spilled out with 'My condolences.'

As they went away, casting him curious glances, Cemal was left at the open door, facing a red-eyed woman of forty or forty-five in a dark dress wearing a muslin kerchief. Something in his face must have rung a bell; her cautious expression relaxed visibly. She took a couple of steps back, feeble hope glinting in dense grief.

'You're Cemal, right?'

'Yes.'

'Come in.'

3

Cemal perched on the edge of the sagging sofa. On a valanced cover that looked dirty even if it was not, a floral pattern in greens and beiges, its flowers unlike any flower. His father's wife placed a plate of helva, made without nuts or cinnamon, on the small Formica table next to him. His father's helva.

Walking through the door, Cemal spotted his father's face bang at eye level, the face that had evaded his memory all this time, the face that made him take an instinctive step back the way he would from a door absently slammed on his face. His father's disembodied head – minus the irretrievably lost mimics – now fitted atop that light, hazy body in Cemal's mind. All that this vacant passport photo face could do was to cover for the memory, which freezes moments without any detail, and which alters as time flows. It was a far cry from representing the vibrancy of the man.

It was the colour version of the photo printed in the missing ads all those years ago. A few more wrinkles, a few more grey hairs. The eyes retreated in an effort to hide their guilt. The stiff lips a little thinner. As Cemal's eyes digested the face of the elusive stranger, the forgotten man transformed from a human being into a quest, as his hands unwittingly reached out to the helva. The bland, soggy pudding grew harder in his throat, resisted going down. He recalled his mother's delicious flaking helva, rich with yummy butter and nuts. He took a deep breath in preparation to speak, the helva went the wrong way and he started coughing. The rusty, creaking sofa joined in an increasingly choking duet. His watering eyes detected a glass of water held out towards him.

'Bless you,' said the woman.

It was impossible to look her in the eye, this woman who had no rights over him, who had stolen all his rights: not only his father, his mother's joy and his own life, but also his inner peace. An unaccustomed anger swelled inside, like something that had been just a duty, accepted, suppressed all these years, like something that would overflow rooms and houses.

'How dare you take that word into your mouth?' he croaked, still coarse from the cough. He had never, ever, in all his life, been quite this confrontational. Staring at the threadbare patches of the carpet, he tried to pull himself together. Compose his mind in turmoil since the cemetery.

'Now, look here, Melahat Hanım. You have no idea what it's like to be searching for your father for twenty years.' They stared at each other, wondering where he had heard the name. Neither recalled the funeral announcement. A spooky silence fell. The grief in Melahat's eyes was crushed by something more urgent, an accusation or an obligation to defend. She stammered.

'Cemal... Cemal Bey. It's hard, I mean. But I...' She either had to start at the beginning of a very long tale, or stay silent.

'I'm only here because I was curious about certain things. I'd been looking for my father everywhere for twenty years. Was he alive, was he dead...'? The account gave way to anger. 'How long have you been here for, for God's sake?'

Melahat was caught off guard once again, as is standard in every interrogation. 'We... not long... A couple of weeks...'

'Where the bloody hell were you before?'

'Eskişehir...'

'A-ha, Eskişehir! Eskişehir, eh; I must've passed through it a thousand times if I...'

Closing his eyes, he took a deep breath.

'And anyway, how the heck are you my father's wife? My father never divorced my mum.' The funeral announcement was recalled by both at the same time. Cemal's voice was beginning to get back to normal as it crashed around the room.

'I mean, like... his wife... after your mother's death...'

'It's only been a year, just over.' Cemal glanced at his father's photo. 'How did he know about mum's death? We never heard a peep from him.'

'He knew someone who had married a woman from around here. They came to stay with her family once a year. He used to ask that bloke.'

He thought about this man he didn't know, his father's spy: a man who had passed by a corner of their lives, carrying whatever he had gleaned to his father; but all the while, nothing came in the opposite direction – an unfair one-way traffic. His father had observed them through a two-way mirror; all they could see had been their own desperate torment, their guilty curiosity, their accusing anger.

'What kind of man… so heartless, so…' Words that eluded him, words he could not say or bear to think of, poked him up to his feet.

There was alarm on Melahat's face.

'Cemal Bey. Sit down, Cemal Bey. Don't say that. He was your father, after all.'

'What a father, though!' A nasty smile spread below the steely glint of his eyes. 'Farter, more like. Did he even want to see me once when he'd got here?'

'Maybe he did. I mean, he always spoke of you. I wouldn't have heard of you otherwise, would I? But he'd had a stroke. Couldn't even speak.'

Cemal fixed his eyes on the corner of the picture stabbed into the green wall.

'So how did he tell you he wanted to come home?'

'He didn't. I did. This is my hometown.'

Cemal looked again at the green walls of the tiny house that was so like his own.

'You're from here?'

'Yes.'

The sofa complained once again. 'Did my father run away with you?'

'Yes.'

…

'Actually, I didn't tempt him. I mean, I didn't say, let's run away. I said, you've got a family and all, but…' She was picking at a crumpled handkerchief soggy with tears. Silence was harder than accusations, harder still to manage. 'I had to get away.'

With a snort, Cemal squinted.

'Why?'

'I, here… I mean, he didn't run away from you. I was in a bad way. I had no mum or dad.' She stared blankly at the walls around her. 'I lived here with my big brother. But my brother… I mean, he gambled a lot. Gambled at home too. His mates all came round.'

'Yeah, sure. You had no other way out but to tempt a married man with a family, to run away with him. Like it was so hard to find a single man to marry!'

Melahat drew strength from his pause, and whatever it was that was stopping her from letting him go. 'No, no. My brother… to pay his gambling debts… making me erm… his mates. I couldn't stand it. Your dad rescued me.'

'So dad's a hero. There was no other way to rescue you?'

'Like… but he… now when you say that…' She blushed bright red. 'He fell in love. I mean, we fell in love.'

Cemal lingered on that word. 'Let's say all right to that too. What about never looking us up, never sending word… Why? What did he have against us?'

'He couldn't face you. He didn't talk much. Didn't really say much at all. In all these twenty years, I've only said once, "Go and see your son." When Cemile was born. When I became a mum too. "I can't face 'em," he said.'

Cemal, who had returned to this long day from an even longer trip with two major decisions, been greeted with indescribable joy at the quietest hour, was invited by a PA to bury his father in fact and not just in his mind, whose sanity slipped away at the abrupt absurdity of twenty years wasted on traipsing after a loss, and was finally offered some closure with a brief summary, gave Melahat a hapless look.

'What? What did you just say?'

'Your dad and I had a daughter. You have a half-sister.'

Melahat pulled out a photograph from the drawer of the TV stand next to her. Suddenly the walls looked far too green to Cemal, a green that wasn't green, the green of confinement, school green, the revolting green of classrooms imprisoning for endless hours of endless tedium the irretrievable time called childhood.

The face of a young girl concealed the yellow-black cigarette burn in the threadbare rug on the sofa. In a lycée uniform, ponytail and a blow-dried fringe, as much pink on the lips as allowed, a precocious gravity in the eyes, heavy eyebrows above Cemal's eyes, Cemal's and his father's brown eyes often mistaken for black. A dark girl like her mother.

'Is she still at school?'

It was strange for her not to be home on the day of her father's funeral.

'No. That's an old picture. She finished school last year.'

'What did you say her name was?'

'Cemile.'

A name that was derived from his own and gave him a faint ache from the ear to the neck.

'So where is she then? Is she coming?'

'She isn't.'

Melahat was crying, but not for her husband. There was something impenetrable in her eyes.

The idea that the sister he had only seen in a photo may also be dead flitted through Cemal's mind.

'Don't tell me she's dead too?'

'I wish!' said Melahat in a bitter sympathy.

Cemal knew what the phrase meant.

'She run away?'

'Yes.'

'Did she get married?'

'Nah.'

He settled back to hear yet another tale soaked in salty tears. A day of new surrenders just when he thought he could surrender no more.

'She was in her last year; some bugger started pestering her. We had no idea. We couldn't buy her things on our workers' wages. He turned her head with gifts and stuff. She was young of course, didn't know no better. Seems he said, I'll ask your father for your hand when you finish school. One day she came home in tears. He'd taken her to his place and had his way with her.'

As if to avoid blurting out family secrets before a stranger, her husband's son or not, Melahat covered her mouth with her handkerchief, stared at the carpet for a while, then shook her head. Her tears had dried.

'She was doing well at school. Had really good marks. Her dad was going to send her to university. "Don't worry mum," she sez, "Zaim's gonna to marry me." Curse his name. "He'll come to ask for my hand," she sez. I didn't make a peep. She finished school. Idled about for about a year, saying she was preparing for university exams. Last year she left saying she's off to the exam, and never came back. Left a letter. "I'm off to Istanbul with Zaim, we're gonna get married there." That's when your dad had a funny turn; he never really got better after that. He loved his daughter, cherished her.'

So Cemal had nothing to teach his father about loss.

Melahat paused for several deep breaths, the way people choke with fear at finding themselves all alone at a point when life presents few, if any, new options. The handkerchief was pressed over her heart now. So it wouldn't rattle around in her chest.

Staring at the photo on the TV stand, Cemal decided his loss was greater than his father's. At the end of the day, you could understand a girl running away from home. The reasons were obvious. Nothing that would leave you in great uncertainty. At worst, it was infuriating. A fury that didn't consume you. Something that a stubborn fellow like his father could shake off unscathed. But a father abandoning his only son and vanishing, never calling again, never wanting to see him or talk to him again, especially as they'd never fallen out or anything...

'Course, he never married her.'

Cemal raised his head, startled.

'Are they living in sin?'

'Nah.'

Melahat paused to prepare herself for the pain of this truth, which she would hear from her own voice for the first time.

'She went bad. Our neighbour downstairs in Eskişehir spotted her at the side of the E5. Stopped and invited her to his car. Gave her advice. He'd have brought her back. But Cemile knows what her dad's like. She waited for her chance and ran away. Must have been scared.'

The thought of his sister gave Cemal a detached sense of sadness. The kind you could feel for anyone, an impersonal sadness. A girl he'd never met, didn't know, a girl he'd heard of only in the snatches of her mother's conversation. Hard to know what she ran away from and what she ran to. She may have taken a foolhardy step in a moment of madness and then found it impossible to get back, or perhaps, she liked what she had let herself in for, and didn't want to get back. Even compassion eluded Cemal's weary mind, nor did have any idea where this conversation was leading. This stranger who was sharing all her secrets, looking for help, and a strange sister popping up into his life at the age of thirty-eight. A vulgar melodrama falling into the core of a no-longer-real world: women being sold for gambling debts, seductions, elopements, and fallen women. Was he really awake, or still sleeping on the sofa in the shop?

'Cemal Bey; she's your sister, even if you don't know her. Find her. Rescue my daughter. She wasn't a slapper; that bugger turned my kid's head. She'll come here straight away if she hears her dad's dead. She won't be scared any more. Find her and bring her back. Don't let her go to waste amongst those scumbags.'

A gloomy light drowned the last corner of wakefulness in Cemal's mind. This tale he'd been listening to with a foolish torpor was actually a plea. The chest-constricting role of the big brother setting off to save his half-sister from the filth she had fallen into. His stomach sank under the increasingly hotter presence of a chestful of air wickedly clinging to the walls of his lungs, refusing to leave. Desperate for a fresh breath, he emptied his lungs noisily. Then his father's halva started burning his stomach. He forced himself to feel pity, something more personal than mere blood ties. It would be needed for this mission.

A new search bubbling up where twenty years of search had ended. Roads again. Questioning total strangers again. An utterly unknown, menacing world. A duty that may be well-nigh impossible. A humane duty. Negated by a sense of imposition. Imposition.

He looked at his father's eyes in the photo, expecting to see a triumphant scorn in that gravity. A father who abandoned his son, and died of grief when his daughter abandoned him.

Istanbul popped into his mind. On hearing 'news' from there some five or six years ago, he had jumped on a coach. The body of a wino found on the street matched his father's description. The police took him to the morgue to identify the body. Cemal had been tense, the inevitable tension of extraordinary situations, despite having seen several dead bodies before and thus inured to that particular fear. The cloth over the dead man's face had been drawn back slowly... and the man's eyes had popped open just then. The petrified constables took to their feet as the attendant shouted behind them: 'It's quite normal, it happens, don't worry, come back.' But the old wino's eyes had held the same mockery behind the mask of stubbornness in his father's photo. As the dead man's face was covered again, something inside Cemal had altered irrevocably.

He was going to Istanbul again. Was he? He had to. He didn't want to. He knew he would. He had not yet said anything. Evading Melahat's pleading eyes, he said, 'Let me think about it.' She knew he would go. Why was he always going, though? How did some total stranger know he would?

Putting his shoes back on, his index fingers used as a shoehorn, he stood up, opened the door and walked out.

4

A toasted sandwich, an aspirin, ten hours of sleep: the morning that followed all this, found Cemal gawping at the wall exactly one minute before the alarm rung at seven thirty. He opened his eyes in his own room after a very crowded, very complicated dream where he and Saliha ran hither and thither, met weird people in weird places, and a shedload of other, now forgotten, incidents took place. He had flung himself out of bed to escape something darker than the darkness, something that had broken off from the top of the mirrored wardrobe in the dark room and flapped its wings in a nosedive aimed at his face. Now he was staring bemused at his suddenly bright bedroom, a raw ache at his knee. Then he realised that the room where he had flung himself out of bed and the one in which he had fallen to the floor were not one and the same. The picture in his brain might be identical, but one was a dream, and the other was real – because it hurt.

Wrenching himself free from the glue of the exhaustion, heartache and tension of the past couple of days, he struggled to sit up on the carpet. One of his slippers had left a circular impression of ache bang on his shoulder blade. His knees were reluctant to straighten up, as if waiting for a tempting promise. It didn't take long for Cemal to find it. Saliha. Gone were knees, wrists, waist, back: his whole being throbbed with an extraordinarily transformative thrill. Chuckling at the unprecedented state of his 38-year-old heart, he went to the toilet. As he peed, his eyes grew serious as if what he was doing – what he was holding – had taken on a totally different meaning.

Applying on his solemn face the brush he had lathered on an old fashioned shaving soap, he decided to shave the solemnity alongside the beard, and indulge the irresistible excitement inside. It was a little new. All his excitement to date had been gloomy, anxious, troubled. Things to shake off as soon as possible. But this was an excitement to cherish, shimmying like the sea in the south-westerly, slapping one into an intoxicated goofiness. Skin stinging with eau de cologne, he got dressed whilst wearing a constant smile and walked out into the warm May morning. Before entering the shop, he sent a low *Good morning!* to Saliha's window, to the netting he often found quite useless, and occasionally, quite chatty.

He set about his usual tasks, shaking his head at the pleasant kookiness of talking to himself. Chocolates and flowers were for Halil to arrange, or rather, Halil's wife; all that Cemal had to do was to wear his only suit and appear at the scene as neatly as was humanly possible. He intended to sneak off to the barber at a slack time.

Ours is the lad, ours is the lass, hey hey hey

Ours is the lad, ours is the lass

The merriment in his voice unaccustomed to singing sounded quite callow. Chiding himself, trying to rein in his elation, he moved on to a more sombre song:

Oh give me a light

For my cigarette

Sway this way

So I can wake

Yes, the intensity of this song that balanced the joy in his voice was more appropriate. Admiring the heavenly image of wife Saliha swaying towards him to wake him, he carried on murmuring between his teeth bashfully.

Tall rise ships' masts

He stopped at this point for a mischievous chuckle. In ones and twos, customers turned up as that grin sneaked over his face.

In between images of her rushing into his mind at every moment of the day, Saliha went past his eyes like a scheduled train, leaving Cemal with countless photos of her face in various lights. She was on her way to the hairdresser, or maybe to buy a dress, had they run out of coffee, or was she going to get a men's white handkerchief... An imperceptible tremble in Cemal's hands rippled the sweet anticipation inside the shop and caused minor, clumsy accidents until evening. People coming in and going out, chats dotted with plenty of repetitions, 'Pardons?' and 'Ehs?' Still in that frame of mind, he closed up early, slipped over to the neighbourhood barber's at the corner, and exchanged some of his hair and a little growth of beard for a Mr Nice Guy face. Went home, washed in the narrow bath until his skin was as pink as his mother's, ironed his snow-white shirt – no creases in the sleeves – put on his suit and fixed his eyes on the minute hand. During the hours and hours it took for Halil and his wife to arrive, it moved an astonishing fifteen minutes.

The next part was recorded in Cemal's mind in gaps. The bit from his house to Saliha's faintly damp hand was missing. Then he had sat with his knees firmly pressed together, rested his hands on his knees, gave unremembered answers to unremembered questions, and when Saliha's father Kadir turned his head at the traditional opening of 'By God's will ...', an impulse to bite his knuckles until they bled rose inside. He had struggled with that impulse for a very long time, too long to recall, before it was whispered to him that being hard of hearing, Kadir could only respond if the question were repeated, and Cemal regained his own hearing. Kadir's lukewarm and noncommittal 'If it is fated,' accompanied by a scornful look, received a glare from Saliha; Cemal's response was sweat trickling down to his chin from the front of his ear. Then came a period generally dominated by Halil's voice, shapes and colours remained indistinct, and a period of incredulity that Saliha was given to him. That period had come to an end with the appearance of the coffee tray and Saliha's suggestive cough. Reaching out in his haste to make up for the wait, he had spilt the coffee on his trouser cuff, sparking off a general wave of merriment.

It was just at that point when everything suddenly became clear and he followed Saliha past the dim landing into the kitchen illuminated by a bare bulb. Saliha was wetting the corner of a clean cloth, placing one hand under the trouser leg and trying to wipe off the coffee stain with the other. The soft dip between knuckles cradled Cemal's shinbone at times, then the pointed knuckles banged against his leg. He couldn't recall if his legs had ever been touched that way. He would have kissed Saliha's glossy hair if Saime had not been poking fun at him from the doorway. Unfortunately, they had to return to the sitting room once the spots had been sprinkled with eau de cologne to prevent staining.

Cemal had then tumbled towards the door amidst Kadir's grumpy *Love is blind, ... Like I'd have given my daughter away to this bloody grocer if she hadn't hit thirty-seven? My precious daughter I'd sent to universities and all!* expression, Halil's chatter hoping to break the ice, Hafize's sighs, 'Wish your mum was here to see the day,' Hafize on the threshold of turning into a mother-in-law, Saime's taunting gaze, Yasemin's silent smiles and Saliha's unmistakable presence, mere presence: along with the thought that she would soon always be there.

Once the door had shut over Saliha's gaze, visible until the very last moment, and Halil landed a customary punch on his back, Cemal noticed the last coolness before summer's heat made a mockery of night-time, the overpowering perfume of the silverberries and the happiness clamouring for attention inside.

Now he was in bed. In the DOUBLE BED he had assumed would always fail to validate the promise in its name. The surplus energy as he turned to the right suggested sleep would elude him for a while yet. The emptiness beside him was no longer an absence or deficit; now it was a space assigned to a loved one. Knowing it was a silly thing to do, he still stroked the spot where a second pillow would go. Inside him rose a desire with the bit between the teeth. A haste. He turned to the left. Hope was exhausting. His eyelids grew heavier. Feeling the hard touch of Saliha's knuckles just above his ankle, he fell asleep.

Cemal was trying to get used to a new status. Getting used to not having to imagine Saliha's scent. Bringing his nose close to her hair at every opportunity to breathe in her haze without closing his eyes or being too obvious with those deep inhalations.

What determined his rhythm was not the speed demanded by daily life or the slowness of the lazy depths of his mind. It was Saliha's brisk, low-heeled gait, so unlike any other woman's. Walking seemed to weigh down the majority of the women he saw on the street. Saliha, on the other hand, appeared to be reconciled with gravity.

Then, occasionally, when they faced someone coming in the opposite direction on pavements narrowed further by trees and tin signboards, he would fall back a step and touch a point between Saliha's shoulders and waist, a touch that made him float like a paper kite. That's when a muscle right over the spine, right where he touched, trembled towards his fingers. Wondering if he'd been imagining it, Cemal would press a little harder and be rewarded with a deepening of the hollow in Saliha's lower back. Once the path had cleared and he was able to resume walking beside her, he would place his index finger and thumb into the hollows on either side of the hard elbow bone, and, in the peachy light, watch the miraculous golden down where her short sleeve ended.

And greeting acquaintances together: that was unlike the greeting by a single person. First of all there was the shyness of novelty. It was also a greeting given by a more crowded place. By a shared life, the power of intimacy, the joy of a start.

Saliha's attempts to forgo 'engagement shopping', something she found utterly unnecessary, had smashed against her mother's wall of indignation; the only negotiation had therefore been over the length of the list. Her mother had finally settled for a few pieces of lingerie, one dress, one pair of shoes, and a ring. So now they were trying to take as long as possible over the shopping, done in this order and unusually, unchaperoned; even though they knew what to buy where, being locals, in a silent complicity, they still spent as long as possible in every single shop.

At times when he had been able to overcome the wonderful pleasure of watching Saliha in silence, Cemal had introduced the matter of Cemile in bits, asking for her opinion as well as a kind of permission for this task he had to get on with sooner rather than later.

'The Cemal I know would never rest easy unless he went.'

'Why do you say that? I may not go.'

'You couldn't not go. You're so kind…'

'You make it sound bad. Like I was an idiot.'

They were sitting, drained of energy, in a tea garden. The yellowish tinge didn't bode well for the quality of the tea. Cemal took out his spoon and laid it in the sloppy saucer.

'I really don't know what to do.'

Saliha gave a teasing laugh. 'You'll never rest until you save her.'

'That's not it. I mean, if I was sure I could…'

'See?' She laughed out loud. Then suddenly grew serious. 'I've never seen anyone saved so far. Nothing can save a person. No religion, no revolution, no work, not even love. If you want to sink, you'll sink all the way to the bottom.'

Cemal's face fell. 'Don't say that. Love's different.'

A small fishing boat was hauling anchor right in front of the tea garden. Tiny explosions woke up the engine, the lines were thrown and the boat moved out. It briefly sliced through the dazzling brightness of the water. Then the light spread everywhere. Cemal raised his head to find a kindly smile on Saliha's face.

'Who's next after you save your sister? Better make you a cape, eh?'

'Don't wind me up.'

Saliha had failed to change the subject. 'Why are you sulking, though?'

'I'm not sulking.'

'You are sulking.' She was hoping Cemal's expression would change at her words as it usually did, but it didn't happen. 'What's bothering you?'

'Don't know.'

A rust-bucket of a village route bus clattered to a halt at the stop nearby. A few people at a table sprang to their feet and hastened towards it. The hissing of the door, the smell of raw exhaust, then the acoustic void that follows a rattle. A fleeting, empty sense of peace.

'Dad left us because he fell in love with that woman. Love makes you give up your most precious things. If that's what love can make you do...'

'Do you think falling in love was enough of an excuse for him to vanish?'

'I guess so.'

Water dripped right into the heart of the light as waves tautened the ropes of the moored boats.

'You mean you've forgiven your father then?'

Lost in thought, Cemal was staring at the tiny rings spreading on water that was nothing more than a golden light.

Saliha laughed. 'Don't tell me you never blamed him?'

'I did. Of course I did. Just don't know if I've forgiven him, though.'

'Didn't love make you forgive?'

Saliha was unprepared for the hurt in Cemal's calm gaze when he looked away from the boats still bobbing up and down.

'Do you think love's something ... unimportant? Can't it change anything in anyone's life? Can't it make life better?'

'No, it's not unimportant. Don't you think it's silly to bang on about its importance? Going on and on about love. Some things just need to be experienced. Why the need for so much talk?'

With endless thoughts rushing into their minds, the couple squinted at the horizon. Cemal focused for a while on the conciliatory finger gently stroking the edge of his hand. He raised his head, but his sweetheart's head was turned away in a little, ordinary, everyday forgetful moment, far away from this moment stretched by his soaring heart.

There was something dark in Saliha, something that prevented her from stretching those moments of pleasure scattered by the day, or extending them beyond what was allowed by the hours. When it came to nice things, she was no good at prolonging, stretching, or sipping at them sparingly. She was too loyal to the seconds, minutes and the commands of a grumpy mind. Pleasures did not get a tenth of the attention wounds did. She was capable of staring sadly at the deep blue sea in the wonderful warmth of May, sitting next to her sweetheart. Cemal beckoned her back with a tug at her little finger.

'What're you thinking of?'

'I don't know. I was looking at these people. Holidaymakers. They rave about this place. It's just a lovely place as far as they're concerned. Just another lovely place. One of those certified lovely places everyone goes to.'

'You never view your hometown in the same way, of course.'

'Exactly. No, it was something else I remembered. All the girls lied at lycée when they went out.'

She opened her mouth as if to continue. Took a restless breath and fell silent. Cemal imagined a scary heap of things she didn't say. 'And went off to meet their boyfriends?'

'No, not always.'

'If they're not meeting their boyfriends, why are they lying then?'

'Because they were never allowed to go just for a stroll.' She played with the tea at the bottom of the glass. 'I remember how oppressive it was as a child and a teenager. That's why I ran away. You've got the sea, but no air. Don't go out, don't look at anyone, don't make anyone look at you, don't make friends with boys, stay at home with the girls. Perhaps Cemile, too...' The end of the sentence hung in the air in an explicit hint. Realising she was talking of someone she had never met, she held back.

'Perhaps. We'll ask her if I find her.'

The prospect of never finding Cemile, or that she might refuse to come back if she were found, was dispiriting.

'The worst things in the world seem to happen to women.'

She continued, seeing the quizzical look on Cemal's face.

'That's not necessarily true. But women are more vulnerable. Simply because of their bodies. Because their bodies can be bought and sold. Because they can be someone else's property or honour.'

Cemal cast an uncomfortable look at his hands.

'I guess you're one of these men who find such conversations awkward.'

'No. Just upsetting.'

That was the moment Saliha realised that Cemal always wanted adoring gazes, all the troubles of the world forgotten in his presence, and hear either sweet nothings or a happy silence.

Unwilling to see her own blues amplifying in the dark mirror of his eyes, she gave his knee a surreptitious squeeze between hers, and was rewarded by the candied apple gloss spreading on his lips.

They got up. Zigzagging between the tables, they emerged into a sun almost as warm as in summer. Saliha extended her hand into the crook of Cemal's arm, which he bent, and they walked arm-in-arm for the first time. Her hand was so light that he clutched it into the crook of his elbow so it wouldn't escape. An overpowering warmth spread below his ribs. Maybe it was May, maybe the dipping sun, the thronging marketplace, the aroma of newly ground coffee, their reflections in the shopwindows walking alongside them, the cat twitching whiskers at a huge crow, or the crow's croaking threat.

Their heads tilted up for an inadvertent look as they walked into the jeweller's, passing cautiously under the sign maker's stepladder.

'Hello, Uncle İhsan, are you changing the sign?'

'Yeah, yeah. It was twenty years old. Got really rusty, ready to fall on our heads at any moment. And we're having to pay twice as much tax because of it.'

'Why is that?'

'Not everyone gets it, girl. They're taxing blue-and-white signs at twice the rate.'

'I don't get it.'

'No tax at all when it's red and white. Other colours, normal tariff. Blue-and-white: double tariff. This bloke's gone and proper lost it.'

Saliha burst into laughter. 'Get away!'

'Funny, yeah? Keep laughing.' The jeweller's senses, honed by years of experience, caught their mood at once. 'Yes, Cemal; you don't usually have much to do with our shop. It's my turn to ask what's up with you.'

'No, no.'

'I guess you're looking for engagement rings then.'

'I give up, Uncle İhsan; read that on our foreheads or something?'

'We-eell, all but. We never heard a thing, Cemal. We thought you were left on the shelf. So this lovely young lady has rescued you, eh? Congratulations. God bring it to a happy end.'

When they walked out of the shop, two plain rings nestled in a tiny box in Cemal's pocket and a small clover in a green gem hung on Saliha's neck, bought over her objections.

The shopping was done, time to go back, steps slowing down. Discussing the fine details of the engagement in a low voice, they carried on walking without a single look at the streets they knew by heart. Being a couple meant being out without taking the slightest bit of notice of the outside world. Cemal was getting impatient the more he thought of this hilly street, or, as he no longer had to carry on searching, other hills elsewhere, of unlocking the door with a clang of keys and entering their own home with Saliha. They were about halfway up when a young girl walked out of Saliha's home, a girl he frequently saw with Saime: her closest friend Jülide.

There was no one about when Cemal entered the hall on the pretext of dropping the parcels. A faint patter upstairs, but the ground floor looked deserted. He was about to walk past Saliha to reach the door when he realised he couldn't. Because she was in front of him and her arms were on his neck and he had inadvertently held her by the waist and clutched her to his chest and her lips were too soft to pass by and her tongue too firm. A creak on the top step and Cemal was outside the door in a flash, a raging riot in his groins. Three steps and he was panting at the grocer's door, his hair tousled, and he'd not even thought of saying, 'See you.' He opened, entered, shut and leant against the door. Then he looked around dazed and opened it again.

5

The north-easterly's taken the gloves off again. Pressing down in its haste to toss the searing heat of the minor continent into the waters of the Aegean. Almost as if it belonged to Andalıç. Not a capricious infantile breeze like the south-westerly, puffing and panting, pausing exhausted one minute and blowing in a frenzy the next, heating instead of cooling, getting lost, and attacking left, right and centre. The north-easterly is sombre, consistent, true, reliable. In summer or winter clothes, it rams Andalıç amidships. Often it rests at night, sleeps, lies down, calms down, its curses no longer heard or transformed into simple rebukes. It's angry, is the north-easterly. It blocks your way, holds you up, squares up to you, shoves you in the chest, stuffs your ears with obscenities. It comes laden with the black bile of the Black Sea, fractious with the perversity of the steppe, chafing and abrading relentlessly. So much so that, occasionally, it doesn't let up even at night. It slaps and slaps to goad trees into a fight and squeezes reedy wails out of the narrow streets between stone houses; 'None shall sleep!' it declares when *it* is sleepless. It dominates dreams and shoves unease down the throat, sneaks in through the windowsills and under the doors, a swarming presence.

At times, when it whips up that sequin-sized bit of sea in between and smashes it over the isthmus, the residents seem to get a bit queasy, feeling as if they were in a ship pitching over a swell; despite the fact that most have never sailed. A sly, imperceptible rise and fall. Nothing weird as far they're concerned; they've grown up with it, and they rarely leave their little town anyway. If they feel giddy, they repeat a word heard from their grannies and grampas: 'porazladım,' I've been touched by the *poyraz*, from the Greek *boreas* for *north* transformed in Turkish mouths.

Andalıç shelters in the south of the peninsula from the north-easterly's fury; it has been blowing for three days and nights. Relentless, guileless, its anger familiar. Refusing to be forgotten even for a moment; it makes you forgetful, enervates, won't leave you alone: always beside you, like a depressive imaginary friend.

The sun sets in a bright yellow rush, hardly reddening at all in the sharp blue sky devoid of a single cloud. The orange light striking the roofs in Andalıç from the side has roused the spirit of the clay and animated the tiles. White walls appear rosy, blues lilac, and yellows and reds could have been kindled by an inner fire. A warm syrup has been dribbled over the town. Illuminated roofs float over streets flooded with dark shadows.

The roof of the house opposite Jülide's is similarly clad in the colour of dying embers. The north-easterly is shaking a loose tile right at the corner. Slipping in through the cracks of the closed window, it moves the yellowing net curtain, shakes the unripe green mulberries off the tree in the tiny garden of the house opposite, tousles the mane of the skinny dray horse lashed to a cart a little higher up the street, clatters the old wooden gate with the loose latch, whistles furiously in the narrow gaps between the houses, wuthers through the needles of the large stone pine to the rear, rustles random carrier bags, sweet wrappers and clumps of dry weeds down the cobblestone slope, displaces anything and everything it can lift, draws a scream out of everything it can, swaggers in an excess of sound and motion.

Staring at the loose roof tile at the corner, the one that has – for just about ever! – been on the verge of falling, Jülide tries to isolate its rattle in amongst all those sounds.

'Oh, Auntie Seher, as God is my witness: I found it like I'd placed it there with my own hands. And you'd said a white cupboard, right? I've got a towel cupboard in the bathroom, white. You know you said on the second shelf, under something… That's where the guest towels are. I lifted them, and blow me down if it wasn't there! God bless you.'

The rattle of the roof tile evaded Jülide's ears, but her grandma's smile didn't. She heard the rustle of the hundreds of crow's feet and lines around her mouth along with the wrinkles on her cheeks and chin as they deepened. Checking her own mouth itching to stretch, she turned back, her eyes glinting with a smile only her grandma could see.

‘That’s all fine, Auntie Seher, but who’d ’a put my bracelet there? Strike me blind in both eyes if it was me. It wouldn’t matter but, I fell out with my neighbour of these many years! Remember the bracelet was lost when her sister-in-law had come over? She’d helped me with the washing up. Thought I’d sound her out, my neighbour, I mean. She twigged at once. Was really cross. God knows, I’ve upset my neighbour of these many years.’

‘Go, talk to her, lass. Apologise. Explain. Neighbours need one another’s sweepings. Come the day, and she’ll be closer to you than a sister.’

A flick of her grandma’s eyebrow prompted Jülide to her feet. When she stood up, the chair with a leg shorter than the others rattled to join the chorus outside. The shadows flooding the streets rising over the roofs had swallowed up the enchanted colours and the yellowish light indoors had also vanished. Jülide was on her way to the little hall, one side of which served as the kitchen, when Şadiye Hanım called out:

‘Hold on, Jülide, hold on. Don’t bother with coffee or anything now. I’m leaving, it’s getting late.’

‘Sit, lass; you’ve only just arrived.’

‘No, Auntie Seher. I’ve left the pan on the cooker. My sister-in-law’s family are coming over in the evening. If you could maybe read her fortune when you have a mo? She has a brother in the army. The lad’s a bit down in the dumps, it seems.’

‘Bring her over, of course. I’ll do it.’

After seeing her off, Jülide picked up the bag Şadiye had hung on the nail by the door upon arrival. Inside was the typical Andalıç coffee: dark, heavy roast, and a packet of sugar. Neighbours made a habit of hanging a bag on that nail whenever they came to have their fortunes read by Jülide’s grandma. They contained a variety of things: rice, flour, soup mix, lentils, beans, chickpeas, pasta, jam. Sometimes they would bring over what they’d cooked or baked, and fight tooth and nail to take their plates back without the customary return gift.

Tucking back into the rattling door the wad of newspaper, which had fallen when Şadiye had stepped in, Jülide placed the bag on the black countertop. She picked up the caddy on the vinyl-covered shelf over the sink, tipped the coffee in, and placed it on the shelf alongside the sugar.

‘She’s a sweetie, is this Şadiye, but tactless.’

This time, Jülide didn't check her smile, lightly biting on her lower lip as she always did whenever she smiled or laughed. Thinking of Şadiye Hanım, of Hüsniye, Nurten, and Hatice Hanıms always made her want to laugh. The ladies who told her grandma everything, down to the finest detail, as if expecting some sort of judgement, about their relations with their husbands, children, parents, siblings, in-laws, neighbours, relatives and all manner of acquaintances. They would start with their bedrooms and end with their kitchens, explain at great length how they cook leeks in olive oil, slap over the bed the latest coffee-table cover they had crocheted, sometimes ask where to decrease the stitches when knitting a baby's cardigan, talk of the miraculous results of polishing glasses with newspaper, concur with all that nothing could wash carpets better than soft soap, and, cheeks gently blushing and eyes flashing, reveal their little tricks which were little different from everyone else's, and, if truth be told, were shared by all. They mooched around at home in a drab old top, a long, gathered floral skirt and a muslin kerchief, changed into outdoors slippers and placed a cardigan over their shoulders when popping to their neighbours; went out in newer versions replacing the faded tops, a plain, long skirt and a floral nylon scarf bought at the market. They had a rounded presence, a constant sense of rolling. A rippling exuberance, plenitude, ampleness on the breasts, arms, bellies, hips, and legs. Jülide liked them all, these ladies she called auntie; she liked their warmth, naivety, sincerity, slyness, envies, gossip, simplicity, quarrelsomeness, and malice.

Her own mother would have been different, though, if she'd lived.

All Jülide could remember of her mother was the extraordinarily white hands. Hands that worked the little miracles of everyday life, extended a small plastic spoon into her mouth, wiped her nose with a soft handkerchief, brushed her hair, occasionally hurting a little, put her cardigan on, fluttered the pages of a picture book, dabbed iodine on the edges of the ever-present wounds on her knees; hands that were always moving, always tending her.

Of her father, only his moustaches, because they tickled her cheek. And the hard, calloused index finger she grabbed when they were walking. He, too, would have been different, if he'd lived. Her parents were certain not to have banged on about the same old things like others did. They would have talked of ancient gods and great battles, pronounced tricky names, mentioned marriages and treaties that bound countries together, and discussed the mysteries thrown up by their latest excavation. Dust, rocks, a searing sun, people laughing and talking aloud: these were the talking photos in Jülide's memory from a very young age. The only thing that was left from her parents was a medallion. A medallion her grandma placed on her neck after the accident, after her parents had abruptly vanished from her life. There was no doubt that this cheeky gaze and wide mouth could never fill the enormous gap left by her parents; all the same, Jülide had not taken off the necklace since the age of five, not even when she was taking a bath. It felt as if her parents touched her spirit and wafted past every time she held it.

Whenever she grasped her medallion lying in bed, throughout the times when she and her grandmother moved from relative to relative, in one-room dwellings rented on a meagre widow's pension plus whatever came from selling their handiwork, living on provisions brought by folk asking to have their fortunes read, wandering from the virtually identical outskirts of one city to another, and at long last, here in Andalıç, where a great-uncle donated them his home, Jülide promised herself she would become an archaeologist. There wasn't a single book on ancient civilisations that she had not yet read in the lifeless Andalıç library, where the only sounds were one's own footsteps, where she would leave without having met anyone: a veritable book cemetery.

'Don't sit idle, lass; pick up your crocheting.' Her grandmother interrupted her musings.

Lifting the valance, Jülide pulled out a green plastic basket with a broken handle. She fished out her own piece from amongst the scraps, balls of wool in various sizes and colours, buttons rescued from old clothes, elastics, reels, and knitting needles in different widths. Tiny motifs that would eventually be transformed into a colourful bedspread. Then she turned on the TV set whose colour scale was limited to purples and greens. As she sat in the chair and fixed her gaze on the screen, the blue yarn wound itself around her finger and the crochet started drawing stitches of its own accord, as if the yarn and the crochet were moving her fingers instead of the other way round. Soon, the smell of sweaty sour metal joined the unerring motion of the hands.

'Wasn't there any songs, lass?' asked her bored grandma.

Placing her work on the sofa, Jülide changed the channel to *Folk Songs and Dance Tunes*. She went to the kitchen to prepare dinner.

*

The whole of Andalıç might be asleep tonight, but the wind has no intention of doing so. It bays in response to the barking of stray dogs. Suspicion dilutes the sleep of fishermen, who had entrusted their boats to the mercy of the night: what if they're sunk by morning? Scrappy is their sleep, as they dip in and out, just like the bows of their boats dipping in and out of the dark sea. The north-easterly sloshes tonnes of water over their minds. Torments them with tiny drops of sensation that never quite grow into a dream. Every once in a while, when something unknown wakens them and they open their eyes, their ears open too, and the fretful storm fills their brains. The squeak of beds in response to tossing bodies joins in all the rustling, rattling and wuthering. And the occasional sound of sleepily-donned clothes and shoes, turned locks, shutting doors, and footsteps clattering over the cobblestones.

Anxiety. The anxiety in the common ancient memory of toppling trees, lightning strikes, floods, and marine accidents. A primitive anxiety that defies all man-made reassurances. The wild wind spreads the cold navy blue of anxieties and nightmares over the topography it erodes.

Jülide lies on a floor mattress. Her eyelashes flicker. She's dancing with someone wearing the mask of the cheeky god in her medallion. Then suddenly, people flock in between them, bashing one another over the head with frying pans. The frying pans keep growing bigger. Jülide wants to get back to her dance partner but the frying pans are terrifying. Then someone touches her on the back and she swings round to see it is him. The masked man hands out something that keeps changing colour, something really important, it's really important to pick it up, but instead, Jülide removes his mask. There is the cheeky god's face underneath. A demented cackle from that wide mouth as his palm snaps shut over whatever it is he is holding. Then he darts behind the frying pans. The frying pans lurch towards her...

By the time she had woken up, the storm was gone and a muggy stillness had settled over the air. They had breakfast in relative silence. Next, Jülide set about readying the house for the neighbours who would be dropping in. Just when she had escaped back into the open air, choking at the fumes of the nitric acid she'd poured down the toilet in the courtyard, someone pulled the rope of the bell at the gate.

Hüsniye, over for morning coffee – fortune reading – slippers shuffling all the way across the courtyard, vanished behind the net curtain stretched over the door.

Jülide knew that Hüsniye had no need for fortune-telling. Her life was a series of identical days, down to the minute: her husband went to the building site in the morning and returned in the evening, her children went to school in the morning and returned at noon, her cleaning was done at ten, she sneaked away for an hour for morning coffee, got lunch ready before the children came back, had a snooze before visiting with ladies, was never late getting back, brewed tea after dinner, sometimes entertained or went visiting, but always and always nibbled sunflower seeds.

Coffee reading was the only extraordinary thing Hüsniye could hope for in life. Which is why Jülide's grandma lay it on so thick.

'Hüsniye, lass; there's a huge kismet over your home. An enormous bird, like a bird of paradise, feathers fluffed up, perching on your house. You have something to do at the state's door in three time: three days, or maybe three months. Look at the door: both wings wide open.'

'Aaa! You've just yawned, Auntie Seher; that's said to mean it'll come true!'

'Of course it will, lass, why wouldn't it? You've got houseguests coming. One of them's tall, with a paunch. Dark blond. And a fat, squat woman. A blue-eyed child, eight or ten years old.'

'Aaa! My sister-in-law in Antalya. They've been saying for ever, we'll come, we'll come, but they never do.'

'They're bringing great news. See here? You'll dance with zils on your fingers. Aaa! A load of furniture is out. Are you looking to move or something, lass?'

'Don't know. Where, though? Maybe if there was work in Antalya ...'

Jülide's eyes were on the clock. Leave her alone, and her grandmother would carry on for another half hour. She knew how to stop it, though. She focused all her strength on her grandma's bladder. Things occasionally did her biding. Atoms, molecules, cells, tiny, invisible things. Her grandma fidgeted a bit, and rushed to finish the reading. Hüsniye would leave soon now. Which is precisely what happened.

'Nana, I'm going to Saime's to study.'

'Fine, but don't be late for lunch.'

'I may have it there.'

'Noo, lass; at a stranger's home? It's bad manners.'

'Saime's not a stranger, is she? It would be even worse manners if they insisted and I refused. Don't wait for me.'

'All right, but don't make a habit of it.'

'OK.'

From the couple of steps leading to the double door of a stone house, water had rolled down the groove in the middle of the cobblestone street; pausing at the spot where it had dried up, assaulting Jülide with her own senses that she had shelved on the way. Her nose tempted by the aroma of the broad beans in olive oil seeping from the neighbour's kitchen as she had walked out, her eyes captivated by the bundle of ginger kittens playing by a small pile of wood, and her ears seized by a baby's scream pitched over her from the open window at the top of the hill: rushing over discrete distances, they crowded her where she stood. Her mind was whole again. Except, that twitchy anxiety inside, that groundless anxiety powerful enough to dislodge all other sensations from the narrow vessel of perception had not yet stilled. Jülide had shrunk piecemeal between the moment of walking out of the door and this moment of finding herself at the bottom of the hill, even as the anxiety had splintered.

The girl who had walked between the two was something less than her, blind and deaf to the world, something with no concept of time. She had stepped into a void and a moment later had found herself here. At 'five minutes to meeting Erkan.'

Lies, guilt, fear. Love? Lies, guilt and fear, which prompt small, rapid steps, sweat-cold fingers, a stinging dryness in the throat, a faint palpitation, and minutes and minutes of wool-gathering.

She sighed, her lungs trembling. Her body, which had taken over whilst she was scattering her senses here and there, was asleep again now that her attention was awake; she tripped over a raised stone. Stumbled. Couldn't help but laugh. Blushed. Being very fair, she blushed easily, and flung her hair back to cover her embarrassment. It smacked against her back. She would occasionally shake her head just because she enjoyed the touch of her hair against her back. She shook it again.

It was an unusually cloudy May day. The stillness in the wake of the north-easterly had not lasted for long. There was a stiffening breeze, which kept changing direction every moment, growing even cooler. An indecisive wind coming from the west, scudding the clouds from the sea, carrying the smell of rain on its back.

Jülide had descended to the rear of the peninsula. The north-facing side where few houses stood. There was a recently-built park consisting of concrete and benches, nicknamed Lamp Park by the residents, who rarely went there. Without a single tree, it was far too hot in daytime, and far too cold in the raw white light of the lamps at night. She spotted Erkan from afar. Her heart started beating a little higher, a little more noisily.

He squashed something with the toe of his shoe and spat on the ground. Sulkily picked up a stone and hurled it into the sea. He turned his head back in a practised move to check the entrance of the park, spotted Jülide, but didn't let on if he was pleased. Gravely he greeted her, gravely kissed her cheeks, and gravely placed a hand on her shoulder. They sat down in a tense silence facing the sea.

'These bugs look so un-buglike,' said Jülide, staring at the bleeding, dying bug on the ground. It was quite big, nearly four inches long.

'Why? Just a bug, that's all.'

'Don't know; it's like it's fleshy. Other bugs have shells; these ones don't.' She raised her head awkwardly. 'Why did you kill it?'

'It was scuttling under my feet. What else can you do with bugs?'

She stared at the insect still trying to move, then at the toe of Erkan's leather shoe, and then at the wet stain of the spit on the ground. Her heart-beat had returned to normal; if anything, the cavity where it beat seemed to be a little tighter.

'Your shirt is too skimpy,' said Erkan.

'Where is it skimpy?'

'The collar. The sleeves are too short too.'

'It's fine,' said Jülide edgily. She felt tiny needles of anger rising from her chest up to her shoulders.

'And it's too thin; you can see through it.'

'You can't have thick summer shirts. Anyway, you can't see through it either.'

Erkan was frowning. 'Don't ever…' he started, but he seemed to be on the verge of a sneeze before he could finish. He opened his mouth and his eyes screwed up over his nose. Ever since the start of this topic, Jülide had been focusing on his nose, convincing a few tiny pollens to enter it and make him sneeze. She wanted them to take their time, though. Erkan's index finger went to his nose, he screwed his face up even more and took a few deep breaths to clear his nose. *Aaa-tchooo!*

'Bless you!' said Jülide with a chuckle. The matter of the shirt was done before Erkan could prohibit it. The weather was getting rougher; the sea was frothing and a rain-laden greyness was rushing over Andalıç.

'And I don't like that medallion either,' said Erkan, 'Swanning about with a man's face on your neck.'

'I've said it once if I've said it a thousand times, Erkan; it was left to me by my mother. I've never taken it off since I was five. It's a memento.'

'He's got a weird look.'

'So don't look at it then.'

'But it's right over your breast. And you don't wear the necklace I've given you either.'

Jülide's heart was nothing but a tight, aching bundle of motion. 'It's beginning to drizzle. It'll probably hammer down. I'd better get back.'

'I thought you were going to stay for two hours.'

'Let's get wet then, shall we? Anyway, you've been criticising everything since I got here.'

'Of course I have. You're my girlfriend. Shall we go over to that café? It's run by my cousin.'

'I can't.'

'Why not?'

'Someone will see me. It's a bar, anyway.'

'We're not going for a drink at this time of the morning, are we? Anyway, let them say what they will; I'll take you to wife when you finish school.'

Annoyed with herself for having given in, Jülide perches at the edge of the wooden chair. There's no one in the bar. They're sitting in the dimmest corner. Erkan's hand wanders on her back, slowly moving forward from her armpit, down her waist, lingering on her soft spots, grabbing her knee from under her skirt and sliding upwards. Sneaking glances around her, Jülide wonders what it is that she finds so discomfiting, what is stopping her from reacting despite that discomfiture, and why she is so yielding. She doesn't want it, doesn't want it, has to do something. But she's paralysed. Maybe she does, does want it after all, but what? Her hands gripping the increasingly warmer bottle of cola.

'Don't, Erkan.'

The attics and coal cellars of the dozens of homes of her childhood, the construction sites next door, forbidden places, playmates, girls and boys a little older or younger than her, the smell of mould, dust, cobwebs, pants lowered curiously and a little shamefully, stolen looks, things not clearly recalled, things passing over the mind like shadows of clouds, things queuing up deep inside to explain the ancient urge.

'Erkan.'

'Huh?'

No windows in the side walls of the narrow, long, stone building that is the bar. The only daylight comes in from the sea-facing side. The walls are painted dark red. It's very cool inside. The walls keep out the stifling heat of the rain. Rattling sounds are heard behind the closed kitchen doors, but there's no one about.

'Do you ever feel detached from everything?'

'Like what?'

'Like you're seeing somewhere for the first time, even if you'd been living there all your life?'

'Nooo. Where do you get these ideas?' Erkan is stroking her hair from the top of her head all the way down to her waist. 'I'm crazy about your hair. Don't gad about on the streets with it loose like that. You'll cover when we're married.'

The noise of the chair alerts Jülide to the fact that she's stood up. She's cross with herself, with herself above all. Her mouth is open but no sound comes out. Taking a deep breath, she closes her mouth again. She'd rather look at the light from the seaward side than at Erkan's bewildered eyes.

'I'd better go now.'

'I'll walk you to the market.'

'No. Best not to be seen together.'

She flings herself out of the door as if she'd dived far too deeply, as if she couldn't find her way back to the surface, as if to save her life. Takes several deep breaths as if she'd just avoided drowning. The rain's still hesitant. A couple of drops strike her here and there before they pause again. She stares at the black door she'd just emerged from in a relentless astonishment – astonishment, anxiety, and anger. As if she'd married Erkan, as if that was her own door, as if she was still underwater. She wants to walk, run, to get away in the great outdoors, to a steppe, on a flatland with an unbroken horizon, to get away, to get away far enough that she becomes a tiny dot in the vastness where no trace will lead to her, no tree, no puddle, not a single identifying feature, to keep going until that dot vanishes, never looking back, never thinking, never being astonished, just going onwards with an infinite strength. Her whole body is ready to bolt, to float off like a kite. A coiled spring. Just then, spotting the approach of a familiar face, she places a formal smile on her lips, ready to greet and flee. Get home before the rain. But a sudden shout nails her to the spot.

'The hell are you doing in a bar at this time in the morning; are you gonna be a whore, you hussy?' An enormous hand, downturned moustache, insults blocking her way, stopping her from running away. 'Couldn't do that if you'd had a father. You're not gonna hang out in bars with ratbags. I'll break your legs if I ever catch you again.'

Three or four times his hand strikes the face she tries to protect with her arms. A sharp ache between her ear and her cheek.

The heavens finally open up over her, where she'd sunk groggily onto a park bench. The sky is no longer as dark; a yellow downpour in columns from the rising clouds. Thunder right over Andalıç rolls away towards the hills to the rear. Puddles already forming on the ground. Little rivulets. Cool freshness dissipating the morning's heat, wet clothes, hair, and the longed-for scent of the wet soil all help Jülide pull herself together. With all that water, it's impossible to tell she's been crying. Tiny streams flow past her feet.

One of those streams is dragging the big, fleshy bug towards the sea. She wants to transform it into a fish, but her powers aren't strong enough for that.

Jülide was drying her long hair with a white towel.

'Son of a bitch!' said Saime, staring at the bruise on her friend's jaw. 'Ruined literature for me anyway!'

Dropping the towel, Jülide started combing her hair. Saime continued to simmer as she circled in the room.

'What are you going to tell your grandmother?'

'I went to a quiet bar with Erkan at noon, the literature teacher saw me when I left and attacked me to save my honour.'

Saime stopped in the middle of the room as if she was about to attack Jülide too. 'Make fun of yourself, not me. How oh how... ?' She growled through a choking throat. 'I mean, how dare he? All right, let's say the school is his patch, but outside...'

'I was already reeling, thanks to Erkan. Two boxing matches in one day? A bit too much.'

'Why can't you dump that swine?' She slapped her own legs. 'Would you look at your calm! You're driving me mad.'

'You're right, I've not dumped him, eh?'

'I'd have said you were one of those marriage-minded girls ... if I didn't know you.'

'Why, I wonder? Why can't I tell him?' Picking up the hairs on the comb, she rolled them into a ball and rested the comb on the towel.

'You're asking me? 'Cos you're daft?'

At long last, Saime calmed down enough to perch on the chair by the desk.

'I don't know. I get excited every time before we meet, but the moment we start to talk, it all goes wrong.'

'You're doing the same thing again, aren't you?' asked Saime with a tense laugh, 'You're digressing. Tempering everything. Not getting angry when you should. Never mind that, you won't even let me swear to my heart's content.'

Footsteps outside. Someone paused outside the door and moved away. The girls waited to regain their privacy as they listened to the sounds of the house.

'Cursing makes you feel powerless. He's always free with his fists anyway. What can we do?'

'It's always the same. All we ever say is, "What can we do?" We could complain.'

'To whom?'

'Don't know; write to the minister, maybe?'

'Think they'll listen to us?' Jülide stared at her long fingers as if pitying their frailty.

'Course they won't, the mother…' Angrily, Saime lowered her eyes away from Jülide's face to the carpet. 'All right; I'm not swearing. Happy now?'

6

Boredom is an indifferent colossus orbiting an elongated oval. Spinning around the distant sun at its back, content to stare at the darkness and the feeble light of stars extinguished hundreds of thousands of years earlier. Its endless orbit ignores the boundaries defined by time and drags its heavy body in the void. An interminable detention that stretches and stretches like chewing gum. At times green, or grey, white or pink; its colour varies along with the wall of the institution you're staring at – whichever school, hospital or barracks. That's because it usually inhabits the universe of enclosed spaces or inescapable situations.

School. Even time zonks out at school; it collapses in a heap between desks and over empty staircases and empty corridors, barely opening its eyes for ten minutes at the tinkling of the bell. Time may actually be fluid, but here it's dried up into something rock solid. Time is a transparent flow prompted by curiosity and pleasure. It refuses to flow as boredom settles into its torpid body. Boredom sucks like a parasite, feeds, is bloated and fattened. Grows until it conquers every last gap in the mind and space. It is everywhere.

It is an uncomfortable wooden bench, eternally green walls, a monotonous voice, and bones of information picked clean of anything of interest. School exists only to teach how to withstand boredom.

Jülide's boredom bounces down the dark steps of her soul like a small grey rubber ball. Growing at every step. Hop hop. She knows how to play with this ball, which had been rolling around inside ever since she was young, and occasionally growing far too heavy. She knows it would become intolerable if she gave it free rein to keep bouncing on the steps. It's best to catch it before it grows too big, before it goes down too far.

First, a little test. A test to recall nice things. The hedgehog, which had squeezed into their tiny courtyard through a crack in the wall, and, unable to find its way back, waited motionlessly amongst the mint for Jülide to leave. Tiny round nose and fearful black beady eyes. The ball hesitated on the step. Another picture to reduce it this time. Hüsniye's four-month-old baby. Lying on the snow-white cloth, gripping Jülide's finger. Frowning and babbling gravely in an incomprehensible tongue. The ball is stationary on the step and a little smaller now.

She looked at her history teacher. Her name is Aynur. Blonde hair. Sickly pale skin. Shortarsed. Head largish, nose long, every feature outsized – except for her eyes. Using the fears and threats perched on her shoulders to hound the kids. Sitting at her desk, coldly tyrannical, expressionless yellow glass eyes. The topic is the Battle of Menzikert. There is little in the way of incidents in the book and plenty of nationalist sentiment. Aynur says, 'Sit; zero,' to Mustafa. Mustafa sits. No one dares to make a peep. Pupils turn their sheer advantage of numbers to relish domineering hapless teachers who show the slightest weakness; but Aynur's venomous tongue has terrorised them all. They cower from her ferocity in the tiny dens of their minds. Using their silence as shields. Trying to hide the fact that they had not studied, that they're not prepared. Staring at their laps for too long is dangerous, as is staring at Aynur too long. Except, she's an expert at sniffing out fear.

As she stared at her history teacher, Jülide recalled a Hittite spell she'd memorised a few days earlier: *Hatalkishna, you are a thorn; just as you are white in the spring and red in the summer, just as you pluck the forelock of the cattle and the wool of the sheep passing under you, pluck out her wickedness.* Jülide wanted to become a magician, to make teachers like teachers, books like books, schools like schools, deflate the ball of boredom, render walls invisible. In silence, she entreated Hatalkishna, that unidentified plant; she pleaded with all her heart and conviction.

She looked out of the window. Dog rose bushes in their white garb on the hillside opposite. Hatalkishna. Why ever not? Given dog rose bushes – rosehips – fruited red in the autumn? Hatalkishna. But no; make hatalkishna something entirely different, an ancient plant, because names are magical. It's better not to know, not to know that hatalkishna is the wild rose. Hatalkishna.

Hatalkishna; please protect snoozing Saime from Aynur's looming long ruler.

But how? What can Hatalkishna, who may no longer exist, do? Jülide locked her eyes on the approaching history teacher's shoe. One step. One more silent step. No one dared to prod Saime awake. The ruler was swinging up and down in a slow arc behind Aynur's back. Jülide's fully focused on the heel of the shoe. Hatalkishna. Hatalkishna. One more step. The ruler comes forward and slowly rises. One more step. Tack.

The students leapt up to their feet at once. Not quite at once, actually; not before enjoying the scene a little first. Then they lifted up their teacher, who had twisted her ankle when her heel had snapped. 'Miss, are you all right, Miss?' Crocodile tears. On Aynur's face something they had always wanted to see: pain. If it's something serious, maybe next week's exam… She was helped to the infirmary. Roused by the commotion, Saime was blinking, gawping at her friend's incantation, 'Hatalkishna.' Jülide was looking out of the window, at the wild roses in their spring whites. 'Are you Hatalkishna? Are you still with us? Or did you vanish alongside the Hittites?'

A greeting came from the wild roses stroked by a gentle westerly wind. Hatalkishna.

Last week of May, last day of the week, last lesson is history, teacher Aynur. Admonitions barely suppressing the exuberance at the flag ceremony. News of the calamity spread to an air of general merriment. *Atten-TION!* came the command. The flag was run up the pole to the tune of the march. The ceremony was over.

Saime was walking alongside Jülide, feeling light as a feather, having escaped the ruler by a hair's breadth.

'Do you have to go to the paper now?'

'Yes. I've only got a week left. Can't get it done otherwise.'

Saime wanted her to come over so they could play her big sister's old records on the old record player, to chat, to talk of anything and everything, to talk non-stop. It was always best on Friday evenings, when two huge days stretched untouched before them.

'It was Supertramp's turn, though,' she said.

'We'll listen to it tomorrow,' said Jülide with a faint sense of guilt she perceived as discomfort. 'Not like it was the first time anyway; how many times have we listened to it so far?'

'I figured out what he's saying in that tricky bit.'

They'd really pitched into English since middle school, just to decipher lyrics. Saime started murmuring, *Send me away to teach me how to be sensible. Logical, responsible, practical.*

'That's probably why school was invented in the first place, see: common sense, logic, responsibility, practicality...'

'Spot on, eh?'

'Especially responsibility, weird thing...'

The mockery in Saime's eyes dripped onto her tongue, 'Yes, it sends you to some rubbishy small town newspaper for prep instead of spending time with your bestest friend.'

'Think we're responsible for everything?'

'For the world's spin, for the seasons to change...'

'No, seriously.'

'Don't know.' Saime continued walking, singing the melody under her breath, then stopped in the middle of the road. 'Maybe you never know what you're responsible for, I mean, other than very obvious stuff. Maybe you just feel responsible for everything.'

'OK; are we responsible for people?'

'How do you mean? If they need care, yes.'

'Not exactly. I mean, how much responsibility do I have for Erkan? For not hurting or offending him; I don't know...'

'A-ha! Now I got it. It all comes back to Himself. We mention ice skating, Erkan, 'cos he's a footballer, right, and ice skating is also a sport. A bit of a stretch, but whatever. We mention foreign actors, Brad Pitt: Erkan, his eyes are similar, yeah, right, just because he's a little fair. Let me think: we mention school, Erkan's not gonna finish. This one, though, is the most extreme example of tenuousness. We get to Erkan from some Supertramp lyrics.'

Jülide was smiling, staring at the ground bashfully. Most of the students had gone.

'At any rate, if He didn't have a training session now, we'd be putting up with His magnificent company. Football, well, all right, I like it too. But when he starts sounding off on women...'

Jülide stared wide-eyed. 'But he used to talk of other things too. Like his childhood memories and stuff. We all laughed at the funny things that happened at training. He talked of the sea, of fishing and stuff... Whatever.'

'I know what you're actually asking, anyway. Just because you're going out with some boy, it's not your *responsibility* to stay with him for all eternity. You don't even need to ask, anyway. No one has such a responsibility anywhere in the world.'

'Why did he change so much, though?'

'He's not changed or anything. He had changed when he met you, when he was chatting you up, and now he's back to his old self. I mean, if you were to spend thirty years with him, he wouldn't be any different from now.'

'All those compliments and everything: gone! He treats me like his fiancée, or even his wife. Terribly jealous. Criticises everything. He's already defined my whole life.'

'What are you waiting for? Dump him, dump him, dump hiiiiim! Don't let me get started on your responsibility. That's not responsibility, that's spinelessness.'

'But I still look forward to meeting him.'

'And when you're together?'

Jülide stared unseeing at her friend, trying to gather her thoughts. 'You're right. But I'm scared he might react badly.'

'So you're carrying on, just because you're scared of him? Bravo. What is he, anyway? How can he hurt you?'

'I don't know; I'm just scared.'

'Of all the reasons why people marry, I never heard anyone doing it out of fear. This is the only thing about you I don't like. You're far too timid, Jülide.'

Jülide replied to the rebuke with a sad look. They had reached the printer's. It wasn't the happiest of goodbyes.

The presses were not running, but the powerful smell of grease was laden with the memory of motion. Rolls of wedding invitations were stacked on the solid old desk in the corner. The exotic interior was mellowed by the golden light of the slanting sun. Silence was the stranger here, the deepening silence of the neighbourhood afternoon between these four walls smelling of grease. The noise was missing from the colossal machine left alone in the room. Jülide ascended the narrow, creaking staircase at the back wall, tapped on the glazed door that had a dusty net curtain on the other side, and walked in.

Countless yellow motes of dust floated in the oblique ribbons of the evening sun falling in through the tall, narrow windows. The empty room with constantly raining dust particles had been enslaved in a warm pause, like a snow globe.

Just as she was about to leave, Jülide heard a faint noise; something moved under the table. One more step brought her into the middle of the cramped office, half of which was taken up by the desk. There was a back bent over the chair.

'Muzaffer Bey?'

The chair was pushed back noisily. A head appeared from under the table: with very short, bright blonde hair; as the face reddened from that upside down position rose, the slender metal frame of the round glasses glinted in the evening sun. Cigarette-stained rows of teeth appeared between the lips separating at the sight of Jülide.

'I am Muzaffer,' said the woman sitting at the table in a sexless, cracked voice, 'So long as you're not going to insist on gender.'

'Oh… Sorry. I thought you were a man when I saw the name in the paper.'

Muzaffer had dived to the floor to rescue a pen, which had rolled into a crack; slipping it now somewhere inside her multi-pocketed waistcoat, she held out her hand.

'Whom do I have the pleasure of meeting?'

'My name is Jülide.'

'Yes, Jülide; what can I do for you? So long as you don't say "engagement party invitation". Not a single local girl turns nineteen as a bachelorette, as you know…'

'No, no; God forbid!' exclaimed Jülide, and saw the vehemence of her reaction in Muzaffer's laughter.

'That bodes well. Fine; the reason for your visit?'

'Schoolwork. What happens at a newspaper? What's working there like? That sort of thing.'

'Let's call it a provincial newspaper, if you like. You kick your heels all day. The paper's only four pages, anyway. One page of ads. The folio on a quarter page. It's a small place. Not enough news even in a week to fill two and a half pages. Large point size, loose spacing. We get someone or other with a reputation for wielding a pen to write the editorial. I write another, using an alias.'

As she reached for a copy of the paper from the shelf behind her, the silence felt as though some priceless antique instrument had stopped playing. Then came a reply from the croaking, harsh, impressive, bruised, yet lively voice.

'Have you ever seen it?'

Her movement doubled up the volume of dust in this room filled with dozens of years of printwork, triggering hasty eddies in the light, a funny sort of tickle in the throat, and a newspaper was placed on Jülide's lap.

'Yeah, have you seen it?'

'Um… not really. I know, I should have done my research before coming, but…'

'It's not easy to get hold of, anyway. Only goes to shopkeepers; it's not sold in newsagents. You may see copies at butchers and dentists from time to time, but not always.'

Jülide was doing a little mental calculation as her slender fingers turned over the toy newspaper: its page layout, typefaces, spelling mistakes, and thin, light presence. 'Thirty-five,' she said aloud. Lifting her head as if she was surprised at having spoken, she added, 'I had no idea it was that old.'

'It is,' said Muzaffer in a bitter, confrontational tone, clearly targeting herself, 'That it is: but take a look at the format before the date if you like. Turn to page two.'

Jülide turned the page of the newspaper whose format had instantly surrendered all claims to credibility; fingers accustomed to regular newspapers moved awkwardly, all thumbs, in inverse proportion to the size of the sheet.

'What can you see?' asked Muzaffer, as if Jülide was responsible for the object she was holding.

'Don't know. There are pictures.'

'Right. Three quarters is photos. Half of which taken at various meetings. I call them laurel wreath photos. The District Governor is never absent. The Mayor, the Commissioner, the Director of Education, or their wives. Anyway. Let's move on to the news.'

Jülide counted slowly, if she were reading a menu to pick a dish. 'The show at the primary school. Ladies' open-air exhibition, two kids selected for the national under sixteens handball team?'

'Sooo; what do you think?'

'Like what?'

Muzaffer gave up. 'OK, move on to page three.'

'Thursday market livelier. Florists from Izmir selling cheap cut flowers. Are those florists from Izmir, then?'

'That's precisely the question this newspaper endeavours to answer.'

Jülide gave her a blank look, as if she were puzzled by the punchline of a joke whose start she'd missed. Muzaffer was laughing. 'I'm a little impatient, right? What I mean is: it's a hollow paper. Hollow. No content whatsoever.'

'But it was interesting, that thing about the boys selected for the national team.'

'And now you'll think I don't like my job.'

'Don't you?'

'Of course I do; I love it. That's the real issue, at any rate. Why would anyone like it? It does have its high points. Like a good run of fish. An item on corruption. You could force a mayor to resign. Not here, in our country, though; you'd have the mafia at your door. Make you regret what you're doing. Here, a few crumbs. At least you could sue. Does it ever end? Who knows, maybe one day…'

Eyes fixed out of the window, Muzaffer lit a cigarette. Yellow dust particles scattered in the smoke. Lit from behind, it licked the sunny half of her face and the glinting frame of her specs as it curled upwards.

The newspaper lay open in the dim office. Goods for sale. Land for sale. A poem by the Library Director. Was that the grey-haired fellow with a paunch Jülide occasionally came across on the library staircase? That middle-aged man who wandered with a kindly haze on his face, a gracious acceptance of this provincial tedium, and an air of having survived an ancient storm with his inner peace intact – being published in these backwater newspapers a bitter consolation for his failure to make it as a famous poet. His lonely footsteps always echoed on the steps of the deserted library.

A photo of a seagull on the back page. A brief piece of text below.

As heavy wintry conditions give way to sunny skies with the arrival of spring, sunrise renews the day and itself every morning.

Seagulls out fishing in Andalıç flap their wings in the sky in celebration of the rising sun. As they fly freely in the sky, they are accompanied by the suns radiance and splendour.

'Tee-hee. How do you like it? It's Mustafa Abi who prepares them. Our Library Director.'

'I guess I see him from time to time.'

'Then you must be the only student in Andalıç who does.' Muzaffer continued to laugh. 'Don't misunderstand; I'm not pulling your leg. I do like him, and this is added colour. Some people just happen to be emotional.'

Jülide turned back to the paper and re-read the text below the seagull.

'How does it strike you? Like a news item?'

Jülide thought for a while. 'Of course, I'm no expert; but probably not very appropriate.'

'See? Even a child gets it. That's not the issue, though: how did I miss that *suns*? I was hoping at least to catch them all.'

'What *suns*?'

'Needs an apostrophe.'

'No one seems to get them right. Not even teachers.'

She carried on reading.

Attention Business Owners

Our printing press is FINANCE validated.

Invoice Bill

R. Sales Receipt Ticket

Despatch Order Expense note

Invoice with Delivery Note Payment Receipt

Various Invitations.

Blowing smoke out of her nostrils, Muzaffer squinted at Jülide.

'Don't put them in then, if you don't like it. You have the last word, right?'

'Says who? I've got an Uncle Tahsin. My father's memento. Inherited along with the paper and the press. Tradition has its place. They're all used to it here. And anyway: take it out, and what're you going to publish instead? Seagulls, flowers, what have you: they fill the page.'

Jülide opened her notebook. 'May I ask a few questions for my homework?'

'Go ahead.'

'Did you want to choose this career? Your education?'

'The career chose me. I was born into it. This printing press has been around for as long as I can remember. A typewriter, my dad tapping on it. He was an important man in Andalıç; he was quite active. He called the shots. Was enthusiastic. It was infectious. Infected me, at any rate. Later, I did study. Worked for years as a reporter after I qualified. Even worked as a war reporter. Then times changed. It all went sour. I came back. It's all right here. Between Uncle Tahsin and Mustafa Abi, it kinda ticks over.'

'I was going to ask if you liked your job, but there's no need now. You obviously do. OK, what do you like most?'

'Most...' She paused. 'I like exposing something that could have remained secret for ever, something that hurt someone. We've done that often here. Not without risk. But there you are. We only live once.'

'Is journalism a dangerous profession?'

'Journalists are the highest number of civilians killed because of their work across the world. I mean, they don't usually face immediate danger at work, like the police and the military do. The risk comes later. Knowledge is dangerous, secrets are dangerous; especially if you put a spoke in someone's wheel or cross a certain line. That's when the threats come. Either you carry on, sticking your neck out, or apply self-censorship. Which is what kills you.'

Having originally come here half-heartedly, just to be done with the term paper, Jülide was now silenced by an unexpected emotion. Not quite sure what self-censorship was, she was about to ask, but stopped herself on realising Muzaffer was lost in thought. She flicked through the paper again.

Sailors compete. Tight contest in the national heats for the Turkish championship.

The white festival on the sea appeared before her eyes. White triangles in the distance that could have been shoving one another. Excited parents waiting on the shore, trying to catch their children with their fingers. The wicked local north-easterly, which suddenly dropped in the middle of the race. A boring wait in the doldrums. A couple of faint puffs barely sufficient to complete the race. She shook herself.

'OK, would you recommend it to young people?'

'No; smart money says stay away. Become models or something – if they're as beautiful as you.'

Jülide blushed.

'I have other plans. I want to become an archaeologist.'

'Now, that could go in next week's news: The first young lady in thirty years to pursue archaeology in our charming Andalıç. Put your photo on page one, and we'll double our circulation!'

Jülide dropped her eyes, downcast.

'Did I offend you? I'm a little tactless, you see. And I like to tease. You'd better get used to my ways. 'Cos I've got something to ask you, too.'

7

With two weeks to go to the engagement party, Cemal wanted the days, which had involved shuffling over to the grocer's in the morning and lazing about until evening, to sprint as if they were going to a date, and scoot off like after visiting the sick. Only the times when Saliha dropped in were allowed stretch till eternity, but sadly, they were in the greatest hurry. Refusing to linger at the grand feast tables in Cemal's heart, the minutes stuck their heads round the door and ran away.

Now that the sea was warmer, he happily resumed swimming. He woke up as usual around six and walked down the deserted streets where only cats and dogs breathed. He usually went in somewhere near Lamp Park and swam north or south, depending on the wind. Hardly a leaf stirred at that hour anyway.

Pausing on the bottom step at the embankment, staring at the cool blue, trying to overcome the recoil from the cold. His body had already lost the warmth of the clothes he had whipped off. The water looked darker, dark and distant. Aware it has no need to entice anyone at this hour. Only the most loyal of lovers come near at this hour, those who have no need of being seduced over and over again. It's only Cemal's body that hesitates; he is loyal to this love, just as he is to all his loves. He goes in.

Swimmer's goggles on his eyes, a childhood habit. The first shiver, the first rebellion. Five or six very quick strokes, maybe even seven or eight. Next, his body stops complaining. The goggles steam up. Even though he had spat in them first; a trick that occasionally needs repeating, so he kicks to float higher. Goggles back in place, he continues. Slow, steady strokes, a breath at every third one.

One right, one left. The noise of his breaths bubbling in the water. He swims in his usual tempo, crowded by the sound of his own breaths and strokes. All thoughts pause as he swims. All he does is move his arms and legs and watch the bottom. He won't entertain a single thought, not even a dream, to swim alongside him in these waters. His mind is totally empty: saltwater floods it with a soft light.

Swimming close to the shore, his strokes break up the ultramarine indifference of the depths. There's no need to swim out; Andalıç's seabed is too deep to be visible. The slope of the peninsula's hills does not continue below the waterline, no; it does not even descend in a plumb line. The mass below the water tapers down to the depths, like an inverted cone, losing its diameter the deeper it goes, narrower, pointier. Countless underwater caves on the inverted cone, popular with divers. 'Iceberg', they call the peninsula, due to its weird underwater geography. No one has ever seen where it is anchored on the seabed, although mariners rumour it's as narrow as the waist of a young maiden. This gigantic mass of pumice stone yaws and pitches in storms as if its narrow waist would snap off, like a never-melting iceberg stabbed into this abyss in the Aegean.

Unfazed by the accustomed dark sea, Cemal continues to swim unconsciously like a fish. Non thinking is freedom. He looks at the darkening hollows underneath the peninsula. Full of thousands of holes like aged cheese. Every time he turns his head to the left, he sees pure white rocks covered with moss, mussels and corals. White enough to dilute the darkness of the deep, light enough to counter the weight of tonnes of water. Pumice stone, the only rock that floats. Featherlight in the hand. Thousands of vesicles inside that capture air.

His eyes, emerging above the waterline, seek out the cracked chimney soaring over the olive oil factory. That's the marker for his return. His usual southerly route. Narrow streets descending straight to the sea flow alongside sun- and salt-bleached stone houses. His strokes cut their reflections into inconsistent, edgy and shivering slices. Agitating the reflections that had settled on the surface in the calm air.

Cemal stops to stare at Andalıç as he always does when he lines up with the tall brick chimney. From the surface of the mirror. Andalıç houses covering the hillside like a stone carapace with their unnatural corners, straight lines and rectangular openings, their reflections softened and animated on the water, and when he dips his head through the silvering surface, suddenly rounded lines beyond the looking glass, the mouths of the caves of varying sizes descending to the peak at the bottom, the ancient architecture of the inverted hillside never touched by a man-made shell. A spectacle all the way from the sky to the bottom of the sea. Cemal pulls his head back through the looking glass and sets off on his return lap.

It was seven thirty by the time he'd taken a quick shower and opened the shop. His hair was wet. Looking at Saliha's closed window, he realised his plans to swim together after they were engaged may need reviewing; she rarely rose before nine.

Concentric rings around the engagement day in the centre of the target board: one week till the school holiday. Then Saturday. Then SUNDAY. At that point, they would be regarded as half-married, and acquire certain privileges they did not as yet enjoy. No longer would they have to cut short those impossible-to-conclude sweet chats during quiet times in the shop every time Hafize yelled 'Salihaaa!' There would be extended strolls arm-in-arm in the warm evenings after locking up the shop, dinners with the entire family once or twice a week as a treat for this bachelor, watching Saliha wandering in her own home, learning about her habits, pleasures and her troubles by seeing, not hearing, dropping in announced, her dropping in announced, that enormous cape of legitimacy which banished the worries niggling away at a corner of the mind, *What would everyone say?*, the relaxation and relaxations of harmony.

Cemal managed to shove the two rotund days fattened on the terrific impatience roused by a shedload of tiny anticipations over the finishing line. At long last, he had reached Sunday; in other words, the countdown was a bit more manageable now, down to just one week, only one. The door opposite him opening and closing all day long, people constantly going shopping and returning, carrying bags with various logos, a profusion of neighbours' slippers lined up outside the door, x covers and y covers carried in bundles and taken back, 'Aaa, sweetie, but this is a must!' trickling out of the window after loud exchanges, Saliha repeatedly giving up throughout the day, raising her hands aloft, coming over to tell Cemal wearily about the preparations that were driving her to distraction, Cemal listening helplessly and attempting to calm her down: all this had taken a day's break. It was evening; he was chatting with Halil outside the darkening shop, all the while serving his regular customers, who were mostly just kids demanding junk food.

These stifling obligations of engagement preparations provided Halil with an endless source of entertainment. His laughter and refrains of 'Women, eh? You never know with them!' proved to be distracting at least, if not a complete cure. Cemal was talking of ceaseless demands and the minutiae of detail, as if telling a joke he didn't quite get himself, when he stopped in the middle of a sentence. A squat woman in a long brown skirt and a long-sleeved black shirt was climbing up the street. She stopped, pretending to straighten her headscarf, and caught her breath.

'Who on earth is this, Mr Cemal?' asked Halil, curious about this personage important enough to interrupt them, 'One of the new relations maybe?'

Cemal didn't reply at once. 'Nooo,' he laughed next and turned back to Halil, 'You could say that. The mother of my half-sister is a relative of sorts, I guess.'

'Why is she coming here, though?'

'No idea, abi. Must be about her daughter. She'd have no other business with me, would she?'

When Melahat finally moved again, facing up to tackling the rest of the climb, Halil made a move to get up, but was held back by a hand gripping his wrist. 'Wait, abi. Stay. This stuff's doing my head in.'

After the introductions and greetings, Melahat fell silent, staring at Halil.

'Don't be shy, Melahat Hanım, say what you've got to say. Halil is like a big brother to me. I've told him, anyway.'

'I've come to ask if you're gonna look for Cemile, Cemal Bey. I've heard from her. She sent me a letter. I know where she is. I'll go if you won't.'

Cemal stared at Halil, as if he couldn't find it in himself to reply. Just then, the dairy shopkeeper İzzet dropped in for his usual half bottle of rakı. As Cemal was wrapping it in a sheet of newspaper, he saw Halil lead Melahat inside. He waited, all ears, for several minutes after İzzet's parting 'Good evening.'

'Were you in contact with your daughter, Melahat Hanım? Only Cemal did say you didn't know her whereabouts.'

'I didn't. But I guess she knew about us. That bloke knows some folks in Eskişehir. She heard about us moving. And about her father dying. Heartbroken, she was. I had left this address with the neighbours there. That's how she must of got it.'

Cemal walked slowly to the door from whence the voices floated.

'Didn't she look you up before? When her father was sick and that.'

'No, she didn't. Maybe she never knew. She'd of come if she'd heard. Devoted to her dad, she was.'

Melahat peered at Cemal's face for a clue to his intentions, then shook herself as if remembering something. Opening a flaking vinyl handbag, she drew up a filthy, creased scrap of paper softened with handling. She held it out, scared that it might fall apart. Gently and equally carefully, Cemal opened it. It was something like parcel paper. Squiggly lines scratched in pencil. Misshapen, practically illegible letters, large and small, wobbly. Swollen in spots as if sprinkled with water.

Mum, my dear mum, my sorrowful mum

No one to stroke my hair. You used to, mum. Your unfortunate daughter. Unfortunate. How [a few illegible words] Ive fallen.

My dear dads gone too. Never hurt me my dad. He was such a good dad. My dear dad. What have I done to you? My eyes are swolen with crying. Never dried,d id they, my tears. My sorry mum.

Who'da thought I'd sink so far? My dad used to call me my beautiful daughter. Pretty as a model.

Mum forget me now: I'm done for. Done for. My ill fortune.

So that was in the cards, falling so low... Who'd a thought it... My dear dad's gone too. Rest in peace. Oh, daddy.

Mum, forgive my trespasses. Rite me a little letter and then forget me.

The address on the envelope was in a different hand. Cemal blinked a few times and gulped once or twice. Handed the letter to Halil, who was watching with a condescending grin. Melahat waited in reverent silence for him too.

'All right, don't bother asking if he's going, Melahat Hanım,' said Halil once he'd finished, 'Our Cemal could never sit on his hands after this letter.'

Melahat waited suspiciously for confirmation from Cemal.

'My daughter's a good girl, a very good girl. That bastard's turned her head. Eh, Cemal Bey?'

Cemal stayed silent, as if he'd already said all there was to say.

'Our Cemal will go, but don't get your hopes up, Melahat Hanım. It's no mean feat to rescue a woman from a pavyon. No one in his right mind would even try.' He cast a worried glance at Cemal, at the stubborn resolve that had overcome all previous decisions and hesitations at every news from across the country of unclaimed dead bodies and demented old men. 'I mean, our Cemal will definitely try.' Not for him to sit back and do nothing after reading a letter like that. He was silent, patient, like all stubborn men.

'Cemal Bey's a strapping fella, God spare him. He'll get my daughter out.'

'If strapping was the only thing needed... God forbid, there's mortal danger here.'

'God forbid! Heaven forbid, Halil Bey!'

They all shut up, thinking of the ominous doings of a dark world they knew nothing about, other than in hearsay or imagination. These all-male nightclubs where bar girls entice the patrons to spend far more on drinks than they would otherwise. Where those girls are expected to entertain the patrons in other ways too.

'God forgive me,' said Melahat, 'Don't want no one's blood on my conscience.'

'Wait a bit, Melahat Hanım, we'll think of something.' It was the first time Cemal announced his intentions out loud. 'Don't write a letter or anything just yet. Keep your powder dry. It might get into the wrong hands. Best do it on the sly.'

Shaking his head, Halil snickered, 'Our superhero's on it, Melahat Hanım. Don't you worry about the rest. He'll sneak over and bring your daughter back.'

'There's a police force in this country, Halil Abi.'

'Yeah, right; the police will go, grab Cemile out, and hand her over to you, " 'Ere mate, here you go!" The pavyons would run out of women if it was that easy. The women are indebted, forced to sign bonds and whatnot. Bound too tight to stir. Anyone who does is shot. Oh, Cemal, grow up!'

Cemal dropped his head. 'What about paying to release her?'

'Say you could buy her way out. Where's the money?'

In the darkness, despair sinking down with the window blinds seemed to have silenced all of Andalıç. A woebegone sigh came from Melahat. Vexed by her desperate frustration, Halil murmured, not quite convincing himself either: 'Hold on. We'll ask around. Someone around here must know what to do. Tomorrow is another day.'

School reports climb up the streets, some waving above joyful children's faces, others stuffed into bags in the hope they'll never be taken out again. Cemal is fetching a stream of chocolates over the counter, feeling better now that he's reached another notch towards the future.

Yasemin, Halil's wife, had already filled a small suitcase with garments obtained after a sneaky little enquiry into Saliha's tastes. Items displayed before being carefully folded into the case popped into Cemal's mind. Things covered in lace and stuff, no bigger than a hand. Nightgowns and dressing gowns of glossy, flowing fabrics. They probably weren't Saliha's cup of tea at all, but he held his tongue. His hand pouring caster sugar into a clear plastic bag shook, scattering grains over the scales. He found himself all thumbs whenever these garments popped into his mind and made him wonder about the parts they concealed. Lately everything was spilling and scattering, rice, flour, lentils, everything. He now knew that certain fascinations caused clumsiness. In any case, fascination whipped up desire into – occasionally – intolerable levels.

Shooting into the little room to the rear, he splashed his face with water. Went out into the plant pot of a garden. Stared blankly at the walls. Rushed back in as quickly. Toured the concrete strip that served as pavement outside the shop a few times. Then sank down to the wicker stool in an impenetrable ache that put the brakes on fascination. He rested his chin in his hand with that weird anxiety, which cooled and slowed down his heart whenever he imagined his sweetheart's nakedness. He stared at the door opposite.

He didn't feel like going home after closing up. Darkness came later and later in June. A turquoise horizon, deepening cobalt skies. The last sad rays hanging over the world without illuminating. Cemal went to the seafront down the stone streets as they released the day's heat. Walked lost in thought as they gradually filled. When he raised his head, he found himself facing a familiar gate. He rang the little bell and stepped into the lit garden. The children were nowhere to be seen. At the sound of the bell, Yasemin had placed her embroidery frame on the wooden table, and Halil, his book; they were both on their feet now.

'Please sit, don't let me disturb you.'

'We-eel! What brings our lord and master here? Do you even leave your own neighbourhood?'

Yasemin was laughing too. 'Yeah, Cemal; it's practically the first time since the winter. I was beginning to take offence; Halil visits you over there, and that's enough for you!'

'Don't say that, Yasemin Yenge. You know I close the shop quite late. And then I'm exhausted. And it gets dark early in the winter, anyway.'

'All right, pal, too many excuses already!'

They sat down on the sofa against the wall. A pleasant chat born of long acquaintance spilled over the stones. Coffees were sipped. The engagement party was discussed. Yasemin talked the most. Painstakingly detailed plans were made at some length. Nothing was too trivial. Cemal's lassitude nestled deeper and deeper as the night spread its navy blue. Yasemin yawned once or twice.

'C'mon,' said Halil, 'I feel like a stroll. Let's go for a walk.'

'I'm sleepy,' said Yasemin with a shrewd smile, 'You two go.'

They set off into the cold white light sprinkled over the cobblestones, picking the quieter streets.

'You're quiet.'

Startled as if caught red-handed, Cemal turned his head. 'Don't know. Am I?'

'Right. You've going to make me drag it out of you.'

'That's why you got up in the middle of the night, right?'

They walked in silence for a while, slipping in and out of the deep shadows under the illuminated trees shining as if they were made of plastic.

'I don't know; I feel a little uneasy.'

'About Cemile? You don't have to go. You know you don't. No one could say a thing either. I've asked around; it's not as difficult as it used to be, but it's still bad news. And who knows what state she was in when she wrote that letter? Maybe she was drunk. Maybe she'd taken something else. You don't know what she's like.'

'No, abi. I mean, that's a problem, of course. I'd be lying if I said I wasn't scared.'

'What then? Engagement jitters?'

'Don't know. A little.'

'A little...'

'Really, a little.'

They focused on the dog standing outside the gate ahead; would it attack? It didn't bark. When they got much closer, it started wagging its tail and then joined them, following a couple of steps behind, sniffing to learn their scents.

'You and Saliha had a row?'

'No, we didn't. Unpleasant subjects pop up now and then, but we've not had a row.'

'So what is it then?'

Frowning and hunched, Cemal was staring at the ground as he continued to walk.

'I was thinking about. I mean, when we get married...' He stopped, looked around. The street went through a vacant lot. And he blurted it out. 'I've never slept with anyone.'

Halil was sniggering. 'Oh, you arse!! You've traipsed up and down the land; why didn't you go to a cathouse? Seeing as it's such an issue.'

Cemal gave him a reproachful look.

'All right, keep your shirt on. Is that the matter then?'

'Yes.'

'Oh Cemal; you're a 38-year-old bloke and you're like a kid.'

'Uh-huh; thirty-eight.'

'Wow! It's true, thirty-eight.'

'Now do you get it?'

They resumed a slow walk. The dog, which had left to sniff here and there when they had paused, started following them again.

'Don't blow it out of all proportion, son. It's quite natural, after all. It gets much worse if you do make a big thing out of it. Just don't think about it.'

'I wouldn't maybe ...' He gave a nervous laugh. 'At one point Mustafa even found me a prostitute. Got her number. I did ring. But then didn't go ahead with it. I couldn't. I changed my mind. That just isn't my way. There has to be some warmth. Interest.'

'Yeah, yeah. It's bad if women do it, and men don't. Look here, Mr Cemal. It's no good worrying it like a bone. No one has to do anything. Some at seventeen, others at thirty-eight. There's no rule, OK? Don't be daft. Then you'll really screw up.'

'Yeah, right.'

By the time he was back at his door after a night of Halil's banter and advice, his heart felt a little lighter. He shooed away the thoughts rushing in. Forgetting to spit as he was brushing his teeth, he burped a couple of times. Dabbed his blurred pink lips. Stared long and hard at the strange eyes in the mirror in an effort to get to know someone he had just met. Pulled apart the line between his eyebrows. Moved his hand lower and gripped his nostrils in the V of his fingers. He didn't breathe at all for a while, then left the bathroom and went to his bedroom. He sank onto the bed, and took a deep breath whenever the constriction inside became unbearable.

Yasemin was carrying a bouquet, Halil a box of chocolates, and Cemal the small suitcase as they walked through the gate at Saliha's house, that had been squeaking open and shut all day long. Cemal was dazzled by the dozens of bare lightbulbs hanging from a long flex. Small as it was, the garden had been transformed into a venue for fifty or sixty. Cemal had seen several types of chairs being carried in throughout the day and these were placed in any available space, and an electronic organ was set up by the gate. Early arrivals – close relations who had come to help – were whizzing around. Kadir's thick, raised eyebrows and thin, glued lips said, *Send her to universities and whatnot, and then go and hand her over to some grocer,* but Saliha's will would never allow these words a voice. Platters laden with wraps, cookies, cakes, savoury pastries, and lentil dumplings were laid out on the long table next to the gate. Mismatched glasses gathered from the neighbourhood. Cases of soft drinks, fruit juices, colas. Lemonade in sweating pitchers.

Taking the suitcase from his hand, Saime said, 'My sister's a bit tense; go see her if you like.' An announcement that tautened the strings of the night. Tense, tense, tense. Cemal's shave-fair face paled a little bit more. He climbed up the creaking wooden steps and paused for a deep breath outside the door. It was impossible to tarry at the doorstep in the endless stream of people coming in and out of the rooms. He tapped on the door.

'I said, leave me alone for five minutes, didn't I?' yelled the familiar voice in an unfamiliar state.

Cemal hesitated before daring to squeak, 'It's me.'

It was like counting the final beats of his heart, which he thought would crack outside the silent door. Lub dub, lub dub, lub dub…

The silent door swung open, drawing in the corridor air. Saliha grabbed his wrist, tugged him in, held on to his neck and burst into tears. Lub dub, lub dub, lub dub… Cemal realised his mouth was too dry, just when he was desperate to swallow. He wanted to see Saliha's face, but didn't dare look. She raised her head from his chest to speak; he saw a twisted, strange, ugly face smeared in make-up. Lub… du dub, du… dub, lub dub.

'They've driven me crazy. For weeks and weeks. I don't want any of this. I'm not normal anyway. Engagement party… All kinds of nonsense. What part of "No" don't they get?' Eyeliner-black tears rolling down on either side of the lips tense with sobbing. 'What I can and can't wear…' she sighed a few times, 'what to buy, what to do, what you're gonna do…' took a couple of breaths, gasping as if there wasn't enough oxygen, 'well, it would be really rude if you didn't dance…' smeared the make-up a bit more as she tried to wipe the tears with the back of her hand, 'well, gotta sit next to Uncle Muhsin… I loathe that tosser called Muhsin, used to give me slobbering kisses when I was little. Bad breath. Disgusted when he took me on his lap.'

Cemal would have pressed her to his chest and stroked her hair gently, but this unfamiliar, solid hairdo straight out of the salon defied the touch.

All he was able to do was to rub her back, as if burping a baby. It took a careful manoeuvre, but he did manage to pull out the handkerchief in his pocket without pushing her away and started wiping that beloved – and now unrecognisable – face back into its old state.

'I can't even stand on these shoes. Mum's insisted…' She kicked one shoe angrily at the wall opposite, and then the other. A little calmer now, she was no longer sobbing. 'That idiot hairdresser turned me into a clown! I keep saying, "Leave it natural," he turns it into a bowl, like a block.' Sitting at the little dressing table, she gazed at the mirror. 'Even this looks better than that stupid make-up. Glitter here, sequins there, lipstick like raw liver. Impossible to remove for love nor money.'

'I understand, my darling, but it's just for a few hours at the end of the day.'

'Intolerable torture, even for a few hours. Better not get married in the first place!' She would have continued, but spotting Cemal's face in the mirror, she stopped.

'You never…' Cemal didn't finish. He shut his mouth tight.

Her chin was twitching. 'I never what?'

'You don't really want to marry me or anything. You don't want me, Saliha. If you did, you wouldn't be in this state. If you did…'

'What?' Saliha got up. 'How would I behave if I did? Dance with zils on my fingers? Shame, Cemal, shame on you.'

Disappointment strummed the tense strings of the night. Nothing of the festive atmosphere outside – not the excited hustle and bustle, giggles, or laughter – could penetrate the walls of this painful globe.

'If you doubt my love…'

Cemal was quick to soothe. 'No, no; not at all. But I do wonder if you want to get married.'

'I'm not really that keen on getting married, anyway. I mean… Oh, I've said it once if I've said it a thousand times, Cemal! Why am I putting up with all this then?'

'Testing… testing…' said the musician, carrying out a sound check outside.

Cemal gazed at Saliha, who no longer was the woman he loved, but one of millions of women about to get engaged. 'I don't know,' he said. He didn't think he could love her if she had wanted to look like this herself, if she were a woman who could be like this. The sense of injustice on the stained face was heartbreaking. 'You're actually right. I mean, all this... tiresome. But... your sweetheart... don't know... you have to put up with all sorts for the sake of your sweetheart.'

A scorching, painful look from Saliha. 'I can't promise you that, Cemal. How can you possibly know what you can or can't put up with? You never know what life has in store for you. And anyway, I can never...' Shaking her head, she dropped her gaze. 'And if that's what you're expecting, you'll end up upsetting yourself. Are you going to doubt my love every time I do something willy-nilly for your sake? That's a big ask. Not one I can cope with. No one should have to put up with anything for anyone else's sake. Neither should we. Don't expect that from me.'

Cemal hesitated for a moment before letting these words hurt him. All those wildly seductive images of sacrifice that enslave the imagination, admirable renunciations, abnegations, underrating oneself, putting up with everything, all those noble things. The noblest and vilest word in the world terrified him for a moment just as much as it had done Saliha. He gave her a kindly look that overcame his hurt, a gentle gaze for the beloved crushed by a pain that he had yet to understand fully. His heart was well versed in waiting and being disappointed every time. He had wandered from city to city, looking for his father; now he would look inside Saliha for that thing he valued so highly – and perhaps do so all his life. Look, and perhaps never find. He would be disappointed, give up, regain hope and start again. He stood at the doorway opening up to the rest of his life, just sensing this series of disappointments, something he didn't quite know nor was able to put into words.

'OK,' he said, trying to convince himself, 'OK,' not particularly expecting to have much of an effect under something this huge, something that had been building up on the back of convictions, habits, beliefs.

There was a tap at the door.

Through the crack appeared Saime's smile veiling her unease. 'C'mon, abla, you're expected downstairs.' One look at Saliha's face, and she added, 'I'll tell them you'll be ten minutes.'

Saliha spent those ten minutes wiping off the hysterics and painting her face in her own way. Every layer of war paint was marked with a sad smile at Cemal. The ordinary strain of an engagement party gradually claimed their faces. When she was done, Cemal held her hand by the blush-smeared fingertips and placed a gentle kiss in the hollow middle of the palm. Pressing his hand on the burning spot right under his chest, he stepped back. Looked her over from top to toe.

'That's much better,' he said, his crushed joy denying him the faculty to find something nicer to say.

They descended the stairs in weary steps, resolved to go through with duty. Every chair was taken in the garden when they emerged as solemnly as if they were on parade. Applause broke out. Saliha took a step back, but Cemal pushed her waist with his fingertips. Helped her regain the will in her feet. The bare bulbs dazzled him again for the second time that night, but it was anxiety that glittered in his eyes now, instead of his earlier joyful anticipation. The organ was playing *Under the Stars*. Saliha turned her head, her desire to run away exposed in the harsh light, and whatever was burning below Cemal's chest exploded, spreading into his belly, when the lights went out. Not just those in the garden or the neighbourhood, but in the entire town. Teasing 'Aaah!'s rose from the guests as children burst into merry screams. Hafize was grumbling at Kadir:

'I told you our fuses couldn't cope, didn't I?'

'Hold your tongue, woman; it's off everywhere. Not just our house.'

Cemal and Saliha raised their heads at the same time to be struck by the dusty light of the stars suddenly ten times in number. Their love of astronomy at primary school, the encyclopaedias they'd read, the book given by Saliha's uncle, the vacant lot on the peak, sneaking away as a group after dark to watch the stars from the spot where the Care Home now stood. All the constellations they had identified and memorised.

Cemal's hurt was crushed by his fear of losing Saliha. Holding her head in both hands before anyone's eyes had a chance to get accustomed to the dark, he gave her lips a fleeting kiss. She was practically laughing as her tense body softened in the magic of distant lights, some of whose sources had long since vanished. The cheeks under his thumbs swelled up.

'Corona Borealis,' said Saliha.

Cemal raised his head to look for it. Then tenderly turned her round, just as he used to when they were children. Once he was certain he'd got the right angle, he knelt down before her. Corona Borealis now shone right above her head in all its glory. The brightest jewel sparkled over her forehead and the others ran down towards her ears.

'You've not forgotten,' said Saliha.

'No, I have not.'

'Neither have I.'

As the hurried scratch of matches and the light of candles spilled out of the kitchen window, Cemal hastened back up to his feet.

'I'm sorry.'

Cemal stayed silent.

'Truly.'

'Don't worry.'

'I sometimes get…'

'It's all right, sweetie.'

Candles were passed from hand to hand throughout the garden. Their flames swayed slowly, unthreatened by the still night. Even their flickering light was enough to dim the stars many times the size of the sun. Individual voices were easily discernible in the dark, silent surprise filling the garden, yet every conversation could also be heard simultaneously. The dark cloak shielding them from the glare of the bare bulbs and the croaking of the organist, the magical inadequacy of the candles illuminating the garden in globes, and the self-preservation instinct that discarded belligerence: it all helped to wash away Saliha's panic. In that miraculous, curative silence, Hasan Dede approached the couple. The deep lines of his face could have been inked in. The flames fluttered in his wake. Once the skittish, pulsating shadows had returned to their places, he – taciturn as ever – nodded at Saime. She ran indoors and came back out, carrying a silver tray covered with a lacy handkerchief.

Privileged by the number of years he had spent in the world, Hasan Dede picked up the little ring from the piece of silk glimmering in response to the candles and placed it on Saliha's finger; next, his ancient hand went back to the tray as though it were considering every move, picked up the larger ring, dropped it just when it was rising, picked it up again, and trembling, zeroed in on Cemal's finger and found the target. The red ribbon tying the rings had been kept long to ensure the union would be a long one, but no one had considered how long it would take Hasan Dede to find the middle. Cemal was happy with this slow-motion ceremony, the unnatural silence, being watched breathlessly by the whole of Andalıç, the sky and the stars, and the middle of the red ribbon evading identification. The silence of the guests intensified under the taciturnity of Hasan Dede, who regarded talking as a pointless occupation. Something new, surrender and hope softened Cemal's chest after all the strain by worries over the future and his recent disappointment. He wished for a long and soft and smooth union, just like this ribbon; and just then a bright star slipped into the sea, leaving a trail of light.

The scissors flashed in the light of every candle. Snip.

'God give you happiness.' The only words that escaped Hasan Dede's lips throughout the ceremony. Metallic applause echoed, subdued by the darkness. Cemal and Saliha kissed Hasan Dede's cracked, bone dry hands first, then shook each other's hand gravely and exchanged kisses on the cheeks. The harsh light of the bulbs abruptly replaced the candle flames in eyes happy to linger in the dim silence. The spell was broken. They laughed.

In unison, every TV set, radio, fridge, dishwasher and washing machine in Andalıç burst into that inaudible hum only conspicuous by its absence. As if they, too, were wired, the humans also grew more animated. The electro organ bellowed over all other sounds. A slow piece in honour of the newly-engaged couple. Everyone was waiting for them to have the first dance to let their hair down.

Unsettled by the broken spell, Cemal glanced at Saliha, wondering if she would dance. He got a faint nod. Their first steps triggered a two-hour marathon of stomping, forcing people to their feet, playing coy, running away and giving into the insistence in increasingly faster tempos of the latest pop songs, folk dances, belly dances, and ending with the *kasapiko,* the butcher's line dance popular on both sides of the Aegean.

After all the guests had been sent away with kisses, Cemal took his leave of the family and walked out of the wooden gate. Lifting his head immediately, he looked for Corona Borealis despite the bright streetlights. Both hands in his pockets, he returned to his solitude, playing with the unfamiliar ring on his finger and his half of the long red ribbon.

8

The more Cemal succumbed to a pleasant lethargy by the warmth of the lengthening days, the dazzling gold of the ring on his finger, and a desire not to stir from the spot he was seated, the more frequent became Melahat's trips to the shop. A week of this increasingly irritating traffic after the engagement party, and Saliha had enough. Thus prodded, Cemal bought a coach ticket, which meant having to get a move on two days hence. Every time he opened his wallet, he tugged at the corner of the ticket, which he then straightened and pushed back. A surging wish to run away, retract, not-to-go, made his decision intolerable, weighed him down.

Istanbul. The Istanbul he had visited twice in the past. Too big, too crowded. He never got why everyone loved it so much; he certainly didn't. There was mud everywhere when he had alighted at the Harem Coach Terminal on a freezing December day five years earlier; too many people to look in the face were all doing their bit like tiny parts of a single creature. His father seemed to be passing on the left when Cemal turned his head to the right, and on the right when he looked left. The diminutive old men seen from the windows of the minibus were wrapped in scarves, berets pulled down to their noses. His father, multiplied by hundreds, was slipping away right under his nose. Wherever Cemal turned his head, he spotted the shoulders, arms or feet of old men turning a corner, entering a shop or boarding a bus. It was much easier to get lost for good in Istanbul than anywhere else.

This ticket contained all the others he had bought in the past, all the roads he had set out on, all the previous searches. Except this time there was an address. There was just the one place to go. It may work, it may not. Beyoğlu. *Moonlight* Pavyon. Street name, door number, all there. Someplace his previous trips never took him: Beyoğlu. The reluctance of setting off on a mission, a threatening uncertainty.

'You look a little subdued.'

'Hm.'

'I said, you're a bit subdued.'

An undeserved, un-June-like heat had settled over noon.

'Probably the heat,' said Cemal.

Saliha cast a look at the lunch tray she had brought. 'You didn't finish your lunch either. Didn't you like it?'

'It was fine. I'm just not very hungry.'

All that could be heard was the buzzing of flies. They sat in silence for a while, their breaths constricted by an inner distress, a tightness over their stomachs; then they both sighed at the same time.

'Why aren't you talking?' Feeling guilty for having offended Cemal at the party, Saliha had been trying to make amends for a week, but nothing seemed to work. She was fed up.

'Don't know. There's nothing to talk about.'

'You always found something to tell me.'

Cemal gave her a tired smile. 'You know everything anyway.'

'You're still cross with me. You're doing this to punish me.'

Laying down the fork that was standing in mid-air, Cemal forced down the last couple of mouthfuls that were stuck in his throat. 'Good God! Where did that come from? What punishment?'

Saliha's eyes were filling. 'I've bent over backwards to make it up to you for the past week. Even baked a cake for the first time in my life. I've apologised too. Why are you doing this?'

'I swear I'm not doing anything, Saliha. I just feel listless. It's all because of this trip.'

'Always the same excuse.'

One of the old wooden cupboards in the shop squeaked out of the blue.

'What excuse do you mean?' Cemal turned to look at Saliha, who had burst into sobs. 'Why are you crying now? Don't cry, sweetie. It breaks my heart when you cry. What have I said now to make you cry?' Gingerly embracing his fiancée, he stroked her hair. 'Come on Saliha, that's enough now.' The sobs didn't seem to be abating any time soon. 'I've got nothing against you, sweetie. People have all kinds of worries. Concerns. Please don't.' He continued to stroke her hair. 'You've been very sweet for the past week.'

'No, Cemal. Accept it. You were hurt, and you can't forgive.' Picking up the napkin on the tray, she wiped her nose noisily. 'But I can't help it. Isn't it unfair to expect someone to do what she can't? All right, so it was a bit much. I couldn't cope. My nerves were shot. But you know me so well; why can't you understand?'

'I do.'

'No, you don't. You wouldn't be hurt if you did.'

Cemal kissed the damp cheeks and swollen lips. 'I do, my darling. I was upset that night, but I'm fine now. You're exaggerating.' The soothing strokes changed over the thin summer dress. His movements grew firmer, his haste overcoming the heat and the lethargy. The smell of sweat seeping out from the undone buttons whipped up the haste. They got as close as two skins could in an unslakeable thirst, whilst their wary ears focused on the shop outside. Quickening breaths and the sour smell of saliva replaced sorrow and pain. They were exploring each other's unknown places, senses sharply focused on a single purpose, excluding the whole world. The world consisted of this searing desire, this focus, this oneness, this twoness. This liquid where no thought remains, a bursting hollow. Beside himself, Cemal's hand moved to his zip.

'Abla.'

Saime sounded so feeble and shy, where she stood at the shop door, that it took them a few seconds to make sense of what they had heard. They hastened to tidy up and get to their feet, then came out of the room to see Saime standing at the door, facing the street. 'My uncle and his folks are here... mum sent me over,' she said apologetically as Saliha glared over the lunch tray.

Saliha left with a nervous little wave at Cemal, who had positioned himself behind the counter the moment he had left the room.

Next morning, on her way to see Cemal off at the coach station, Saliha was squeezing and releasing her fingertips one by one. Her dress, which had been getting looser on her by the week, suddenly seemed to have tensed up; it no longer fell in loose folds. Words attempting to sound cheerful were filling with an inner heaviness and escaping her throat in a laden, muffled tremor. Raising her right hand over her sternum, she rubbed her neck. Cemal was too tense to pay attention to her, but caught up with her tale halfway through.

'My uncle and his folks got in. Pulled out the woman and the man from the bathroom. "This fella looks nothing like our Süleyman Bey," says my uncle to himself.'

'But what happened, though?'

'I've been telling you for half an hour! Gas poisoning. Their neighbours were poisoned by the water heater. The kids were screaming. They had to break the door to get in.'

'And?'

'Ooh, Cemal! She'd taken her lover in! Locked the kids in their room.'

'A-ha!'

'A-ha, exactly. Then they were poisoned by the fumes in the bathroom. She was a covered type and all! Of course, it caused no end of gossip.'

Cemal chuckled. 'Bold as brass, eh? What did her husband do?'

'What do you think? Divorced her.'

'Could have shot her, even.'

'Of course; his property, right? He can shoot if he wants.'

'At least he was a civilised fellow.'

They laughed.

'Look, she took her lover in; you've yet to take me in, Cemal!'

Saliha was laughing, but Cemal grew serious.

'Soon as I'm back, God willing,' he said.

The crows pecking at some invisible fare on the ground blustered until the last possible moment before taking to wing with defiant squawks. Engine chugging noisily, a lorry sped from behind. Cemal tugged Saliha gently by the arm and took up the outside on the pavement.

'Mother always made me walk on the inside when I was a child,' said Saliha, 'And she took the outside.'

The coach station's entrance came into view.

'Turn back here,' said Cemal.

'Why?'

'Don't know.'

'Don't want me to wave? Look, I've even got a white handkerchief!' Pulling it out of her pocket, she waved it with a smile.

'OK, come along then. I don't know. I feel a bit weird this time. I really don't want to go. Like I'd never leave if I saw you there.'

'Then you'd stay here and sulk all day, lost in thought.'

They walked through the huge entrance hung with a wide metal plate emblazoned ANDALIÇ COACH STATION.

'Good God, it's so hard to leave you, Saliha!'

She laughed. 'You'll be back in a couple of days if all goes well; don't know if I can wait though.'

With an uneasy chuckle, they looked around.

'What I want to do is to hug you and cover you with kisses; that's why I told you to go, Saliha.'

'Wouldn't it be better to hug me and kiss me, though?'

'But look; I know everyone here!'

He exchanged greetings with the buffet kiosk holder. Waved at the old 'uncle' selling tickets for the village buses.

'I don't care. I'm not going anywhere until I've waved this handkerchief. Kiss me if you like or don't; your choice.'

The driver started the engine. 'Istanbul passengers, all aboard!' yelled the assistant.

Cemal shook his fiancée's hand formally and kissed her on both cheeks, pressing his lips just a little more firmly than usual. Just as he was about to turn round and climb onto the first step, she tugged at his hand. Placing her mouth on his ear, she said, 'Cemal. Cemal. Don't do anything risky. Don't. Come back at once if you sense anything like that. Fast. Just come back.'

This time Cemal turned, grabbed her tight and gave her cheeks several long kisses. A broad smile opened up below Saliha's welling eyes. The coach set off just as Cemal put his foot on the first step. He remained standing whilst the white handkerchief remained visible before settling into his seat at number 15, churning with emotion.

He alights under the orange lights of the ugly city that takes hours to cross. Amongst high buildings with blazing windows. He feels under attack by it all. Blocks of flats whose walls echo and amplify the traffic noises, the starless darkness above the lights, faces trained to avoid looking, and that constant flow, which will only slowly abate as the hours pass. He is not familiar with the city's night. Accustomed to asking for the past twenty years, he consults strangers and locals: which bus, where? Some are strangers here. In the belly of the monstrous city. Tickets? In the little kiosk. Taksim? That second bus. A sudden start. He apologises to the elderly auntie he has banged into. Glaring, she turns her head away. Crowded. One of two women gripping their bags speaks. 'Thankfully the bus isn't too crowded.' Crowded and cramped. The city passes by in slow motion. People hurrying over pavements. A bit of cool air mixed with the odour of exhaust comes in from the little fanlights. One of the two women calls out, 'Shut that window, brother, it's cold.' Less and less air every second, and hotter too. A sudden brake. Everyone is flung over one another. A sudden start. Everyone is flung in the opposite direction. This time, he stands fast and avoids smashing into the elderly auntie. It's weird to see people walking in Istanbul; as if nowhere could be within walking distance. Could you walk to Taksim? No, it's too far. The city shakes them all without touching their feelings much. It has its own time. It gives the same route different times, sometimes half an hour, at others, one hour, or even two. The city determines jams and flows. Whom to hold back, whom to release, when to hold back and when to release.

His weary head resting on the arm hanging on the rail. Tsss. Passengers alighting and boarding. More cramped. Tsss. Shouting shopwindows. The bus submits to the city's time and shortens its steps. The ancient engine rattles the windowpanes. It coughs. Everything standing up. Weary feet.

After too long bloated on the heat, the crowds and stuffiness, the bus seems to pop its cork and decant its entire contingent in a plaza. Last stop. Taksim. It's nine o'clock. Not yet dark. One of the longest days in the northern hemisphere. A cool, dim blue hangs over the unraised heads of the crowd moving back and forth on vaguely the same lines, like blood pumped through the veins. A thin, faded crescent over them, Mars and the Evening Star too. Cemal manages to place the unfamiliar city under the familiar sky somewhere on the compass. His stomach is rumbling. He enters İstiklal Road from one end, that thoroughfare tramped by thousands shoulder to shoulder in parade formation. Maintaining his own pace necessitates zigzagging. Swarms of people flow past on either side, like ants from a kicked anthill. Some flamboyant, striking; others, in a calculated, bizarre scruffiness, and others, recognisably ordinary.

Turning his travel-weary head right and left, Cemal walks along the tram rails. The lights are dazzling. As he stares at the drained face over the sachets of lavender, a sudden yell makes him jump out of his skin. The madman, his one thrill scaring people by sneaking up from behind for a shriek, walks past, looking pleased with himself. He yells at the top of his voice again a little later. Two girls in front of him jump. They swing round terrified, see the madman, and break into giggles.

Cemal's stomach is rumbling. He finds big restaurants a little intimidating. Crowds flocking in and out. A queue outside one. It must be cheap, but the idea of queuing outside a restaurant is quite unpleasant. He walks, hunching his shoulders and ducking, turning his body left or right as needed. A constant stream in and out of side streets. Pubs, taverns, tables on the street. People sitting, getting up, eating.

Cemal's stomach is rumbling. Doing the least advisable thing in a big city, he stares at faces. Worse still, at eyes. He's on a hunt for smiles. As he always does to warm up, whenever he goes somewhere new. Single people walk past in familiar tempos on auto pilot, their faces closed, lost in familiar thoughts. You need to look at people in groups when you hunt smiles. Definitely not women with children. A sullen face, a shrill rebuke, frowning eyebrows. Lovers may seem to be the ideal choice, but the drunken bliss stretching lips across slackened faces is more a fixture than a real smile. At any rate, lovers often wander around in a state of loud tension. Laughter bursting in peaks of banter amongst groups of friends is hindered by an exclusionist group spirit. The hollow laughter of men in suits and ties after work is laden with a groggy exhaustion. The wicked grin on the faces of whispering women suggests Schadenfreude-inducing gossip. But what Cemal is looking for is a genuine smile. Like the one falling on Saliha's face unbidden when she's lost in a favourite book by the window. Something that will bring him closer to this city than the stars. A city with inhabitants who know how to smile. He finds a bitter smile on the hissing lips of a middle-aged couple. The manifestation of a practised argument, homely after years soured together. Toxin spreading from tense nostrils to squinting eyes.

Cemal's stomach is rumbling. He has the reluctance of people who grew up dining exclusively at home. It's impossible to pick a restaurant and go in. Faces stand out from the crowd flowing past the shopwindows, tensed into an almost-smile by acquisitiveness, features washed out by the bright lights. He thinks he might have found what he was looking for on the face of a woman nodding with a distracted smile as she listens to the man beside her, but then changes his mind; maybe she was just being polite. Just then, he catches the twinkle on the face of a youngster admiring a small painting behind the expanse of glass belonging to an art gallery. Was that a studied expression? He can't be sure.

Cemal's stomach is rumbling. He spots his prey by the telephone cabins at Galatasaray. A willowy twenty-something with tousled dark blonde tresses. She clutches the handset to her chest before replacing it. Slowly opens the door and leaves, keeping her face hidden. Before taking a step with her right foot, she bounces lightly on her left. Cemal finds the smile not on her face, but on that bounce. She turns into a side street and enters a restaurant. A small spot popular with tradespeople. Cemal dives in after her and the little bell on the door rings. He can't see her at any of the tables, but soon she comes over with a smile, pen and paper to take his order. His eyes follow the progress of her agile heels where the smile still hangs. Gentle enough to float. Stares at the white hands placing the dishes before him. He has a couple of hours to kill to get closer to midnight. He chews slowly. His jaw opens and closes, daunted.

Rested and hunger satisfied, he feels brighter, more energetic, and even more reluctant. He's never even seen a pavyon in his life. He spins the salt shaker, staring so fixedly that he could be using his gaze and not his fingers. The heavy ceramic makes a deep rattle as it spins on the wooden table. Again and again.

'Would you like some coffee?'

The girl, whose smile had dimmed in stages as Cemal was eating, brings over the coffee. The froth has a hole in the middle. Then money. Then the street. He still has nearly two hours to kill. Once he's located the pavyon, he starts wandering aimlessly. Dives into back streets to escape the crowds. The darkness is much more intense now. He passes streets mainly populated with males. One has a funny name: Giraffe Street. Funny street, too. Women in the shopwindows. Half-naked women. Gawping, grinning men. Pre-moustache boys. Some of the older women loudly advertising themselves. 'It's a job.' Occasionally someone goes in, picks a woman and goes upstairs. Occasionally someone leaves, face not looking particularly relaxed. Pale-faced callow youths tremble as they are shoved through the door by their mates. 'It's a job.' A man spits at the ground and wipes his moustache with the back of his hand right in front of Cemal. 'There are women with children here. It's a job.' Cemal mostly stares at the kids forced to come here to pop their cherries. He can't look at the women. He can only look at their faces. The moment he does, he doesn't want to look any longer. He's got heartburn. At one door stands a young woman, who resembles Cemile's photo in his pocket. A crowd in front of her. She's fanning herself with a newspaper to cool down. She stares at the men in front of her like a scene she's hardened to. Lifts her short skirt and lethargically scratches her hip. A wave amongst the men. One of them nods and goes inside with her.

The night that refuses to cool down settles heavily on Cemal's neck. There is a numb spot between his eyebrows. Needles and pins on his wrists. He stops before a relatively quieter house. Behind him, the baleful pulsations of lust for sale, the hum of strange voices. He pats his wallet. Stares at a strapping blonde who could be an immigrant. Approaches the door. 'It's a job.' He doesn't find her remotely attractive. Sweat pours down his back. The head he lifts up to the starless orange night is spinning. Turning back, a fierce throbbing in his ears, he runs away from the street. The street.

The street. The streets. Cemal wavered outside when he reached the pavyon again. It was close to midnight. He was back by this terrifying door once again, after a hesitant, idling orbit, entering a pub each time he wanted to sit down, and downing a beer or two. Passing between pale jackets worn over a threatening swagger and broad shoulders, he went in. His hand on his wallet as if he needed one more look at the photo in his pocket, to make sure, he stood somewhere in the middle of the hall. Then he changed his mind. He looked for that picture on the faces of the women accustomed to being stared at and picked. Trying to place the young girl's face under the bleached hair, heavy make-up, and the weariness of bondage.

There were tables, women at the tables. He had to get closer in the dim light. To take a closer look. An accustomed tension and a fleeting lethargy swam side by side in the atmosphere cheapened by the flat singer. Cemal lurched from one table to the next, like a fish in the south-westerly.

'What'sa matter, handsome; can't find one to your taste?' Shrill, croaking women's laughter.

He knew he couldn't afford to sit down and drink. Silenced by the voice screeching his ears and pinching his brain, he made for one of the women. As he pulled out the picture from his pocket, murmuring something, he saw her alarmed gaze. A hand touched his back.

'This way, mate.'

The amount of muscle behind him grew as he walked towards the door. The moment he stepped outside, he bent double with the two punches to the stomach. He sat up, winded, and another punch caught him on the right cheek and temple. Then a kick to his calf. One more, this time to the kidneys, when he fell down. Two men grabbed him by the arms and pulled him up to his feet. 'Drinks, yes; women, yes; questions, no. Fuck off. You won't get away so easy if I catch you again,' said the thug and delivered one more in the belly for good measure.

Once the footsteps had gone away, he pulled his arms from his face and stared behind the bouncers. He was lying in a narrow street, surrounded by rubbish stinking in the summer heat and ragged cats – blind in one eye, or missing an ear tip. An ugly ginger moggie with a coat so grey that it could have been covered in soot, was calmly licking its paw. It carried on, ignoring Cemal, then reluctantly got up to sit a little further away, and turned its back.

Cemal sat up. His right temple was throbbing and warm blood seeped from his lip. Suddenly he felt violently sick, turned to the side and vomited. He was sitting next to his own sick, unable to summarise his pains, when a touch on the shoulder made him jump.

'Are you all right, son?'

A man well past middle-age, in a pale suit and a red carnation in his buttonhole.

'You got a real working over.'

Cemal was trying to stand up in all the pain. The man held out a hand.

'Can you walk?'

'Ah wull,' rolled Cemal's mouth, 'Thank you, uncle. You carry on.'

'Come on then, let me see you walk. Let's make sure nothing's broken.'

Cemal hobbled for a couple of steps.

'Where do you live? Let me put you into a taxi or something.'

'I don't. Not here, I mean. I'm from out of town.'

'Don't you have anywhere to stay?'

'No. I'd not got around to looking. I was going to go back straight away.'

'Where is home?'

'Andalıç. Do you know it?'

'And how! Andalıç, eh? Well, well, well. Andalıç.'

The ginger cat jumped into one of the big bins. A sudden screech, and an even scrawnier cat shot out.

'Come with me then, seeing as you've got nowhere else to go.' Cemal's hesitation was so obvious that he felt the need to add, 'I won't hurt you. My name is Hakkı. Known as Baba Hakkı.'

'Who did you fight with?'

'I don't know.'

'How do you mean?'

'I mean, I don't know them. I don't have a personal issue with anyone.'

Hakkı nodded before pausing.

'So what's the issue then?'

A flash of white caught Cemal's eye, the belly of a seagull flying over the powerful streetlights. 'Seagulls fly here at night too?'

'Eh?' Hakkı looked up. 'Mean the seagulls? Poor things don't know night from day.' He waited for a little longer, but there was no change in the scene; Cemal was still standing in the middle of the street. 'Aren't you coming?'

'The issue is a woman. I'm looking for a woman. Heard she was working in a pavyon. Moonlight Pavyon, it was.' They set off slowly. The stitches of the story were unravelled as they proceeded in quickening steps before pausing again. Aches thinned out words, interrupting sentences and silences that could have turned permanent.

Hakkı pointed a little down the street. 'Look, that's where Moonlight Pavyon is. This is a long street. Looks as if it ends here, at this bend. Did you check the number?'

'The address didn't have a number.'

'Well, come with me now, and we'll figure something out.'

'No, I'd better not. I don't want to be any trouble.'

'Don't worry, son. I'm an old man. How can I hurt you?'

As darkness deepened, the faces, clothes and postures of the people on the back streets changed. There were bodies who moved as effortlessly in the night-time back streets as fishes in the water.

'Don't misunderstand, Uncle Hakkı.'

Hakkı raised his hand.

'We'll fall out if you call me *uncle*. Everyone calls me *dad* around here.'

'Hakkı Baba.' Black blood stains on his shirt, a thousand and one aches all over.

'You can't put a foot into anywhere in this state. Let's get you sorted out first. I know what it's like. The things I've seen! Wish I hadn't, but there you are.' He resumed walking without looking back, just turning his head a little to hear footsteps. 'You're skint, aren't you, Cemal, son? You're a stranger to this world. Eh? Come along; let's get you cleaned up. Find you a shirt and a jacket to borrow. I'll give you a few words of advice. Then you're free to go wherever you want. Fatherly advice.' He turned round when the footsteps stopped. 'Sorry, it just came out. Is your father alive?'

'No. He died last month.' Cemal resumed walking.

'Sorry for your loss.'

Cemal was sitting in the cramped lounge of a small bachelor's pad, his damp hair brushed back, face washed, lip swollen and a faint bruise on his chin. Clumps of aches in various parts of his body made him grimace at every move, tied his tongue and deepened the furrow between his brows. Now that he was surrounded by the unmistakable familiarity of a poor home, however, he relaxed a little.

'So you're going to take her back. Letter, et cetera, et cetera,' said Hakkı, placing one beer bottle in front of Cemal, and another in front of his mate sporting several days' growth of a greying beard, sitting in pants and vest. There seemed to be some sort of patron/supplicant relationship between the two.

'Then best not to ask anyone; eh, Sadun?'

His friend shook his head.

'You can't just go in there looking with a photo in your hand and stuff. Gotta sit down like a regular patron. But even a glass of beer will cost and arm and a leg. And what if she's not free?' Another shake of the head, and another sip of beer. Cemal had yet to hear Sadun's voice. 'If you were to go back tomorrow, you'd be ruined.' Hakkı stood up, turned the radio on and searched through the stations until he found classical Turkish music. '*The final stage of our lives, our final spring...*' he accompanied the lyrics. 'Every classical song is a sad one,' he conceded with a long, deep laugh.

'Aren't you drinking, Hakkı Baba?'

Sadun spoke for the first time. 'Sworn off.'

'I promised my son and daughter-in-law. Went to rehab. It's a long story, this shit and me.' After listening to the entire song with a contented look, he looked back at Cemal. 'They force them to sign debt bonds. They give 'em money first, right? But the pimps blow the money. It's the girls who have to pay it off. If they're in debt, they're pursued. Some pimps are nasty pieces of work. God forbid, they can and do kill.'

Having heard it all before, been warned time and again, and having thought it through, Cemal made no objection. 'Can't leave her there, either,' he murmured feebly.

'Cemal, son; are you married?'

'I'm engaged.'

'You'll get into trouble. Don't say I've not warned you. Isn't that so, Sadun?'

Sadun nodded. 'Trouble.'

'We've made it to one o'clock! Go over about two-ish. You'll speak to her if you can find her, if you can get anywhere near. If you can't, scribble something here. You'll find an opportunity to tuck it into her hands.' A siren in the distance drowned out the radio. 'God help him, whoever he is.'

'Amen,' said Sadun. Belched. Rolled up his vest and wearily scratched his belly.

Squinting, his split lip stinging with the beer, Cemal nodded.

'I never complain, weeping instead at my state…' Hakkı was clearly in the habit of reciting the lyrics like a poem. With a moue that said, *Will you listen to these lyrics!* he shook his head.

'Tell it, Baba.'

'You've heard it so many times though, Sadun.'

'To the lad.'

'What's the lad gonna do with my tale?' He turned back to the song, raised one hand and recited enthusiastically, *'I fear the curtain of gloom is drawn over my fortune…'*

Sadun's beer was gone. Sitting back, he belched once more. Lit a cigarette.

'How old are you, Cemal?'

'Thirty-eight.'

'Wow! I wasn't even your age then.' And the tale began. A rich father, a yalı on the Bosphorus, the finest cars of the time, factories… Hakkı had done it all. All that money could get, all the women money could buy; he'd toured Europe, got back to carry on gadding about here. He had neglected the business, and all advice went in one ear, come out the other. A girl was found so he could marry. The daughter of a similarly rich family. He went along with it, since he viewed it as a mere formality, since he had no intention at all of changing anything.

'It was a month before the wedding. There was a spot behind the pavyon where you were beaten up. We were there with my mates. It was called Lalezar. A new place called Tulip Garden, eh? I was struck the moment I walked in. A woman like…' Pursing his lips, he slowly waved a hand. 'Her name was Lale. Probably not her own name. She never told me. A fresh young thing like this girl in your picture. Dark eyebrows, dark eyes, long dark hair. Something wild. You'd have thought she was lassoed out in the sticks and brought into the city. If you were to ask me if she was beautiful… I couldn't say. People were fighting over her every other night. People slashed, shot in the street, had their faces rearranged like you. You know when we say *woman,* she was nothing like that. She was something completely different. Doesn't talk. Never goes with anyone. Didn't have a pimp or a lover. Took her time to turn round for a look when you called.'

He scratched his large, red, pockmarked nose with a sound like crumpling paper. A woman who was quite a handful, one who sits on a lap but runs away from the bed, one who can tame the worst brute into a lamb with a single glance – a strange animal who breaks hearts everywhere.

'I knew her figure like the back of my hand. Like every old hand. Never saw her laugh out loud, simper or flirt. She could down a whole bottle of whisky and still stay sober. Never accepted gifts from anyone. No diamonds, no brilliants … nothing. Women are strange creatures, in other words. More fool you if you think otherwise.'

Hakkı had cancelled the wedding and everything. Not that he'd been putting a foot through the door of the factory, anyway. And the managers he'd left in charge since his father's death had failed, grabbed what they could of the sinking ship and announced bankruptcy.

'I didn't give a fig about the world. One day, whatever made me do it, I invited her to tea. Funny thing, she accepted. I was handsome, of course, even if I do say so myself.'

Cemal glanced again at the young Hakkı in swimming trunks in the photo on the wall.

'We met at a tea garden like school-age lovers. Ended up going to every tea garden in Istanbul over time. She's in conservative outfits. Even a little scarf over her hair.'

He had blown it all in the pavyon, his whole fortune, everything from the bank accounts to the office buildings and flats that were sold.

'Man: you can do anything, and never know why. I proposed, but she refused. I couldn't figure it out. She didn't give me a sniff, other than holding her hand at the tea gardens and copping a feel at the pavyon.' He stared at Sadun's empty beer bottle. *'Scared to smell you, my lovely magnolia … '* He went inside. Brought out another beer. 'You've not finished yet, have you, Cemal?'

'Nah.'

'Where were we … Oh, yes. One day, there was a brawl again. Some hulk of a man grabbed her. Thinking he could drag her out, I guess. Everyone's hammered. A twenty-something athletic fellow jumped in to protect our girl. I was inured to this sort of stuff by then, I was staying out of it. The bloke's got a huge flick knife. I didn't see what happened, or how. One moment.

One moment Lale had got up, the next she was on the knife. Did she try to intervene, grab the knife, or…'

Still puzzled by this secret, he paused. 'They always play this *Makber*. What a gloomy song!' He got up and stilled the crackling of the radio. 'I rushed over. She was lying on the floor. No one dared to get near. As if they were all slashed. I lifted her head. We're just frozen there, like in a Turkish film. The knife rises and falls with every breath. She was about to say something. I bent down. Thinking she'll tell me she loves me in her last breath. "Tea," she said, "Tarabya's is the best." Those were her last words.'

Surprised that his pain had dwindled over the years, Hakkı laughed.

'You know why I'm called Baba Hakkı? Nothing to do with fatherliness or anything. I was pining away at the time. Pater's fortune is dwindling in the meanwhile. My mates used to ask whenever they saw me, "Did you get what you wanted?" I'd shake my head. They kept taking the piss that I'd been fucked again, "Hakkı's gobbled the *baba* again." You know the saying. So I'm now Baba Hakkı. Not *Paternal*. Not because I did anyone a tiny bit of good all my life. *Fucked Over* Hakkı.'

'God forbid,' filled Sadun's mouth in an evidently customary tone.

Wearing the borrowed jacket and drunk more on this conurbation and everything he received – the beating, the help and the advice – and heard so far – the stories and the melancholy songs – than on the beers downed one after the other, Cemal walked into the Moonlight Pavyon. The kind of place where a bruised face elicits respect, not suspicion.

A belly dancer shimmied between the tables, unhurried hands tucking tips into her costume here and there, her movements intermittently revealing a sparsely populated hall, possibly because it was mid-week. An aggressively stunted sexuality was on display *en masse*, about the same level as good family girls might indulge in with their intendeds in nooks and crannies. Buying a woman was enough for the men here. They didn't even need to bed her.

The dancer tarried a little by Cemal, but as his eye strayed to the rear, she resumed her perambulations. A lone woman sat at a drunken angle at one of the tables at the back, forehead resting on her hand. The only woman in the room whose face was obscured.

He traversed the length of the club in an unintentional swagger: hobbling slightly to favour his aching calf, arms held away from the ribs, and head tilted back each time his eyes lost focus in the golden haze of the beer he'd consumed. An error in calculation as he approached made him take one extra step and he banged noisily into the chair. The woman's hand slid from her forehead to her temple, her eyes blinked open and she scrambled to replace the sleepy stupor on her face with a sham focus. Mustering a phoney coquettishness, she flicked the scraggly ends of her long peroxide blonde hair. Her elbow slipped on the table and she nearly hit her chin. Straightened up with a laugh. The dark circles under her dark eyes showed through the foundation.

'Sit down, big boy.'

The stitches to the right of her upper lip had altered the shape of her mouth. The nose was the same.

Cemal pulled the chair he'd banged into, centred it in two moves, and sat down.

'What happened to your lip, darling? Who'd ya hurt?'

The sound of the dancer's zils hurt his head.

'A real man talks little. I like a quiet man.'

The dancer was still moving around the hall. She came over; the fringes on her costume amplified the movements in impossible parts of her body. Distracted by the undulating flesh before his eyes, Cemal struggled to visualise the photo in his pocket. Matching the photo to the reality was proving to be difficult. A leg peeking out through the tulle, something shimmering immediately above it, and fringes that come close enough to poke his eyes before swinging away. He resumed his inspection after the dancer left.

'And so handsome too, God bless,' said the sitting woman. She brushed his hair back, 'Eyes, brow, and tall too. A sight for sore eyes, once in a blue moon.' The waiter had come over. 'What're you having, husband darling? I'm on the whisky meself.'

'Whisky.' And then, 'How long have you been here?'

She waved the question away, 'Neeever mind. Even I can't remember. A year, five months? So long as we have a good time; makes no difference.'

Cemal's 'How did you come to fall into this place?' rang much too loud, falling as it did into the abrupt pause in the music and the dancer's zils.

The whole room turned to stare. Some of the women laughed out loud.

'Made 'em laugh! Don't worry, heartthrob. That's the key question for all the tarts here. What everyone wants to know. What a lark.'

The music began again. A woman took to the stage, singing as she stripped. The underage violinist had been seated with his back to the stage.

'Something about you, big boy. I've taken to you. I'd take you home this minute if it wasn't for our Zaim.' Cemal flinched: she was slowly stroking his leg under the table. 'Don't be shy, lover, touching's allowed.' Her hand kept creeping ever higher.

'Where are you from?' His eye slid to the woman on the stage, to the now bare tits.

'Eskişehir. What, we're neighbours now?'

'Cemile!'

Her hand stopped, 'Think I look like someone else? They call me Gülümser.' She stared, suddenly sober, occasionally glancing at the man looming at the entrance.

The memory of the clobbering, the coquettish laughter, the frisky music, and the fondling at the increasingly busier tables washed over Cemal in a wave of torpor. Too tired to insist. He downed his whisky. He saw curiosity amongst the less charming things on her face.

'Gülümser: just listen. My name is Cemal. I'm looking for my half-sister, but I've never seen her. All I have is her photo.' His hand reaching for his pocket halted at the memory of the pain in his neck. 'I thought you looked a little like her. I'm sorry.'

'A little,' she said with a bitter laugh, 'a little.'

'Her mother asked me. Her mother wanted me to look for her. "Find her and bring her back," she said. If you know her… if she wants to, I'm here to take her back to her mother.' The music stopped again.

With a loud laugh, she waved at someone behind them, making Cemal's heart miss a beat, 'Bring 'em over, Necati, two refills here.' The music struck again. 'Can't sit here without drinking, big boy.'

'Then I'll have to leave, Gülümser. I haven't got a lot of money. And if you don't know Cemile, there's no point in me staying either.' He pushed his chair back, but she grabbed hold of his knee, and wouldn't let go.

'Sit down, heartthrob, what's your hurry? Samet Abi here will give me what for, grumbling I've lost no time to scare off a customer.' The whiskies arrived. 'Throw your arm over my shoulder; don't worry, I won't eat you.'

Cemal was at a loss what to do, unable to read her face or the pulse of the club. Unable to read the kanun player with the pasted-on gold-capped grin, the solemn waiter plying amongst the tables, the clarinettist wandering around the stage waving his long instrument, the men groping the women at the tables, the women groping the men, or the heavyset bloke towering at the entrance. 'Look, sister, I mean it...'

'Ooh, now we're brother and sister, are we?' Another peal of laughter. 'Perhaps you've got a sixth sense. Do I really look like the picture then?'

'I'm not sure. The scar on your lip...'

'That's Zaim's doing. I once fell for a hunk, just like you. I tried to run away. He shot the punter in the heel. And cut my lip. Gripped it and made me watch as he did.' She giggled as if at a jolly memory. 'Zaim's my pimp. Pimp Zaim. Loses it when you say that.' She raised her tumbler, 'All right, lover, what are we drinking to? Can't just clink for no reason!'

Cemal leant against the table and covered his face with both hands. 'I want to go,' he said between his fingers.

'Take those hands down now! Are you crying? I hate men who cry when they drink. You think it's easy to pinch a woman from a pavyon, my lamb? If you begin blubbering like this so fast, well, we're in for it!'

'Are you Cemile?'

'Where do you come from, big boy?'

'Andalıç.'

She began toying with the tumbler on the table. 'Cemal, hah? Cemal.' She peered at his face, 'So you're taking Cemile back to her mother?'

'Yes.' Cemal's right leg was twitching and there was a faint ache in his ribs. 'Yes.'

'What if she has a pimp?'

'So?'

'What if he's trouble. Wouldn't let her go.'

'How would he know she'd gone to Andalıç?'

'What if he knew her mum and dad were from Andalıç.'

He stared at her, 'How would he know?'

'If Cemile had told him once. Once.'

Cemal looked down in his customary patient resolve.

'Say this man followed Cemile. Would you shoot him?'

He raised his head in a panic, 'God forbid. No way. We don't kill people.'

'So you'll let him do whatever he wants with her, is that it?'

'She's run back to her mother, not to another man. Why would he kill her?'

'How else does a pimp make a living? He'd be left high and dry if his capital asset ran away.'

In unison, they took a sip of their whiskies. The man at the entrance kept staring restlessly.

'Brother mine, so we've met after all these years, and no hug or kiss?' Cemal hugged Cemile and kissed her on both cheeks.

'So you're penniless too, hah? Still a grocer?'

He replied automatically, 'Yes, still a grocer,' before staring in surprise, 'How do you know?'

'Course I do! Dad always told me, whenever he received news. He'd only tell me though, not mum.' She scanned the club, then said, 'Put your arm around my waist.'

'Are you coming?'

'Do as I say. Samet Abi's glaring at us.'

Reluctantly, Cemal wrapped his arm around his half-sister's waist. The soft, warm bubbling under his hand made him pull back instantly, as if he'd touched something revolting, but Cemile's right hand had grasped his tightly.

'You're determined to treat us as a sister. Half is no sister, babes.'

Vision blurred by the red lights, and temper rising, Cemal snapped, 'How come? Of the same father? What else would you be?' He was frowning in earnest now. 'Are you coming, I've asked.'

'I'm thinking about it.'

'So why'd ya write the letter then?'

'I don't know; must have been pissed, don't even remember it now. Necmi the waiter said the next day, he'd posted it. He's got a thing for me, you see. See how his face falls when you hug me. Silly bugger.' With a merry laugh, she rested her knee against Cemal's.

'Let me go if you're not coming. This isn't my sort of place.'

Cemile's increasingly coquettish gaze lingered on his face.

'All right, bugger it. I've had it with this life, anyways.' She stroked the bruise on his chin gingerly. 'How'd ya get that? It's swollen, too.'

'I went into the wrong place looking for you. That's where it happened.'

'You got beaten up for my sake, hah?' Cemile simpered, tilting her head one way and the other, 'My big brother got beaten up for my sake. Blessss...'

Feeling sick at the overwhelming smell of cheap perfume, Cemal flinched.

'What's with the ring? Engaged?'

He nodded.

'When's the wedding?'

'September.'

'Aaah, not long now, then! How'd your fiancée let you go? What's her name?'

He glowered, 'My fiancée is like no one else,' somehow reluctant to pronounce Saliha's name. The flat singing of the woman drew his eyes to the stage again. Saliha filled his mind with so much longing that it left no room for anything else. Not for sounds, scents, or lights... It was only the sharp pain in his thigh that made him notice the soft weight on his lap. He wanted to get up, but his knees gave way.

'Course I'll sit on my big brother's lap; if not his, then whose? I used to sit on dad's lap just like this too. He'd stroke my hair. Does mum really want me back?'

'Yes.'

'Well, you know what they say, a girl's best friend is her mother.'

'Get off!'

Cemile curled her bottom lip like a kid and burst into tears. Once her sobs had quieted on his shoulder, she whispered an escape plan. Where they'd meet and when.

By the time Cemal was completely awake, he was sitting next to Cemile in a coach speeding towards Andalıç. He recalled as if in a dream waking up on a bench in Taksim Park, finding his wallet empty, sparing his blushes thanks to some loose change in his pocket when he wanted to pay for a cuppa in the tea garden at the corner, returning the jacket to Hakkı, cringing as he accepted the fare tucked into his hand after explaining what had happened, leaving Hakkı and Sadun after eating and noting down their address and telephone so he could pay them back, waiting outside the grocer's facing Cemile's place, tailing her when she walked out of the door and nodded in a silent *Follow me,* boarding the same minibus, and buying tickets at the coach station.

He looked at the dressing on his arm. It had cost them a few hours, but here was Andalıç, finally coming into view over the crest of the hill.

He smiled, albeit a little uneasily, at the sight of Cemile sleeping with her head on his shoulder. The seat next to him was occupied at long last. For the first time, he had found what he was looking for. The woman he had rescued was in the seat which had either mocked him, remaining untaken throughout the journey, or bored him to tears with the nattering or grim silence of strangers. A twenty-year-old sister he had found twenty years later. He cast a happy glance at the sea as the coach traversed the isthmus, an evanescent joy tottering over suppressed concerns. Day had broken long ago; it was mid-morning by now. He had tasted the pleasure of finding, albeit just the once, and despite everything.

As the coach entered the hangar, marching tunes were blaring out of the town's loudspeakers. Prodded gently by Cemal, Cemile sat up, her curiosity overcoming the grogginess: she had never seen her father's hometown before.

'What's that big building at the top?'

'The Care Home.'

As the doors opened, an enthusiastic Military College March flooded in. They descended. Picked up Cemile's suitcase. 'What's the date? Which holiday is it?'

'I don't know.' Suitcase in Cemal's hand, they walked towards the exit. Taxi driver Hasan was drinking tea in the coffee house next door. He chuckled from afar at first, but after a more careful look, he came over.

'What happened to you?'

'Long story.'

'What happened to your arm?'

'On the coach…'

'An accident or something?'

'I mean, yes, a kind of accident, quite out of the blue. There was a butcher in the seat behind me. He'd wrapped his sharpened cleavers and knives and stuff in a newspaper and popped it overhead. The coach swerved in a bend and his cleavers rained down on me. Thankfully not over my head or eyes.'

'Wow! Someone up there likes you, mate. You've had a lucky escape.'

'You can say that again!'

Hasan's gaze kept straying from the dressing on the arm to Cemile's décolleté. He cleared his throat at Cemal's silence. 'Yeah, lucky escape,' he said, unsaid questions peppering his face.

'Fine, Hasan. Excuse us. We're bushed. I'll take Cemile to her mum. See ya.'

In the plodding, lurching steps of the shipwrecked, the pair unconsciously picked up the march rhythm and proceeded amongst the flags wrapped around poles and hanging from ropes stretched over the road. They were dragged by the fluctuating waves of sound from one loudspeaker to another along narrow streets, indifferent to the synthetic jubilation of deliverance that belonged to a generation incapable of even imagining what occupation and war meant.

Shallow grandchildren of grandfathers who had come from all four corners of the land and who had denied their progeny even a single tale about the liberation of Andalıç were lolling about in their shops or homes. The heroics of other places had failed to take root or flourish in this alien soil. The dearth of living memory did not allow for anything deeper than inculcated emotions. All that remained of Andalıç's past rested in stone; it had buzzed off along with the hands that had laid those stones. Words, emotions, and vibrations, which could only be conveyed by those with actual experience, had faded, their truth gone.

Scenes of tearful embraces between mother and daughter, and Melahat's prayers still warm in his mind, Cemal went on to Saliha's home. Rang the bell. Told Saliha's anxious eyes pausing on various parts of his body everything, down to the last detail. He sat in the cool stone room, relieving his split lip with iced lemonade, his eyes with Saliha's eyes and his ears with her voice; he sat there until the sun hit the window and started to warm the back of his neck. All he could think about on his way home was to preserve the sensation on his cheeks.

9

The shade in the street fled from the rising sun towards the printer's shop. Streets deliberately kept narrow, barely the width of a horse cart, in order to remain cool for as long as possible, thick, stone-walled houses snuggling up to one another, walls high enough to keep the shade surrounding tiny courtyards, wetted courtyards. July. The hottest time in Andalıç. Affronted by the complaints, the implacable north-easterly has made itself scarce. Not a whisper nor a breath for days. Dawns that break before the earth has had a chance to cool down. The sun, which makes a mockery of all that distance to the earth as it rubs its scorching back on human skin, and begrudges even a single relaxed breath as it smothers mouths with its golden pelt. Hours that crush the human body under their weight, like individual loads pressing down one by one, one, two, three, four, five.

For the past four days, Andalıç residents had been subdued, weary and expectant. No amount of attention to the weather forecast hastened away the high pressure from the Arabian Gulf. People would continue to toss and turn between sweat-damp sheets for a few more nights, dipping in and out of sleep. The sun was the sun, fine; but the real traitor was the night. Refusing to cool down even a little.

The hottest time in Andalıç. Scrawny stray cats sleeping in the shadiest nooks and crannies, stretching their limbs as the heat rose, sleeping a little deeper, and occasionally lying on their backs, their bellies exposed to the sky. Their floppiness easily serving as a thermometer.

Jülide was sitting beside a black-and-white tomcat covered in scratches and bruises; he was sleeping too deeply to even bother to prick his ears. The stone step was cool.

She had swept the concrete floor thoroughly first thing in the morning, not that it did much to dislodge the soft coating of years of dust sticking to grease. She had also dusted the office. The unnamed absence she had noticed on her first visit was now gone: the printing press was clattering away. Rahmi was wiping his sweaty brow with a sweaty wrist and trying to cool down by fanning his dripping shirt. Once the wedding invitations had been printed, he came, sat next to Jülide and lit a cigarette.

'July: no July passes without weddings.'

Now used to hearing this complaint several times a day, Jülide smiled. Her fingertips were stroking the neck of the limp cat.

'Where did Muzaffer Abla rush off to?'

'To Soma.'

'To Soma? What on earth for?'

Rahmi was thirty. Half his life had been spent in this printer's, which he had originally entered as an apprentice. Despite his constant moans, he must have found something to his liking in this job, given he had never looked for another. He would grumble at Muzaffer all day long, possibly to conceal his respect and love for his boss, but would never let anyone else speak ill of her. He would even happily get into a fight if necessary. His grave eyes held a reassuring glimmer.

Just like the black-and-white cat, he had long since stopped counting the days. The sense of time came from the seasons. As far as he was concerned, time was something that rotated continually rather than being a linear process. Like the cat, he knew hot and cold, and where danger and food would come from. He was caring and he liked the soil. Enjoyed the exuberant fruitfulness of his tiny garden with its rows of onions, lettuces, hanging tomatoes, peppers, aubergines, mandarins, and lemons, which avenged the sweet aroma of their blossom with the tartness of their fruit.

He'd had no family other than Muzaffer's all his life: her father had found him idling, taken him into the printer's, taught him the trade, treated him like a son, and even donated him a little hut with a garden outside Andalıç. He had also tried very hard to marry the lad off, but for some reason, Rahmi had dug his heels in: there was no one to his liking.

'Your intended's on his way, lass.'

Jülide sat up with a short intake of breath.

'My cigarette break is over. Best start on the circumcision party invitations. Then the engagement. It's July, isn't it? Blooming July.' Rahmi went inside. Another funeral announcement came from the loudspeakers. Repeated every morning, these announcements stacked a gloomy crowd of the dead over the town, exceeding the number of the living, and pressing down on the old in particular. The clatter of the starting press drowned out the announcement.

Erkan perched next to Jülide, frowning deeper than ever, having brought along all the weight of the dismal heat of the street. His hair was wet.

'How was training?'

'Good.'

She wanted to circle that dark thing rising towards his lips. To find a way of distracting or silencing him, but it was too hot.

'I don't want you to work. Our women don't work. A woman's place is her home.'

Jülide didn't reply; she was staring at the door opposite and gently rocking on the stone step. Trying to focus on the monotonous clatter of the press.

'... haven't I told you ... besides ... a bloke ... alone with some unmarried bloke ...'

Erkan shut up when she stopped rocking and suddenly swung her head. Her blue eyes flashed with the wild phosphorescence of the heat and her lips were stretched menacingly, like a hissing cat.

'I'm working here because I like Muzaffer Abla, I like journalism and I'm earning some pocket money. You can't decide where I may or may not work. As for Rahmi Abi: he's like a big brother to me.'

'What do you mean I can't decide. You're like, my betrothed.'

'I'm not your betrothed or anything. Neither do I have any intention to be so.'

'Like what?'

'I have no intention of marrying you or anyone else. As a matter of fact, I want to split up now.'

Erkan leapt up to his feet.

'What the fuck are you saying? You're not splitting up or anything. No one splits up with me.'

His hand, which was grabbed by Rahmi just at the right time, was held up in the air.

'You can't raise a hand against women.'

'Mind your own business! You can't interfere between lovers. I can beat her up and I can hug her. My business.'

'Why are you going to beat her up?'

Stronger than suggested by his diminutive build, Rahmi's grip was like a vice, even though the youth was half a foot taller and nearly twice the size.

'She wants to split up.'

'Right.' Erkan was trying to free his hand. 'Since she wants to split up, you're no longer lovers. Which means I can interfere. I'm not letting anyone raise a hand against people working here. All right, mate, away you go. You can't force these things.'

That serene authority forestalled Erkan's anger from transforming into curses or punches. Shaking like a leaf, terrified of a punch-up, Jülide interrupted in a calm voice.

'Erkan. I've thought long and hard. It's not going to work. You interfere with everything. You're too possessive. You're far too conservative. I can't take any of it. Please don't be like that. Let's part as friends.'

Rahmi released the arm slackening in his grip. A furtive, destructive energy was rising inside Erkan, who appeared to have given up, his head sunk into a moment of silence. As they stood still outside the printer's, Jülide heard the sound of the spring being wound. Sensed which arm Erkan would swing. She beckoned the cat from his deep sleep. The cat got up lazily. Leapt up between Erkan's legs just when the youth was about to charge at Rahmi. Erkan stumbled in mid-attack, unexpectedly swift given his unbalanced forward momentum, and his fist swung past Rahmi's shoulder into the glass in the door. The pane exploded in a thunderous clatter in the heat-silenced street, waking up not only the neighbourhood, but the grumpy north-easterly too. A hot breath rolled down the street as blood spurted out of Erkan's arm.

'Can't leave you alone for a couple of hours!' said Muzaffer, staring at the fresh putty of the new pane, the greasy fingerprints on it, and the blood on the wall. The sun had turned to shine into the printer's and the north-easterly had picked up. The top one of the newly-printed stack of engagement invitations was opening and closing, on the verge of falling. 'You've not even started on the newspaper. Who'd you chop up here?'

Since Jülide's guilty silence wasn't going to break any time soon, it fell upon Rahmi to tell the whole story, how it had taken so long to take Erkan to the hospital and get his hand stitched up. That's why the newspaper was late.

'Clueless, this lot: they've no idea how to hook up, or how to break up. Good job the paper wasn't printed, though. We're changing the front page. Looks like we're here for the night.'

COUNCIL IN SHADY COAL DEAL

A stink rises from the Council's so-called winter coal assistance for needy families. The third-grade Soma coal handed out by the Council turns out to have been purchased at second grade prices.

This paper has evidence that the Council purchased the coal from Mayor Vahdet Topçu's cousin Necdet Topçu, a coal wholesaler in Soma, in what is effectively a profiteering deal for Necdet Topçu. For experts' report on the coal samples and copies of the invoices presented to the Council, please turn to page two.

The press ran until midnight in the increasingly raucous north-easterly, which at least served to cool the night. The clatter of steel had stopped by the time a laughing Muzaffer picked up the top copy from the stack. All three exchanged happy and equally exhausted glances. 'Come on, Rahmi, let's walk this lass home,' said Muzaffer. Squinting, they hit the climb.

Seher was still awake, waiting for Jülide. 'Are you done, lass?' 'Yes grandma, look!' Proudly, she handed the paper to her grandmother, whose dry fingers sought a pair of specs in the gap between the pillow and the wall. Unfolding them slowly, she placed them on the tip of her nose and began to read with an index finger under the headline. 'Coun-cil. in Sh-ady. C-coal. D-deal.' She peered at Jülide over her specs. 'Black flecks floating over my eyes. Eyes, hah! What do they call it, cataract or something?' The film over her blue eyes was growing thicker. Her granddaughter picked up the paper and read the article.

Folding her specs gingerly, as though they were creasable, Seher gave her chin a thoughtful rub. 'Yes, fine, but it's a good council. Topçu's a kind man. Hands out coal for the poor and needy. What will they burn all winter long if he doesn't? Wish you'd not said this, lass. What will we do this winter if they don't hand out coal?'

The wind, having only just become fresher, was waving the curtains in the open window.

'No one ever thinks about winter in the heat, eh? Like it's never going to get cold.'

Jülide shook herself, wrenched her gaze away from the curtain and looked at her grandma. 'But can't you see, grandma? He's enriching his own relative under the guise of helping the poor. Think we should stay silent just because he gives away coal?'

Stream-rolled, crushed and crumpled by her seventy-eight years, Seher gave her a sympathetic look. 'Oh, my sweetie, my lambkin. If only you'd seen the things I've seen. Like I care if the mayor's nephew was rich or not. He's not the one who's going to be shivering all winter long.' She stared into the distance. 'Your parents tried so hard. Like they could change things. Things have always been this way, and always will be. She'd come back in the evening, like you. Tell me all about it, all excited. My poor Sabriye.' Her face showed the weariness of waiting until unaccustomed hours. Untying the muslin kerchief she only ever removed in bed, she laid it on her pillow. The collar of her threadbare flannel nightgown, faded from years of washing, framed a desiccated pigeon chest. She tugged at the sleeves sagging at the elbows and made her dry arms looked like twigs. Jülide gave her noisy kisses on the dry, bony cheeks covered only with a soft layer of crepey skin the way she always did whenever she saw those arms.

'You big softie.' Happiness sparkled in Seher's misty, sunken eyes. Then she felt a little sad, watching her granddaughter getting ready for bed. 'You used to visit your dad in prison when you were a baby. Sabriye would cry for ages when you two got back. Nothing changes, lass. Nothing ever does. The poor may get a little help, and that's too easy to lose. Doesn't do the poor any good to talk too much.'

'Was my dad in for long, grandma?' A question whose answer Jülide knew very well; but it would pave the way to other stories buried in her grandmother's memory, other details, and the remnants of a civilisation lost for all eternity.

'Two years and eight months.' Every time her grandma cut it short, every time stories refused to flow, Jülide asked questions to chivvy her along.

'So, what did mum do then?'

'She worked. Even worked in a shop. There's no money in their profession. Then she got a job as an assistant... well, you know it all, lass. Why make me repeat it?'

'Never mind, tell me again.'

Seher was playing with the patches in the sheet; old sorrows were obviously flooding back. 'Things were better then. Your grandpa was alive. Your mum was working. Your dad started working too, when he got back...' The memories were snapping, flung about back and forth in time. 'After the accident, your grandpa passed away too. Oh, İbrahim. If only you were here with us. Oh, lass, why rake it all up now?'

Jülide didn't have the heart to let her grandma go to sleep in this state, not before her favourite story. The moment she started playing with her medallion, memories gathered around it.

'It was like a festival when your dad was released. Your mum decorated the whole house. Cooked your dad's favourite dishes. Wouldn't let me do anything. Dressed to the nines. Dolled you up, too. We could tell, even then, that your hair would be so thick. She tied up two bunches with pink ribbons. I remember it like it was yesterday. I'd knitted you a pink dress. You looked lovely in it. She'd dressed you up in it. You two went, picked him up and came home. Your mum had invited a couple of friends who weren't inside. They sang. Drank. Sabriye's eyes shone with joy. You fell asleep in the armchair. Your dad picked you up. Carried you and tucked you in. It took a while for him to come back. I saw his eyes were red. Must've cried. He was a good lad, was Tahir. He sat down a while, and pulled himself together. Dinner was done, and it was time for the cake. Crazy lass – she'd decked it out with candles. That's when your dad leapt up, "Oh, I forgot!" A tiny stone or something in his hand. We didn't know what it was. This thing on your neck now. He'd pestered your mum for quilting needles all that time. He made this medallion for her, using whatever he could to carve it: forks, spoons, needles. She never took it off.'

Jülide glanced at the slender inscription on the reverse: *Sabriye.* Put it to her lips. She didn't want to make her grandma talk any longer. She fell asleep under the gently blowing north-easterly.

The exposé rocked Andalıç for two days. *The Voice of Andalıç,* which would normally languish unwanted under other magazines on the low tables in waiting rooms or in forgotten corners, now wandered in the streets, was tucked under arms, carried home, and even made a second edition. Throughout this time, a gleeful Muzaffer chattered with friends and visiting tradespeople, waxed lyrical over her trip to Soma and how she got hold of the invoices and exposed the corruption, cackled liberally, and cheerfully blowing smoke, said, 'Let's see what they're going to do now!' The only fly in the ointment was the telephone calls. Calls she listened to with slow nods, a brave smile drawn over the anxiety on her face, calls she put down saying, 'Wrong number,' when there was someone else around. She told Jülide and Rahmi to 'Be careful for a couple of days,' without explaining what *careful* meant.

After two days of refreshing joy dotted by an ephemeral concern, Jülide and Rahmi were sweeping glass from outside the printer's again. Shards of both the new pane in the door and the big window in the front. The strong north-easterly occasionally drowned out the monotonous crunch before amplifying and spreading it throughout the street. A wriggle of kids impossible to move away, their mothers yelling, 'Come home, quick; you'll cut yourself!', old men resting on their sticks to watch the printer's on their way to the coffee house, women resting their shopping bags on the ground, pretending to stop to catch their breaths across the street, and the cats suspiciously sniffing at the bins filling with glass shards… Hands akimbo like a commander, Muzaffer was chattering to the firemen, police constables, the Neighbourhood Headman, and the tradespeople in the vicinity, arguing with anyone daring to suggest 'This newspaper's a danger to the neighbourhood!' At every possible opportunity, she shooed away the grinning crowd of kids as if they were watching a play, although it was always in vain. It was impossible to tell them; they would chuckle and snigger, scudding outside the shop like low-flying balloons until they got bored.

The neighbours, who were rudely awakened by the noise of exploding glass just when the wind had dropped in the middle of the night, felt their hearts jump into their mouths at the sight of the crimson flames framed in their windows. Grabbing a bucket, they had run over with the instinct of people who live cheek-by-jowl in narrow streets; as a result, the fire had only consumed the wooden shelves in one corner and the invitations and newspapers printed earlier in the day. It had blackened the walls and the ceilings, but been stopped before it could reach any of the valuable equipment or the office upstairs full of books, old magazines and newspapers. That the workshop had not burned like a torch, not been reduced to ashes, was owed entirely to those neighbours with their buckets, who had kept the fire occupied until the arrival of the fire engine.

When Muzaffer had rushed over at three in the morning or so, the orange light of the fire engine, which looked as if it had shoved the houses out of the way to get in, was pulsing on whitewashed walls, on a background of scared faces beginning to relax, striped pyjamas, floral nighties, torn slippers, and dishevelled hair. Something warm was bleeding inside at the sight of the battered body of her dearest. Her father's desk: was it burned, the desk where he sat with a grave face, writing his articles with his black fountain pen in that flawlessly neat handwriting, occasionally removing his thick-framed spectacles to rub his eyes, and those spectacles she still kept in the drawer? What about the copy of the first newspaper they had published, the first copy of the first edition which had come off the press? That first edition he had placed as he would a newborn on the lap of her mother – who had flicked her plate up with her thumb, scared by the door he had slammed when he had walked in, waving his newspaper? The Jules Vernes Muzaffer had read over and over again when she was a child, hiding in the tiny cubbyhole of the desk, those books she had rediscovered, covered in dust on one of the high shelves years later on her return, and started reading again? Never mind the machinery; but the office was different. The articles in faded ink on yellowed sheets – her father had never really taken to a typewriter – his correspondence with ministers and MPs, the letters he wrote to his daughter, following the pedagogical tenets of the time, and poems, some of which had been put to music by his friends, had all been boxed and placed in the cupboards in the office because her mother hated mess at home. Muzaffer enjoyed dipping into them from time to time; they enriched the crumbs of her memories.

On one occasion, before her father's hair had gone white overnight, she had found tense correspondence and threatening letters spanning a couple of months. The last one of those anonymous letters held threats against Muzaffer. She remembered her father's hands trembling as he lit his cigarette, spooned his soup, or stroked her hair. Her mother's pleas, 'Close down that newspaper, let's get away, let's move to Izmir.' Muzaffer had been taken from school, sent to her aunt in Izmir, and returned once things had quieted down; but she had lost that year.

Having raced to the stairs at the back in the smoking shop, which smelled of burnt wood, she relaxed at the sight of steps that were only scorched halfway up. The office door, although sooty, still looked solid. She owed it all to the striped pyjamas, floral nighties, and eyes with bright whites.

The next morning, she came to work as usual; now she sips a cup of tea offered by a neighbour, happy like a shipwreck who comes round on the shore, sitting on the stool where a still wide-eyed Jülide had plonked her down, watching glazer Mustafa apply the putty around the glass panes. The glazier can always find a way to deepen the dimples on his chubby face.

'Muzaffer Abla; we'd be going bust but for you, I swear!'

'Not my fault last time, Mustafa. Lovers' tiff.'

Jülide runs inside, beetroot red.

'They've come round to our shop and asked for the paper. My assistant handed it over whilst I was away. Seems they're confiscating all the copies in Andalıç.'

'Let them. A copy's already gone to the prosecutor. Too late. So sorry,' she chuckled.

'Abla, no offence, but... why don't you go on holiday or something for a few days? I hear they're saying you'd better mind yourself and stuff. You never know with these bastards. Eh, abla?'

'Never mind. We've heard it all before. Caution to the wind and all that. All we have is one single life.'

Finished with the putty, Mustafa packed his tools.

'That's all very fine, abla, but we'd go to the wall if you went down! Think it's you I'm worried about?'

Laughter tames danger. Shrinks it, renders it unimportant. Pushes it to the back of the mind.

Rahmi and Jülide keep going in and out, bringing out unusable items.

'Lover boy's curse must have worked.'

Jülide scuttles away to the bins, bright red again.

'Turned out all right, though,' says Muzaffer, 'This place did need a good overhaul. It's like an armoury upstairs. All that dry paper. They'd never manage to put it out if it had leapt upstairs. It needs sorting out. Donate some things to the library, for their archives. Send some of it to the paper factory.'

Pulling up a stool beside her, Mustafa sits down.

'They did succeed once, you know. It's been twenty years or so. Not even Rahmi here knows about it. Dad used to keep all his documents at home. Mum grumbled. He dug his heels in. Just as well he didn't bring them over. That's how everything was saved, but there was nothing left of the printing press. We used to have a much bigger place behind the market. When he saw what happened to the printer's, though, dad was scared, and moved all the bits and pieces here.'

'Ladies don't like junk around. Or rather, not their husbands' junk. Got lots of their own crap, though.' Mustafa paused. 'What's the police say, abla?'

'What do they always say? They'll look into it. As if there was anything to look into. It's all obvious.' She lowered her voice. 'They're alleging it's her boyfriend. Could he have done it out of spite, ya di ya da. That's not to say I've not asked around about him. He, too, is one of those…' She didn't finish when she saw Jülide return.

Mustafa teased her again. 'Abla, publish something about the District Governor's smelly feet next week, so I can get another early sale.'

Evening: the hammering of new shutters being installed. Muzaffer, Rahmi and Jülide were watching the men at work from the steps of the house across the road. The metallic noise was amplified, smashing against close-set walls, blows bruising the horizon that was beginning to decay from its corner.

'Go home now, Jülide. What's the point of hanging around here?'

'I'll go in a minute.'

'Refurbishment will probably take about a week or so. I'll send you word with Rahmi.'

An exhausted, distracted Rahmi nodded, scratched hands clasped before him, cigarette in his mouth.

'Country's full of bastards.' A line he'd been repeating since the morning.

Her eyes tiny now, Muzaffer couldn't be bothered to nod this time. 'Bastards outnumber decent folk, Rahmi. Decent folk wouldn't be left alone in this country. Speak out, and you're silenced.'

Rahmi nodded again. Covered as he was in soot, he looked like a coal merchant's apprentice. He threw the cigarette to the ground, too tired to stub it out, though, he left it smouldering.

'Jülide, you've been a little out of sorts since the morning.'

'I'm upset, Muzaffer Abla.'

'Is that all?'

Two deep, white lines stood between Jülide's eyebrows. Her blue eyes glinted as if they didn't belong on the sooty face. She was all eyes. A pair of floating eyes.

'I don't know. I've been wondering ...' She hesitated and fell silent.

'What?'

'Erkan. Could he have done it? He threatened us so badly the other day.'

Muzaffer gave an exhausted laugh. 'This is far beyond him, lass. Someone like him, probably. Young, et cetera. What matters is who's behind it. People who want something like this done never do it themselves. They'll find some stooge instead. Erkan, Hüseyin, Ayşe, Fatma ...'

'Uh-huh. But it would be so easy to use Erkan in something like this. He'd jump at the chance.' Two sad, white lines glimmered on her sooty cheeks in the dusk. Muzaffer pretended not to notice.

'Don't think so, Jülide. It's obvious who's responsible for this shit. So many others in line before we'd come to you. At any rate, even if Erkan had done it – which I don't think he did, not with all those stitches in his hand. Wrapped in dressing. They wouldn't send an injured bloke to torch a shop. Anyway. Even if it was him, it doesn't matter. They'd have found someone else, if not him. This isn't about your life; this is about this town's life, this country's life.'

Rahmi nodded again, lost in thought. 'The country's life,' he murmured, then remembered to add, 'Country's full of bastards.'

'Shit is so much easier than accepting you're wrong. We've seen so many shitbags. So much shit. You will, too. I wish you wouldn't, lass. But you will.'

What her grandma had said a couple of nights ago and what Muzaffer was saying now; despair like a bucketful of ice water over the thrill of that first night. The black-and-white cat rubbed against Jülide's legs. She wanted to stroke him, but was reluctant to soil him with her sooty fingers.

'Can't something be done? Anything?'

'I don't know. We used to think you could. Still occasionally think so.' Loath to give in to so much despair, Muzaffer paused. 'Perhaps a few things are being done, but ...'

Rahmi turned his head. 'Scaring the kid.'

'So what? I'm scared too. Aren't you?'

Rahmi nodded slowly once again. Reached for the pack in his pocket. Dipped his fingers a little deeper than usual. Fumbled and fumbled. 'Must've run out. Have you got any, abla?' He took the cigarette Muzaffer extended. Lit it. 'You're scared when you're alone. Scared of the crowd.'

They said nothing more until the shutters were fixed shut. As they were leaving, Muzaffer gripped Jülide's arm. 'Watch out for that punk, Jülide. Look out for yourself for a while.'

They set off for their homes, the north-easterly's commotion to their back, shifting shadows on the streets ahead, their steps silent, their ears pricked for the slightest noise, and a callous weight over their hearts.

10

Another mid-morning chat, each successive one a minute longer countering the shortening days, as Cemal and Saliha sat with their backs against the wall in the little rear room. No longer enjoying quite so much of her mother's doting attention, a distracted Saliha was enlarging the hole in the *pala* kilim with her finger as she waited for Cemal to return from his latest sale. The calm cheer pasted on her face when she was talking to him was replaced, again, by the unease evident in the static gaze and the preoccupied action of her finger. A troubled gaze fixed on the enormous map of Turkey Cemal had stuck on the wall opposite. Although a hole in the ground, a cloud in the sky or the rocks Cemal had moved from the shelf to the garden could have easily replaced the map, since what she was staring at mattered not a bit.

These sudden chills that froze the warmth of her nearest and dearest with an icy breath, these senses of distancing, these dissociations with herself first and everything else next, these steps into a void and tumbles out of the earth which came upon her whenever and wherever and ripped through the happiest moments... she shivered. August was reluctant to relinquish its heat.

All the spring calla lilies' yellowed leaves were lying on the ground. A carpet was beaten next door. The dusty weight of the noise tickled her throat. She coughed. Then there was total silence. For a couple of seconds. The customer in the shop, Cemal, objects and hands all stilled, waiting for the vibrations in the air to subside. The futile flailing in the void stopped. Absolute silence for only a few seconds. Then a glass broke in the kitchen of the house where the carpet was shaken out; slivers shattered the silence. Someone was torn off a strip. A tight window was prised open in another house. Cemal's cheese knife struck the board. The customer placed the jingling change on the counter. A lorry horn brayed at the bottom of the hill. Two tomcats fell down the wall into the tiny garden and went at each other with feral shrieks. Saliha got up and clapped her hands to shoo them off. Then she stood frozen on the doorstep, her palms stuck together. Silent under the sky in all the sounds of the day, the unceasing humming of the day. If Cemal's approaching steps had not been checked halfway by the sound of a young child, she would have had to turn round, separate her hands, sit back down on the sofa, speak and look and laugh – forgetting this episode.

Her eyes did not follow the large black bee buzzing robustly past her in a flash of metallic blue. She would have to turn round. Immediately after the sweet wrappers were torn in a hurry. Two steps to the sofa; she took two steps back, her palms still together, her gaze fixed on the crack in the garden wall. The broken glass was being swept into a pan in a jangle, the sound of ancient guilt. She would have to turn round. A startling touch on her shoulder. She was saved from the trap.

'What a silent approach.'

Reaching over, Cemal kissed her on the cheek. 'Did I scare you?'

'No, no. You didn't.'

'What were you thinking about?'

'Don't know.'

Unaware of the transfusion of resolve he was making, Cemal sat her back on the sofa. Stared at her face. A little puzzled.

'Your lips are pale. Something wrong?'

'No.'

The map on the wall was a new game. A game stemming from the idea that grocery was a universal profession, one that could be done anywhere. Mountainsides, lake sides and lacey coastlines were all places one could go and settle in. Hatay sounded nice: the variety, the difference, being on the border. But it was too hot. The Kızılırmak often tempted, that enormous tail curling in the heart of Anatolia. Was it really scarlet like its name? Living near a colossal river, which never dried up even in the summer, crawling delicately like a living creature. In Amasya perhaps. Cemal had happened to pass by on one occasion, and liked it a great deal. Tombs carved into sheer rocks and all those ancient buildings. The allure of Lake Van, the islands dotting it. They knew they could never be parted from the sea, no matter where they looked.

The future waited to be formed, barely one step ahead. To be formed with plans, desires, fantasies, and decisions. Saliha was happy to join in when it started out as a game, but drew back the moment things seem to get serious, the moment a decision looked imminent. Into the secure shadows of suspicions, concerns and indecision. Nothing frightened her more than the risk that a lasting change would be a bad one. Questions lined up. What if it's really conservative? What if we don't get on with the locals? What if we don't like it? What if we don't settle in? What if we're left all alone?

'Would you rather we stayed here?' asked Cemal once again.

'No.' Something like revulsion appeared on Saliha's face.

'I don't understand why you hate this place so much.'

'We've discussed it so many times Cemal; it's small. Everyone knows everyone. Everyone interferes with everything.'

'It's the same everywhere. All small places are alike. That's what happens as soon as you get over the first stage of being new. You can only really relax in big cities. No one interferes with anyone there, but it's hard to make ends meet.'

'I don't like big cities either. I was never happy in Izmir. I wish we could just wander from place to place, like staring at a map.'

Cemal laughed. 'Then we'll become mobile grocers. We'll sell the shop and buy a caravan. We'll tour every village.'

He was actually joking, but Saliha seemed to like the idea.

'I think that's the best. We won't stay anywhere for long. We'll chat to people whenever we stop. And we'll get away before the usual gossip, envy, etc. has a chance to start. And we'd be seeing everywhere, too.'

'Would you really like a life like that? You're not that keen on travel.'

'I would… I guess. But those villages will have their own grocers. We have to sell something else. Could we fit in to the caravan, as well as the goods?'

'I don't know. We'll buy something big. Are you serious?'

'Yes. We'll be nomads. No one can put their nose into our business. All we need is to make enough for the petrol and the food.'

Cemal shook his head with a smile. The map now asked to be seen as a continuous line instead of dots. An endless line connecting villages and towns. A long line connecting all the places where he had looked for his father and many others besides; transform his life into a river, his marriage a secure raft on that life.

'All my life, I dreamt of going away. Living a different kind of life. But this had never occurred to me, to be honest.' He squinted at the distances that looked so easy to cover on the map, but in real life took forever. 'All the same, if you …' He looked around. 'I've never really left this place. Your hometown is something else. Familiarity, at the very least. Even if you curse it, even if you don't like it.'

Whenever they made such half-serious, half-playful plans, some unsaid unsayable things hung in the air. What the doctor had told Saliha: to avoid sudden changes and not resume working until she was completely cured. To avoid stress.

'You'd always stay here if it was left to you, Cemal. I want to go away.'

'That's fine, sweetie, so do I. Always did. I was an arse not to go to university. But all I can do in this blooming life is buy and sell.'

'Oh, Cemal. You're a man, so it's up to you to put food on the table, right? We could move to a big city, if we can't do anything else. I can get a job in a bank. I can look after both of us.'

This comment always drew a nervous laugh from Cemal.

'And what would I do at home all day long? I'd look after the kids if we had any. Housework is no biggie, but then, there's the boredom. And then, what would I say when your friends ask? I'm a househusband.' Another laugh.

Tugging at the hole in the kilim, Saliha stayed silent for a while. 'I wish there was something in the middle, something between being nailed to a spot and wandering all the time.'

The Sellotape holding the top corner came away again and the map rolled down with a rustle. A damp patch showed behind it, yellow darkening into brown in waves.

'Wish we could go over those tracks.'

The still air intensified silences. Cemal saw something mysteriously disturbing on his fiancée's face. As though the lid of a usually shut wardrobe had creaked ajar in the middle of the night. Inside were objects one never knew about, even though they shared the same house. Objects rendered indistinct in the darkness, their boundaries lost, objects unlike anything.

'You're a bit out of sorts today.'

A hasty smile scrambled to reach Saliha's eyes, which didn't immediately return from the distance that had tempted them.

'Is there a problem? Is something bothering you? Sweetie?' His long fingers brushed back his fiancée's pale blonde hair falling on her forehead.

A dog in the distance barked on and on, and another replied. Struggling to dig out the words that just wouldn't come, Saliha squinted at the gloom inside her. 'I don't know. I sometimes get this way.'

'How do you mean?'

'I don't know; you… I mean, I feel distant from everything. There's a void inside me.'

Cemal took a deep breath, feeling something stinging his lungs. 'Whenever we start to make plans, whenever we start to think about the future…'

'Cemaaaaaal…!'

The familiarity in this strange female voice coming from the shop drew a quizzical look from Saliha.

'Abiiii…'

'Come, Cemile; we're at the back.' He got up and went to the door.

Curiosity mingling with displeasure at the tone of the voice tossed into the shop, Saliha stared. High heels clattered on the flagstones. As the two women shook hands, they exchanged looks from top to toe far more informative than any length of acquaintance.

'Welcome,' said Saliha with a chill in her voice that Cemal didn't recognise, 'Are you settled yet?'

'Yes, like I had a choice, right? Happy to be back with mum. But I'm cross with you, abi. You've never called round to ask how I'm getting on since I've come here.' A gaze feigning hurt dropped beneath a coy flicker of the eyelashes.

'I'm sorry. I would have, but I open the shop really early, and close near midnight. I wouldn't want to disturb at that late hour.'

'Who'd mind the hour between brother and sister?' Pursing her full lips, she glanced at Saliha. 'I've got it, though; you can't leave your *pretty* fiancée.' It was more than obvious that pretty was the last thing she believed.

Cemal, who was flustered by feeling no reciprocal familiarity, didn't even attempt to laugh it off. He said nothing. The room wasn't big enough or filled with enough detail to occupy the eye at such moments.

'I was bored at home, and I thought I'd go see my big brother. Just as well I did. Got to meet my sister-in-law too.'

Fidgeting as if she'd sat on something sharp, Saliha gave a polite smile. Cemal had caught a sense of the extraordinary tempests inside her, and was trying to figure out what was going on, looking at one, and then the other. 'Anything I can do for you or your mum, Cemile? Something you need, perhaps?'

'No, thanks.' Cemile was still standing. 'Aren't you gonna ask me to sit, though?' Her heels click-clacked. Holding the slit of her pencil skirt, she sat down on the sofa.

'As you've just said. You're not a stranger. Does one need an invitation from her big brother?'

Cemile's teeth showed between her lips in a yellow sauciness. 'Sure. My big brother's my closest, after me mum.'

The silence triggered by Saliha's nod and forced smile settled into the middle of the room in the still air, when the tab of Sellotape holding the other top corner of the map came off, and the huge sheet rolled down with a noise that made them all jump. Cemal, who was on his feet, bent down and slowly started to fold it.

'Sooo, when's the wedding?'

'Like I said, Cemile. In three weeks. On the first of September.'

A hand not quite curled due to the long red nails knocked on wood. 'God bless. How lovely, you're going to make a home. We're not so lucky.'

The envy, regret, faint jealousy, and reproach in her voice could have been tacked onto another emotion, but, being badly attached like the map, the bare wall underneath peeked through. As far as Saliha was concerned, at least.

'Why wouldn't you be? So long as you want to.'

'Don't say that, sister. Who'd marry a woman like me? I'm not like you. Gone to schools and everything, never had no bad reputation.' The same wall showed up under the ostensible self-pity and self-reproach. Saliha had diagnosed the insincerity under the peeling paper, but not yet understood its contents.

'That's life; you never know. Isn't there anything else you want to do in life, other than get married?'

As he watched them sitting on either end of the sofa and sniffing each other from a distance like two tense female cats, Cemal was alert to the fact that this was no civil, ordinary conversation.

'What else though? Every woman wants a home and a family.' The prim and proper virtue in the voice dripped over mascara-heavy eyelashes.

'I don't, to be honest.'

Candour blurted out by tautened nerves, confrontation shattering tranquillity and putting everything back in its place.

'How can you say that, sister? Don't you want to marry? Have children? Every woman wants children.'

'What an earth for?'

'Well, it's natural! Innit, abi?'

Well aware that there was no room for a third player in this table tennis match, Cemal was rooted to the spot, still clutching the map. With no help coming from him, Saliha spoke on her own behalf again. 'Just because it's natural doesn't mean it's for everyone. And that's not the only reason you marry, anyway.'

'Of course! You actually marry for love,' simpered Cemile, managing to catch Cemal's eye as she pronounced *love*. It was meant to deflect the anger in his eyes away from herself and direct it at Saliha's words. She crossed her legs, releasing the split in her skirt she'd been grabbing all this time. Cemal pretended not to have noticed, rushed to the garden door and turned his back. 'You'd do anything for love,' added Cemile, her gaze on Cemal's slowly stretching broad shoulders and long neck tilting first one way, and then the other. A gaze timed by Saliha, like a diligent coach timing her athlete. A gaze that stretched like a sticky pleasure.

'That's right. You'd even whore at a pinch.'

Saliha and Cemal's eyes sought one another, like two little children lost in a forest; when they did meet, there was reproach on Cemal's face. A stranger to them both, this reproach, cross, condemning. Saliha looked into herself for a moment. At the anger, jealousy, the need to rebuff, crush, annihilate. She was annoyed with herself. That's when Cemile's merry laughter chimed. 'Well done to my sister-in-law! She can call a whore a whore. Bad arse chick.'

Cemal turned back to the room. Saw at once how Cemile used her life like a weapon to win such cheap victories. Saliha's cringing face slamming shut transformed his anger into pity. They all waited, frozen in silent discomfort. The hole in the kilim over the sofa was right beside Cemile's hip.

'Neighbours and that, Cemile? Hope you're not bored.'

'Oh, I swear I'm bored to tears. What good are mum's neighbours? A load of old women.'

Cemal hesitated to ask the question that had popped into his mind, but the silence was more unnerving. 'Do they know… erm?'

'Mum's big mouth never stops, does it? She blabbed to everyone.'

'Hm. That's not great.' Cemal was frowning.

Cemile gave a brazen laugh. 'What'sa matter, abi; offended your honour? Should'a never brought me here then.'

'Best thing. Everyone was happy with their lot.' Saliha's calm voice was cold enough to chill them all, even in the heat of August.

'Why would it offend my honour? But if you're bored, if you're not happy here, of course you can go back. Who's holding you back?'

Cemile sighed. 'Only the blokes you don't want. The ones you want, never do.' Silence again, until. Cemal's ears longing for the tiniest patter were finally rewarded. Footsteps, and then a customer entered the shop. How much he'd been longing to get away only sank in when he walked out of the door and emptied his lungs in a long breath. All the same, there was a tiny worry, tugging at this relief from the corner. Those two were alone inside. With all his attention fixed on trying to listen to the rear room, it took him three times to understand the customer's order.

No matter how hard he strained, though, Cemile's malicious whisper was too low.

'You're not in love with my brother, are you?'

Startled away from the tiny, parched garden, Saliha swung round and peered into her eyes. Cemile did not look away this time. They stared long and hard, like two wild animals about to strike a mortal blow.

This hostile freeze was released by Cemal's entrance.

'Ah, my handsome brother's back,' simpered Cemile, rearranging her features into something completely different with a simple magic trick, 'And I was just telling my sister-in-law how I'd met the Commissioner.'

'Oh, yeah? You needed the police?'

'Well, we've got form, yeah? Our card's marked.' With a blasé chuckle, she watched the guilt waving over their faces. 'Noo, my God! He's mum's aunt's son. She took me over to meet him, see if he can help, find me a job or something.'

If she had expected the explanation to relax Cemal's face, she was wrong.

'Well, looks like he wasted no time at all. Watch your step, all the same. He doesn't have a great reputation.'

'Oh, well, that one's no good, this one's no good. Like you're the only good guys in the place.' She paused, evidently tired of this petty game. 'Whatever, let me know if you need anything. I've met important people since arriving here. I think he looks all right. Nice or not, he's a man, ain't he? Anyways, I'm off. I'll be waiting, abi. Bring my sister-in-law too.'

The room was really quiet now. Someone was cooking mince in the same neighbour's kitchen, banging the pan with a wooden spoon every once in a while. Cemile's perfume lingered in the tiny room with an insidious shame.

An incomprehensible shame for Saliha and Cemal, who exchanged sad smiles. A staccato noise came from the neighbour's knife as she chopped something on a board. Saliha was experiencing the initial effects of the venom dripped into her ear with such spell-binding blatancy. Love. Once more: love. She cast Cemal a suspicious glance. The neighbour called out from her window, 'Hafizeee? Hafize, lass! Come over for morning coffee if you're done.' The reply came at once. 'I'll turn off the pan and come right over, Nurten Abla.'

After they had finished talking, the approaching noontime heat swallowed the sounds of the neighbourhood once again. Even the constantly dripping ancient brass tap over the small cracked washbasin seemed to have succumbed to the overwhelming stillness of August. A drop wavered at the greenish mouth of the tap. The moment it overcame its indecision, it slid silently over the aged rust stain in the basin. There was a thin forked crack on the blue wall freed of the map, and like all newly bare walls, it held the gaze. Midges orbited around one another in total silence. Everything and everyone – Nurten Hanım, Hafize Hanım, tomcats, bumblebees, water droplets and the whole world – was quiet, leaving Cemal and Saliha focused on their own minds.

'Didn't you think her clothes were too…' started Cemal hesitantly, as though testing whether the stillness would allow any sounds at all.

'Too what?'

'You know. Skimpy.'

'She can wear what she likes. Not going to ask us, is she?'

'But no. Not around here. She'd be uncomfortable.'

'Maybe she wants to be uncomfortable.'

'But she'd sworn it off.'

'You heard her?'

'I mean, she said she did. Said she'd sworn it off.'

'I'm not so sure. You might like to take that with a pinch of salt. She's a weird one.'

'Don't say that. It's an awful life. I saw it with my own eyes. Really awful. Not saying it just because I'm narrow-minded or anything. Honour's a personal thing. Why would it offend mine? But being bought and sold like an object, like a slave, no freedom.'

'Who's free, anyway? Are other women? Am I free?'

Cemal's crow's feet deepened in pain.

'But I… I mean, I've been feeling really free since you've come into my life. Don't you feel the same?'

Saliha turned towards him, sadness quelling the dogged cruelty inside, yet unable to repudiate what was on her mind. 'I don't know. I can't understand it right now. Time will show. You're very important for me, Cemal, but that's not enough for you.'

'Just because you're in love with me…' He glanced at Saliha like a child lost in a crowd. 'Anyway, never mind.' That cruel thing inside, that timeless enemy constantly wearing down and grinding, gave a disdainful steely glare. Cemal's eardrums pounded with his racing heartbeat: bang bang, bang bang.

'That's fine, Cemal, but when you do that…'

Someone entered the shop noisily, 'Whoa, Cemal; where are you?'

It was Halil.

Saliha pressed her hand over the heart capable of freezing even in the heat of August. She recognised the pain she caused, but failed to heal it; numbed by its own groundless pain, her heart just would not warm up.

'Wow, lovebirds.' Halil dived in, pasting a smile on his face and peering at theirs. Saliha and Cemal pulled themselves together and forced a smile in response.

'Cemile passed by in the marketplace.'

'How did you recognise her? You've not met yet.'

'I used my powers of deduction.'

Cemal attempted to cheer up by teasing Halil. 'Our Halil Abi – a dirty old man. Don't be fooled by his decent looks. Yasemin tried to divorce him so many times, but well-wishers intervened.'

Halil blushed, surprising in one so carefree. 'Ya silly git, you keep mum all the time and drop the worst clanger when least expected. Douchebag.'

Cringing for his sake, Saliha changed the subject. 'We saw her too. She was here.'

Halil gazed at them one by one, sensing the tangible unease in the atmosphere. 'Did she stir things up here? Your faces are like a wet weekend.'

'Nooo!' they replied in unison, before looking at each other.

'Perhaps she did,' said Cemal.

'Soo, what happened? Come on, tell us.'

'Nothing much, in actual fact,' said Saliha. 'Cemile's a little… a little provocative, annoying.'

'Ha, ha. No one complained in the marketplace, though!'

Cemal grunted, recalling his earlier anger. 'So long as she's not annoyed.'

'Well, *you're* definitely annoyed,' said Saliha, 'You're taking this big brother business much too seriously. *Isn't that right, handsome abi?* A total stranger; she can do whatever she likes. Mind your own business.'

Halil intervened as the atmosphere grew tense. 'Don't say that, Saliha. They share the same father and the same surname. Any impropriety would ultimately get back at Cemal. The lad's right.'

'Sure; he had to go and bring that impropriety here.'

'Now, there you're right. But that's our Cemal. He couldn't say no. Would he listen, though?'

Cemal gave Saliha a hurt look. 'But you're being unfair. Didn't you tell me to go? I said I'd stay if you'd asked me to.'

Halil may have been always ready to enjoy listening to a good argument, but something on Cemal's face suggested it was time to change the subject. This was obviously not the real issue; a disproportionately huge row seemed to be brewing.

'You two can scrap all you like after I'm gone. I can't be breaking up a lovers' tiff. I'm already pissed off, anyway.' Cemal's hurt look at the word *lovers* did not go unnoticed. 'You know about that kilim course? At Public Training.'

'I do. Jülide was going too,' said Saliha. 'She'd woven a beautiful kilim. I saw it when I went there with my sister. The other ladies had also done some lovely, colourful things. So, what's happened?'

'I'll tell you what's happened. Remember all those bigwigs who came here to celebrate Andalıç's liberation? County Director here, Governor there, our District Governor, obviously, Mayor, Commissioner. Our Director of Education, up and hands the kilims to these blokes, never bothering to ask anyone for permission. Like it was all his property. The ladies hit the roof. All those months of work, puff!' He put his fingertips together, flicked them open and held his hand up in the air for a while. 'They're saying, "If only he'd asked!" There was an exhibition; the next morning they saw it was all gone. No kilims, no nothing.'

'No way! Are you sure, abi?'

'The ladies were on the warpath, at his door, not that it did any good! Is the bloke gonna say, return the kilims? Never mind that, the poor things had all bought their own materials.'

Saliha shook her head, staring distractedly at the floor. 'Shame. What a shame. Jülide was going to sell it to pay for her courses. Anything can happen in this country.'

'I know, but why should it, right, Saliha? They shouldn't be able to. It's easy to boss women around. No one can match them when it comes to bullying.' Stroking his ginger moustache, he gave a nervous laugh. 'And that is the head of our education. Just imagine the rest.'

Shaking her head again, Saliha looked up, said, 'Just a sec,' and went out. A faint sound of tearing swept past Cemal's ears, distracted by Halil's ranting and raving. A pen scrawled something on a sheet of paper, a notebook was opened and shut, Saliha returned, listened to Halil for a little longer, made her excuses and left.

Halil's arsenal of curses wound down along with his anger, as it finally occurred to him to look for something in Cemal's eyes squinting on the light outside.

'Don't worry, mate; everyone has these little rows. Spice up your marriage.'

'Yeah, yeah. No marriage as yet, though.'

'Yeah, what's going on there? Wasn't it Saliha who was telling you to go? Now she's taken up against Cemile. What happened in just one meeting?'

The concern on Cemal's face seemed to be glued, impossible to shift. 'I don't know, abi. Was she jealous because Cemile flirted or something? Not something I'd have ever expected of Saliha.' He paused with a silly grin that washed off the concern. 'She was jealous. Proper jealous.'

'Why would she be? Half-sister or not, Cemile's still your sister, isn't she?'

'No, abi. You've not seen her. Doesn't behave at all like a sister.'

Halil sniggered. 'So don't behave like a brother, dude.'

'God forbid! You'd be struck down!'

'Ha, ha, ha. Thought I was serious, eh?'

'Abiii!'

They set about shoving and pushing like they did when they were kids, the whole world, their ages, seriousness, everything: forgotten.

Cemal swept the rattling rice grains from the scales to the plastic bag with the edge of his hand. Raziye stood opposite, down from her tower overlooking the whole of the hill. Gatherer of everyone's secrets to later circulate them to everyone else, a veritable magazine on legs, she was peering at Cemal's face under her muslin kerchief and behind thick lenses. Her face could have been emblazoned with some news item about Cemile, who tottered on the cobblestones in her high heels, Saliha, who left the shop with a face like thunder, and Halil, who tormented him like a child. Cemal felt awkward, as though such an article actually existed and he was unable to hide it. Raziye's specs and the eyes behind them – less like eyes, more like a weird instrument – seemed to possess the faculty to read minds.

Lifting his head, he saw Saliha watching him from between the curtains. Raziye usually acted so fast the moment she got wind of anything at all in the neighbourhood that spotting her anywhere could have heralded something. Cemal's restlessness took a break from grumbling under the involuntary smile spreading on his face. He knotted the clear plastic bag. Raziye, who had obviously marked Cemile's card, was not in the least satisfied with the terse replies to her indirect questions. But Cemal grabbed the credit book to cut the interrogation short: Raziye always settled when her son in Ankara sent money.

Resigned to her failure to pump him, she probed for another topic to extend the conversation. 'You know that girl, Saime's friend. That pretty girl with long hair…' Cemal denied her Jülide's name. 'She was seen with Jale Hanım's son.'

'And?'

'And, that's it. She was seen.'

'Fine.' For some reason, the news of Jülide being seen with Erkan was vexing. A scrap of paper flying out of the hastily opened book floated down to the floor. Some writing showed up when the fold opened a little. In her annoyance with Cemal's indifference, Raziye missed it. Cemal looked up: Saliha's curtain closed with an anxious quiver. Instead of diving for it at once, Cemal kept the scrap at the edge of his vision, logged Raziye's rice, and quickly added the margarine, as if the credit book would be impossible to open again once it was shut.

Raziye shot him a reproachful look for being so incompetent and taciturn. The grocery was the only place with a higher footfall than her home; if only she were the owner of such a spot, frequented all day long by every woman and man in the neighbourhood, she'd drag such gems out of every mouth! When it finally hit her that she wasn't about to get what she had been hoping for, she stopped lingering and walked out.

Cemal knew he was being watched from behind the curtain. He went outside, as if he had not seen the scrap of paper at all. Hiding his simmering curiosity behind a calm façade, he looked at the sea shimmering in the afternoon sun at the bottom of the hill. Sat on the stool by the door and flicked through the newspaper. Then he took his time to walk to the rear room, which wasn't visible from Saliha's window. He squatted down the moment he was out of her vision, crawled behind the counter, picked up the scrap, and crawled back to the rear to avoid having to get up in case anyone came into the shop. Gingerly, pressing his thumb pads on the pointed corners of the paper folded in two, he opened it.

At 8 in the evening.

Staring at the thumbs trembling on the wings of the piece of paper, he wondered if he would feel this searing excitement if Saliha's parents weren't visiting a sick relative in Izmir.

At precisely eight o'clock, the door opened only wide enough to let him in before he'd reached for the bell. He was holding a single branch of the red geranium he had cut from the window pot. On his body scrubbed red, a set of clean underwear, a white shirt still bearing its packaging folds, and beige trousers. A pair of arms on his neck, incredibly soft lips on his lips.

He could feel the cool of the stone under his socks, perhaps it was the chill that trembled up his legs and made his spine shiver. Yet his shirt's underarms were damp, and with still a couple of steps to get to the door, he had had to wipe off a thin drop of sweat with the enormous handkerchief his mother had insisted he carry at all times. He had opened it and wiped his face, neck and palms. But for the pungent scent of the geranium on his fingers, he would have forgotten the blossom he'd laid on the windowsill. Apprehension honed over the years reining in his absent-minded excitement, he had scanned the windows in the street, with particular attention to Raziye's. Thankfully everyone was at dinner. Not a single head showed in any window. The lights were just being turned on, which meant that the thick curtains hadn't yet been drawn and the interiors were visible. The sharp, metallic sound of forks striking plates echoed on the walls and cobblestones in the silent August evening, weighing down anyone caught alone with an intense gush of loneliness. Yet on this occasion, the clatter of cutlery heard whenever he walked past open windows and the dim desolation of the street at dinner time, failed to affect him.

With a strange agitation concealed by joy and excitement, he sat down on the old wooden sofa. The rest of the seats in the room were armchairs. He sensed, rather than heard, that low creak always made by this sofa whenever anyone sat on it, and the mattress whose covers were replaced from time to time and which was occasionally sent to the cotton carder for a good fluffing ever since he was a child. Then the sofa creaked once again.

The light was off in the room. The last droplets of light gently fluttered the curtain as they spilled into the street and dissolved in the iridescence. The room was constantly changing shape as it lost the light, turning into something mysterious and strange, imposing the sad silence of darkness. Ignoring her melancholy for once, Saliha pushed Cemal towards the cushions at the back, and the sofa gave a few more creaks.

'Saliha,' said Cemal. His voice rang in the room, strangely clumsy, surprising him, since he had no idea what to say.

'Yes?'

She was wrapped around him like a lifebelt; he held her tight. Kissed her forehead, eyes and cheeks.

'Remember Mari?' One of those memories you never knew when, where and why they would resurface.

'Of course. Uncle Hasan's foster daughter. Whatever made you think of her now, though?'

'Don't know. Just popped into my mind.'

'Poor, naive thing.'

'Uh-huh. She'd go anywhere if you gave her a little sweet. Neighbourhood boys would lead her up to the ruined church at the top.'

'And Uncle Hasan would go looking for her. Poor fellow. We called her Mari, but they called her Mine or something.'

'He used to yell. "Mine, you bastard's spawn! Come out, wherever you are!" Everyone sniggered. They all knew where she was. Never made a peep if you gave her a sweet, poor lass.'

'Then she fell pregnant.'

They paused, discomfited by this interruption. The topic hung in the air, inappropriate, one end still open.

'When they led her to the church, you know, to... And we'd go to watch.'

'You'd refuse to take me along. I used to get very upset. I didn't understand it either at the time.'

'We didn't take you along because you were a girl.'

Cemal had no idea why he was talking, why he was holding back on everything, why he was spoiling the moment, or what he was trying to delay. Saliha reached for his lips and drew back, astonished at the hardness she found there. At the utterly unfamiliar tension and worry on her fiancé's face, she gave him a hurt look.

The disappointment gathering in her eyes prompted Cemal. 'Saliha…' He was choking on words that clung to something inside, refusing to come out. Struggling to get round to what he really wanted to talk about. Saliha sat up slowly and drew back. Resting her hand on the sofa, faced him, peering.

'I…' A pause. 'I'm a little tense.'

'Yes. It's obvious.'

'It's the first time we're alone. I'm not entirely sure what to do.'

'You don't have to do anything.'

An uncomfortable silence. Saliha stood up and lit a cigarette. Sat down in the armchair opposite.

'But you don't get it.'

'What do I not get?'

'I mean, this… I mean, I never… never had sexual intercourse before.'

Saliha's face brightened by a smile quickly composed itself at Cemal's gravity.

'So what?'

'Don't, Saliha. I'm thirty-eight.'

'And?'

'You're not a man, so you have no idea what this means. Once your mates get wind of it… They ask all the time. Find you prostitutes. Try to get you to lay someone. I only got away by lying in the end.'

'And?'

'Do you seriously not get it? I'm scared. You've been with others before. I… I mean, what if I fail? What if it's not good?'

'Don't be silly, Cemal. You're one of the least hung-up men I've ever seen, but even you…' She paused. This was clearly not going to alleviate the worry straining Cemal's face. 'So what? What's the big deal? There's always a first time for everything. Relax a little.' She put out her cigarette. 'Good God. The things you worry about.' She got up and sat down next to him. Gave him friendly kisses on the cheeks and hugged him tight. 'Take me, for example: I've cooked beans in olive oil for the first time in my life. Eating that could prove to be far more daunting a prospect.' They laughed, rose from the whingeing sofa and went into the kitchen.

Until the first light of day, silence remains unremembered by summer nights in Andalıç. Sounds of fun in the distance. Circumcision parties, engagement parties, weddings, and the bars, discos and night clubs that pick up the baton after that lot's dispersed. The sounds of the distant bass slicing time on such still nights. Even the full moon rising over the roofs resting against one another is not as cold or alien as it is in the winter. Yellowish and flashy. Doesn't silence the summer night as it does the winter night. Its light falls on the bed under the window. Illuminates the sweat trickling down Saliha's neck. Cemal can't tell if it's his own. His hands trembling in excitement just now, when he was removing his clothes, lifting the top sheet and reaching out to an unacquainted intimacy, now gently trace the line of the shadow on Saliha's left breast. The finger dipped in the sweat on the neck follows the shadow all the way down, silvering the softness. Even after having performed all the moves nature has endowed his body with, an uneasy tension remains on his temples. He stares at the strangeness of his hands on Saliha's breasts. Doesn't dare look her in the eye yet. Hasn't found his own voice yet. In any case, her face is in the shade, in the bit made pitch black by the sharp full moon. Below her knees too. Cemal's finger slowly circles around the damp belly button.

The eddies he had created draw his attention below, to the place he had just come out of. He slides down in the bed. Gingerly prising her legs apart, he starts inspecting like a scientist. He is startled by a giggle; lifts his head to see Saliha's eyes translucent in the moonlight and her mouth curved in a childish shyness. She sits up.

'You're hilarious. All right, so you've never seen one before, but that's a little much.'

Parting his dry mouth, Cemal takes a little breath. The moonlight licking his face reveals the smile.

'We-eel. It's fascinating.'

'Like what?'

'I don't know. It's quite intricate.'

Saliha falls back on the pillow, giggling as if she had been tickled. An indistinct light on the facing walls, a pale glimmer on the frames. Everything is alien, momentary, as though it all came into being now. Everything that is well known and constantly touched, and which is now invisible, gives an indistinct sigh in the inherent magic of the moon and the moment.

'You might be better off looking in daylight.'

A dog's claws click on the cobblestones, a pause to sniff the rubbish, a moment's indecision, then steps interrupted by the smell of another dog or the cat staring from the trellis by the door. Water noises from next door's bathroom. Then the dog again, click click click.

Silently rehearsing the question, Cemal asks timidly, 'How was it?'

Saliha rises once again into the moonlight, eyes serious, mouth smiling. 'Do you want the truth?'

Biting both lips, Cemal nods. He stares at her, his chin resting on her bone, feeling that strange, damp tunnel right next to his carotid. 'Was it too brief?'

'Hard to say,' says a giggling voice, 'Do you think two and a half minutes is fine?'

'Don't pull my leg now.'

'It may have felt like ages to you, of course...'

Cemal sulked.

'Well, I'm happy. You tell me, how was it?'

'Don't know. Feels a bit overrated.'

'Ha, ha,' said Saliha, a little put out, but didn't let on. 'Hold on; this is just the beginning.'

'But I asked...'

His head is tugged up by Saliha's hands and his voice is imprisoned in his mouth.

'If you like,' top lip, 'we'll try,' bottom lip, 'once again,' an invading tongue, 'I'm not quite sure I got it,' and a night that will pass with little tests, until they are exhausted, until Kadir's rooster crows in the dark, as is its wont, well before daybreak. Until the moon leaves the window, until only desire is left in the darkness, until the chill that raises gooseflesh wherever sweat dries. Until the arms, legs, organs that suddenly seem to have multiplied, reluctantly let go of one another like octopuses after making love, until clothes are donned again unwillingly, until the door opens silently and Cemal steps out into the last of the dog barks, a bracing ache in his chest.

11

A sudden clarity in the colour of the sky at the end of August, a summer crack that swiftly repairs itself. The smell of September. The north-easterly's evidently due to break out in the morning. It's just around the corner. It'll wake up now. And replace the sleepy breaths only audible to the most familiar ears with that primitive tune.

It was in the trumpet vine in the garden that Jülide spotted this minuscule, naughty autumn seeping into the summer. A single yellowing leaf with tiny green dots. An apparently confused ant hesitating on its surface. Bees dipping into the orange cones of the trumpet vine and buzzing out, the yellow sacs on their legs a little fuller.

Distracted by the lizard slithering past with a rustle of leaves, she remembered the folded floor cloth on her squatting lap. Her hands were still resting on it. A claret and green marl cloth, bleached, threadbare from countless washes, a new hole at the edge. It was so old that she didn't even remember her grandma knitting it.

Putting a finger into the hole, she showed it to her grandma when she went in.

'All right, put it down there. I'll mend it today.'

She laid the cloth on the floor. Started clearing the table. The things splashing about on her face had retreated to her eyes since coming in from the courtyard, but the greasy cutlery, olive stones and bread crumbs also helped.

Sitting in her usual corner with a leg tucked under, the other bent upright, Seher swept her hand over the deep wrinkles in her mouth.

'Come on, stop feeling so sad. You can make another, now you know how.'

'What if they take that one too?'

'They won't.'

'Anyway, it's not the same. All that work, all the materials and everything...'

Her face broke again. She had cried all night long, angry, helpless tears. Biting her lower lip, she took the breakfast stuff into the kitchen and lathered a cloth at once to suppress the trembling in her throat, but there wasn't all that much to wash up.

'But they didn't even bother to ask.' A high-pitched, angry voice echoed in the kitchen.

'Make some coffee so we can enjoy it together. I'll read your fortune,' said her grandmother, hoping to distract the girl a little. She wasn't keen on reading her granddaughter's fortune, even when the girl begged her to. 'Have we still got some coffee? Make two cups. No one does it like you. Miss Coffee.'

Seher pricked up her ears as if she could read her granddaughter's mind from the rattle of the spoon in the coffee pot. Untying her muslin scarf, she said a *besmele,* flicked back the skinny braids reaching down to her waist and re-tied it. She lit the first of her Birinci cigarettes brought in cartons by the neighbours, as though they were visiting a prisoner. Like an endless, single cigarette, there would be a permanent fixture at the corner of her lips throughout the day. Listening in to the noises from the kitchen, she thought she heard the coffee rising. The wrinkles on her cheeks deepened as she sucked. An index finger that no longer had any flesh on it rubbed slightly damp eyes, which had sunk into prominent cheek bones and were going a little opaque to boot.

'Did mum make good coffee too?'

'I never made her do any housework. Not a stitch. I just wanted her to get an education.' She gave her granddaughter a sad smile. 'Her coffee was lousy. I sneaked inside to make it when your father's family came to ask for her hand.'

'Fine. Much better. Better be rubbish at it. Like doing well does you any good!'

The cigarette clamped between two lips was only removed when it was time to put it out – the smoke apparently absorbed instead of blown out. Like pulling out a cork, Seher removed out the last third of the unfiltered cigarette from her mouth with two dry fingers and blew the smoke out to dispel the acrid odour of heartbreak in the room. Once again, she wouldn't know what made Jülide's eyes water on the smoke-obscured face.

'Don't say that, child. Whatever you do, do it well. Your mum did everything well.'

'But she died.'

Breaking a habit of a lifetime, Seher stubbed out the cigarette instead of lighting the next one from the end.

'She didn't die because she did what she did well.' She stared at her granddaughter in astonishment. 'What's the matter, child?'

Jülide shrugged.

'When you do something well, it's lovely. Why live at all if there wasn't loveliness? You're lovely too. Lovely to look at.'

'Nothing looks lovely to me these days, grandma. Everything's ugly.'

Seher spun the overturned cup to dispel this unaccustomed edgy gloom. The first stiff attack of the north-easterly lifted the net curtain, and a diminutive cloud passing over the sun suddenly lowered the light.

'Bad things happen in life, lass. Everything passes. Fate. No use rebelling like this.'

'What could be worse? You know what Erkan's done; the paper was torched, and now months of my work's gone down the drain. I'm starting my final year. What will I do if I don't get into university? How will I pay for it if I do?'

At a loss for something to say, Seher looked at her granddaughter, unable to find some words of comfort. She glanced at the cup again. Frowned at the intricate shapes in the grounds.

'It could have been worse, lass. You need to count your blessings.'

Jülide's attention was shaken by the ominous tone in the platitudes heard since childhood.

'I buried two children. Your dad was like a son to me too. I buried my husband. I'm still alive, lass. The things you and I went through together. You can't die with the dead. Life goes on. It is what it is. Grieve all you like; to what end? I'm going to die too. I won't be here with you for ever.'

Jülide glanced at the white china between the dry fingers, as if it was the cup making her grandma say all this. 'Stop smoking, nana. You smoke too much. You never listen to me.'

'I've turned seventy-eight. Like it would make a difference if I packed it in now?'

'Never mind nana, don't bother with my fortune now. I'm off to the paper now, anyway,' said Jülide, worried, with a sudden glance at her grandma.

'That would never do, lass! We've opened it now. You never close it without reading it first.' She carried on. 'There's something breaking off, like a drop. Whatever it is, it keeps coming up in every woman's cup these days. Grows thinner and snaps just where it is thinnest.' She peers deeper into the cup. 'It's quite confusing. Ruined buildings and stuff. A crowd. Look, that's where you are. Long hair and everything. You're on your feet. You've come from a bendy curling road. A tough road. A tough time.'

'Aren't you there, nana?'

'Nothing to say I'm going to be around all the time everywhere.'

'Don't say that, nana. You never used to say things like that. Heaven forbid! You've been saying awful things all the time today. Isn't this cup done now?' The cool breeze coming in from the curtain covered her arms in gooseflesh. Rubbing them, she looked at her grandmother with eyes like saucers.

'You'll have enemies, child. There's a big fellow. But you'll have friends too. I've not seen her, but I wonder if this lady is Muzaffer Hanım? Glasses. Sandy hair.'

'Muzaffer Abla's blonde.'

'Right. She'll help you a good deal. There are others too. You'll be upset, it'll be tough, but it will all come out all right. You'll ride it out. There's something on your back. You're lifting a load. Holding your hand out to someone. The ground under your feet's not that solid, but you're standing firm. You're holding something like a sword, Jülide. A power. Something.' Seher suddenly lowered the cup. 'Oooh. The older I get, the more I forget how to read fortunes. Go on, lass, go wash it. Enough of the fibs.'

Jülide walks in a daze, bewildered by her grandma's predictions. The things rushing into her mind smash into one another and fall down. There is a vibrating electric void. Humming. All she can hear is Erkan's footsteps risen from the coffee grounds and made flesh and bone. Right behind her. The harassing, menacing footsteps that tail her every morning on her way to work, and every evening on her way back, footsteps that she pretends not to notice. She likes enlisting the roots of fig trees, cobblestones and weeds sprouting in the gaps to trip them up. Likes hearing him stumble, his balance disrupted, and sensing him falter until he regains his walking rhythm. The most enjoyable part of the game is to make him stumble three times, this agile Erkan, who can dominate a flighty ball and use his feet better than his hands, but she doesn't have the energy today. There's a crowd in the square. Shouts. She crosses over at once. Away from the watching throng.

'Was it you who wove those kilims, you pillock?' Looking up at the familiar voice, she sees Halil, one of her teachers, in the middle of the crowd.

'Who the bloody hell are you, you bastard?' The red face rings a bell. She peers more carefully. Remembers the opening of the course. The ceremonies at national holidays, and recognises the National Education Director. The man she'd been spitting at in her dreams for the past few days. She clenches her fists.

'What gives you the right to hand them out, when other people's kids spent months weaving those kilims, you pillock?'

The Director's voice a little feebler now, a little hoarser. 'How dare you call me a pillock? You're done for. You'll be posting cards from Şırnak next year.'

'So what? Isn't that part of this county? Threatening me instead of apologising. Cheeky git.'

'Fuck off. I'll get you charged for insults.'

'I'll get you charged first. For thieving. Corruption. Stealing people's labour.'

Two burly youths square up to Halil. 'The fuck are you saying to the Director, you bastard?'

'What's it to you, eh? Are you his brothers or something?'

'Shut up, arsehole; know your place.'

Jülide recognises one of them. Erkan's teammate.

'Apologise to the Director, you bastard.'

They start pushing and shoving Halil.

'What for? Shame on you too. Raising a hand against your teacher. So that's how low you've sunk.'

The Director turns towards the open door of his official car; reaching for him, Halil tries to free himself, but his hand strikes one of the boys in the face. The boy tugs him by the shoulder and lands a stiff punch. The police constables at the door of the station a mere twenty metres away watch, unperturbed.

Nobody in the crowd makes the slightest effort to break it up. Halil is under a rain of punches and kicks. When the police, whose patient wait for a quota was rewarded, slowly approach the crowd, the lads who had been battering the teacher slip away into a suddenly opened gap and vanish. Nobody knows or can identify them.

That venomous hiss came again as Jülide entered the printer's. 'My eye's on you. You're mine. I'm not letting you go to anyone else.' It's only when she heard him that she realised she must have resumed walking. Maybe when Halil was put into a taxi right in front of her to be taken to the hospital.

Rahmi raised his head from the newly-printed paper for a glance when she walked in. His eyes fell back to the paper and he sprang up. 'What's wrong, lass? You're pale as a ghost. Is it that punk again?'

Fresh ink glittered on the headline of the top paper stacked on the table.

BIG SCANDAL AT PUBLIC TRAINING

It has come to light that the kilims woven by the ladies on training courses were presented to senior officials by National Education Director. The ladies are incensed.

'Whoa! We're talking here! What's wrong, lass? Not even a good morning?'

Lifting her tearful gaze, Jülide saw that the everyday had suddenly left Rahmi's eyes, an extraordinary sparkle had spilled out of a permanently closed door, a gossamer-fine gauze had settled on his usual stance and the way he held the paper, and raised his head, transforming him into someone else. She would have run away from this disconcerting gaze, when the tiny deviation in its angle alerted her to a new presence. Her head turned unbidden on the axis of his gaze. A woman she had never seen before stood at the door; an intimacy curtained in her green eyes. Traces of occasional closeness in their bodies. The formality in the movements of their hands, arms and lips was obviously artificial. Her breath alone, full breasts rising and falling nervously above her narrow waist, turned this defensive unfamiliarity into a social game. Feeling like a third wheel, Jülide went outside.

'Welcome,' said Rahmi, a sleepy, yet watchful fear in his eyes, 'What is it?'

'I'm here about the boy.'

Fear flared up in his eyes. 'Something happen to him?'

'No, why should it? He's getting circumcised. Haven't I told you already?'

'You didn't.' He scanned the shop as if looking for his voice, but all he could drag out was a moan. 'Zeliha... Need to sort it out, Zeliha. Can't carry on.'

'Are you nuts? Like you don't know!'

'But this is circumcision, Zeliha! You don't get it. Circumcision. Circumcision's different.'

'How is it different? He's reached this age under your nose. You've seen him walk, seen him talk, put up with it all, but you can't put up with this now?'

Rahmi paused. Crumpled the paper in his hand and threw it to the floor. A vein on his temple was throbbing. 'He called me Uncle Rahmi.'

'What was he going to call you instead?' Zeliha lowered her voice. 'Baba?'

'Yes!'

'Hush!'

He continued, speaking between clenched teeth, 'All your fault. You should've got divorced. You should've got divorced.'

'We've discussed it a hundred times,' said Zeliha, glancing around fretfully, 'Not here. The whole world... Someone will hear. Oh, Rahmi, oh my darling, we'll discuss it later.' She was using fear to pacify this fellow she knew so well.

'My son calls me uncle. All your fault. All your...' The green veins in his neck were swollen.

'Rahmi, please. Please keep calm.' She moved closer and held his elbow. Felt that little relaxation in the tense body. 'I couldn't have got divorced. He'd have killed me. You know it all.'

'Why couldn't you get divorced?'

'They have their customs and stuff. They never get a divorce, unless it's them who want to. Never divorce a wife who wants to go. Like you don't know.'

'No, I don't know.' He tugged his arm free grumpily. 'You don't know it either. You never tried. It's easy to call me your lover when you snuggle up to me though. Lover, huh? That's not love. I don't know what they call yours, but me...'

'Rahmi...' She was pleading.

'Don't call me Rahmi.' It was his own voice, going beyond the limit of secrets and Zeliha's eyes looking anywhere but him, that calmed him down. A creak came from the office upstairs. The window was opened with the usual strain. Glaring at the world shrunk by his frown, Rahmi took pity on Zeliha's hands. Pale, slender, trembling, sweaty hands, clasping each other to hide their trembling, opening suddenly in a white torment, seeking solace in each other again, the small, beautiful hands whose fingers he had kissed over and over again, never tired of playing with in his palms.

'Unless it happens to you, you never know what it's like.' The final echo joining the chain of the last ten years.

'You too. You never know it either.'

Their softened voiced stirred kindness. Their eyes seemed to gather the courage for tenderness, the way they did after every row. Rahmi's gaze was fixed on the mother-of-pearl button done up over the top of her cleavage.

'You've been missing for a week.'

'My in-laws are here for the circumcision. They'll stay for a few more weeks yet.' Zeliha took a step towards the table. Watched the drop of sweat trickling down from Rahmi's neck to his chest in the silence redolent of grease.

'It's too hot,' said Rahmi, tired of sweating.

'I like you getting sweaty.'

Rahmi shivered, as if an invisible butterfly had rubbed the place where the sweat slid down. He resigned himself to the words which did not leave Zeliha's mouth, which only his ears could hear, words nobody else knew.

'Abdurrahman was going to come. I said I'd go. Just to see you. Just to see you for five minutes. And now look what you've done. Made me regret I've come.' He sniffed this fruity, reproachful breath. Lowered his head towards her lips to smell better.

'For the invitation...'

'The invitation is the easy part. We'd be delighted to see you at our son's circumcision party. Mother Zeliha Çetin. Father Rahmi Çetin.'

After Zeliha had left, Jülide tottered back in to see the copy of the invitation in a shaky hand:

We'd be delighted to see you at our son's circumcision party.
Mother Zeliha Kesmikerek. Father Abdurrahman Kesmikerek.

Rahmi stood by the shelves at the rear, motionless as if frozen by a sudden gust of icy wind. Jülide wanted to tiptoe upstairs to avoid disturbing him in this tiny place, but nothing seemed to rouse him from his reverie, not even the creaking stairs.

'What's the matter; you're all pale?'

'Oh, yeah? That's what Rahmi Abi said just now, too.' Even the forced smile left Jülide's face quickly.

Muzaffer's eyes tilted below the reading specs once again as she turned back to the newspaper in her hand. Gesturing Jülide to take a seat, she continued to read. 'Pah! They still have no idea how to write a news item. Headline: Turbaned Girl Holds Demo Outside College. First line: Turbaned N.E. held a demo, sitting outside the university gate to protest being denied continuing her education. Pah! Just like Lucky Luke. Jolly Jumper thinks of something, and Lucky Luke repeats it. In exactly the same words. And that's how they pad it out.' Her eyes rolled up behind the specs again. Tilting her head and pointing at Jülide like a teacher, she started a lesson, 'Look Jülide, if you want to become a journalist…'

'I don't, Muzaffer Abla.' A sudden outburst carving a shocked cavity of silence in the room.

'Oh,' Muzaffer couldn't find anything else to say. 'You look very determined. May I ask why?'

'I don't like newspapers.'

'Good God. Must have been our fault; we've put the young lady off. Since she knows of no other paper. What is it that has put you off, pray tell?'

Blushing brightly, Jülide looked down. 'That's not it, Muzaffer Abla.' The sour stink of rubbish uncollected for several days sneaked in through the window. She was frowning at a fixed point, as if this stink were tangible, standing somewhere in the middle of the room. The morning's north-easterly had stilled. 'I think the wind's going to change.'

Removing her specs held by a cord and letting them rest on her chest, Muzaffer leant back impatiently. 'I give up, Jülide. You don't have enough respect for me to answer. And you think you can distract me.'

'Oh, no, Muzaffer Abla. I was… thinking. I mean, thinking about why I'd said it. I wasn't sure. I just blurted it out. I'm sorry.'

'Spill the beans instead of apologising.'

'There's no beans or anything. Seriously. I don't know.' Pausing, she looked down. 'Fear all the time.'

Having waited in vain for her to continue, Muzaffer couldn't hold back. 'This is like pulling teeth, lass. What fear?'

Unaccustomed to expressing herself in such matters, Jülide was tugging at her fingers nervously as she sought the words. 'They're either reporting on an old fear someone had, or warn about a fear in the future. I mean, something horrific happened the day before, someone was hacked with an axe, raped, or killed by their relatives. Or wars or something. The war dead. Or the economy on the brink unless something is done. External enemies about to do something. All the newspapers are like... a terror factory. And nothing changes anyway. Whatever they write. People... people are so...'

'I take it you've not been looking at the papers much recently.' Muzaffer raised the paper in her hand. 'There's a damsel in a swimsuit. Here's what x celeb said to y celeb. There: whatshisname's fling. Not that I don't find all this far more horrific. I guess I could agree with you on one thing.' She hesitated at the sight of the deep anxiety on Jülide's face. 'The newspapers don't make it up, Jülide. All they do is inform people.'

'But Muzaffer Abla, don't you agree it's an awful profession? Just like being a doctor. You earn your money from pain.'

Muzaffer's mouth opened to say something, and stayed open when she failed to say anything.

A couple of clicks came from the loudspeaker hanging on the power pole nearby, before the day's funeral notice spilled over the narrow streets. The two women listened until the end of the announcement about a woman they didn't know and her close relations, all named one by one.

'My classmates think there are too many deaths in Andalıç. Is it true; are there more deaths here than anywhere else?'

'Aaah, Jülide! You're a real ray of gloom today!' Muzaffer couldn't hold it in any longer. 'Do you honestly believe that? Anyway, what's the matter with you? Like it doesn't happen anywhere else? They'd be in real trouble if they tried the same in a big city.'

'Exactly. Publicising compounds the effect. So the newspapers too...'

'Aaah but…' Briefly thinking, she turned to Jülide, having remembered something. 'Now look here; what did that mutt say to you when he was going?'

'But you… how?' In a nervous tone.

'I know everything. I'm a journalist. Turn your nose up all you like.'

'Oh no, Muzaffer Abla, that's not what I meant. Just that it wasn't for me…'

'All right, all right. Sooo, what did that ratbag say?'

'The usual. Threatens me. You either belong to me or to the black soil, etc.'

Muzaffer threw her hands up. 'Would you look at him! Like it's just a normal thing to say. Like it's easy!'

'Yes, but what can I do? What can I do?' She swallowed the sob filling her throat. 'And then there was grandma's fortune reading this morning, anyway. And then Mr Halil.'

'What's happened to Halil?'

Just then footsteps boomed over the stairs groaning as if begging for mercy. Jülide jumped and ran behind the desk. Shielding her with an arm, Muzaffer sat up and faced the door. A massive cloud of dust rose outside the window as a sudden gust of wind rushed into the street. The footsteps stopped, the door opened, and a slam was heard, then a smash. Jülide and Muzaffer swung round to the broken pane before seeing who it was at the door.

'Oh, fuck!'

They swung back to the door in unison.

'Oh, Jülide's here too. Sorry, child.'

Never happy to show any alarm, Muzaffer sought her usual reproachful teasing. 'Well, well, well; never mind us! Jülide's been humming and hawing all morning. So this was the matter of Mr Halil!'

'Sorry, Muzaffer; we've broken your glass too. Something's off today – let's hope for the best. But it's not my fault, it was the wind.'

'Never mind the windows and what have you. Glass panes don't stick around here, anyway.' She shook her head. 'Oh, Jülide. Oh, Jülide. You should've run over to let me know. Here we are, styling ourselves as journalists. Our friend's face gets smashed in, and he's the one who has to tell us. Bravo, what can I say?' Realising that Halil had nothing worse than a few aches and pains, she gave a genuine laugh this time. 'Whoever's rearranged your face did a fair fist of it.'

'A couple of strapping youths. The new generation's a little beefy, I guess. Otherwise…' Forgetting himself, he laughed, tensing the lip as if it would split open again. 'Uh uh uh! We're getting past it, Muzaffer. Lost our touch. I, who had made short work of so many hulks in my day!'

'Yeah, right.'

Muzaffer stared at the open flesh reduced to the mortal essence of all creatures walking this earth: wrapped in dressing, sealed in bruises, torn, crushed, the outer layer making him a human being stripped off. Flesh that slowly ages, grows old, scares the evanescence hitting its wrinkles, and rots and vanishes once it's gone.

'Do you want something to eat or drink?'

'No. Lost a tooth, too. Nothing to eat until evening. Nothing cold, nothing hot. I saw the paper in the hospital and thought I'd drop in. On my way, anyway.'

He had the inexplicable euphoria of people who'd just had an extraordinary experience, albeit a nasty one.

'I'm taking that geezer to court, thought I'd tell you. Let's see if he can exile me before I've dealt with him. We've got courts and judges in the country. We're not letting them get away with it.'

12

Dressings and stitches removed, bruises turning yellow, Halil was sitting slumped outside the grocery in the manner of a war veteran or a pensioner.

'How can you tell it's the south-westerly?'

'It blows from the rear.'

'Say your eyes were covered. You were spun over and over again. Didn't know where you were facing.'

'No idea.'

'How come?'

'I probably couldn't tell in that case.'

'Well, doesn't it have a smell?'

'Who says the wind has a smell?'

'Of course it does! The south-westerly smells of boiled pasta.'

'Yeah, right.'

'Have a sniff.'

'You're right; it does, a little.'

Halil was now able to laugh without worrying.

'Grin all you want. Of course, only two days to the wedding. Think about the photos with a witness in this state!'

Cemal's grin continued to spread.

'Stop dreaming all day and chat a little, mate. Whenever I come, here's this grinning type sitting here. I'll see what you look like in three years' time. Kids at your trouser legs, dragging you one way and the other…'

The grin vanished at once.

'Saliha doesn't want kids.'

'Don't you believe it. No woman "doesn't want children". She might say that at first, but she'll change her mind later.'

'No, she's determined. She really doesn't want any.'

'Bravo; smart girl. Bring them up, then go and hand 'em over to some boor. I could cheerfully drown our daughter's hairy-arsed boyfriend.'

He glanced at the dry tips of the misshapen vine leaves hanging from the wall opposite. Swung round to Cemal as if reminded of something by the silence.

'But you do, right? There: it's written all over your face. Gone is the charmer who was here just now…' He giggled. 'Doesn't make the slightest difference what you want, mate. Women take all the decisions. You'll never again buy a pair of socks or a shirt she doesn't like. You can't eat the food she doesn't like. You can't make a peep about the colour of the walls or what colour bedsheets to buy.'

'But why doesn't she want them? Doesn't a woman want children with the man she loves? All women go gaga over kids.'

'Oh, Cemal! Have I been wasting my breath all these years? And I thought you were smart. Is there just one woman on Earth? Are we zebras? And even zebras might have different characters, who knows? There was a lion who didn't eat meat, for instance, I read about it in the paper the other day. They'd place a lamb next to her and she'd cuddle it.' Laughing, he squinted and peered at Cemal for quite a while. 'I'm wasting my breath. Two hours gone, and still sulking.'

'Leave me alone, abi. Is it that strange to want a family?'

'It's not the "wanting a family", it's treating "wanting a family" as an indicator of love.'

'Isn't it the little things that show whether someone loves you, though? Like you wouldn't have been cross if Yasemin hadn't wanted children! Like we don't know what you're like.'

'Get away; you know nothing. Yasemin didn't want kids either. She stuck it out for four or five years. I said OK, fine. It kinda suited me anyway. Then her mum and all and our lot: they just wouldn't leave her alone. Hints, innuendos, placing babies on her lap. Sounding her out about whether I can't get it up. Digging into whose fault it is. Refrains of "You'll regret it when you're older." At long last, they swayed her. Then she had our daughter, and had postpartum depression. She was about to throw the baby out the window one day; I had the devil of a time stopping her. You have no idea. All I'm saying is, get off her case.'

Enervated by the heat of the south-westerly that so rarely grabs Andalıç, they shut up. Halil inspected his aches and pains, turning his head right and left.

'Well, well, well. Your lady sister honours us.'

'Where?'

'Hard to tell what you can see if you can't see her!'

Cemal's sulk darkened. 'It would be better to see a little less of her. Blessed thing drops in whenever she's bored. Don't know what she's after.'

Halil glanced at Saliha's window. 'Your sister, isn't she? Half- or not.'

'Yes, but ...' Cemal fidgeted nervously. 'She's said to have taken up with the Commissioner. His mistress.'

'Says who?'

'Auntie Raziye.'

'Ah! In which case, it's definitely true. And our news source has just taken up position on the cushion placed over the windowsill. Does she just get a hunch, or does she have other methods? Maybe just a really keen sense of smell. And she'd have caught Cemile's smell all the way from the bottom of the hill. Which is not necessarily a major feat for any normal person. When the wind is right. This Auntie Raziye's got a mortar – I've known its sound since childhood. There was a time when everyone borrowed it. She was pounding garlic just now. Bang bang bang. Now, if she's got the scent over the smell of garlic, then she deserves congratulations.' Cheered up even more by something akin to a smile on Cemal's face, he said, 'It's not for nothing we train' and, eschewing the need for a full stop, tacked to the tail of the sentence, 'Welcome, Cemile Hanım.'

'Thank you, Halil Abi.'

'How's the Mater?'

'Fine.'

'And your other relations? Abdurrahman Bey etc?'

Cemile simpered. 'Oh, d'ya know Abdurrahman Bey?'

'Who wouldn't? The august Commissioner of Police.'

'Yeah. I've kinda recently met him. He's a very nice person. Helps us a lot. Otherwise, us feeble women ...'

Playing with the scab over his smile, Halil rubbed a fingernail on his teeth as if to soften it. 'You seem to be really devoted to your relations, Cemile Hanım. You keep looking up Cemal too.'

They all drew back a little to give way to a horse cart with rubber tyres. Its eyes down, the scrawny beast was struggling to pull a load of wood. The woodman was walking beside him to lighten its burden.

'Oh, poor thing!' Both hands on her cheeks, Cemile stared at the horse with genuine compassion. 'So many horse carts here! Narrow streets, right? But I've not seen no phaetons.'

'Everywhere has its own customs, Cemile Hanım. Everywhere has its own fashions and behaviour.'

Trying to hide his blush, Cemal undid and re-tied his shoelace; he wanted to look at Saliha's window, but for some reason his eye wouldn't go higher than the doorknob. He stared at it, lost in thought.

'Oh, Halil Abi, you're a right one! So formal and all. Cemile Hanıms etc. I'm not used to such stuff. And we're almost family, anyway.'

'Yes. Family. And with our thanks to you… Sorry, thanks to you, we're now related to Abdurrahman Bey too. He's much loved around here. Anyone who ends up in custody takes his name with a prayer of gratitude.'

The noise of the cart was gone, along with the horse's torment. All that remained was the acrid smell of horse droppings.

'You're such a sweetie, Halil Abi. You know what. No one has a moustache like yours in the whole of Andalıç.'

'We-eel, sister, growing a moustache is not for the fainthearted.' He glanced at Cemal, who was tilting the stool's legs and setting them back down. His face was utterly blank. The only clue was the swollen blue veins in the hands gripping the side of the stool. 'Cemal, my lad. The missus's expecting me. I'm off now. And anyway, we've not offered Cemile a seat – shame on us!' Getting up, he offered Cemile his stool.

'Thanks, Halil Abi, but I can't sit here in this skirt, anyways. Can't we sit at the rear, darling abi?'

Cemal followed her into the shop, his feet going backwards – as the saying goes – like a lamb to the slaughter. He glanced at Saliha's window. The curtain swelling in the south-westerly momentarily revealed an empty room. Filled with chagrin, like all absences. A sudden sense of abandonment, followed by a hope that Saliha might be coming downstairs.

His gaze averted from Cemile's bare shoulders fell, smashing against the bra visible under the thin blouse, the broad belt cinching her waist, the wrinkles of the tight skirt digging into her hips, the slit that started a full handspan above her knees, the white dimples behind her knees, the ankles tensing over the high heels, and finally, at the bottom of those heels. Cringing, wondering why they didn't turn towards the cheeses, lollipops or crisps, his eyes struck the floor and remained motionless, enervated by a primordial sense of defeat. His gaze continued to crawl on the floor a few inches behind the high heels, stumbling on the tiny white mosaic stones amongst the tiny holes of the dark grey concrete floor swept daily.

'Oh, my ankle!'

Cemile's ankles, which had traversed (and done so with the expertise of an acrobat) the town's cobblestones polished by centuries of footsteps into a round, shiny slipperiness, couldn't take this excessive caution any more and let go on the shop's flat floor; as they did, her body, instead of losing its balance towards the side as might be expected in the case of a twisted ankle, spun around itself in a neat arc to turn 180 degrees. The moment he recognised the feminine softness falling into his instinctively extending arms, and over his leg that had taken a huge step, he tried to extricate himself as if he had been thrown a hot brick. In a rapid, mechanical move, he retracted the forward step he had taken. His arms shoved Cemile by the shoulders as far as they could reach. The half-closed eyes that were raised up to his face a moment ago and the lips extended in a slight pout were now at a safe distance, but the sharp smell of rakı that had pinched his nose just now was still lurching in the air.

Once he was convinced that balance had been restored, he shook his hands with exaggerated hurry like shaking off some dirt and clasped them behind his back; the obviousness and defencelessness of this pose moved his hands back up to the sides as if to form a footballers' wall, and surprised by this bizarre desire, contented himself with wiping his hands on his trousers instead. Just like all those times when he received a public scolding whenever he failed at an oral exam at school, or disappointed his father in anything at all.

'My handsome abi,' said Cemile, gazing at him in a drunken delight Cemal attributed to the rakı.

'Have you had rakı so early in the day?'

'A little. Are you cross, darling abi?'

Cemal sighed fretfully, uncomfortable with standing in the middle of the shop this way, being stared at this way. Yet, the rear room held a daunting sense of intimacy. Hence his reluctance to move. Then Cemile swung round and set off into the store and his anxiety rose like dark, choppy seas.

The moment his shuffling feet crossed over the doorstep, some obstacle prevented him from walking further, something soft leant against him, just below the chest, and grabbed him tight just above the waist, and his nose sank into hair crisped by a heavily-perfumed spray. He had inadvertently thrown his arms up and was now gawping at this strange object wrapped around his body. He stammered, 'You… what are you doing Cemile? Are you too drunk to stand?'

His words beckoned his wits, and his wits beckoned his willpower. He tried once more to push away Cemile with his fingertips, as if touching an unfamiliar creature he couldn't be certain was not venomous. But she was gripping him far too tight to be dislodged by fingertips. When he succeeded, at long last, to push her wrists away in a panic, gripping them tight enough to bruise them, he grabbed her just above the elbow and led her to the sofa by the wall like leading a criminal, madwoman or a patient, like leading someone not free to act on her own to a courtroom, cell in an asylum or to her sick bed. With a tug, he seated her down. Throughout this time, the drunken grin slapped on Cemile's face ever since she'd set foot inside the shop never vanished.

'Let me make you a strong Nescafé.'

'It's not that kind of drunkenness.'

Standing in the doorway with an eye on the shop entrance and realising that Saliha wasn't coming, Cemal was no longer able to contain his anger.

'I've been minding my own business all this time, but there is a limit! What's all this rakı drinking in daytime and all? This outfit, all this paint. What about all this gossip about Abdurrahman Bey? Is that why I've brought you here? All the things you'd said, all that you'd sworn off…' He stopped, surprised by his own anger. 'Oh well, none of my business, anyway.'

'No, my handsome abi. You can't say none of my business when it comes to these matters. This is honour, after all.'

Eyebrows lifted, he gave his half-sister an astonished look. 'No one's honour is my business. You were the one who was crying, "I want a decent life." But you were drunk then too, weren't you?'

'So I only want to be decent when I'm drunk. Shouldn't it be the other way round? Everyone lets their hair down when they drink.'

'Yup. And you've obviously let yours down now. So you never can tell.'

'Cemal.'

His name suddenly rang in his own ears like something very intimate. He shifted as if to run away from his own shop.

'Come and sit down, why don't you? I'm not gonna eat you. I got a problem.'

Hesitating, Cemal continued to stand at the door.

'How can I speak when you're standing like that?'

He went and sat down. As far as away as he could, at the other end of the sofa. 'Fine, I'm sitting down now. Tell me what your problem is.'

'You know you said about Abdurrahman Bey. There's gossip. Why would I hide from you what God knows, the punter got me a place, I'm his kept woman now.' Cemal took a deep breath, his eyes like saucers. 'My kind always gets lots on our tail.'

'Well, if you will dress like this, and flaunt it ... Give me strength!'

'Like it would be different if I didn't? It's already written on our forehead.'

'I give up! That's just too... Do you really believe what you're saying, Cemile? If you'd been dressing and behaving like the women here since you've come here, nobody would've bothered you, would they?'

'Do you think I'm the kind of woman who wouldn't attract attention if I dressed different, then?'

'Let's say you did. All the same, nobody would dare to approach you this way. They might be more serious. You might have a suitor who wants to marry you.'

'And what will he do when I tell him about my past?' Rubbing her neck and throwing her head back, she looked at him. 'Or should I not say anything?'

Cemal looked at the ivy animated by the south-westerly.

'Course you've got nothing to say. Once you're a whore, they won't let you live unless you whore. Either you're going to say yes to them all or you pick someone who keeps them all at bay. There: you're a kept woman. If you have no honour, you need an owner. Or you're in the shit. Can you own me, for example? What can you do? Would you beat someone up to get rid of him? Would you shoot him? If you were stabbed in the groin in some dark corner… My lot doesn't get decent blokes.'

He was looking out when he felt a warm touch on his leg. Cemile had come closer unnoticed. He was cornered at the end of the sofa. The soft pressure invading his body was spreading.

'As for my outfits. That's the only thing that I enjoy. I don't have any other pleasures in life. You want me to wear a floral frock?'

'Of course you don't have any other pleasures. You don't have to wear a frock. There are elegant things that are also quite modest.'

'Oh, no, no! I can't wear stuff that looks like men's clothes, like your fiancée.'

'Keep Saliha out of it.' The voice striking his gritted teeth grew louder.

Cemile's grin spread even wider. 'I'm sorry, darling abi. Don't you want to know what my trouble is, though?'

'Your trouble is obvious.'

'Oh, but don't say that, you'll hurt me. See, it gives me a right turn when I think about it.' She undid her top button. 'See how my heart's beatin'.' Grabbing Cemal's hand, she pressed it on her practically bare left tit.

Cemal leapt up as though he had touched naked flames and yelled at the top of his voice. 'Have you lost your mind? Look here. This is a small place. You can't just do whatever springs to your mind. If this is how you want to live, go back to Istanbul. I can't be defending you all day long. And I'm not your pimp. And I don't feel like your big brother either.'

'Oh, what honey flows from your mouth!'

All of a sudden, his back was against the wall, Cemile's legs pinning his, her lips on his, her hand between his legs. This time the reaction came from his body and he shoved her off with all his strength. He strode towards Cemile, who had fallen on her arse. Grabbed her by the arm and lifted her to her feet. Dragged her to the door. She was guffawing. 'She's not in love with you. Your one true love's not in love with you. It'll hit you one day. I'm the one who's in love with you.'

'Stop. Stop talking.' He saw his raised hand. Grinning again, Cemile did nothing to protect herself from the imminent slap on her cheek. 'You're a maniac.' Clenching his hand, he slowly lowered it and shook Cemile out the door as if she were a panful of dust. 'You're a maniac. Don't let me see you again. Get lost.' Just as he was about to go back in, he heard a hiss.

'Zaim's here. He's been asking about me. He's here to kill me.'

The smell of old cheese, detergent and pulses coiling in the shop strangely turned Cemal's stomach.

'Maybe that's for the best. I have absolutely no intention of getting between you and your pimp. Your Commissioner can protect you. I mean it. I don't want to see your face again. Do whatever the bloody hell you like.' He had not turned towards her as he spoke. He heard the needling noises of the thin heels disappearing behind his back. Grabbing the wall and the shelves in a sudden fit of exhaustion, he went to the little washbasin. Splashed his face with water when he heard a voice. 'Anyone here?'

A strange male voice, which briefly alarmed his topsy-turvy mind. He didn't even notice drying his face with the back of his arm. The water drops on his eyelashes made it difficult to recognise the new arrival. A stoutish shadow, of average height. Cemal weighed his options at once. Took a defensive pose. Then the voice and the vision combined somewhere in his brain, triggering a sense of familiarity.

'Hakkı Baba, is that you?'

'Yup, in person. Didn't you recognise me?'

'Of course I did. How could I fail to? Just that ... erm ... just now ... anyway, sorry. Welcome.'

'Thank you.'

Glancing over the shop, Hakkı laughed, peering at Cemal's face.

'A lady was leaving just as I arrived. I'm guessing it was the sister you'd gone to look for.'

'Yes, yes. My sister.'

Hakkı pulled out the handkerchief peeking out of the top pocket of his beige suit jacket and handed it to him, laughing again at Cemal's blank look.

'You've not started wearing lipstick, have you?'

'Lipstick? What lipstick?' Cemal's eyes opened wide. He ran over to the broken mirror over the washbasin. His lips were smeared with what looked like the blood of a weird prey, a smear of pale red giving him a greedy expression. Returning the unused handkerchief, he gave his face a good wash with soap.

'Cemal, son; I'm in my seventies now. I've been around quite a bit too. I know anything's possible in this world, but: isn't she your sister? Look, you're getting married in a couple of days. I beg of you, think carefully. Love is a sensitive issue. You're half-siblings, you've grown up apart, you could be strangers... Don't upset your fiancée, son.'

Cemal's outburst was drowned in the towel. 'Oh, Hakkı Baba, what are you saying? God forbid! How could I ever...' He paused. 'She...' Clutching at a word not generally associated with males, a word he wasn't sure he knew, 'I mean, I... I don't want anything like that. I didn't. I mean, she forced...' Then it all hit home at once, and it all poured out: why his eyes were stinging before he washed his face, the sense, the distress and shame of being violated. 'She grabbed me, tried to kiss me. I pushed her. She fell. I chucked her out. Then she says, just as she's leaving, that her pimp's here, come to kill her. Argh!' The filth that had been choking him burst out. 'She... she's a maniac... she's nuts. Or has no concept of decency or modesty.'

'Wild women are sometimes great, but not like this. Anyway, now that you've chucked her out, she probably won't come back again.'

'I don't know: she doesn't act like normal people.'

Cemal glanced at the little dry garden and the profusion of blue thorn apple flowers wrapped around the telephone pole. Their faint, sweet scent flowed into and out of the room in the dropping wind.

'Oh, Cemal, it's not worth worrying about. She'll leave you alone once you're married, don't worry. Everything gets sorted out, except for death.' A paternal rub on Cemal's arm. 'You'll cope together, so long as you and your fiancée love each other.'

Cemal looked very pensive. 'We do, of course we love each other.' He sounded very faint. 'She said... this Cemile...' The flowers were shaking gently.

'What did she say?'

'That Saliha's not in love with me.'

'Sooo?'

Realising what he'd just said actually meant, Cemal pulled himself together. 'I mean, how can she say anything like that?'

'Let her; so what? Haven't you just said she was nuts? She's not sane, so why take any notice of what she says. You and your fiancée know each other. Nothing else matters.'

Cemal seemed to pull himself together in the faint breeze cooling his damp face. 'Yeah, sorry, Hakkı Baba. You'd looked after me so well, and here's me, not even offering you a seat. I'm in such a foul mood that I'd join you if you wanted some rakı.'

'I'm not sure. Perhaps one glass won't hurt.'

Early evenings, which pick at the flesh of the day to build the longest night, linger on the warm pink horizon as they delight in the imminence of September. The sun sinks right over the tip of Andalıç. The Care Home casts its shadow over the narrow isthmus. Matching the speed of the sun leaving the Aegean behind the big Greek island on the other side of the water, the peninsula's shadow climbs up the hills opposite until there is no light left. The olive trees denied a single drop of water for three months hide from the sun in their dusty plain grey cloaks; now they can take their first cool breaths. The faint shiver as they exhale ruffles the sea, reaching all the way to Andalıç. Through Cemal's small window, it descends into the lounge, spreading the heady odour in the glasses raised to celebrate all joys and sorrows.

'I'd come here thirty-five years ago, on honeymoon, when I was thirty-five. I'm seventy now, less one day.'

'Tomorrow's your birthday?'

'That's what it says on the ID card, but mum always said I was born at Hıdrellez. Spring celebrations. Older generations didn't keep precise records of birth dates or anything. My aunt used to say she was born when the Greeks were running away. Mum was born at Bocuk.'

'What's Bocuk?'

'There's a saying in Thrace: like a Bocuk pig. Maybe a Christian festival near New Year's. They must have fattened the pigs for the festival.'

A morsel each of melon and cheese. Long silences dotted the night, which became warmer as it darkened, as if even talking would make one sweat. Hakkı was still tired from the journey. He sipped his rakı with an old longing, and a shiver.

'You never came back then, Hakkı Baba.'

'No, son; I didn't. But that one week... It's been a lifetime, and I never forgot it.' Memories clearly outweighing his desire to speak freely, he hesitated on the threshold of the story. He rarely thought for so long before indulging his lust of talking about himself.

'She was known as Lovely Cevriye. I'd heard her voice first. Can't remember her face or anything now. Just her voice. Sometimes I jump out of bed, hearing her say "Have you locked the door, Hakkı?" But it's a dream. Just a dream...'

His tarnished blue eyes had darkened like the waters, matching the darkening sky. He pushed back his thin white hair without putting his cigarette down first.

'Marriage is sometimes the worst thing in the world. Sometimes the nicest. Ours was lovely. As lovely as Cevriye. She'd know what was wrong from my eyes. It was such delight, such a celebration to get back home to her. I'd given up frequenting taverns within a couple of months.' Blowing the smoke to the side, he took his time to stub out the cigarette.

'By God, women are taught so much! They arrange all of life. They bring their trousseaux and lay it all out, choose the furniture and the food... The design on a plate, the line on a fork handle, the lace edging the cambric pillow cases and duvet covers. Especially if she's got good taste. And my Cevriye had great taste. The house was like a picture, too lovely for words.'

Cemal looks around at his place, wondering what Saliha's signature is going to be like. He was so used to his mother's plain, clean, neat style that it was difficult to guess whether he would welcome change, or feel sad. All the same, he was hungry for whatever came from Saliha.

'All this time, Cemal, I've never told anyone the stuff I told Cevriye. She was the only person who knew me. You wonder if your fiancée loves you or not. Even tormenting yourself. Doubt is a strange thing. A little is good at times. A little doubt, a little agony. Especially whether you're really loved. It makes you restless, makes you suffer, but it also shows how much you really love. That you don't doubt yourself at all. The worst thing in these matters of the heart is doubting yourself. But making small demands, sulking when she forgets something, or expecting more... it's tiring. Tiring, but lovely. You feel you're in love. I mean, so long as you don't torment her, there's nothing strange in wondering like you do.'

He took another large, hungry sip of rakı. 'Oh, this blooming thing... has it been fifteen years, I wonder?'

'But no, Hakkı Baba. I never say anything. It's all inside me.' He paused. 'I don't know. Sometimes she's too distant.'

'Pull her close, then. Don't just watch from a distance, son. You said she had issues. Don't take offence at everything now. You need to be a little thick skinned when it comes to love. Where's pride gonna get you?'

Tiny bats flitting about stirred the evening's colours.

'Now this Cevriye: she was my everything. What a woman! Beautiful, smart, competent... it would break your heart just to look at her. And her mezes! And she was a great mother too. Two boys she raised, diamonds, both of them. Oh, Cemal; children are something else. You'll understand if you have them.'

Cemal downed the glass he'd been staring at for a while.

'But sometimes... I mean, something happens. Suddenly you no longer see your wife or kids. It was around the time the boys had just started lycée. After getting married, I'd pulled my socks up and turned around the business. The money was pouring in. You never know where to spend it. House, summer place, cars, travel. The more I earned, the more I took to gadding about on my own, never mind the family. You know what they say: the leopard can't change its spots. I'd got myself a convertible Ford, gallivanting about. Next thing I knew, I took up with some woman. A common piece. Not pretty or anything. Wasn't a patch on Cevriye. Whatever the bloody hell I thought I found there, I got more and more involved. Set her up in a place and all. It all got out of control.'

With a long sip, Hakkı downed his glass too. Cemal reached for the bottles at once. The rakı clouded into white in veins.

'Of course it finally got to Cevriye's ears. She turned me out. Divorced me in one single hearing. Bang. Like a joke.'

Cemal pressed his lips together and raised his eyebrows, then cast his eyes down and sighed sadly.

'You know what she did next?'

'Got married again?'

'No. I wish she had.' Hakkı pulled out another cigarette from the pack on the table, in three slow, staccato moves. Placing it in his mouth, he clicked a lighter engraved with his initials and scratches acquired over the years. He took his first drag and laid the cigarette on the edge of the ashtray.

'She imprisoned herself at home. If only it was just home. Imprisoned herself in bed. Wouldn't answer my calls. Returned my letters unopened. I asked friends to intervene, she refused them all. Her sisters, her friends: no matter how hard they tried, they couldn't convince her. She made herself into a bedridden patient. Wouldn't even take any notice of her sons. In the end she died at the age of thirty-eight, of kidney failure. She slowly killed herself. Willed herself to die.'

Cemal sought for some indication of how the old man had coped with this dreadful guilt; all he found was a strange calm.

'You have to betray someone if you want to know whether she really loves you, Cemal. At first I thought she was doing it out of love for me. I felt guilty as shit. Thought I'd killed her. Along with a sick sense of pride. 'Cos she died for me, yeah? I lived with the guilt of having killed the one person I loved most in the world. I became an alcoholic. My sons disowned me. Took over the business and turned me out. Thankfully I had my pension. But it was years later, one morning when I happened to be sober, that I noticed something.' Flicking the ash off the cigarette he had forgotten on the ashtray, he took a drag. Looked at the darkness. 'Cevriye never loved me. She chose pride over love and killed herself just to punish me. Or rather, didn't love me like I thought she did.'

Cemal grimaced.

'You never can tell if someone loves you unless you betray her, Cemal. All the same, best not to test it. Better to think you're loved than remain ignorant if you've never been loved. Got to own your love. Not that there's any point in being loved by someone you don't love, either.'

Untroubled by human concerns or joys, the crickets started filling the night with their song. A bead of sweat rolled down from Hakkı's temple to his crepey jowls and vanished into the white hairs on his chest. He waited and waited until the last drop in the bottle fell into the glass.

'Since then I never had a sip of alcohol, not for fifteen years. This is the first. This place is different. This wedding. Cevriye. New bride Cevriye.' He lit another cigarette and smoked it in silence till the end. 'It's the things you most want to protect that you lose most easily. A demon prods you from inside. Like you want to know if you can lose it or not. It's possible to lose anything and everything, Cemal. Even the things you thought you never would. But even losses are good. Maybe even better than wins. At least you can't fool yourself then.'

Enticed by these words, all those thousands of years of Andalıç's losses flooded the night. Fermented the heat and the dark, dimmed the stars, and forced windows open one by one. Threadbare bedsheets split just where they were thinnest under nightmare-laden tossings and turnings. Hair stuck itchily to sweating necks instead of fanning out on pillows, as troubled dreamers waited with evanescent hope for the elusive voice or the face of a past love. Old muslin headscarves, washed with the tears of grandmas when they recited the Koran on anniversaries, were tucked into children's vests. All those lovingly safeguarded mementos too precious to use radiated the pungent odour of waiting from the cracks in wardrobes. In the stifling heat, weighed down by loss, during blissful or restive sleep full of everything that will remain lost for ever, all of Andalıç gave a deep sigh.

13

That sigh heralded a muffled rumble from the depths of the earth, a heave that would balloon into a colossus as it rose. Birds were the first creatures to run away from this surge that presaged an eerie future, flocking, screaming, oblivious to the darkness. Next, dogs howled over a hushed fear that dilated cats' pupils, raised their hackles, and arched their backs. Terror and anguish, which had seeped into the ground and pooled there for a century, rattled the ordinary, intent on extracting it. The faces of the dead sought resurrection as the glass over their framed portraits hanging on walls shivered with a thin fever. Windows, display cases and glasses in cupboards plunged into a low wail like a taut wire, in a frequency outside the range of human hearing. Water shivered too, in concentric rings in glasses on bedside tables, in pitchers on tables, in buckets in bathrooms, and sleeping on the shores of Andalıç. Early risers spotted a weirdly coloured illumination piercing the darkness of the sky.

The next reply to the earth came from dead trees, as they recalled the one- or two hundred-year chunks cleaved out of an eternal motionlessness unknown to man: chairs, tables, cupboards, doors, and frames. Activated by the suddenly enlivened ground underneath, they started shaking from side to side and bouncing and shrieking in unheard-of creaks. The howls drowning out the roar, the crashes drowning out the howls, the creaks drowning out the crashes, and the beds transformed into cradles rocked by terror, ripped through sleep. Later risers saw the walls shake and not just the beds, plaster fall and cracks open, and doors recede into the distance.

Stones, bricks or roof tiles: there was nothing left in Andalıç not inculcated in how to scream. The faculty to make sounds and move in response to a single command, which was acquired all at once by the entirety of inanimate objects, opened cupboard doors and flung out the contents, overturned tables, chairs, bookcases and wardrobes, and transformed homes into traps of endless falls. Chandeliers, the ceilings where those chandeliers hung, and the walls holding up those ceilings dropped their hefty bulks over humans in what could only be described as a deranged wrath.

Garish and imperious, the tremor continued to ascend towards its bumpy summit, silence, resolve, wits, and endurance smashing against one another in its sack. Andalıç's low stone houses erected by builders of old gave their inhabitants time to run outdoors; but the five- and six-storey blocks erected on the seafront during the apartment boom were not as merciful. The particles gripping one another for goodness knows how long suddenly shrugged off their links; as they turned adrift, a choking cloud of dust filled the air. Motes of dust fell everywhere, in particular, into eyes, mouths, and lungs: soft, damp, delicate tissues.

As the tremor dawdled in an incomprehensible frenzy, people waited with muscles tensed by a primeval fear, seconds beyond the capacity of petrified minds to count distended into minutes, and all strength to scream or move a step was gone, a faint, feeble snap was heard from the depths, a noise everyone who heard it another would later recollect as if in a dream.

A snap only distinguished by a peculiar feebleness in the midst of this portentous commotion. A teeny, unique, quiet snap, which managed to seep into ears in the midst of that ferocious din, that sound of a break, of an eternal change, of irreversibility rather than one signifying a disaster or period of grief. A lonely single snap, whose meaning and memory would only come into focus after daybreak. The gigantic cone of pumice stone in the sea lurched one last time, or perhaps twice, before finding its balance as the inanimate recalled their status and, taking the animate along, returned to absolute stillness. The houses remembered to stand on their foundations, the roofs on their walls, the roof tiles on their roofs, and humans on their feet.

It's over, oh my God it's over.

On course for a long trip, an unknown destination and an extraordinary nomadism, and, until daybreak, under an illusion of immobility, Andalıç let go of the breath it had been holding for thirty seconds. But mothers could not let go of their children, nor husbands of their wives, or siblings, of one another; all those people who had all been rendered mute as all sound vanished from the earth. All movement vanished from the sky; townsfolk rendered immobile contented themselves with staring for a long while. Staring at the darkness behind the settling dust.

My God; what was that?

There was neither moon nor a single star in the sky. In the absence of all light, even the dust came down in an invisible black.

The townsfolk waited in a daze until the first voices returned to earth as moans.

My house is still standing, it's still standing.

Piercing the dust in yellow lines, torch beams turned towards the walls of the houses. On walls roughed up yet still standing, or collapsed.

Not too much damage. Next doors're also standing. But those across the street...

Once again, it was time for the living to move. They called out, shut up and listened. Sweated for hours to replace the stones, bricks and rubble, which had been placed on the ground by those thirty seconds.

My hands are bleeding.

Bending down, rising up, carrying things from hand to hand, running home to grab blankets and water.

One house has collapsed in our street; not too bad in the higher neighbourhoods but those on the seafront...

A nervous daylight returned to a world it had entrusted to darkness. Accustomed as it was to be gazed at like a miracle instead of an everyday occurrence, dawn had fallen from grace this time. No one looked up at the sky filled with the arid smell of terror. A silent light peeked in the east, which had lost its bearings. People lifting their heads briefly to wipe their brows were baffled, a barely detectable sense of finding something not quite where it had been placed.

Heard about taxi driver Mustafa? There was no room at the hospital. He was taking his mother to Izmir. Seems the road's collapsed. The poor fella's sunk into the sea.

Rescue work at the occasional collapsed property in the neighbourhood was nearly done. Survivors pulled out from the rubble were taken to the hospital, and the others ... to the school's sports hall. That the sun rose at all was still a miracle for those who had spent all night tearing their hands to shreds in the dark, in car headlights. The tip of the sun appeared in the golden glow of dawn, which invariably paled at the first sight of the earth. The olive-clad hills behind which the sun rose seemed to have gone farther away. Folks setting out to see how much of the causeway had collapsed noticed a gap twice or three times the length of the road between themselves and the land.

I wonder if the shore's sunk too; it looks farther away. So aid won't arrive at once. No problem; it'll come by boat. By ship. By helicopter. If the breakwater holds, if the skiffs stay moored... God forgive my soul, the shore seems to be moving further away, like we're moving.

The sun continued to climb in the sky, dragging behind it all manner of illusions. The telephones and wireless sets were silent, but not the car radios.

7.9, they say; and a 7.6 in Greece a short time later... the odds are a million to one. They're talking of aftershocks, but we've had none here.

Andalıç was floating in the middle of the motionless sea, its reflection symmetrical, the entirety of its communication buried in the rubble. It would have looked pretty similar if the waters were to recede: a larger inverted cone stuck to the bottom of the cone above. A sky island floating in the air.

The olive oil factory on the shore was never visible from the top of this hill. Wonder if a house collapsed at the bottom?

Wrinkles on the sea started from the furtively diminishing shore. Enveloping Andalıç, they stretched towards the horizon, but the surface of the sea on the landwards side remained smooth, occasionally dotted by tiny eddies like a wake. The townsfolk stared at the weird flatness that had replaced the causeway; instead of connecting them to the shore, it was pushing them away a little more by the second.

They're saying Andalıç is set afloat... Yeah, right... They've really lost it now.

Its east, west, north and south at the mercy of the winds and the currents, Andalıç drifted towards Greece in a slow spin like a floating magic roundabout.

So where's the island then? That huge island...

There was no longer any doubt that Andalıç was moving downwind. The olive trees were growing smaller as the land seemed to grow bigger, stretch and spread, covering ever more of the world. With a tremendous awe, which suppressed the receding fear, increasing anguish and the extraordinary poured over life, the residents watched the movement of their floating island. A moment of hearts in mouths. Like an enormous hand had lifted them and dropped them back on the water. They saw a huge swell racing across the sea. It rose and rose as it approached the shore, a wall of sea towering between them and Turkey, but only for a moment, until it collapsed with a thundering crash as fast as it had risen. The sea had joined in the earth's show of strength, unwilling to lose the challenge, and thus proven its mastery of wrath.

Oh, Lord; huge olive trees are floating in the sea. It's like mud. The chimney of the old olive oil factory's collapsed, and some of the walls too... hard to make it out now...

Just then the island staggered. In the newly fragile sense of security, a wave of terror swept through the place. A large column of water was spurting up into the air where the tremendous noise came from. The collapsed blocks at the seafront had just sunk into the deep waters of the Aegean, leaving behind an arc like an enormous bitemark. Sunk together with their residents. Despair reigned supreme. Once realisation and grief had run their course, the townsfolk noticed that the sun had risen all the way to the top. It was very hot, it would only get hotter still, there was no time to waste. Glancing at the land, now really faint and distant in the noon sun, they set off for the cemetery.

They used a digger. Couldn't cope with shovels, could you? One hundred and fifty-three. Oh, dear oh dear oh dear! Some look so big for their charges.

Forgetting its shock, Andalıç remembered its pain and prayers. Soil dug out was replaced. The dead were hidden. The last sobs vanished. The cemetery fell silent. The sun dragging the island westwards ran away. Exhaustion trumped anguish. All those same beds in the same rooms, familiar for years and years, grew distant, became strange, as if this were the first night in a foreign country. The wuthering north-easterly eschewed its usual windows of entry. Ursa Major was not in its usual place. The darker black shade of the sky, the unfamiliar sourness of the sweat on the pillow, the glass shards swept until late at night, leaving deep cuts in the mind, the trousers waving behind the door as if they would quicken, the cooler scent of the north-easterly scudding over, not the land and the olives, but the sea, its scent that chilled those cuts in the mind, the silence of the ever-dripping tap, and the deserted and ominous night emptied of the familiar sounds of the dogs now too scared to bark... Eyelashes denying rest to weary bodies rustled softly on pillows. That barely perceptible tremor was new, the body's demand for the continuation of the basic routine despite the disaster was new, heartfelt mourning for losses not one's own was new, helplessness, frailty, the everyday that had ended with a single puff...

After many a struggle, Andalıç finally fell into its deepest ever sleep; its cradle rocking in a barely perceptible rhythm. Having spent their first night away from the national grid, with candles and gas lamps, with transistor radios that lost their customary weak reception of Turkish stations altogether as they drifted farther away, and talking to one another over and over again – like it was the first time – about the terror they had just lived through together, the people of Andalıç succumbed to the demands of their bodies. Longing to wipe from their minds a surreal day spent as if sleepwalking, as if it were one of the most bizarre dreams they had ever had, and awaken to resume life where they had left off, they allowed their breaths to deepen. The deeper their breaths and sleep became, the deeper they sank into the pitch-black waters of the Aegean.

In the darkest part of the night, Andalıç stopped still for a moment. The wind, which had been dropping for a while, was no longer felt either. The island was tarrying right over that great absence, which had triggered astonishment time and again throughout the day's conversations. The gigantic inverted cone below the waterline had met another peak many metres below the surface. The rough pumice stone had settled on the summit of a sunken Greek island, and as the current dithered over which side of the peak to pass it, the island pondered in the middle of the sea.

What kept the dark Andalıç there may well have been the glow in the deep. An unworldly glow at the peak of the island that asked to be seen. The windows of the mountain houses on the sunken island were ablaze like a wedding venue. Millions of micro-organisms flooding into the houses emitted an eerie luminescence; the shadows in the extra slow movements of a last dance appeared even in some windows. But there was no sleepless Andalıçian to witness this underwater wedding party. Having abandoned their branches to the curiously dense wind of the sea, the trees, marooned into a salty death in the dark waters, echoed the shadow dance in the windows. Shocked into doldrums by the presence of so many creatures that need air to survive, the waters needed Andalıç to bear witness. The sea had not yet accepted the sunken island; it would take thousands of years for that, thousands of years to gently wear it down, adorn it with its water-breathing creatures and turn it into one of the thousands of hills. Hence the extra aberration.

Triggered by one of the aftershocks continuing on both sides of the Aegean, the island suddenly sunk into a deep crack in the sea bed, shrugged Andalıç off in a single move. Another snap spilled into the depths of the sea, identical to the one twenty-four hours earlier; but the sound heard in the midst of that tumult the previous night went unnoticed by any of the sleepers, muffled as it was in the silent sea. The micro-organisms rose from the trembling windows of the sunken island like millions of tiny glow-worms. Rose ever higher and clung onto the inverted cone. Andalıç continued to drift in the middle of the stygian sea, a scoop of pitch-black ice cream in a cone ablaze with light.

14

Never one to indulge lethargy, the sun tugged away the amnesia veiling Andalıç. Seeping into strange rooms through windows it had never touched before, it transformed unaccustomed eyelids into a scarlet translucence, and dotted rainbows over twitching eyelashes.

Jülide shaded her eyes with her hand first, then instinctively turned over; but this tiny move had already stirred the great anxiety within her, which had barely been soothed by sleep. She woke up in a room which held, at least for a few minutes, a sense of ordinary continuity; but this impertinent sun, this pesky sun, which had never stepped into these corners at any time of the year... Sitting up suddenly, terrified, she looked at her grandma, who seemed to be in very deep sleep. Silently Jülide went over and bent down to bring her ear close to her grandma's nose. Her racing heart only calmed down on hearing the faint breathing; except that Seher's breaths were almost too faint to stand between her and death. She was definitely alive, albeit without stirring or opening her eyes since the earthquake.

Urged on by the slowly rising north-easterly, the sun moved faster than ever on the wall, almost fast enough to be followed by the eye. The wind no longer contented itself with roughing it up a little as it passed over Andalıç; now it dragged the town wherever it wanted.

Convinced now that her grandma was still alive, Jülide got up silently, went to the kitchen, and absently turned the tap in a little move carved into muscle memory.

'Ah! Here I go again! There's no water! Silly billy! It's off, it's off.' She slapped her forehead a couple of times. Ever since Seher had abandoned all activity except breathing, Jülide had been talking to her grandma or herself whilst at home. She was hoping to hear her grandma whenever she stopped talking, pricking her ears at the strange silence in the house and waiting for a while. She poured a little water from the small can into the kettle.

'I'm putting the tea on, nana, wake up now!' This time she called out loud. Uncertain whether to put one or two teaspoonfuls, she hesitated with the second still in the caddy before tipping it into the teapot with a resolve that checked her welling eyes.

'We're running low on tea; better get some more,' she called out. She stared at the kettle as her lips opened and shut with a cold sigh. There was no sound other than the trees rustling in the wind. Her mind sought the name of this absence. There was no clatter from the neighbours accompanying hers, not the sound of water running in the kitchens adjoining the garden to the side, nor singing, nor any of the familiar, barely noticed sounds that made a morning into a morning like any other. She was surprised at herself for lighting the cooker, placing the kettle on the ring, thinking of having breakfast, and feeling hungry. She was still unaware that these tiny stains of forgetfulness and stargazing would spread and eventually paint all this pain in the colour of ordinariness. She didn't know that she would live, continue to live until her body abandoned her, get over everything she'd imagine to be impossible to get over, and that not even the greatest anguish or grief in the world could end life. She brewed the tea. Listened to her grandma's breathing once again. Unable to lift her mattress and place it on the bed, she rolled it up and shoved it to the bottom of the wall, gloom swelling inside, too big to contain. She emptied her lungs. Three teardrops sank into the cotton mattress. She pressed her fingers on her eyes and patted her face back into shape. Pulled back her eyes, cheeks, eyebrows, both corners of her lips. Tried to find something akin to a smile.

She gave Seher's shoulder a nudge. 'C'mon, grandma, come to the table.'

She fetched the cheese, olives, jam, two forks, and the two glasses she'd poured in the kitchen. Her grandmother was still lying motionlessly. Jülide prodded a little more firmly this time. Then gave her a rough shake. 'C'mon, then, grandma. Wake up, wake up now.' No movement. Jülide went to the table and sat down in a chair with her back to her grandmother. Stared at her tea glass glowing like a copper lightbulb in the sun. Her gaze slipped to the roof of the house across the road. The loose tile in the corner that had been shaking, on the verge of falling on someone's head at every gust of wind, was gone. Her shoulders started to shake, first slowly, then faster, but not even a single muffled sob escaped from her throat.

'You don't eat, you don't drink water, I can't get a doctor. They're all busy with the injured. I can't take you there. I'm stuck. I'm stuck. Wake up, nana… wake up now.'

Staring at her cooling tea until she regained her composure, she got up in a fury and sat down on her grandmother's bed. 'Well, I'm not gonna have a single morsel until you open your eyes then. There's nothing wrong with you. You can get up if you want to.' She got up, went to the window, came back and sat down again. 'What's wrong? Oh, God, if only I knew what was wrong with you. Can't see into human beings, can you? If only you would open your eyes, though!' She paused for a moment. Her face brightened as if she had hit upon something. She pleaded with her grandmother's eyelids, an urgent request, nay, a command. She poured her entire being into this request, in an effort she had never known before. She felt as helpless as water crashing against a wall before her grandmother's resistance. There was movement in the eyelids, but in the opposite direction, as if they were trying to squeeze shut even harder. Cottoning on to that sly, elusive mischief, Jülide doubled her efforts. Squeezing her eyes shut against the stinging beads of sweat gathering on her forehead and trickling past her eyebrows, she loaded her will like an unfamiliar weapon. She loosed her shot and opened her eyes when she felt a release heralded by a little bit of freshness in the air. Seher was gazing at her granddaughter with a rebuke clouded by cataracts. With a joyful scream, Jülide collapsed on her grandmother's chest.

'Jülide, my lovely child. My time has come now.'

'Don't you dare say that! What time? You were scared by the earthquake, nana. So was I. You'll be fine in a couple of days. We'll go to Ankara, to my great uncle's when help comes. You'll be right as rain once you've seen a good doctor.'

'You're still young, child; you don't know. Some things you just feel. I'd go if only I could leave you. These are my last efforts.'

'That's nonsense. How can you know you're going to die?'

'Some do. I do.'

'No, nana. Don't make yourself get into this state. You're doing it. There's nothing wrong with you. Do you have any pain or aches anywhere?'

'No.'

'See? I told you.'

'It's not that kind of thing, child. I can feel it. It's close. Get used to it. You can't tell by looking from the outside.'

Scared that she might actually tell by looking, Jülide turned her face away. 'I don't believe it. That's nonsense. You were scared. Scared, that's why. I won't leave you. And you can't leave me, either.'

'Of course I can't. Oh, Jülide; if it weren't for you … I'd never have lived this long.' A feeble cough. 'But this time, want is not going to get.'

'Want it anyway.' She stroked the hennaed white hair. 'Come on, get up for breakfast.' Gave her grandmother an anxious look. 'What? Can't you move?' Touched the motionless body beside her. 'Can't you even lift your arm?' She was shouting now. 'What's the matter, nana? What's this? What?'

Like a novice planet slowly learning to spin, Andalıç follows its alien route. The sun hangs above the peak. It casts shadows that skim over the walls here and there on the façade of the Care Home – one of the few official buildings still standing. Concealing the tiny cracks from the eyes below, the colossal edifice poses, grandiose, officious. As for the lycée, the new courthouse, town hall, police station, library, and one wing of the hospital: piles of rubble, either partial or in whole. The Care Home, however, stands firm, its lawless foundations gripping the rocks underneath. It gazes at Andalıç marked by ugly gaps like a battered jaw, and at Anatolia, now a long, grey line on the horizon; at the threatening void on the other side; scanning every square, street and house from its highest spot in Andalıç. The streets could have progressed from mere existence into thinking. Thinking of the collapse of the illusion of permanence; the ruins obstruct their basic function by blocking them here and there; cutting and dividing them. Now, they feel the absence of wheel rattles they had grown accustomed to over hundreds of years; the new sun that violates even the most intimate shadows; the flow of the injured and the dead; and the quick whose eyes are fixed on the horizon and the sky, waiting for deliverance. The streets are thinking of the end. Of drifting like a floating mine, eroded by the air, sun and the water, or sinking to the bottom of the sea. The streets, who age but never die, recognise death.

There are queues in the shade on four of the narrow Andalıç streets. Each queue is two to three hours long, starts at a fountain and stretches for hundreds of metres. Hopes of spotting a shorter one are dashed to the ground. As the rising sun invades more and more of the shade, the queues slink back to the walls, shoulders rest on windowsills, people perch on doorsteps. The narrowest of streams flows from the council fountains and the waterline rises ever so slowly in the can. All the talk in the queue concerns Andalıç drifting, never mind the earthquake now: the help that will come any day now, the uncertainty awaiting them when they're taken back to the country, the dead they will leave buried on the floating island, the injured in the hospital or at home, the sardine-packed hospital corridors, the help that will come soon, the water in the big reservoir that will last until then, the power cuts reminiscent of old times, the help that will come today, at the latest tomorrow, the help that will definitely come…

Resting against the peeling plaster on a house, Jülide was thinking about her grandmother. Faint laughter coming from somewhere to the rear swung every head round for a look, as if laughter was a recent discovery. The closer one got to the front, the louder sounded the monotonous babble of water, exacerbating the anxiety over its scarcity, and, under the hot weight of the midday sun, inspiring silence. A street cat slunk past, sidled up to the trough and had a hurried drink with a scared look at the people filling up after every mouthful. There was no longer enough water in the trough for the animals.

Jülide was startled by a scream. The woman in front of her was yelling at a youngster ahead. 'Couldn't you find any more cans at home?' The kid was carrying four. 'The neighbours' house collapsed; they're staying with us. We're nine now,' he said, blushing.

The queue moved a little more and Jülide bagged a spot on a stone doorstep.

'Doesn't pumice sink?' she heard herself asking.

The lady next to her took it upon herself to answer. 'No, it doesn't. It floats.'

Jülide recalled the pumice stone she'd thrown into the pond in Saime's garden; it lay at the bottom a few days later, but didn't say a word. When the queue moved again, the elderly lady behind her joined her on the doorstep. 'Haven't you got anyone else to carry water for you, auntie?' Jülide asked before realising how loaded a question this was and giving the lady a terrified look.

'My son and daughter-in-law had gone to Bergama. Three days ago. I can't think of anything else. I've not heard a peep, girl. Left here all by meself. If only I knew they were fine! Who'd mind about carrying a can of water? Not like we've never done it, pot after pot. Oh, lass, not knowing is terrible.'

'Was it difficult in the past, when there was no running water at home?'

'Of course it was! But we didn't know any better at the time. We'd never had anything different. There used to be so many fountains in the streets; not that many are left now. We used earthenware pots. Us girls. We'd stack the washing in baskets, sprinkle with wood ash, pour water over it; it would come out whiter than white. These detergents are useless. We used to wash our hair with clay. We'd buy *pirina* to do the dishes.'

Having heard all this from her grandmother, Jülide's attention wavered. It was as if someone who wanted to send them back in time had pressed a button, demolished the new buildings, cut the power and the water and left the cars out of action. They had been tossed back a hundred years and were now waiting for someone to come with help, today, tomorrow, soon, and carry them back into this century. This trip in time suited Andalıç well, given its centuries-old houses. The old woman's gaze settled on the mosque across the road.

'These mosques used to be churches. There were more Rums than Turks here. We had lovely neighbours. Someone rang the door the other day. Their grandchildren. They were visiting their grandfather's hometown. They spoke a few words of Turkish. I cried.' She paused and looked at the mosque. 'It's awful not knowing. If only I had some news!'

The queue advanced a little. They got up and moved along the wall, one step at a time.

'The birds have gone, have you noticed?' asked the lady in front.

They looked up at the trees and into the sky. 'That's right,' said Jülide, 'I wonder if it's just here? Can't say I noticed round our way.'

They were at the fountain now. The lady in front started filling her can.

'I hope the children are all right,' murmured the old auntie, staring at the trickle of water going into the can.

Jülide helped her back with the water can before returning to her grandmother. Seher was in a deep sleep. Carrying a bucket, Jülide went down to the seafront to get water for the toilet. She took three breaks up the hill on her way back. The bakeries weren't working and the majority of the grocers were still shut. She put the last of the lentils and bulgur on the boil and sat down with her grandmother, who had been awakened by the noises in the kitchen.

'I popped into the hospital in the morning, nana. None of the doctors can go home. The hospital is chock-a-block. Patients even in the corridors. It took a while, but I did manage to find a doctor and tell him about your condition. He said it wasn't urgent and to wait until help comes.' She straightened the blanket over her grandmother. 'So you'll have to be patient for a couple more days. Then great uncle will take you to a big hospital or something in Ankara.' She had to turn her head away at the eloquence in her grandma's welling eyes.

'My little Jülide, my precious lamb. I hope so, but I'm not particularly convinced. If something happened to me...' Jülide got up to sit by the window. 'Don't be cross, child. That's life. It is what it is. Go to Ankara anyway, if something happens to me. Get into a university there. You can stay with your great uncle. He's in my will, anyway.'

'No, grandma, no. Don't say such things.' Taking a couple of sniffs, she ran into the kitchen. 'Oh, no! I've burnt the bulgur!' Turning off the flame and shutting her eyes, she stood by the counter, biting her lower lip. 'How do you prepare for something like this?' she murmured.

Just then the doorbell rang. It wasn't neighbours visiting her grandma; it was Muzaffer, holding a couple of bags of provisions. Jülide's eyes sparkled with a sudden surge of joy.

'Welcome, Muzaffer Abla. You shouldn't have! We'll never eat all this, not in a month!' Then, realising she was keeping her guest at the door, she said, 'Do come in, please. Sorry, my mind's all over the place!' Picking the bags, she placed them on the counter. Her smile wavered and all of a sudden, she found herself sobbing her heart out, clutching Muzaffer's neck.

'Whoa! Give me a moment to sit down first!' As she led Jülide in by the shoulder, the bed caught her eye. 'Oh, well done, Auntie Seher. Why upset this kid so much? Shame on you, at your age too!' she rebuked, 'What's this, "I'm dyin', I'm dyin'?" We're all gonna die. We're all dumbfounded anyway. Laid out our dead in rows. Shame on you. Tormenting this poor little kid...' She shook her head with a *tsk tsk*. 'She's got no one else but you! Pull yourself together, get back on your feet for this kid.'

Seher looked a little shamefaced. 'Is there much damage, Muzaffer Hanım? Many dead?'

'I've just told you, nana.'

Seher's eyes sparkled as Muzaffer pulled out a pack of cigarettes. 'Stick one in my mouth, lass.'

'There we are!' cackled Muzaffer, 'You don't know what they're like, the sick, Jülide; the moment they ask for a cigarette, you know they're getting better.' Lighting two cigarettes, she placed one between Seher's lips. Every time she took a drag, she also pulled out the cigarette from Seher's lips, and then placed it back. 'I've got used to unfiltered. These filters don't feel like a cigarette. Now don't you go burning the lentils, too, Jülide!'

Muzaffer looked suddenly graver the moment Jülide went to the kitchen.

'I've had a stroke, Muzaffer Hanım. I'll never get better now,' said Seher in a voice as faint as a breath.

'There are people who lie for years like this.'

'God forbid! A burden to everyone.'

'Hold your horses. Let's get a doctor first. They may get you back on your feet in a flash!'

'Don't I know myself, Muzaffer Hanım? Now look, if something happens to me, Jülide's in your hands. I have a brother in Ankara. I looked after him like a mother. Take the lass over to him. I've asked him as a last wish; he promised me, he'll see her through college.'

'Now, stop it, Auntie Seher. Jülide's like a daughter to me. Don't you worry. And there's no need for wills or anything. I'll see her through college if necessary. Never you mind all that; just get better as soon as possible.'

Just then Jülide came back in. 'What are you two whispering about?'

'Your grandma says, "Let's get this Jülide married off, find some suitable prospect, a footballer or something." She wants to see your blessings.'

The two women had a good laugh at the furiously blushing girl.

Muzaffer was forced to stay for dinner. Afterwards, Jülide used up the last of the coffee. Seher had been propped up for the meal. The resolve to die on her face may have persisted, but the smile, which crinkled the corners of her eyes, was back. Accustomed to keeping a cigarette permanently fixed on her lips, she was smoking, only letting go when the ash had to be flicked.

The conversation eventually turned to coffee reading. Muzaffer objected a little at first, before joining in Jülide's game. This was the one thing Seher was able to do, after all, using only her eyes and mouth.

'There's a crowd, but it's not a merry one. It's like a fight, like a brawl. A closed space. Two people hiding, it looks like. They're cowering, here. There's a place with lots of doors. A big building, on the hill. Some folks are sitting there, doing something.'

Unable to take her eyes off the patch in the carpet, Muzaffer asked, 'What kind of fortune is this, Auntie Seher? Where's my kismet, where's the official business, where's the three days or three months?' It took a while, but she did succeed in cajoling a smile as well as a look. 'And here's me, thrilled that I might be in for a good kismet after all these years! You mean I'm destined to stay an old maid?'

'I swear that's what there was, lass.'

'Soo, when's help coming then? Can't you see any help there?'

'Not today or tomorrow or anything. See, there's a snake here. Snake means an enemy. There's someone who wishes you ill. Look out.'

'Oh, nana! My fault for asking for my fortune now. You've only spoken of bad stuff. Not that anything could be worse than what's happened so far.'

Having easily secured permission to take Jülide out for a breath of fresh air, Muzaffer led the way towards the spot where the causeway split from the mainland hung over the void, a spot that had become a constitutional for the entire town. The north-easterly was dropping down noticeably in the mild September evening.

'Wherever the wind blows or the currents drive. Like a cheap day ferry.'

Yellowing vine leaves with coppery veins rustled in nooks and crannies, shredded bit by bit at the edges and tips. Jülide slunk against a wall as she skirted a pile of rubble and focused on the dry leaves. Muzaffer, on the other hand, didn't avert her gaze from the faded pillow corners, broken clock dials, toy car wheels, bent forks, and dusty sheets. Although there was no one around, they could hear conversation. The intense hum of the intercity road and the nagging of electrical appliances had given way to human voices and animal sounds.

'Don't you think it's fantastic? Being on a floating island like this. Who'd have believed it was possible? How extraordinary, in an age past miracles.'

'But so many died. And there are injured too. And my nana…'

'True. True. The devastation at the break will be far worse. We have no idea what happened on the other shore. Everything shook, snapped, broke, sank. The world's geography is altered. But we were still breathing in the minute immediately after it. How weird. This is really weird. The losses will be forgotten, but this incident will go into history.'

'*Fire burns where it falls.* My nana's breathing stopped for a few minutes; then it started up again.'

Muzaffer gave her an annoyed look. 'Forget about your nana for a bit. Just for a moment. And stop torturing yourself. I understand, you're scared of being left alone. But I'm here, you've got your uncle in Ankara. Auntie Seher is seventy-eight. Even if she is all right now, she won't be in a few more years. People go away. We can't cling to them. We can't keep hold of them. It may be hard to accept it now, but… Don't do that, Jülide. All right, I know: you feel awful, you're terrified. You've gone through a great deal just recently. We all have. The possibility of losing our loved ones is unbearable. Death is a fact; yet you can't accept the possibility of your nana's death. But why? Because it's people that make us enjoy life. I've not been able to suss it out all these years. My father's dead. My mother's dead. I was devastated each time. But there must be a way to accept it as natural, to acknowledge it and get over it more easily. We have to prepare ourselves. Why are we so unprepared?'

Jülide cast a restless glance at the dusty laundry forgotten on a line between two windows.

'Is she in a bad way, Muzaffer Abla? You sensed something, didn't you?'

'How would I know, child, just by looking? If help is delayed, we'll get a few people to help us carry her to the hospital, like in the coffee cup. Don't forget, Jülide; if the worst came to the worst, you're not alone in this world. I'm here. There's Rahmi. There's Saime.'

Jülide stared at the old causeway's teeth sunk into the sea. 'Even pumice stone sinks, Muzaffer Abla. Saime and I once…'

'Aaah! That's enough, now, Jülide! There are no signs of sinking as yet. This isn't one of your tiny scraps of pumice stone. Can't you at least enjoy the fact that we're floating right now? We're floating, lass, look! It's a miracle.' Turning her head, she saw the bitterness on Jülide's face. 'Oh, blast it! You're such a terrible apprentice. Best give you to that footballer and be shot of you. He does such a grand job of smashing glass, anyway.'

Astonished for the first time, rather than hurt, Jülide watched the island's wake. 'We'll be picked up soon. We'll abandon your miracle.'

'Don't you worry; this place would be transformed at once into a touristic whatsit. And don't you place all that much trust in help, either. Greek radio stations announced that Andalıç had sunk, just like their island. Who'd have thought it would don a lifebelt and go swimming!'

On her way back home, a pensive Jülide was startled by a voice she was beginning to forget.

'Hello.'

She hesitated; but then, in view of all that had happened, what had taken place between them seemed quite silly and unimportant.

'Hello.'

'Anything with you or yours?'

'Grandma's paralysed; she can't move.'

'I'm sorry.'

'Thank you. And you?'

'My big sister and her family…' A short sob, which he quashed with a cough. Jülide gave him a blank stare. 'The baby,' said Erkan, his voice catching in his throat, 'the baby's all right. She's with us.'

15

Cemal returns from the break point, the scab that the entire community feels compelled to pick at several times a day. For the first time in twenty years, he doesn't need to keep shop: he has handed out all his stock. He goes for walks, reads the classics forgotten on a shelf at home, frequently stares at the horizon and the sky like everyone else has been doing for the past week, fetches water for the house, meets Saliha at every opportunity and rolls up his sleeves whenever there is some gruelling task. There is no sign as yet of the help expected any moment now. On returning home, he finds Hakkı at the table, hitting the bottle – having transferred to his home the shop's entire stock of alcoholic drinks the day after the earthquake.

'You've started in the morning again, baba. Broke your word for good, it seems.' A tiny crack in Hakkı's silence, on the nail of the ring finger he's tapping on his lower lip. Tap tap tap tap. Cemal stares at the old man's red face, swollen nose and red eyes. 'Your daughter-in-law's gonna skin you alive.'

A recent refrain, this dialogue, albeit with a minor change or two. 'Oh, son! I've not touched a drop for years and years, leave me alone to drink for a few days now. I'll pack it in again when I get back. She'll never know.' Taking another sip, he watches the unchanging horizon that offers no hint to the island's spinning motion. Cemal moves towards the kitchen to prepare lunch, but Hakkı pins him to the threshold. 'Cemal…'

'Yes?'

'A bloke turned up just now. Looking for you. I didn't like his looks.'

'Who is he?'

'Zaim, he said.'

'Zaim… Zaim…' Cemal rubbed the anxiety on his forehead. 'Cemile's thingy…'

Without turning his head, Hakkı looked at him from the corner of his eye.

'With everything going on... What's he still want with me? We've broken off, drifting, lots of people are dead, the whole place is in ruins. What more does he want?'

'Who knows?'

'Like the whole world's not changed beyond recognition.'

'I said he's dead. Cemal's dead.' He fell silent and took another sip. 'God give you a long life. Don't think he bought it, though. Just as long as he stays away until help comes. Everyone's gonna go away then, anyways.'

'Fine, but why?'

'Who knows? Maybe he's bored. He can't get anywhere near her with the Commissioner, so he's gonna take it out on you. Who knows.'

'As if...' Cemal sighed. 'Beans; there was a lorry load of beans left in the vegetable market. They were distributing it. That's what I'm going to cook.'

'No meze?'

'Oh, baba! What more do you want – jam on it?'

Cemal started stringing the beans at the table, occasionally glancing at the empty horizon or the sky.

'Son, you have a fiancée. Why doesn't she come over and cook for you?'

'That's not on, Hakkı Baba!'

'Good God! Why the hell not? Of course it is.'

A sharp rap on the door made them both jump. Hakkı would have got up first, but Cemal gestured for him to stay seated and went to the door, still holding the vegetable knife. He took a cautious peep through the crack and hiding the knife behind his back, opened the door wide when he saw it was Halil. A bundle of nerves as usual, Halil was grumbling non-stop, wrapped up in his own agenda. 'Here's us, thinking these scumbags called for help. There's no wireless nor nothing, mate. The wireless was gone in the earthquake. Those buggers were staring at the skies like us for a week.'

'Soo?'

'So what? There's no help nor nothing on the way.'

'But why do we have to call for help? Shouldn't they send help anyway?'

'The whole place is razed to the ground, my lad. They think we've sunk. Seems Greek radios say so.'

'All the same, abi: what about aircraft and ships and everything? One is sure to pass by. This can't go on for ever.'

'Where, though? It's been a week, and nothing's passed by! Where, Cemal Bey?'

'Don't lose your temper, abi. The wireless wasn't nobbled by those blokes, was it? It's an earthquake, after all. All those dead – why would the wireless survive?'

'Are you defending those blokes, mate?'

'Absolutely not.' Well aware of Halil's temper, Cemal shut up and carried on stringing the beans. As he made for the kitchen once he was done, he said gently, 'Anyway, seems there's enough provisions for a month.'

Halil yelled as if hurling something behind his back: 'The water in the reservoir's down to a half. What does our lord have to say about that, eh?'

Nothing flies over or sails past Andalıç. The accretion of days chips away at the sense of impermanence. Old routines, still vigorous, blend with new ones to create a sense of continuity, almost one of permanence. Daily life tumbling in increasing apprehension. Rising panic over water and food in periods of permanence gives way to apathy shaded by a long-term uncertainty when transience tips the scales; as the parched soil unslaked by a single drop of rain for months turns to dust under feet, heads turn up to the skies in search of a cloud or an aircraft.

Houses filled with all the same old furniture, streets and buildings pretty much identical to before with a few exceptions, all the familiar faces missing one or two, and the unchanging commands of eating and sleeping sustain the illusion of eternity; at times, hours go by without mentioning when help might come, or going to the window or door, talking instead of how many packs of pasta, how many days' worth of legumes and how many kilos of rice are left. No one would be surprised at the suggestion that the floating island is invisible. Naps dotting idle days end with waking up to the now or the past; concerns swap places and dreams seep into the day. At times, people talk to the dead as if they were there, in the same room; the touch of a faint breeze on the cheek is transformed into fingers missed so much; on waking up with a start, the sofa mattress feels so snug, so warm.

Distant relatives hardly remembered for ages, grandmas and grandpas gather fruits and vegetables in lush green gardens, mothers cook delicious dishes, the stream that had been concreted over and turned into a road cascades freely, and the splashes of bathrooms and rain fill the gaps between sleep and wakefulness. To the extent that wakefulness is even drier.

Shaken to the marrow, having rediscovered a replica (but in a different form) of the world they had lost, and grown apathetic due to the sense of impermanence, Andalıç residents are granted deep sleep rich with dreams, which twist this shattered reality even more, by the dropping autumn wind, the lean sea stretching like a grey mirror, the light island moving ever so slowly, silence and idleness. They make pilgrimages to the spot where the umbilical had snapped, pass through hospital corridors in weary compassion, dine on much reduced rations, and sleep. Daytime conversations are as sparing as their meals. It's only when darkness settles, covering the world in flighty shadows, that tongues are loosened. In the light of strangely numerous stars, they speak of their dreams in soft voices. The darkness fills with a non-existent crowd. They only feel a little better when the imaginary spookiness quells the spookiness of real life. They sit and snuggle under the stars.

Somewhere in the vicinity, a pure elegy, mingling with night-time waters, cuts through the cracking of sunflower seeds, painting the island all the way to the end in its blackness. Sleep settles over Andalıç with the pain of that one song. Come morning when the day starts to grind, now they are on an island, no, now they're on a peninsula; reality wins now, no, dreams do; disaster triumphs now, no, normality does. Swings between poles that melt the residents' will and interest in their own destiny, swings that exacerbate indolence.

One morning, a wake-up call exploded into their silent world:

> DEAR ANDALIÇ RESIDENTS: UNFORTUNATELY, ALL EFFORTS TO REPAIR THE WIRELESS DAMAGED IN THE EARTHQUAKE HAVE FAILED. IT HAS NOT BEEN POSSIBLE TO GET IN TOUCH WITH OUR COUNTRY. WE HAVE HEARD THAT OUR TOWN IS BELIEVED TO HAVE SUNK. A BIG BONFIRE WILL BE LIT AT THE CARE HOME HILL TODAY TO ATTRACT ATTENTION. EVERYONE IS REQUESTED TO CARRY ALL THE WOOD THEY CAN GATHER.

At least Andalıç now had its loudspeakers, thanks to a rudimentary generator, a few idle electricians and copious quantities of diesel in the petrol station. And so, every piece of wood that was found was carried uphill throughout the day. By the evening, a massive pile rose in the car park to the rear of the Care Home. A new announcement was heard when the sun sank:

OUR COMMUNITY IS INVITED TO THE BEACON LIGHTING CEREMONY TONIGHT.

As dictated by entrenched custom, all the dignitaries were lined up by the woodpile in national holiday protocol. Well aware that even the tiniest ceremonial obligation counts as selfless service, these notables couldn't stop themselves from making emotional speeches in what may well be the town's final night. Suppressing a sob with manly willpower, the Mayor pronounced his last syllable, struck a match at the dense smell of gas, and dazzling flames shot up, forcing feet back by several steps.

Tongues were tied by the infallible magic of fire, fire transforming what only a week or ten days ago were doors, frames, chairs and tables. The crowd watched with due respect this stupendous, yet reined in, force. As all the experience and years of use were converted into light and ashes, those present gradually backed away from the heat. No matter how far they got, however, it kept scorching faces, the light brought tears to the eyes, and the smoke seared throats. That night, the smoke they attributed solely to their bonfire settled over the entire Aegean as a dense fog. The aircraft they were expecting to fly over them were parked on aprons and the ships were moored in safe harbours. Unaware of it all, at the threshold of a new future, and with the childish thrill of playing with fire, the Andalıç folks continued to watch the ingenious solution that would rescue them from this temporary life. As the hours advanced and the fire retreated, first the elderly and the children abandoned the watch, then everyone who loved sleep, and finally, the dignitaries who realised that the crowd was now too small to make it worth their while. Not a single star sparkled in the white darkness covering the island after everyone had gone home.

By the time the bonfire had turned to embers, there was no one left. A subdued dawn, smothered by low clouds, had just started to lighten the edge of the night, when two sleepless shapes appeared. Having captured the whole of Andalıç in a damp invasion, the sooty smell of burnt wood had no intention of lifting. Dreams were tumbling in the ashes of minds silenced by the smell.

Embracing Saliha from behind, Cemal buried his nose in her hair. Sniffed and sniffed. 'My favourite scent. I know of none finer. The smell of burning hasn't got here.' These words came from lips which moved on Saliha's neck; and she heard him with her skin, not her ears. Held the hands encircling her waist. Silence had become much easier of late.

'I,' she said, her voice hissing like water poured on the embers, 'I'm not that well.'

'Who is?'

'Not like that. You know.'

'I'm not that well either. If that earthquake had happened a day later, we'd have been married. Away from here. I'm not well either.' He grabbed her tighter and rested his cheek on her neck. He placed his softest voice right into her ear to shorten the distance to her heart. 'I'm here with you. I love you. Love you very much. It will all be sorted out. We'll soon get away from here. We'll start a new life. Just be a little patient.'

Saliha's voice was so faint that it would have flown away in the slightest wind, but it got stuck on the burnt soot. 'I don't want to live.'

Cemal suddenly released her and drew back. 'You don't love me. What's that mean, not wanting to live? Don't I mean anything to you at all?'

'No, not like that. Of course I love you, I do, but…'

'But what?'

'Don't know.'

The brightness rising in the east was white, not blue. Even the faint breathing of sleepers was audible under the heavy blanket of low clouds: volatile sounds unable to escape into the skies and evaporate.

'How weird would it be if sound stayed where it was, like objects. If we could hear everything that was said wherever we went. The past would never die.'

'It would be noisy. If everything was heard all at the same time.'

'No, only one thing will be heard at any one time.'

'At random?'

'Uh-huh.'

'There'd be no need to record songs either.'

'Screams. There'd be screams,' Saliha gave the wounded town below a frightened look.

'You always find the worst in everything. Of course you wouldn't want to live if that's how your mind works.' Cemal started digging a hole in the ground with the toe of his shoe. 'You break my heart. You really do.'

Imams deprived of their minarets started climbing up to high points to chant the call to prayer in the old fashion: in their own voices. Saliha waited until the ezan had finished. 'We'd probably go mad. If we heard everyone. Everyone we knew, and everyone we never knew.'

'We'd walk around with earplugs, or something would have been invented to block out the sounds of the past.'

He moved to face Saliha, held her face in his palms and looked at her smouldering eyes in anguish. 'Your pupils are huge, enormous, like they've covered your entire eyes. Dark. Why?'

Lowering her eyes that put even the embers of the bonfire to shame, Saliha felt the inner chill capable of dousing anything. 'I can't love,' she said in a panic.

Cemal swung round and kicked the embers angrily. Sparks flew. He watched them fall, his insides squirming.

'This is the illness. I'm sick. Doesn't concern you.'

'What does that mean, it doesn't concern me? Everything of mine concerns you. I don't have a single thing that doesn't concern you. How easily you say, you can't love. If all this stuff hadn't happened...'

'You don't understand.' Cold fingers grabbed Cemal's wrist. 'That's not how it is. I can't help it.' Her tears were streaming in two rows. 'I... why am I like that?'

His anger cooled at once, Cemal embraced his fiancée again. 'Don't cry. I don't like you crying at all. Don't cry. If it is an illness, there will be a cure. Don't worry. You'll get better.'

Sitting on the wall side by side, they stared the ashes, which were fast losing what little scarlet glow remained. They said nothing until the dirty brightness in the east paled and surrounded the whole island.

'Cemal.'

'Yes, sweetie?'

'I'm pregnant.'

Unsure how to react, Cemal gave her a blank stare. 'Are you sure?'

'I'm three weeks late.'

'Why didn't you say anything all this time?' He paused to rack his brains. 'Yasemin once thought she had a baby on the way. She was a month late. It turned out to be a false alarm. Maybe that's how it is.'

'I'm sick in the mornings. Been feeling sick all the time for the past couple of days, in actual fact. I'm sick all the time.'

'Saliha...'

Her face now clearly discernible, her torment laid bare, Saliha gave him an anguished look.

'This baby...' He fell silent. 'Don't you want it?'

'No.'

'Are you sure?'

'Yes.'

An unequivocal yes, ringing with a resolve that would not wither under the motionless fog.

'Fine. You know best. I would have wanted it, if you were to ask me. But you don't.' A reproachful silence. 'When help comes... if you really are pregnant... we'll do whatever you want.'

Saliha retched, crouched at the bottom of the wall and emptied the bile in her stomach. The acrid smell of vomit replaced the smell of burning in her nostrils. The irritation in her throat was on fire, just like the one in her soul. Eyes growing darker in the increasingly brighter day pierced Cemal.

'I'd rather die than have this baby.'

Unruffled by even the faintest *meltem* for three days, the Aegean is still, unable to shrug off the thick mass of clouds settling over it. The thermometer does not move down by one degree at night, nor rise by the same amount in daytime. The whiteness, which thins out the night-time, blurs shapes and lowers the light. The light softens in the thick layer of water vapour and is amplified enough to tickle the eye with inscrutable reflections. People wrenched from their own lives are further estranged from the world by the suddenly shallow vision, the inability to even determine where the sun is on this island that has lost all sense of direction, the overwhelming, lingering smell of the bonfire, and the mist that absorbs sound like a velvet curtain. No sea, no sky, no ends to the street; all that can be picked out is the wall of the house opposite, and that only just, a pale wash of colour. Only the interiors are familiar, but they're infiltrated by the silence of mist. Misssst. Shhhh. Everyone walks on tiptoe; the few words that are exchanged are done so in whispers. Something intimidating outside, something that suppresses everything. The roads walked on take shape out of nothingness and return to the same nothingness. The mist is a bivalve, which vomits the town metre by metre before swallowing it back again. It's terribly disconcerting to move between these two mouths that swallow the before and the after. White distress at home, white restlessness outside.

For the past three days, Andalıç has forgotten why it lit the bonfire, where it is, or what it's waiting for. Even breathing outdoors feels strange. Faces are constantly smeared with the sweat of the clouds. Footsteps are a little less balanced, a little more cautious. There's something astonishing even in the firmness of the ground. The island refuses to see or be seen. The secretive mist keeps everything from everyone. Alters the faces passing by the window. Prevents recognition. Forces everyone out of hiding.

Cemile entered the bare-shelved shop, where Hakkı and Cemal had failed to find respite from the boredom of sitting at home, and were now marking increasingly longer gaps between sentences with long sighs. 'It was sixty-two. In Ortaköy; misty like this again ...' Hakkı spluttered, repeating the same tale for the past three days. He shut up when he looked up and saw her. Then Cemal snapped.

'What are you doing here?' Hakkı attempted to rise, but Cemal grabbed his arm and sat him back down. 'No, Hakkı Baba. You're not going anywhere. This woman doesn't have the face to see me. She can beat it.'

Unperturbed, accustomed to being shooed away, Cemile remained at the door.

'Can't you hear? No more sister and brother, either. Buzz off home.'

The chilly mist kept sticking its head through the door that had let Cemile in and then drawing back again. Sensing there had to be more to her hesitation than plain old cheek, Hakkı intervened. 'Hold your horses, don't lose your rag so fast. Let's see why she's here first. She can go afterwards. Not like she's gonna attack you or anything.'

Cemal gave a nervous laugh. 'Of course she is, and how. I know why she's here.' He sounded much harsher after all those recent gashes on his soul. 'We now have her pimp to contend with too, like she wasn't bad enough.'

'Oh,' Cemile finally broke her silence, 'Oh, be careful! Stay away from him. Watch yourself.'

'Mind your own business! Never you mind about me! Mind your own business!'

Accustomed to all types of rage, drama and disaster, Hakkı paid no attention to this rude outburst. 'What makes you say that, child?'

'He swore to kill Cemal, uncle.'

'Fine; you've said what you had to say; now go. There's been an earthquake, the island drifted off, everyone's suffered, the wedding's delayed, the ba...' Cemal checked himself. 'So I'll die at the hands of that pimp. Like I care. Buzz off now!'

Cemile still stood at the door. 'Be careful. He'll sneak up on you from behind. You'd never know what hit you. Uncle, you tell him. He doesn't understand these things.' Then she swung back and vanished into the mist.

'All this misfortune came after I fetched her. She's the one who pushed Saliha away too. All her fault.'

'Don't be silly. It wasn't she who shook the earth, was it?'

'I never had it easy, but this time... It's one thing after another. I can't take it. I'll go nuts at this rate.' The gradually darkening mist dozed on behind the window. 'No one knows who or what will come out of this bloody fog. No one knows where we are, where we're going, how much longer we're gonna be here. And now...'

Hakkı staggered up. 'C'mon, let's go out. Let's go for a walk. And I've got a story to tell you.'

They moved slowly in the tangible air that was no longer transparent. Head bowed, Cemal was frowning in painful shock. Hakkı launched into his tale.

'I was here in Andalıç thirty-five years ago. No Care Home on the hill. We're staying in a hotel overlooking the square, me and my wife, my young bride. Cevriye's so lovely she turns heads over all the time. Old ladies murmur a *Maşallah*. Sometimes I like it, feel proud; at others, I'm jealous, wrings my innards. I've hit thirty-five, she's only eighteen. If I sound a bit tetchy, and she's all attention, she gets it. Sometimes she laughs at me like I was a child.' They continued walking, lost in thought, listening to the sound of muffled footsteps. Then Cemal noticed something was missing and raised his head.

'Soo?'

'I'll tell you in a minute, when we get there.'

They reached the corner of the soap factory.

'We were taking a walk. Climbing this hill. Cevriye's on my arm. It was May. I've always loved May. Air like sherbet. "Delightful," she said. Always used to say that. The afternoon sun highlighted the auburn strands in her hair. I was just watching her. Pure glow. A sleepy peace in her eyes, her lips always ready to break into a smile. Her cheeks glowing peach red in those four or five days. I can still see her dress. Turquoise. A broad belt on her waist. I was in raptures, feeling faint inside. No amount of rakı could hit you like that. I was grateful. And how. Here, we got to this house at the right. There was an old woman at the window. You don't appreciate youth when you're young. It doesn't come back. Anyway, Cevriye raised her head. They exchanged a look. The woman's face was covered in wrinkles. There was a climbing rose at her window. May is the month of roses. But what a rose! In full bloom, perfuming the whole street.'

Cemal was all ears now.

'They didn't speak. The woman picked a rose and threw it towards us. Cevriye put this chiffony, floaty rose to her nose and raised it up like a glass to her. Then tucked it into her hair, like it always belonged there. She turned to me. The evening sun hit her clear eyes all the way to the bottom. The most beautiful eyes I ever saw. I must have been staring so passionately that she gave a shy laugh. Her teeth like pearls. Just then a nightingale burst into song. She turned her head to look. One petal broke off and landed on her shoulder. I picked it up and put it in my wallet. It was the happiest moment in my life.'

The tale hanging in the mist echoed in Cemal's mind for a while. They were staring at the yellow painted house. He gave a soft laugh.

'This was my grandmother's house. My mother was born here. So was my aunt. Halil Abi's mother. Grandma would bring us an armful of the white rose when it bloomed every spring. It would perfume the whole room. Her face was covered in wrinkles. Halil Abi and I would pinch them until she got fed up.'

It was Hakkı's turn to stare at the house. He pulled out his wallet. There was a folded square of paper in one of the pockets. He opened it gingerly. It held a darkened, dried rose petal, cracked in several places. 'People die. Look, the rose has dried too. Such inanimate things last. Even after us. What if this house had collapsed? What would I do then?'

Five sets of hurried footsteps resonate on the cobblestones. The inhabitants of the houses they pass by are drawn willy nilly to the windows by a sense of the extraordinary – but in vain. There's nothing to see. Those impatient spectres are long since gone. The two in front can barely make out the road, and the two at the rear, those in front. Not that they're looking at one another much. They're all grabbing the edges of a blanket. Cemal, Halil, Rahmi, and Muzaffer at the corners, and Jülide somewhere in the middle, at the centre with her grandmother. Her face is the same colour as her yellowish dress; her long hair (which looks the colour of dust in this light) is undone and dishevelled, her blue-green eyes a dull grey in the mist, her lips are drained of blood, and her nails gripping the blanket are almost whiter than her skin. A snow-white statue of panic in the mist, in the fog, made of fog, about to dissolve starting from the outlines. The most spectral of all, the most hurried. 'Rubble ahead, we're about to go over it; careful now,' says Cemal's voice.

The feeble light of candle flames flickering in the houses hang like a yellow plume of smoke in front of some windows. The mist captures the movement of the light, stills it, and dissolves the shadows. Everything is two-dimensional, faint, volatile.

'Left, left,' shouts Halil.

They hurry along the main road, lifting the blanket so it won't drag on the ground, it takes no effort at all, it's so light, so very light. Jülide's just being dragged along.

'Muzaffer Abla, careful: there's a stone.'

Jülide looks at her grandmother's closed eyes, wrinkled and drawn face, sunken mouth, and dry fingers clasped over her belly. She doesn't even remember when she had first seen the black baggy trousers with the red floral pattern; it's more familiar than the legs inside. The evening's denser cloud drowns out her panting breath.

'I'm older, I'm older, Rahmi …' gasps Muzaffer. Addressing only him, as she knows no one else can hear.

'It's the cigarettes, Muzaffer Abla, the cigarettes.' Rahmi's voice also hurts his lungs.

The silhouette in front of them takes shape: a horse cart. With skinny wheels and peeling paint. When it raises its head to shake, they see the horse too; its nostrils give that trembling grunt. They stop to call out for the carter. No response.

'I'll drive,' says Rahmi, 'We'll return it later. We're not stealing it, are we?' Seher is laid in the back. Jülide sits in front, next to Rahmi. Cemal and Halil stay behind. The rattling of the wheels carries on even after the cart vanishes from sight.

'Think she'll live?'

His footsteps slower, Halil replied without raising his head. 'I thought she'd already died. This girlie's got no one else here. She's our charge now.'

16

The north-easterly was slapping into Andalıç, every gust rippling the firm navy blue of the sea. It had started in the morning by chopping into the fog, pieces of which it then scattered, and let loose the raw autumn sun into streets that had forgotten their shade. After three days of forced dreams and forgetting, the whole of Andalıç was fully awake. Awake, sober, compos mentis. Water was carried, food was cooked, and even the cleaning jobs neglected at first with bemusement, then waiting, despair and finally, forgetfulness, had been tackled; the houses were washed and scrubbed as if people would continue to live here for days and days yet – except it was done using salt water, salt water that would not lather, did not clean all that well, and left white marks. Throughout the day, the word 'help' fell from thousands of lips ten thousand times, a word that had all but vanished from the lexicon of the community in the clutches of a strange lethargy. What to do? What to do? Questions were flung into the wind, answers were grabbed and seized at. A few hours later, however, when the north-easterly whipped up in earnest, and in fact, exceeding its usual violence, grew into a massive storm scudding the island like a sailboat, all those captured answers were ground into dust and vanished. The residents were imprisoned back in their insular lives inside the walls erected by the storm. Then those walls rang with an announcement, some of whose words were dragged away by the wind:

DEAR ANDALIÇ RESIDENTS; AS THE AMOUNT OF WATER IN THE RESERVOIR IS RUNNING REALLY LOW, A PREVENTATIVE MEASURE OF LIMITING SUPPLY TO TWO LITRES PER PERSON A DAY WILL BE IMPOSED. TAKE NOTE.

People hearing it shook their heads with a smile. No north-easterly storm had ever run for longer than three or four days. Help was sure to come after that.

Only the north-easterly does such a thorough job of clearing the air in the autumn, crystal clear, like it would ring if you flicked it with a fingernail. Only when it's hastening to sweep the summer off from the world. Wearing down every surface it touches, it scours. It removes the warmth from the sea, the haze from the soil and the mist from the air. It broadens the limits of vision all the way to the ends of the earth.

The cleanest section of the glittering Aegean stretched as far as the eye could see under the crisp azure sky. Seen from the Care Home hill, the planet consisted of a perfectly round plate of ultramarine. Not a single bump or point marred the monotonous circle of the horizon. Eyes granted a tremendous freedom after days of fog scanned over and over again the blank shades of blue before returning, annoyed by this useless liberty, to familiar stones, faces and hands. To streets with whirlwinds of dust, scrawny cats and dogs, cookers, pans, forks, plates, sofas, beds, pillows. Wherever the eyes turned, a faded copy of life carried on with an increasing sense of reality, aspiring to something like permanence, complete with all its daily sounds and rituals. Children's shrill screams bounced off the walls of the town, which had lost so many of its voices, as gurgling babies and smiles that only found sorrow on fading began to chink away at the thick, hard carapace of mourning. Exhaustion to the point of being unable to raise an arm; a coffee table, a table cloth or the corner of a curtain suddenly blurring behind tears; going into the back room to look for something and returning after staring around blankly; the way mornings continue to stretch in a chewy disquiet; sighs; long periods of holding on one's lap a half-picked over tray of rice; eyes fixed at an indistinct point above a finger hesitating before picking a darkened grain of rice; the way rooms felt quite narrow, streets quite broad, insides quite lonesome, outsides quite crowded: and the way every conversation rang with an absence, with unimportance: yet another coat of forgetfulness varnish, increasingly dulling every day it is slapped over.

Where grief thinned out and the scabs started to heal, anguish faded into sorrow. The shared grief over the whole town was intense enough to be visible to the naked eye; its holes were getting bigger; the patient erosion of the days and the impatient fastidiousness of the wind joined forces to imprison suffering in individual homes and hearts. Andalıç is all alone in this catastrophe and in its pain, all alone in the most deserted part of the sea. It has no other way out but to get better.

Jülide squints against the frothy sea giving the island a barely perceptible tremor, the piercing sun that lays everything bare and the fine dust whipped up by the storm. She's leaning against the wind to avoid being knocked down. The north-easterly is bending even ancient cypresses as though they were mere saplings. A chilly breath redolent of resin wuthers amongst the sombre green, dark enough to be mistaken for black. The same yellowish dress, a baggy green cardigan, a brown headscarf with grey flowers, rubber slippers on her feet. Jülide presses her finger into the amber resin set in the crack of a cypress. It is irritatingly sticky, but she continues to press, knowing full well she won't be able to get it off without paraffin. There is none at home.

The wind is so wild that she had to tie two knots in her headscarf; all the same, her long hair falling below the scarf is being blown behind her. Her skirt is secured, caught between her legs. All she can see is her fingers and the resin. The honey of the hundred-year-old tree. A muffled creak from the branches overhead. And the noise of the shovels throwing soil. They dive into the pile with a sharp, metallic sound, then the rattle of the soil on the wooden strips, and the sound continues until the rattle on the wood gives way to the earth's muffled pulse. Sometimes inaudible in the wind.

'Let's go now,' says Muzaffer.

'I'm staying until it's done.'

Opposite, Cemal, Halil and Rahmi are standing shoulder to shoulder by the grave, unable to look her in the face. Erkan stands a good distance behind them, occasionally casting a sneaky glance. Saime is gripping her arm as if she would run away. Words chanted in a foreign tongue wander amongst the trees and the stones. The imam has been clutching his turban since picking it up from where it had been blown into the grave. His bare head rocking back and forth in time with the chant in Arabic seems to detract something from the sacredness of the ritual. The turban pressed over his belly grants him no more say over a sacrament than anyone else. Jülide recites the *Fatiha* in silence, repeating it as soon as it is finished, hundreds of times. Iridescent green flies land on and take off from the ever-smaller pile of soil. Blown away every time they take off, they seek somewhere in the lee. The grave fills shovel by shovel. The rising dust is scattered.

'The only trees are here,' says Jülide, staring behind the departing imam, 'This is where they forget the trees along with the dead.' She looks at the mound. 'All I have in life is two litres of water.'

Something dark pierces her, something that the harsh wind had been unable to tug out. The little procession climbs up the hill, their steps hastened by the storm. Two women beside Jülide. The grief that is beginning to release the town cascades into her like a stream that has found a tiny tunnel.

*

TO THE ATTENTION OF OUR DEAR COMMUNITY: THE ADMINISTRATION HAS REQUISITIONED EVERY FOOD STORE IN OUR TOWN. PROVISIONS WILL HENCEFORTH BE DISTRIBUTED EQUALLY TO OUR COMMUNITY BY THE ADMINISTRATION.

Rahmi rolled over onto his back. His sweat had chilled in the wind seeping in from the gap in the window frame. An artery was throbbing in his groin. He lit a cigarette. The branches of the ancient fig tapping on the window sent deceptive chills into the room, as if someone wanted to get in. He handed the cigarette to Zeliha. Taking a drag, Zeliha pulled the cover all the way up to her neck.

'It's suddenly got cooler.'

'Uh-huh.'

Rahmi was staring at the quaking aspen in the distance. The branches of the colossal hundred-foot-tall tree were bending with amazing flexibility, returning to their old position after every gust, and then bending again. The leaves turning over were as pale as the trunk. Rahmi wrenched his gaze away from the milky whiteness of the tree. He pulled the cover away from Zeliha. 'It's been two months. Don't cover.'

'I have no idea what I'm doing here after all that's happened.'

Rahmi grinned at her. 'So, you have no idea?'

She laughed.

The old frame rattled every so often. The wind pressed against the door. 'You did bolt it, didn't you?' Raising herself on her elbows, she was watching the door anxiously. 'Is it worth all this terror, oh, God? God forgive me. Forgive my sin.'

'Just this once, don't ask this question. Just this once.'

Feeling guilty that she was there, and that she was surprised at being there, Zeliha pulled the covers over her again nervously. Glanced at her clothes folded on the chair. Light streamed through two large windows into the airy, whitewashed room. Snow white bedsheet and cover. A white sheepskin on the vinyl floor. Zeliha's skin. Rahmi's teeth flashing between his parted lips, his skin even darker after idling outdoors for days and days.

He put his hand on Zeliha's plump leg. 'Look at this! You're like white cheese. I've not seen anyone whiter. Nor prettier.'

'Get away! The girl at the printer's is very pretty.'

'So what?'

'Nothing.'

'It was her grandmother's funeral today. Poor thing's got no one now.'

Zeliha's cheeks tensed up. 'Full of pity, eh?'

'Soo?'

'Nothing.'

'You have no right to be jealous, Zeliha Hanım.' She stared at the dark hand circling her belly, as if she was vexed that her rights to jealousy were denied. 'This is jealousy. You can't tell it what to do.'

'Then get a divorce and marry me. And I won't look at anyone else.'

Zeliha grappled for the upper hand. 'I know about your carryings-on, anyway.'

'So what should I have done? Waited for three years whilst you were in Malatya?'

She reached for the cover again, but Rahmi stopped her.

'She's got no one, poor lass; I thought I'd marry her. What do you think?'

The storm was howling under the door. Zeliha tried to get up, but Rahmi pulled her back with a laugh and covered her whole body with a frenzy of kisses.

There was a fragile peace on his face when he stretched out next to her, slick with sweat once again. 'Have you screwed him?' he asked softly, as though he were murmuring sweet nothings.

'Why're you asking that now?'

'Because it drives me crazy when I think about it.'

'Don't think about it.'

'Have you?' The peace was shattered.

'He's my husband.'

Rahmi sat up like a jack knife. Lifting a corner of the pillow, he leant back and lit up testily. He drew away to the edge of the single bed to avoid touching her.

'Like you had to ask this question every time!' said Zeliha, getting up and dressing in a hurry. Her hand was on the door knob when Rahmi said, 'Wait. Stay a while; don't go away now.' She stood with her hand on the door knob, avoiding his gaze. Hesitating between an irritable desire to run away and a passionate one to stay. Confused and indecisive, as usual.

'I'm fed up. With lying, with hiding. With the fear of being caught. With never getting together. And now you're giving me a hard time.' She was sobbing.

'Here we go!' Rahmi grabbed her and sat her down at the edge of the bed. 'Don't go crying now. Don't cry.'

'That's all I can do. You knew – know! – my situation. If the children… And before then I was too young. Oh, God…' She burst into deep, heaving sobs.

'Oh, dear! All right, all right! Sorry.'

The storm was no longer heard. The sobs gradually abated. Zeliha blew noisily into her handkerchief.

'I'd best go now. I've left the children with Mine Abla. And now… you know, normal hours are gone. He could come any time.'

'Of course he could,' he said bitterly, then looked at Zeliha's clumped eyelashes. 'Not that he'll be done that easily. District Governor here, Mayor there. Took over the Care Home. Announcements and what have you. Like we're gonna be here for good.'

'Better to run out of water and let the stores be ransacked then?'

'Help's gonna come any time now, my girl. Those blokes are just bossy. They're playing at governing. They've adopted that place as their palace. And they're sultans now. So long as they're not at each other's throats.'

The fig was pressing hard, as if it would break the glass. They listened to the wild howling of the north-easterly.

'Rahmi.'

'Yes, my precious?'

'What's gonna happen when help comes?'

'We'll hop on board and go.'

Zeliha gave him a cross look. 'Where? Then what? What's gonna happen to us?'

'How would I know? Let's get away first. We'll set something new up somewhere.'

'What if you can't come where we go?' With no reply from Rahmi, she sighed. 'Maybe that's better. We can't leave him. He'll leave us.'

'I might as well not bother chasing you, if that's what you think.'

Zeliha's chest fluttered as she took a long breath. Her eyes were fixed on the sheepskin on the floor.

'You have an opportunity this time, Zeliha. Your husband's got a mistress. He wouldn't dare oppose if you said you wanted a divorce. He may well agree, since he's the guilty party. He can't bully you. Are you still not gonna do anything?'

'What can I do?'

'Of course you can't do anything. Just sit there. I don't know; tail him. Catch him on the job with her. Raise hell. Get the police to raid them. To be fair, that's a bit tricky. But no one would ask a woman in your situation why you're divorcing. This may be your last chance, Zeliha.'

'I don't know if I can do it, though.'

'Of course you can. When the ship comes – or helicopter – we'll hop on and get away. You'd get the children too under the circumstances. You can file for divorce the moment you set foot on land...'

'But there's nowhere for a helicopter to land here.'

Rahmi shook his head irritably.

'I've got it. Well you might cry. You don't want anything to change. Away with you now. If you won't do anything this time, I'm done. Not gonna pursue you.'

Hot despair swelling in her chest, Zeliha looked at him. Pecked his cheek, crushed by the possibility that this might be the last time she would ever see him so alone, so intimately. She got up, put her shoes on and drew back the bolt. With a quick glance outside, she ran for her life down the bushy path between two houses.

*

'She never shed a tear.' Muzaffer was stringing beans. She bent down to whisper, as if sharing a secret, the moment Jülide's footsteps had gone. The north-easterly may have lost its initial violence, but it was still howling. Halil shook his head with a grimace. 'Would've been better if she had.'

'Yes, but you can't force her to cry, can you, though?'

They were sitting in the spacious kitchen of the old stone house. A cushion propped open the window overlooking the yellowed garden.

'You know, Muzaffer? No offence, but your hands aren't made for these things. Cemal was stringing beans the other day, and even he was doing a better job.'

Muzaffer gave something between a smoker's cough and a guffaw. Her reading specs had slid down to the tip of her nose. 'Well, mother never taught me. I had to learn later. That being said, we still cook for ourselves here; we don't have our own chef like you, Mr Halil.'

'Shucks! People who live in glass houses and that! Except, I always help Yasemin. I'm great at stringing beans, for example.'

'With those sausage fingers?' Muzaffer pushed the pan over. 'Give us a hand, then.'

'Walked into it, didn't I?' Halil laughed as he set about stringing the beans. 'If you don't mind me asking: where did you get them?'

'From the garden. My father's seeds. He used to plant them every year. I've been doing the same, so the seeds don't perish. They've all dried up with lack of water, but I managed to gather enough for one meal.'

His thick fingers occasionally tangling, Halil continued to crack the beans at both ends. 'Good job your garden was spared. You know Memiş Ağa, by our corner? His garden was ransacked. Poor fellow was sobbing his heart out. I said, we're leaving any time now, don't worry. Survivor psychology's weird.'

Shaking her head, Muzaffer carried the prepared beans to the sink. Rinsed the dust with a pitcher of sea water. 'We're scared. It's in our genes. We're a people who live like we'd lose everything any moment. Scared if we don't have anything put aside, a roof over our heads. Remember the time when there was no coffee? A ghastly thing called chickpea coffee popped up. Oil queues, petrol shortages.'

'My mother loathed chickpea coffee,' said Halil, remembering days so long ago that they might never have happened. 'Like they're gonna stay here for ever. Ransacking gardens. Looting supermarkets. Brawls at water queues. Funny.'

'It's not funny.' It was unlike Muzaffer to be so serious and apprehensive. We're stuck here. No contact with anywhere. What's going to happen if there's no help in the next five days? Everyone will be at one another's throats, I swear to God. Would have been better if we'd sunk.'

Sitting at the window, Halil mechanically looked up at the sky for a long while. His eyes settled on the ungainly form of the Care Home coiled up on top of the hill. The loudspeakers clicked as if mocking the shortages on the island.

DEAR RESIDENTS. A CENSUS WILL BE TAKEN TO PREVENT DISPUTES DURING THE DISTRIBUTION OF WATER AND FOOD. ONCE THE NUMBER OF INHABITANTS PER EACH HOUSEHOLD IS IDENTIFIED, CARDS WILL BE DISTRIBUTED TO OUR COMMUNITY. WATER AND FOOD WILL HENCEFORTH BE GIVEN BY RATION CARD. ONLY ONE PERSON FROM EACH HOUSEHOLD NEED APPLY.

'Ha, ha! All we needed was a census. This lot's really off their heads now. How much longer do they think we're going to be here? They're so bored, they don't know whether they're coming or going. Playing government.' Halil glared at the Care Home. 'The Three Stooges ruling Andalıç from above. They've placed a couple of guards outside food stores. Policemen or community constables or whatever. Who recruited them, and where? Patrols and what have you!'

'We've got our work cut out with this lot unless help comes. Censuses, ration cards, guards. God knows what's next.'

'Don't you start, Muzaffer! Of course help will come, why wouldn't it? It's been nearly two weeks. Any time now. How can a huge island go unseen?'

'It's not that; this thing with guards and all, that's bad. They're armed, too. God save us.'

'Oh, come on. You're a smart lady. They can't do a bloody thing. Let them play. They've even given themselves a name: The Administration. Let them play. They'll be put in their place if they overstep the mark.'

DEAR RESIDENTS. THE CENSUS WILL BE TAKEN TOMORROW. THERE WILL BE A CURFEW FROM SEVEN A.M. YOU ARE REQUESTED TO COMPLY WITH THE CURFEW. NO ONE WILL BE GIVEN WATER OR FOOD UNLESS THEY ARE RECORDED IN THE CENSUS AND HAVE A RATION CARD. PLEASE LET'S NOT MAKE IT DIFFICULT FOR THE OFFICIALS.

With a bitter smile, Muzaffer started peeling and chopping onions.

'Are the onions from the garden, too?'

'No, I'd bought them at the door before the earthquake. Five kilos. It'll last for a month or two. Prudence, that's our name.'

'Daughter of these lands, after all.'

Wiping her eyes with the back of her hand, she turned to Halil. 'I've seen awful things in this job. I was always at the worst place at the worst time. There was a time when it seemed as if nothing good would ever happen in the world.' She paused, continuing to chop the onion. 'Do you think the odds of someone noticing us are higher than the island floating?'

'How would I know? It's not something you can calculate.'

'The huge sea.'

'Oh, come on! This is the Aegean, little more than a pool!'

'Not exactly. All you can see is the void.'

His mind on the sea, Halil mused. 'The weird thing is, there's no fish in the sea. I held a fishing rod for three hours the other day. Not a single thing.'

'I can't get my head round that one, either. No one going fishing bothers with a bucket any more.'

There was a commotion outside the high garden wall. First, a couple of number three haircuts popped up briefly, then two foreheads, and finally four dark eyes. 'What're you doing up there? Buzz off!' bellowed Halil in his most schoolteacher-y voice.

'I guess the pomegranates, pears and apples have been marked now,' said Muzaffer.

'It's a wonder it took that long.' His eyes were on the street. 'Look here. They'll come here tonight and steal the lot. Shall we go out and gather them all?'

'Ha ha. Look who's talking!' Muzaffer was chuckling. She mimicked him: 'Like we're gonna stay here for ever?'

'Bloody hell! Caught out! Thanks to those greedy brats. My game's up.'

Adding a little tomato sauce to the fried onion, Muzaffer put the beans in the pot, seasoned it and covered it with the lid. She sat back down in the same chair. Lit a cigarette.

'Worse still, there are no cigarettes. You want it all the more when there's a shortage. I hid a carton. You never know.'

When Jülide came, Muzaffer and Halil were staring anxiously at the Care Home. She drank a glass of water. Placed the glass back on the counter without a rattle. Sat down in the chair next to Muzaffer. Jülide was looking out as well, but at the pomegranates barely turning pink now. The tree was unable to hang on to all of the heavy fruit in the violent wind. Unripe pomegranates dotted the ground below it.

'Nana loved pomegranates, but she had no teeth left to eat any. I used to squeeze the juice for her whenever the neighbours brought one.'

They all stared at the pomegranate tree. The green fruits were refusing to let go of their branches despite the brutal wind. Yet the branches looked so slender, and so flexible at the same time.

'There's one turning pink now. Go pick it if you like, let's see if it's ripe.'

'No. I mean, I don't want it.' The porcelain hardness of her face was blotchy with a pink rage. Embarrassed by her vehement reaction, she blushed even deeper. 'But I'll go pick it if you want.'

With an arm over Jülide's shoulder, Muzaffer looked her in the eye. That kindness was so flattering, yet it so rarely got to settle there.

'No, child; I'd meant it for you. Leave it if you don't want it. At any rate, it's not quite ripe yet.'

Halil was spinning the knife on the table with a finger. He glanced at the pomegranate as pale as Jülide's cheeks, repeatedly buffeted in the wind: coming close to smashing against the wall and drawing back again.

'Don't you like pomegranates?'

'No. I mean, I eat them; but I don't want one now.'

'But this pomegranate is a very good fruit.'

On the threshold of boring advice, Jülide gave him an unwilling look.

'Pomegranates have magical powers. Come on, ask away.'

'What?'

'What sort of powers they have.'

'What sort of powers do they have?'

'They change lives, and for all eternity, too.'

Magic meant despair for Jülide. No one capable of solving anything through ordinary means would need magic. Magic was thick with distress, fears, disappointments and desperation.

'Do you think magic is a good thing?'

Halil laughed. 'Depends on the magic. Maybe there's no such thing. Maybe it's us fooling ourselves. Maybe it's all the extraordinary stuff in our lives.'

The polish on the old table had long since gone, but buffed with years of use, the softer sections had worn down, leaving harder parts raised like veins. Jülide's index finger was absently trailing over these ridges. She kept her eyes down to hide the pain.

'Except, pomegranate's magic is permanent. It lasts a whole lifetime.' Halil's attempt to don a mysterious air failed miserably, given the smile which so rarely left his face. Her usual fascination with magic dulled by pain, Jülide only gathered a polite degree of interest in her eyes.

'There's a lovely pomegranate in our garden. Dad had planted it; took a sapling from Muzaffer Abla's father. That huge pomegranate's baby, the one by the wall.'

Muzaffer nodded with a laugh. 'How they liked to work at it! Take cuttings, grafting new strains. Everyone wants a bit if there's anything marginally different. It's planted in yogurt pots and sent over. The finest vegetables are left untouched. They're saved for seeds. A slightly different tulip bulb or a plum sapling spreads the following year. Folks used to love gardening, Jülide; no one does these days.'

Outside, the beans waved sadly on their poles, some of the leaves speckled with white spots, and a few branches on the verge of drying out.

'Nana was never happy until she'd planted a couple of peppers, a tomato and some basil in that handful of a garden.' Her grandmother's slender, wrinkled fingers covered in soil popped into her mind.

'But you're getting side-tracked! This is my pomegranate story.' Halil adopted a childish whinge to cut through the gloom. 'Now then; I loved pomegranates, twenty-five years ago, when I was at university. Still do, anyway. But this one was a rare beauty. Bright red, huge arils, soft seeds, sweet. I knew I'd never forget it when I went away. Never saw the like.'

Muzaffer's burly tabby appeared on top of the wall just beyond the pomegranate. Scanned the garden cautiously. Then turned back to glare at the street, where he had just come from. At long last, he must have made his mind up, leapt down to the garden and sauntered to the open window. His hefty body materialised on the windowsill. He exchanged a stare with Jülide for a silent moment.

'Welcome, Mr Mestan,' said Muzaffer, but the cat ignored the greeting, took his time to leap onto his own chair, and curled up.

'His mistress may let us, but not Mr Mestan.' Halil started stroking the neck of the charismatic animal sitting in the next chair, a deferential cuddle. 'Where were we? Oh, yes; so, one year, I'd loaded up here. Gone to Ankara with a sack full of pomegranates. I'm scoffing one or two every day. Without necessarily offering them around either. Very carefully. Anyway, I'd eaten them all, except for one last one. I loved Swan Park at the time. It was a bright autumn day. All right, sez I, I'll sit on a bench by the pond and eat my last pomegranate there. When I got to the park, though, all the benches were occupied by old codgers. The rest were grabbed by women with babies. Three men on one bench. Bachelors. You could tell their marital status straightaway, that obvious. Only one half of one single bench was free. A young girl sitting on the other half. Who could ask for more? Far better than making up a fourth by the three bachelors.' As the story wound on, Jülide transferred her attention from her snow-white fingers to Halil's face. Her eyes occasionally smiled at Mestan's purrs, so incongruous with his formidable personage. Only her eyes though; an old habit, an unnoticeable smile.

'As I approached the girl, I perceived that the gap in the park was in just the right spot. Mercilessly overtaking the elderly auntie in front, I settled on the bench at once. If that auntie had sat down, there would have been no room for anyone else; just overtaking her took a while. Anyway… I'd grabbed the seat next to the girl and the auntie walked past. I'm no shy youth, but chatting up a girl so openly is no easy feat. She has a chunk of bread in her hand; tearing bits off to throw into the pond, but that's all I can see. It takes a good deal of mettle to go up past the elbows.'

The memory of awkward glad eyes seemed to brighten Jülide's cheeks into a smile.

Muzaffer was chuckling. 'Don't be fooled by this false modesty. Halil was the fastest heartthrob in the neighbourhood. The moment he appeared at the end of the street, every girl would flock to the window.'

'No way! Spurious allegations. Don't pay her any attention, child.' Noticing the tetchy flick of Mestan's tail, he drew his hand back. 'What was I saying? Oh, yes. When I finally managed to look up past her elbow, I saw huge tears on her cheeks. Poor thing was crying in silence. Now this matter of women's tears is a bit complicated. You want to take her under your wing at once. It's a man thing. And scary at the same time. You can't just dive into conversation. She's still holding the bread. I'm agonising next to her. Others looking for somewhere to sit are ogling the bench. Time's running out.'

Jülide's smile took shape, along with her piqued interest.

'I put my hand in my pocket. I had this baggy cardigan. With huge pockets. It was our pomegranate. The last pomegranate. A really difficult moment of decision. On the one hand, a sad girl. On the other, the last pomegranate; that's it. Of course it was my chivalrous spirit that won. Pulling out my flick knife, I split the pomegranate in half. A few arils fell down, wasted. Impossible to eat this stuff without spilling, anyway. I held one half out to her. She gave me a suspicious look at first. But our pomegranate was a handsome fella; she couldn't resist for long. We enjoyed chewing sitting side by side, without saying a word. Every single aril, careful not to spill a single one. We started talking afterwards. That was her favourite fruit, her father was poorly, her name was Yasemin.'

'Never forgot her name then, sir?'

Muzaffer croaked as she got up to turn the heat off under the beans. 'I guess you weren't listening to the start of the story. Remember what he'd said? Pomegranate's magic lasts a whole lifetime. Now ask Mr Halil what his wife's name is.'

Jülide's smiling eyes asked the question, not her mouth.

'Yasemin,' said Halil. 'Yasemin.' He was laughing, with his head down.

Hypersensitive to any activity on the cooker and the counter, Mestan had risen on his hind legs, front paws resting on the cupboard door, staring at the cooker.

'Like we're cooking for you!' The smoker's voice softened whenever Muzaffer addressed the cat. But the Mestan tone altered when she said, 'I have a pomegranate story too.' She came back and sat down. 'It was some thirty years ago.'

Halil gave a wicked chortle. 'Oh, well; you're revealing our age now.'

Exhaling with a smile the half breath she had taken to continue her sentence, Muzaffer went on. 'We were in Beirut.' Halil's face twisted in dark memories. 'We had a colleague known as Deaf Nazif. Photo reporter. He wasn't usually sent into the thick of battle or anything, but for some reason he had been sent there on that occasion.'

'Hold on though; how would this kid know about Beirut or anything. It was the symbol of war in our day. All that devastation, all that loss ...'

'Thank you, Sir,' said Muzaffer; it was her turn at mischief. 'Hard to explain what Beirut was like at the time; it was a blood bath. We're doing our job, but we're scared shitless. Israel's the usual Israel, of course. Beirut's a ghost town. You won't know about him Jülide, but there was a writer called Refik Halit.'

'Yes, I do. I'd picked up his books from the library and read them.'

'Then you know how wonderfully he describes Beirut, where he was exiled at the time. It was known as the Paris of the East. Something that's said about anywhere half decent, to be honest. It was like a beautiful girl whose face had been ravaged in a terrible accident. Heartbreaking. Anyone with money had run away. Only those who didn't stayed behind. The buildings were pockmarked with bullets and shrapnel. A sight that is hard to forget. I guess I'll never forget it as long as I live.'

She stared for a long time at the pomegranate tree, picturing the scene. It was beginning to get dark.

'Anyway. Never knew what made us do it, but one day Nazif and I were caught in cross fire. Nazif's deaf, right, so he doesn't mind. Bullets whizzing over our heads. Reflecting off the walls of the buildings nearby. Huge explosions in the distance. We're slinking behind the thick wall of an old house in a garden. Can't even put our noses out. Fuck knows how many hours; seems to die down a bit, and then picks up again in a fury. We're waiting there, hungry, thirsty. Maybe we'll die the next minute.'

Looking at the peacefully sleeping Mestan on his chair, far from the reach of words, Jülide stirred. She glanced at Muzaffer from the corner of her eye. The journalist's profile appeared harsher in the twilight as she blew smoke towards the window. The smell prodded Jülide's grief, which had been quietening in her fascination. She sighed.

'I was desperate for a pee. But it's impossible to stir. Nazif's sitting calm as anything at the bottom of the wall. No need to shout if I want to say anything. A whisper's enough, since he reads lips. I keep thinking the bullets will find us if I raise my voice.'

Even Halil looked sombre now. He resumed stroking Mestan's neck.

'There was a pomegranate tree, right by our side in this garden. A young sapling, three or four years old. One single pomegranate on it. Its first ever, who knows? Nazif keeps pointing at it. We're thirsty. I keep mimicking *NO*. They're still firing, I say. The pomegranate had split down the middle, an enormous thing. The tree had given its all to this one single fruit. We're both fascinated by it. Our mouths are watering. Nazif tries to reach, I hold him back. Then the firing slowed down. No guns were heard for fifteen minutes, maybe twenty. I was just rising to look over the wall when Nazif got up, picked the pomegranate, then a hum, he stumbled and sank to the ground. Bleeding from somewhere at the back of his head. Terror in his face. I bent down, but must have emptied my bladder too. I'm shouting. Nazif's eyes keep growing wider.'

A sudden gust of wind dislodged the cushion propping the window and the window slammed shut, making Jülide jump. Stroking her hand, Muzaffer bent down, picked up the cushion and secured the window shut now that the wind had cooled perceptibly.

'Nazif gestured for me to shut up. I did. He's clutching the pomegranate. He pointed at it. I didn't get what he wanted. "Pomegranate," I said. He gestured for me to repeat it. "Pomegranate," I said. His face twisted in agony. I'm having kittens there. There's nowhere to ask for help, you can't carry him away. Poor bloke's dying before my very eyes. I met his wife. He's got a young child.'

Jülide couldn't stand it any longer. 'Did he die?'

'Hold your horses!' Muzaffer was laughing. 'No, he didn't. He wasn't even in pain just then. Only, he'd started hearing. Wherever the bullet hit. It's still there; they didn't remove it; it was more risky to remove it. But later he told me something really amusing. He said until then, he only knew the shapes of words; but that's when he started hearing them too. At first, they flooded his mind in a jumble. He was terrified. Hearing for the first time in his life. He felt something like revulsion.' She paused, a little embarrassed. 'He said he'd smelt an awful stench of piss, then the sounds came, and it all combined in his brain. To be fair, both the smell and the sounds were coming from me; so he was right, in a manner of speaking.'

Both Halil and Jülide chuckled, relieved at the ending. Mestan's ears flattened, showing his displeasure with the noise.

'A few hours later, in the ambulance on our way to hospital, Nazif held out the pomegranate. I cracked it in half and we laid into it. He was tormented even by the noise of his own teeth. The pomegranate was the same colour as the dried blood on his neck. But it was so delicious. I don't think I ever had any like it.'

'So what happened to Nazif afterwards? Did he get used to sounds?'

'Ha, ha! The bloke became a clarinettist! A professional, even. He stopped photo journalism and everything. Went all the way to New York and played in clubs. Bizarre. One pomegranate. One bullet.'

'One pomegranate. One bullet,' repeated Jülide. She looked at the sky, which was really dark now. The tree was nothing but a black skeleton ahead. The pomegranate was being blown about like a black ball.

17

The morning stretches over the sea holding its breath. Stillness, akin to peace in the absence of the storm, beckons everyone to the streets. Strolling in the slanted autumn sun, listening to one's own footsteps rustling through the fallen leaves; listening to the tiny whispers of things that move of their own accord after the frenzied chorus of the wind. Inner peace rises by the buzzing of flies circling outside windows opened to let in the sun. The muffled *pats!* as skinny cats jump down from high walls and the scratching of dogs dissolve in the clear air. With little movement to focus on, the eyes lead to a refreshed opening in the mind. For the first time in days, there is something like peace in Andalıç.

DEAR RESIDENTS, THE CENSUS IS DUE TO START SHORTLY. YOU ARE KINDLY REQUESTED TO STAY AT HOME.

Cemal and Hakkı are having breakfast, picking at a little cheese and slightly stale bread bought a day earlier. The calm sea visible over the rooftops looks grey. The tea is bubbling on a really low flame. Behind the island, opposite the horizon they're looking at, a barely visible freighter far away steams north. To the Marmara, perhaps, or even the Black Sea. But they're gazing eastwards, where the sun, which illuminates half the table, rises. The only thing to the rear of Andalıç is the cemetery. Attention at the Care Home is focused on the census, on the town lying in silence below. There's no one to pivot and scan the horizons.

'I've seen a good deal of funny stuff in my life, but this census probably takes the biscuit.' Staring absently at the morsel of cheese at the end of his fork, Hakkı shook his head. 'And it's a sin to eat this with tea.' He threw half of his bread to the scraggy dog wagging its tail and moaning creakily under the window. 'They'll even eat cats if they're starving. Throttle sheep if they can manage it.'

'No way! This mangy thing…'

'Not on their own, but they would in a pack.'

'Well, bullying's easier in a crowd.'

Seeing the cups had emptied, Cemal went in to fetch the teapot. In the kitchen, his foot kicked the bottle of rakı that was finished the night before; it rolled away noisily. When he returned, Hakkı was still sitting in the same pose, staring at his morsel of cheese on the fork.

'I know I get cross with everyone, but I'm scared witless I'll run out of gas. Should be able to get bottles, though.' Paused for a moment's reflection. 'Or maybe not; who knows?'

The dog was still grovelling after scoffing the bread in one bite. An orange butterfly with brown spots flew in, like a scrap of paper blown in the wind, settled on the windowsill and started opening and closing its wings in the sun. 'Seems like years since I last saw a butterfly. I guess there aren't any in Istanbul. Not around our way, at least.'

Cemal squinted looking at the butterfly. 'Saliha's not well at all.'

Tugging downwards at his swollen nose, Hakkı blew forcibly twice. Raised his half-closed, bloodshot eyes to Cemal with difficulty. 'Saliha.'

'Perhaps if we'd got married…'

'Perhaps.'

'And we'd have gone away too. We'd have been somewhere else. Not cooped up here. She could've done what she wanted then.'

'Who does, though? Who does, and doesn't pay for it?'

The butterfly must have decided it had rested long enough and shot off.

'If only it was a day later. The earthquake, just a day later.'

'There's always an excuse, anyway.'

The tea he poured into his empty glass dribbled down the spout and dripped onto the vinyl. A brown track on the porcelain indicated all the wasted drops.

'Always.'

Tired of wagging his tail and having given up hope, the dog stretched out. When Cemal threw the rest of his slice, it sprang up happily and wolfed it down.

'She's fed up here. Really fed up. She was biding her time, knowing we'd leave. We stayed. Why the hell didn't we get a date a couple of days earlier?

What for? We were told to pick the first of the month. Why do we have to listen to everyone, anyway?'

'Because everyone talks. Everyone talks. Everyone gives advice. You'll take one if not the other. That's life. You get to the end; you see others lived half of it. You've lived as others told you to.'

Cemal placed his spoon on the edge of the saucer. Gingerly took a small sip. Looked at the dog, which had moved into the shade for a nap now that the meal seemed to be over.

'But does it all have to be one thing after another? This much?'

'Yup. That's the way life goes. Could have been far worse. Anything could happen.' At long last, having popped the cheese into his mouth, Hakkı was chewing slowly.

There was a knock on the door. Erkan and a friend came in. They perched on the clean side of the table a little timidly. Erkan had the neater hand, so he wrote down the address in a large notebook that didn't look particularly official. Adding the inhabitants' names below the address, he asked for their signatures. He then wrote their names on individual ready-stamped, thick pieces of paper and handed them over.

'The date will be noted when you get water, and the official will sign it. One loaf per person a day.' He closed the notebook carefully. 'Dried beans will be distributed tomorrow. The quantity will be determined once the census results are in.'

'Who's appointed you?'

'The District Governor,' Erkan hesitated before adding, 'The Commissioner and the Mayor were there too.' He flicked his head in the direction of the Care Home.

'Jobsworths, nothing more. Like we're gonna stay here for all eternity.'

'Don't say that, Cemal Abi. One of the stores was looted the other day. That's unfair. What if there's still no help? And who knows, they might flog it on the black market soon.' Erkan was at the door, putting his shoes back on. His mate was already out and was glaring at Cemal.

'Regardless. How dare they bang people up, threatening them with hunger and thirst?'

Erkan shrugged, tucked the notebook under his arm and went next door.

It got quite warm as the sun rose. By the time Cemal knocked on his fiancée's door, it was stifling hot. Saliha's room being out of bounds on this occasion as her father was at home, he went into the sitting room. Someone called up. As he waited for Saliha, he listened to Kadir's uninterrupted monologue on the merits of a census and establishing order.

As he shook off his awkward absent-mindedness and turned his head, Cemal realised that Saliha had come and sat down by the door in total silence. She looked, again, as if she were far away, caught somewhere, unable to get away. Cemal was upset once again by the thing that her family referred to indifferently as her 'strange ways'. Just as he had failed to find his father in any of Turkey's cities, he was failing to find Saliha in her own body for the past couple of weeks.

'How are you?'

'I'm fine. Fine. You?'

'Me too. It feels heavy today. Oppressive.'

The grandmother clock on the wall no longer interrupted the silence. It had fallen and broken in the earthquake, but habit still drew the eye. It had stopped at three fifteen.

'Saliha, c'mon girl; make your fiancé a cup of coffee.'

Cemal would have enjoyed the irritated crow's feet appearing at the corners of Saliha's eyes at this command; but it vanished without spreading over her face. She made for the kitchen obediently, her lethargy caused by a strange pain no one could fathom – least of all her.

'He's good, is the Mayor. I voted for him. He's a distant relation,' said Kadir.

'I heard he'd been trained in the camps,' said Cemal, not in the least bit confrontationally, 'Never left home for ten years after the coup. Used to stab his mother with forks and things. You'll know the truth of it, of course, being related and all.'

With a feeble, 'That's all gossip,' Kadir tried to brush off these claims, whose veracity he, too, believed.

'You may like his poetic side, though.'

That the poems read on the council loudspeakers by the Mayor came from his own pen was common knowledge.

'Of course, he's talented. And a patriotic fellow too. Not to mention being lord bountiful.'

Cemal was unable to suppress his laughter. 'Of course, he distributes free coal to the poor. Well done. Pretends the third-grade coal he buys from his cousin is first grade and pockets the difference.'

Kadir was beetroot red in the room where the absence of a functioning clock was palpable. 'Slander. They can't stomach the fact that he helps the poor. Posh scum just want it all for themselves.'

Cemal had also gone red. Normally happy to stay silent and keep his opinions to himself, something prodded him this time, and he was prepared to cross swords with his father-in-law. A conflict which caused inner turmoil, a strange unease mixed with satisfaction.

'Of course, it could be slander. We can't be sure. What is certain is that he plonked that Care Home on the hill, ignoring every court case, after forcibly collecting donations from everyone. And now he's settled in there. Must have had second sight.'

'Well, that's also service; we'll go there when we're old,' said Kadir automatically.

'We might have if we stayed here.' Cemal was looking only into Saliha's eyes as he picked up his cup from the tray, despite the risk of spilling his coffee. 'Our turn would never come with all your *sosyetiks* in the queue.'

Saliha had pricked up her ears in the kitchen; she lingered before Cemal a good deal longer than necessary as she offered his coffee. Her eyebrows kept rising, clearly trying to say something with her eyes. Cemal didn't get it. Was she upset that he'd had words with her father? Was she telling him to hush? Just then, Kadir spat out the enormous sip he had taken with a slurp.

'Bloody hell! She used salt instead of sugar. My fault for asking her to do anything. Got to her thirties, still can't make coffee.'

Placing his cup on the coffee table to staunch the rebuke, Cemal said, 'I'd like to take Saliha out for a stroll, if that's all right with you.'

'Go, go,' Kadir waved his hand as if shooing a fly, 'Don't want to see no daughter no nothing. Take Saime along too.' Cemal took his leave with a nervous laugh.

They went out, all three, and walked together for a safe distance. Then Saime peeled away to join Jülide; the two girls being inseparable now. The moment Saliha had learnt that Hakkı had gone down to the seafront, she practically dragged Cemal to his home.

And attacked him with something more like rage than desire as soon as they were through the door. Cemal made love to her mechanically, quickly, with an unease that pinched at his desire. When he had sank down onto the pillow to rest, he heard Saliha get up and get dressed in a hurry. He didn't want to open his eyes. But on sensing she was leaving the room, he sat up in a panic, and caught up with her at the door.

'Wait. Where?' Grabbing her arm, he sat her down on the sofa. 'If you're going, how about a goodbye first? And what's the hurry, anyway? Who's chasing you?' He paused, a dizzying sense inside of sinking or losing altitude. 'You don't... you never talk to me any more.'

The autumn warmth had not penetrated the chill indoors. Saliha gathered her legs under her and drew away to the far corner. Sitting in the middle of the sofa, Cemal gave her a helpless, weary look.

'I watched a documentary on the day of the earthquake,' said Saliha, her eyes fixed on the carpet. 'On hippos. The waters of a huge river had collected in a lake. But really clear. Like a crystal-clear pool. In a bright green forest. A mother hippopotamus and her tiny calf. A sweet little thing. Everything looks wonderful. Like paradise. Swimming in the clear water. Underwater photography.'

Cemal closed his eyes to visualise this peaceful haven. A baby hippopotamus with its mother in a perfect pond. All those lovely, happy animals in distant corners of the earth. 'I love your voice.' Opening his eyes momentarily, he looked at Saliha, asking for something even he could not name. He thought he saw a degree of softening, something like a what he was hoping to see, but only for a moment; the tale continued under a frown.

'Anyway, they were swimming when another big hippo arrived. A male. The mother tried to attack and drive him away. But she wasn't strong enough. She lost. The animals were so huge that the sediment at the bottom was blown up and the water got murky. The male went to the baby. Caught it as it was trying to get away.' She paused, her voice breaking. 'He bit the baby and pushed it to the bottom. Held it there until it drowned. The animal thrashed and thrashed and then died.'

Cemal pressed his fingers on his eyes.

'Once he was sure it was dead, the male hippo went away. The female was left with a dead baby in the murky pond. She wasn't strong enough. She couldn't protect her young. Just stood there.'

Cemal drew his hands away from his face, as if convinced of having adopted the desired expression, and looked at his fiancée.

'I'd never cried watching a documentary before. It keeps popping into my mind for days and days. I can't forget it.'

'Aaaah!' Cemal went inside, got dressed and came back. 'Why are you torturing yourself like this? Animals kill one another. Cats kill mice and birds; tomcats strangle their young. Why does that upset you so much?'

'I don't know. I don't feel at all well.' She looked blankly at the house that seemed to grow stranger, not more familiar, the more she stayed there. 'The baby…' She paused. 'The baby's making me really…' Cemal reluctantly waited for her to talk, but he did not have the energy or resilience to encourage her.

'I love you. You upset me. I… I have no idea what to do. How to help you.' The words all seemed to be too ineffectual, too artificial. 'Can't you try to get better for my sake, Saliha? Please.'

She gave him a cold, blank look. 'I don't know. I'll try.' Her voice, devoid of the slightest note of conviction, echoed in the room with a chilling despair.

On the second morning of the doldrums, Andalıç residents leapt out of bed at the sound of an aircraft, but all they could spot was a tiny dot high up in the sky.

Faces were washed with a handful of water. A pitcher of water was taken to the toilet. Bodies unwashed for days began to stink and itch. Without the wind to blow everything away, all the smells of the town stuck around. The smell of rubbish piling high, the smell of unflushed toilets, the smell of bodies untouched by soap for days. Self-consciousness made everyone keep everyone else at arm's length; everyone tried to maintain enough distance to avoid awkwardness at homes, coffee houses and mosques. Attempts to wash with sea water were abandoned once bodies so cleansed stung and itched even worse. Water rations being only sufficient to drink, food was now cooked with sea water. The heat of the still autumn days was more oppressive than summer's, making everything feel soiled, sticky and sickly. Hands only soaped when they got really dirty fouled every object they touched, which in turn fouled every hand.

Eyes on the horizons again: rain or help. Water or water. Salt-free, clean, cleansing, fresh water. The townsfolk regretted cisterns they'd closed up after the council had connected domestic properties to the water supply system. Only a few houses had wells, now with long queues before them. At any rate, the water ran out after drawing only fifteen or twenty buckets, and what little seeped into the well was always just a little less the following day. Dry, yellow leaves spread over the bone-dry soil. Tomato, aubergine and pepper plants now no more than a crisp stick. The town ever poorer in moisture as the sun claimed its tax. Cats and dogs snoozing in the deepest shades throughout the day, horses and donkeys glaring fiery rebukes at their desperate owners, and flies and insects swarming around the water drops in washbasins.

The aircraft that flew over without spotting them in the morning, the ship floating like a dream behind the midday haze, and the absolute disconnect of so many days had given the townsfolk a sense of invisibility. Everything would pass by, over, under their nose, but no one would see them. They might be slowly starving and dying of thirst on their serpentine route, leaving an ominous wake of animal carcases, but their plight would go unnoticed by the millions on either side of the sea. The dirt sticking to them would increase layer by layer and they would start to rot well before exhaling their last breaths.

An announcement followed the midday call to prayer that was broadcast to the whole town:

DEAR RESIDENTS; THERE WILL PRAYERS FOR RAIN FOLLOWING AFTERNOON PRAYERS. EVERYONE IS INVITED.

Until the afternoon, Andalıç watched the two small white clouds standing still on the unmoving horizon. Once the afternoon prayers were over, the town's men streamed out of the mosques and climbed to the arid land by the Care Home. They pleaded for rain, one hand raised to the sky, the other turned to the ground. The deep voices of this crowd of men echoed down the hills. They pleaded so they could lie beside their wives without revulsion, cuddle their children and go visiting with their neighbours.

The old cisterns were remembered. The sounds of buckets emptying cinders, trowels plastering cracks, and brushes filling pans with dust and dirt were heard until darkness fell. Night descended on Andalıç, which had cooled down in a flash at sunset. But by then, the stink of bodies which had toiled in hot, cramped cisterns was unbearable. Open windows failed to catch a single draught as sleep daunted by the stink eluded the people at the edges of their beds, avoiding one another.

Pale with revulsion rose the sun over Andalıç again. It illuminated the town with a fastidious hesitation, a white veil drawn over its face. As it rose high at noon, it forgot once again it was autumn, and set about searing the town mercilessly. It buried the stinking townsfolk into a giddying abandonment as all their effluvia and waste reeked together. They prayed for a drop of water as they listened to the call to prayer from the loudspeakers, filled their mosques, performed their prayers in a hurry and flung themselves outdoors. Faces drawn and wretched, they walked down the streets, hoping for clouds to fill the blank horizon or help to come. The island abandoned by man and God kept drifting on the greyish waters of the Aegean like a floating mine.

DEAR RESIDENTS, AS THE WASTE CONTAINERS CANNOT BE EMPTIED, THE RUBBISH EMITS AN UNPLEASANT SMELL. EVERYONE IS REQUESTED TO CARRY THE CONTAINERS IN THEIR NEIGHBOURHOOD TO THE SEAFRONT AND EMPTY THEM INTO THE SEA.

The streets were swamped with the hollow rumble of wheelie bins. The men were trying to push the heavy metal bins without tipping them over, as women and children followed with the bags that had been left beside the overflowing bins. Holding by fingertips those bags festering for days. A constant sound of retching rang out.

The smell of rubbish didn't leave the streets, hands or clothing, even well after all the rubbish had vanished from sight, reluctantly carried away by the feeble current. It was smeared on fine nostril hairs. Even washing was useless. Everything was filthy with the intolerable stench of rotting, from the water drunk from a glass through to the bread sliced on the table. Not even their meagre rations could whet appetites that night. This sense of being violated by their own filth, this sense of writhing germs invading their alimentary canals and settling in their stomachs, just would not be shaken off.

It was nearing midnight when Cemal went out in the hope of finding a fresh breeze in the darkness. He saw thin blue cigarette smoke coming out of Saliha's lighted window and picking up a small stone, he threw it at the window. First, her shadow appeared on the net curtain, which was drawn to reveal her face, a little indistinct in the dim gaslight. Her hair was longer, but not long enough to hang it down to enable her lover to climb up. She pointed at the garden gate. Cemal slipped into the dark garden as soundlessly as a cat. The newly-risen wedge of the moon cast a pale grey light into the night sky behind the dark house. Saliha came out of the kitchen door on tiptoe. Standing at the spot where the engagement rings were placed on their fingers, she looked for him. He picked out her silhouette and rustled the dry leaves under his foot in the corner where he was sitting. His sweetheart was in his arms a second later.

She shrank back as if she was hurt after that first hug. Cemal, who had been trying to understand, solve and eliminate her depression for days, didn't even need to ask. But Saliha felt the need to explain. 'I stink.'

'No. You still smell lovely, as always. Even in this drought.' He placed his sweetheart on his lap. 'I love everything about you. All your smells.'

'I know, but I'm revolted by my own smell. And everyone stinks anyway. I was retching the whole day. Thankfully I now have an excuse.'

It was Cemal's turn to feel uncomfortable. 'I'll stay away if you don't like the way I smell.'

'No. No. You smell fine. I like even the smell of your sweat.'

They were whispering, their lips sweeping each other's ears.

'You're wearing a skirt.'

'A nightie.'

'And lovely it is too!'

They stopped for a moment, pricking their ears.

'How noisy is a zip!'

They stopped talking. Entrusted their bodies and breaths to the guidance of their ears. On the stone bench, amongst dry leaves, without rousing the still night.

'If... this earthquake... was to happen a few days later... like this... outside...'

'Don't you ever… shut up? And … anyway, you're not complaining at all…'

The pointy corner of the moon rose over the roof just then, giving Cemal's teeth a bright white gleam. 'OK… oh…' 'you're right, I'm not…'

The thick bright slice rose rapidly and broke away from the roof. They were sitting side by side. The moon's chill flattered Saliha's coolness.

'It's enchanting, the moon.'

Cemal hugged her tight. 'You seem to be a bit better tonight,' he said timidly.

'I am a bit better at night-time. When everyone's asleep. That's when I think no one's suffering.'

They watched the moon run behind the thinning, forked branches of the apricot as they breathed in each other's smells, new sweat, old sweat, soap, eau de cologne, and fluids beginning to dry.

'The way I am… I mean, the way I behave… it's not because I don't love you, Cemal.'

'But you can't say you love me either; I don't recall you ever saying it.'

'You know I don't like saying things like that.'

'It would have been nice to hear it once in a blue moon.'

'Then you'll have to wait for the blue moon.'

A cool breath passed between them. Cemal took his head in his hands. The south-westerly swishing the dry leaves on the branches breathed on his dejected forehead. Like blowing on a pan of milk so his gloom didn't boil over. Dipping his head into the sweet scent of the wind, he took deep breaths.

'At long last the wind's risen. Smells so sweet. Like it's come over from flower gardens.' She placed her cool lips on Cemal's temple. 'If something happened to me, know that I love you; know that it doesn't have anything to do with y…'

Cemal shot up angrily. 'I'm sick of this chat. You don't love anyone.' He strode to the gate, never mind the noise. Swung round as he was about to leave. 'People live for their loved ones. All right? For their loved ones.' He slammed the gate on his way out.

Just before turning into his street, he slowed down, sensing a presence in the darkness. Someone rubbed past him. He smelled sour breath. The man's footsteps halted before long. Cemal carried on for home. With a tetchy sense of being followed. His hackles up, his shoulders hunched, and his back hollowed. Trying to silence his own footsteps as much as possible, he moved, all his attention focused on his hearing. As he approached the door, he suddenly sped up and threw himself down just before something whistled past in the air. He leant against the door and stood still. He bolted the door for the first time since his mother's death, checked the windows, and rushing past Hakkı's alcohol breath, which overpowered everything else, he flung himself into his room.

With tiny licks like a cat, the south-westerly started cleaning Andalıç's foetid air. Piled up before the moon, came thick clouds redolent of rain. First their edges silvered, then the clouds combined into a thick grey cover. With deep black shadows inside, they descended like the rugged surface of a planet about to strike the earth. Having forgotten its manners in the meanwhile, the south-westerly slammed open windows first, then rolled away empty containers and plastic buckets with a rattle, before shoving anything it could through the streets in a thick cloud of dust and dumping them into the sea. The sea, which was stirring like an uneasy flock of sheep, was strewn with newspapers, carrier bags, yogurt pots, and slivers of wood. Frothing as it brought up any trace of whiteness, it grew darker by one more shade. The town was battered by a wind which repeatedly raised and slammed tin roofs, removed loosened signs, swung rotten garden gates, and tugged away the last remaining leaves from the trees, and then was illuminated by a flash of lightning somewhere close. Thunder roared but a moment later, shocking everybody out of bed. Flashes of lightning flickered on the patterns of drawn curtains.

The first drops left a warm tune in everyone's ears. A crowded patter grabbed the world. The rain descended, raising the thin, soft dust accumulated by the drought. The smell of dusty water roused everyone. Lightning illuminated heads in windows. Everyone rushed out into tiny gardens or courtyards, grabbing every bucket, basin, cauldron, pots and pans they could lay hands on. The sound of plastic basins and tin cauldrons joined the patter of the soil, trees and roof tiles. Bodies craving for water had no wish to go back in once they were outdoors. Laundry piled up in baskets was fetched and laid out on branches, lines and flagstones. Olive oil soaps and shampoos were grabbed from bathrooms. The whole of Andalıç – men, women, children – began to wash as one, lathering under the rain falling hard enough to hurt. The smell of soap overpowered the smell of wet earth. Everyone washed, with their clothes on, shivering, teeth chattering. Washed, laughing out loud. Calling out to one another. There was so much water, so unrestrained. Overwhelmed by a great sense of waste, they watched it run down the streets to the sea. Every street in Andalıç was washed with soapy water cascading under garden gates and terrace waste pipes. Floods ran down dry stream beds. Clean, laughing people ran back indoors to dry. They snuggled under blankets with a happy shiver. The world was clean again. Rocked by the gentle regret of the receding thunder, dropping wind and slowing rain, they fell into a deep and peaceful sleep on their damp pillows.

18

Peeking through the slit in the horizon, the sun cast its orange light at the bottom of the grey clouds covering the sky. Despite the dropping wind, the restless motion of the leaden sea, which refused to reflect the light, continued unabated. Then the horizon closed over and the sun vanished from view. A light drizzle started. The whole world consisted of grey as the clouds descended even lower. Cool grey light fell on minds as two helicopters flying over the thick grey layer were heard. This time they were imprisoned under a glass bell made of clouds. Still torn away from the world.

The damp seeping into houses carried the unmistakable chill of autumn. The rich odour of naphthalene smothered the paucity of breakfast tables. Eyes were shutting as if about to fall asleep again in the indolence offered by the rain and the dark, blankets waited at the ready on the edges and arms of sofas, and bodies pitched this way and that, jolted by some unknown weight. Woollen cardigans, jumpers, blankets, snuggling sleepy bodies, and cool faces gently pinched by the damp. But for the constant grumbling of their stomachs, Andalıç residents would have felt just like contented cats; except, the plummeting mice population had made a huge dint in the feline happiness stakes too.

Mealtimes were now marked by windows firmly shut against mewling and barking; yet the food taking up ever less space on their plates still refused to go down. Whenever some of the starving beasts failed to wake up from the sleep where they spent the majority of their time, their bodies were carried to the shore by pangs of conscience, and released into the all-embracing waters of the sea.

The drizzle fell on heads, backs, roof tiles, into gutterings, buckets, cisterns, tanks, and pots. Wretched as they might look with dripping hides glued to their skeletons, the long-thirsty animals were still happy. The soil was gulping the water being sprinkled on it. Getting heavier as it did. Tonnes of water collected on Andalıç, pooled instead of flowing down, and was absorbed by the soil. Like an enormous, bone dry sponge, Andalıç guzzled greedily.

It rained non-stop for an entire day and night. The dense grey clouds never let up and the island grew heavier. *Yalı* gardens were dissolving in the sea, only a brown stain to mark their place. The benches at the seafront had sunk overnight. The inhabitants of the sinking invisible island rushed to the shore. Houses were flooded too. What little remained inside was evacuated, carried from hand to hand. Their occupants moved in slow, cautious steps, as if visiting a strange planet, dragging their water-heavy skirts and trouser legs, moving out with dark, glum faces, but without forgetting to pull the doors shut behind them. Staring with a fond sorrow from a distance at the homes where their grandfathers had lived, and which they had thought they would leave to their grandchildren.

But the main issue wasn't the few seafront houses or the sinking coastal road. The sea was climbing the walls of the half-submerged houses inch by inch, right before the eyes of the community that had flocked to the shore. The sea wanted to drag down this colossus that should never have floated, pull it down to the depths like all non-floating objects and settle it at the bottom. The rain, their best friend only a couple of days ago, was now their greatest enemy.

ATTENTION, DEAR RESIDENTS: OUR ISLAND FACES THE RISK OF SINKING. THE WATERS HAVE RISEN BY A METRE. PEOPLE WHOSE HOMES HAVE BEEN FLOODED WILL BE WELCOME AT THE PRIMARY SCHOOL. WE INVITE ANYONE CAPABLE OF WIELDING A SHOVEL TO HELP LIGHTEN THE ISLAND.

Once the panicked inspection at the shore was done, small groups started gathering by the collapsed houses in every neighbourhood. The few surviving horses, donkeys and mules were lashed to carts. Shovels and pickaxes rose and fell. Under the intermittent drizzle, stones, pieces of concrete and metal were carried to the carts. Rubble slick with wet grey mud taught unacquainted backs what carrying stones meant – a surprisingly painful lesson. The beasts struggled to haul their heavy loads over cobblestones, reached the shore, unloaded and went back up again.

Rain mingling with his sweat for hours, Cemal used the back of his wrist to brush away his hair now long enough to get into his eyes. His aching hands were slick with mud. Raising his head, he spotted a dark man watching him from about fifty metres away. A black pinstriped suit, black shirt with the buttons undone over the chest, dark skin competing with the black of his short hair. Cemal felt the same shiver he had sensed in the dark two nights earlier. The difference was, this time he was able to see what he had only sensed then. When Hakkı, who had been throwing small pieces of concrete into the cart, came over, Cemal prodded him with his elbow and pointed with his head.

'Is that Zaim?'

Hakkı peered from amongst the bodies rising and falling. 'Yes, I guess that's him.'

'I guess he was the one the other night then.'

Hakkı shook his head. 'Can't do anything though. Just being an arse.'

'Not so sure. I thought something had whizzed past my ear.'

Erkan helped Cemal carry a big stone to the cart. The rickety structure shook ominously when they had managed to heave it in next to the other stones. Erkan's eye caught Zaim. 'You know this bloke, Cemal Abi?'

'I don't, but I know *of* him. What gives?'

'A couple of PCs brought him over to the Commissioner's office the other day.' His head pointed at the Care Home. 'But he left on his own.'

Going back to the ruins, they set their sights on a big block of concrete. Wood was collected elsewhere; it wouldn't be thrown away. Lifting the block together, they carried it to the cart, huffing and puffing.

'Why doesn't he give a hand instead of gawping like a dickhead?' Erkan was exhausted, covered in mud all the way up to his long, curling eyelashes. 'Who's this geezer, abi?'

'Some pimp.'

Erkan laughed. They turned back to the ruins. His exhaustion forgotten in his anger, Cemal felt strangely strong. He lifted three moderately large stones one after the other and carried them to the cart. Once it was full, the skinny horse was whipped into very slow action. The men all squatted as one. The rain had stopped again. Hanife looked out of her window, saw they were taking a break, and came out with a tray of tea. A pleasant warmth spread from their throats to their stomachs and thence to their chilled backs. Cemal was still sipping when he spotted Halil across the road. His cousin was wearing a yellow raincoat and wellies. Cemal flicked his head back when Halil reached him, before they'd even had a chance to say hello.

'What are you pointing at?' asked Halil.

'Can't you see the bloke behind?'

'Which bloke?'

Cemal swung his head round. 'Aaa! He's gone.'

'Who's gone?'

'Zaim.'

Squatting next to Cemal, Erkan gave him a reproachful look. 'Why'd you not tell me just now, abi, seeing as you know his name?'

As if he had not heard, Cemal scanned the whole area, as did Halil. Shivers replied to sweat cooling in the drizzle. Smelling a rat, and reluctant to breach the need for silence in the caginess peculiar to males, Erkan continued to sip his tea. Halil looked around irritably for a little longer before shrugging this topic off. The anger on his face was strange. Thin drops of rain trembled on his bushy moustache when he spoke.

'What do you think you're doing here, Cemal?'

'What do you mean? Can't you see: we're removing rubble. To lighten the island.'

'Are you going to do everything these bastards shout from the loudspeakers? Use your bonce: what difference does a few scraps of concrete make, next to the weight of tonnes of water?' He glared at Erkan. 'He's in their team, fine. Ignorant kid. You?'

'Now, that's out of order, sir!' glowered Erkan.

'I'm right though, aren't I, son? Aren't these geezers your big brothers, chiefs, whatever? And he has the cheek to square up and everything!'

Erkan scowled, his eyes down.

'Instead of asking them, "What are you doing there? Where does this authority come from? How are you taking these decisions?" et cetera ... Shame on you.' When Halil raised his head, he got a few drops of the quickening rain in his eye. He pointed at Hakkı impatiently. 'And what's this venerable man of the world doing here?' He carried on, staring at the top of Cemal's head, as the latter remained squatting. 'Instead of dealing with Zaim and what have you, remove rubble then. Bravo Cemal. Like the island's not going to sink if it's meant to.'

'Don't say that, sir. It might help. How do you know?' Lifting his head, Erkan gave Halil a furtive glance.

'It's obvious it's going to help, but I couldn't say who it would help.'

'So what should we have done, Halil Bey? Swan around like you when everyone else is working?' Cemal was cross.

'Oh, far be it from you, Cemal Bey, to stay out when everyone else's pitching in?'

Cemal glared, brushing his wet hair back.

'Stopping these blokes from working too, for example; doesn't that occur to you?' The schoolteacher's mocking tone subdued Erkan most of all.

'We're a nation of soldiers, Halil Bey, son,' interrupted Hakkı, who had been listening from afar. 'We don't disobey orders from above.'

'There! That's precisely what I've been saying,' said Halil, before yelling at the group of volunteer labourers covered in sweat. 'Gentlemen, use your logic. How could the island get lighter if you threw a few cartloads of rubble? Isn't all this effort wasted?'

'Of course it does.' Kadir's clipped moustache seemed to be delaying the words. 'How many tonnes are here? We're sitting on our hands at home anyway. What's the problem with throwing a couple of shovelfuls?'

'Uncle Kadir, please don't, for God's sake. There is so much on this island: houses, trees, soil. This lot here's hardly worth mentioning!'

'Of course it is. Every little helps. And it's not sinking that bad yet. It may rise again once we've got rid of this lot, who knows?'

'Let's say it may. Two helicopters flew over the clouds just this morning. There'll be no cloud tomorrow, or the day after. They will see us. Help will come. You think the island can't hold out for a couple more days?'

'Only Allah knows. He can make it float, and He can make it sink.'

'Sooo… if He can make it sink, you're wasting your time.'

Kadir's eyebrows rose. 'Noooo. First precaution, then resignation.'

'Words fail me.' Simmering, Halil turned to Cemal. 'You're going to carry on with this pointless thing, along with your father-in-law?' Cemal's hesitation made him lose his temper. 'Carry on, lad. Don't you dare leave the flock in case the wolf gets you!' Spinning angrily on his heels, Halil dived back into the street he had come from, chuntering aloud all the while. 'Looking for a single sane man in the whole of Andalıç!'

As the rain started to come down harder, it got darker and darker. Cemal looked at Hakkı in a silent plea for a decision.

'Gentlemen,' said Hakkı, rising to his feet, 'You'll all get sick if you carry on for much longer in this rain. Don't worry, the island won't sink in one night. You can carry on tomorrow where you'd left off. Go home and get changed. And it's nearly evening, anyway.'

As if this was what they had been waiting for, the small crowd dispersed without complaint.

Cemal hastened through the darkening streets in the soft rain, which seeped into every crack, nook and cranny. His body felt cold after that rest. The wet shirt was sticking to the middle of his chilly back and the sleeves, to his arms. He was dragging himself despite the exhaustion, which hampered the movement of his aching muscles. The damp, muddy trousers clung to his calves as his eyelashes weighed down by tiny droplets fell over eyes struggling to see in the twilight. But he knew these streets well enough to find his way blindfolded. Left to his feet, they'd have covered Andalıç from one end to the other. All the same, when he halted before a house he'd never entered before and lifted his clenched hand, he hesitated for several seconds, maintaining those few inches between knocking on the door and himself.

The whole island was in the grip of a silent and gentle drizzle, a mere whisper, broken only by the irregular patter of drops falling from the roofs, eaves, and corners of wet objects.

As he stood in the silence of the town behind him and the house in front, a huge drop broke from the eaves and went down the back of his neck. He shivered. He was about to relax that fist and draw it back before he surprised himself with the force he rapped on the door. The rain drowned out the noise that had sounded so loud to him. Fists at his sides, he waited for the approach of the woman's silhouette in the frosted glass. The glass behind the iron grille of the old door opened a crack. Immediately below the suspicious single eye, the lips drawing back enough to reveal the teeth flashing in the yellow light. Shutting the peep window swiftly, Cemile opened the heavy door.

'I knew you'd come in the end.'

Another drop rolled down Cemal's back, but he didn't move even when Cemile drew back.

'Come inside, why don't you?'

'No. I'm just going to say a couple of things and go away, anyway.'

That weird smile kept playing on Cemile's face. 'You're wet. It's raining harder too. You can't just stand at the door like this. The neighbours…'

Hesitating a little, glancing left and right, Cemal took a reluctant step inside. The door shut, leaving them a hair's breadth apart in the narrow vestibule. A gas lamp on a high side table between two carved armchairs cast a powerful light onto the stained glass in the double wing doors opening to the hall, spreading the colours on the whitewashed walls. Cemal leant back against the wall to distance himself as much as possible and perhaps even draw a little strength; light filtered by a green pane of glass transformed his angry face into a restless ghost running away from the torments of the other world. Cemile took a step back too, and the whites of her eyes shone scarlet. Her right cheek was marked in thick veins by the pattern in the red glass. She looked away from the wild green glints in Cemal's dark, interrogating, judging and executing eyes and to his shirt turning transparent where it clung to his body. A long muscle from the left shoulder to the elbow, the right nipple, a soft curve like a caress right over the belly button.

'Don't stare at me like that.' Cemal's voice was more terrible than his eyes.

Cemile protested. 'Why not?' She knew very well she'd come to no harm. 'Can't I fall in love? I've been wanting you ever since I first laid eyes on you at the pavyon.'

'You were too drunk to see the tip of your own nose. Anyway, that's sick. You're mad, you are.'

'Yes, I'm mad about you. 'Ere, I swear: my name's not Cemile if I die without shagging you once. You'll tire of that cold bitch one day.' She moved her finger on the glass as if writing something down.

'You really are a maniac.' His anger was replaced by his frustration with silliness. He leant his wet head back against the stone wall. Its chill passed through his wet shirt and reached his lungs. 'I don't want you; even if we weren't siblings.'

'No problem. You don't have to. So long as I want you.' The patterns in the red glass swept over her face like a blazing fire when she moved.

'Stay away! Get back!'

The only sound was the bare noise of the drops falling onto the stone steps from the eaves. Cemal took a deep, angry breath. 'What's Zaim doing with the Commissioner?'

'Ah! That's why you've come.' A scoff to suppress her disappointment. 'How do you know about that?'

'Never you mind. Tell me what they're up to.'

'What could they be up to?' Leaning back against the wall again, Cemile spoke in an unconvincing tone. Not even irritation could warm her. 'He'd been on my tail. So I told Abdurrahman Bey. He had him run in, a word in his ear, like. That's all.'

'You're well shot of him then. Good.' Bowing his head, he laughed. 'He was going to stab me the other night, but that's my business.'

'Bastard! Don't you worry...'

Just then a key was heard turning in the lock. A potbellied man squeezed through the door that wouldn't open fully with Cemile in the way. The thick eyebrows frowning in the purple light falling on his bald head turned towards Cemal, who was close enough for their elbows to touch. The eyes flanking the large, flat nose squinted. Cemile intervened before he could open his mouth.

'My big brother.' The jealous hatred on Abdurrahman's face thinned out into an ordinary suspicion.

'I'd been wanting to introduce the two of you all this time. Good, I'm glad.'

The two men shook hands ponderously in the uneasy narrow vestibule.

'I insisted so much, but he won't come in.'

Staring at Cemal in an indecipherable silence, Abdurrahman was trying to figure out his intentions, character, and what he was doing there. He peered at Cemile's innocence under the white light, now that she had moved aside by a step when he had come in. Still trying to detect any possible lies, he bent down to unlace his shoes.

'I'll make tracks if I may. I'd only dropped in to see if Cemile needed anything.'

Abdurrahman raised his protruding eyes as if looking down, even though he was squatting. 'Thank Allah we're here. She won't need nothing no more.'

'Sure, absolutely. Good evening.'

As the door shut behind him and a drop falling from the eaves hit the tip of his nose, he heard the sound of a slap. Followed by a growl. 'Abi or no abi; I'm not putting up...'

Heading back to Turkey in the moderate south-westerly, which had been blowing for the past two days, Andalıç left the shipping lanes once again, returning to that deserted void in the middle of the Aegean in grey anticipation, shock and despair. Leaden waves nudged the island under the overcast sky; breaching its own limit, the curious sea climbed onto the land millimetre by millimetre. Clutching their ration cards, the townsfolk waited for hours in long queues. A law enforcement agency comprising policemen, community constables and some of the youngsters operated in flawless discipline, intervening instantly in any brawls that might flare up, leading away anyone complaining about the meagreness of the rations, and squaring up to anyone expressing loud objections to any new measure. There didn't seem to be anyone carrying an ounce of spare fat as a result of this enforced diet in this land of short, plump people. They were on starvation rations, for which they counted their blessings. They all did whatever the announcements said, queued, threw rubbish into the sea, hauled rubble, and never objected. Exhausted with heavy labour and half-starved, they were too weak to even glance at the horizon for entire days. Anticipation dwindled and slowly died; the situation overtook and overpowered everything.

ATTENTION, ATTENTION. EVERY MALE IN THE TOWN IS ASKED TO ATTEND FRIDAY PRAYERS.

'Cemal, come on, son. Take a sip. Look, we got milk today. I made you sweet porridge; here, nice and warm. Come on, son.' Hakkı's spoon fails to hit Cemal's mouth.

Cemal can't open his eyes. His ears buckle sounds, glue them together, stack them up. He is sweating. The back of his neck, his neck, armpits, then his whole body suddenly breaks out in a downpour. He doesn't know what the voice is saying, nor whom it belongs to. He wants to open his eyes. Doesn't know he does. Shivers, clammy under the thick duvet. His teeth chattering.

'Oh, Cemal. You're burning up, son. What was the point of strolling in the rain in the evening!'

Suddenly he feels unbearably hot. Thrashes about. Flings away the duvet with a single move of his weak arm.

'Don't, son. You're covered in sweat, anyway. You'll catch an even worse cold.' Hakkı stumbles as he bends down to retrieve the duvet.

He feels a slightly cooler weight placed on him again. He struggles with it, a terrible sense of being smothered. He shoves it away. Down to his waist.

'I've fetched the doctor, Uncle Hakkı. Once he's examined him, we'll go get the meds. That will lower the fever straightaway.'

'I hope so, girl, I hope so.'

He still can't make out the words, but there is something in this voice that soothes him, that penetrates. Then a cold metal wanders on his chest. He is dragged up by the arms. The cold metal goes to his back. The cool thing they place between his teeth warms up at once on his tongue. He wants to spit it out.

'It's over forty. Prepare a cool compress straightaway. I'll give him an injection.'

Something stings at the top of his hip. He wants to shake, but is held down. When he is released, he thrashes about again feverishly.

'You never said he was so poorly, Uncle Hakkı,' says a worried voice.

The injection and the worry prise open Cemal's eyelids.

'Sssa …'

'Yes, sweetheart?'

Squeezing the excess into a small bowl, Saliha spreads a damp handkerchief on his forehead. Rubs his joints and groin with cool cloths. Changes his underwear, her cool hands on his body. Lays a muslin square on his back. The scent of fresh linen replaces the sour reek of sick man. He comes around and sees medicines at his bedside. A hand stroking his hair. Raising his upper back with pillows. Feeding him warm spicy tomato soup, spoon by spoon. Laying a thin blanket over him when the fever returns and bringing the duvet when his teeth begin to chatter. Opening the windows frequently to keep the room fresh. A sweet voice reading him a novel.

'You've lost a lot of weight.'

'Everyone has. You, too, Cemal. Don't tell me you like 'em plump?'

'No, but don't you get sick now. Don't come that close.'

'Don't you worry. Just get better as soon as you can.'

'Still got morning sickness?'

'Not as bad as you, though. You've not kept anything down.'

'Have you had something to eat?'

'Of course I have. Can't go round hungry.'

He drifts off before coming round again to the kindness beside him.

'Where's Hakkı?'

'Gone to Friday prayers.'

'Good God! Hakkı? Prayers?'

'They came to the door to fetch him.'

'Who did?'

'The neighbourhood lads. Erkan and that.'

'Whatever for?'

'Never you mind now. Just sleep and rest a while.'

Reeling at the smell of medicine on top of his urine and sweat, he lowers his numb back onto the bed once more. An aching exhaustion renders all his joints immobile wherever they're laid down. The body enervated by the incarceration that is illness longs to make sudden movements. He feels something heavy on his chest. Opening his eyes, he sees a large tortoiseshell cat. It's bigger than his chest, reaching all the way down to his stomach. It grows to the size of a dog, no, a donkey, pressing him down.

'Shoo! Shoo!'

'What is it, Cemal? Do you want something?' Saliha's voice, right beside his ear.

'Cat. Get the cat off me.'

'What cat? There's no cat here, Cemal.'

'On my chest. On… me. Really heavy.'

'All right, sweetheart, I'll take it away now.'

The fever slowly regains its hold, until the next dose of medicine, refusing to be gouged out. It releases nightmares into his mind to stoke the fire.

'Awful, staring like that, without seeing.' His ears catch this murmur barely louder than a sigh. His eyes begin to see half an hour after another pill he must have swallowed.

'Hakkı?'

'Here I am, son, here.'

'Why'd ya go to Friday?'

'They came for me, so I went.'

'And?'

'Just regular Friday prayers. Prayers, sermon.'

As soon as Cemal's eyes turn towards a glass of water, the glass comes to his lips.

'What does the imam say?'

'I don't know. How can you remember all that stuff?' Hakkı stands at the foot of the bed, looking at Saliha, who sits beside Cemal. 'That obeisance is a great virtue, crucial at times like these, the soil of the motherland is sacred, and on and on. My father died in the War of Liberation. Do these people have any idea what the "soil of the motherland" even means? Anyway.'

Another pillow slid under Cemal's head, 'What else?'

'That the south-westerly is blowing. That the island's changed course, and we're returning to our country. That so long as the wind stays, we'll be back within a fortnight. That we have enough water and food. That we'd be better off not signalling. As if the waters were teeming with planes and ships. Where the heck does all the shipping go, anyway?'

19

The warm breath of the south-westerly carries a whiff of spirit to breakfast tables. Purple words in a neat hand on straw paper. They have entered houses under doors and through open windows; they swing like sticky-out ears or long tongues, pinned on doors they have failed to slip through. Those that fail to cling on are dragged along streets to tangle between the feet of winded hill climbers and fuming bread queuers. The warm caress of the south-westerly on their hair seems to be whispering into their ears; quiet murmurs everywhere. Like the chatter of tiny animals hiding in corners. The sheets rustle softly in the damp air and dance, dropping and rising as directed by the capricious wind. Jülide's neat handwriting demands to be seen. Hundreds of copies from an old spirit duplicator.

> IT HAS BEEN REVEALED THAT THE PERSONAGES WHO HAVE TAKEN OVER THE CARE HOME ARE EXEMPT FROM RATION CARDS. THE DIGNITARIES OF OUR TOWN CAN OBTAIN AS MUCH FOOD AND DRINK AS THEY LIKE, WHENEVER THEY LIKE, WITH A SINGLE WORD. IT'S TIME TO SAY STOP TO THIS INEQUITY. CITIZENS ARE KEPT IN THE DARK ABOUT THE PROLIFIC QUANTITIES OF FROZEN MEAT AND VEGETABLE STOCKS IN THE COLD STORAGE UNIT NEXT TO THE COACH GARAGE. ENOUGH OF THIS UNQUESTIONING OBEDIENCE. CLAIM YOUR RIGHTS.

The eyes behind the mirrored windows of the Care Home see everything. Binoculars scan the faces of the public, faces astonished by the duplication papers. They could almost be making the writing out too.

At any rate, sheets collected from the streets are laid out on desks.

The wind ferments anger throughout Andalıç. The evaporating spirit could burst into flame at any moment. Scrawny cats and dogs skitter away. Stomachs grumble louder as acid levels rise. The grumbles don't rise all the way up to the Care Home, but the frowning eyebrows of the men slamming their doors and making for the coffee houses are clearly visible.

TO THE ATTENTION OF OUR DEAR COMMUNITY: DUE TO HYGIENE INSPECTIONS, ALL COFFEE HOUSES WILL BE CLOSED TODAY.

The announcements spread in waves on a tail wind of rising anger. A few burly youths prevent anyone from entering the coffee houses. Minor brawls keep erupting. Men turned away unceremoniously gather under the statue of Atatürk in the town square. They talk with sweeping gestures. In loud, excited voices. Fingers flying in the air point at the Care Home. Next, attention turns to the cold storage unit. The crowd grows.

ATTENTION, ATTENTION! THE NOTICES DISTRIBUTED IN THE MORNING ARE FULL OF LIES. DISPERSE AT ONCE. ANYONE WHO REFUSES WILL BE KEPT UNDER LOCK AND KEY UNTIL WE RETURN TO OUR COUNTRY. BACK HOME AT ONCE!

A restless stir seems to quiet mounting grumbles. Over the stillness rise several voices. They lead the crowd towards the coach station. Rumbling like a landslide from the depths. Few people appear to be speaking. The intimidating sound of this great total comprises the muffled patter of thousands of feet, the inaudible squeak of moving joints, the gentle ruffle of trouser hems and shirtsleeves, and the warm whistle of breaths quickening with movement. This colossal male animal – with just a sprinkling of women – covers the corniche, stalked by the birds of prey above. Apex predators know they need to split the herd.

Halil is at the forefront. He raises his booming teacher's voice to eliminate any hesitation. Muzaffer at his shoulder, Rahmi a few rows back. Marching. Some hands still clutching the duplication papers with purple lettering. Countless heads rise when the cold storage unit comes into view. Primed and ready to attack and be attacked, fear deep inside. Twenty or twenty-five armed men outside the iron doors of the cold air store.

ATTENTION, ATTENTION! BACK HOME AT ONCE! OUR FORCES HAVE ORDERS TO SHOOT. NO DISOBEDIENCE WILL BE ALLOWED. ANYONE DISRUPTING PUBLIC ORDER WILL FACE THE MOST SEVERE OF PUNISHMENTS.

The crowd slowly pours into the square by the coach station from the road. Confronting the armed men. Its fragmented, hesitant purpose wavers before the steel-reinforced resolve of the handful of henchmen opposite. A determined wait wavering between rumbling stomachs and the fear for life. Stubborn gazes stretching out from bodies nailed to the spot. A few regretful eyes in the crowd look for a retreat. The resistance to disbanding is very feeble.

The mirrored windows of the Care Home see this wish to disband, this restless stirring, and the shakiness of this impromptu rebellion pinned together by male pride.

ATTENTION, ATTENTION! THE DUPLICATIONS DISTRIBUTED THIS MORNING BY SOME EVIL FORCES INTENT ON SOWING SEDITION DO NOT REFLECT REALITY. THEY ARE NOTHING MORE THAN FABRICATIONS. PLEASE RETURN TO YOUR HOMES FOR THE SALVATION OF OUR TOWN.

They are trying to partition the common will by exploiting the weak sections of the seemingly endless ice floe that is the crowd.

'No!' Halil's robust voice rises before the loudspeaker has stopped crackling. 'If the claims are spurious, open the doors and we'll see what's inside. We'll go away if there's no food.'

A roar goes all the way to the rear, 'Open the doors!' Growing louder. 'Open the doors, open the doors!' Angry chests square up, the seams no longer visible. The ranks grow tighter, fists are clenched. 'Open the doors!'

'Next we'll check the kitchens of these people perching over our heads!'

'Open the doors!'

Thousands of feet take a couple steps behind Halil. A few of the youngsters at the doors pale, raised guns trembling in their hands. Sneaking glances at their mates' tense faces, they adopt gauche emulations of scary expressions. The order, which knows it would be destroyed the moment it allowed disorder, readies itself to spill blood, drawing strength from the shiny eyes of the Care Home at its back.

ATTENTION, ATTENTION! OUR FORCES HAVE ORDERS TO SHOOT. BACK HOME AT ONCE!

Unconvinced that unfairness in this game would warrant spilling blood, the crowd remains stubborn, equally unwilling to be crushed so blatantly. It does not disperse.

The elderly, the women and the children in every house in Andalıç are all ears. Some are outside their doors, other pray indoors. Those unable to spill into the battleground convert their inertia into an accusation. Some swear at the Mayor, who is personally reading out the announcements; others, at the Commissioner, who has armed the kids; yet another group berate their own foolish husbands, sons and daughters. They're cracking their fingers, chewing their nails and repeatedly undoing and retying their kerchiefs. Sweating blood, Cemal is trying to push away the bed that has grasped him. Saliha and Hakkı watch him in growing helplessness. Jülide goes to the door, puts her shoes on, but turns back at the gate, goes back in again, goes out again, goes back in again. At long last, she decides to leave, unsure quite what good it would do. Every lethargic person in Andalıç counts the seconds under the weight of this sudden burst of peril.

ATTENTION! FINAL WARNING! DISPERSE AT ONCE!

There was total silence outside the storage unit when rounds were loaded into the barrels. The situation, which had got out of hand, surpassing every individual, resigned itself to an oppressive common logic, giving Andalıç a nightmare reality.

'What's that rifle doing in your hand, Erkan?' yelled Halil. The blanched lad was trembling like a leaf. 'I'm your teacher. Are you going to shoot me? There are your neighbours and relations here.'

'Don't get closer, sir. We'll shoot,' screeched Erkan guiltily.

'Why?'

'We have orders, sir.'

'So what? Are you a soldier or a policeman? Who's giving the order? On whose authority?'

A wave moved over the crowd to the rear. A low growl travelled all the way to the back rows, losing volume, and eventually fizzling out. Halil took one more step. Muzaffer moved along with him, but the others stayed where they were.

'Don't come, sir. We have orders.'

'What are you protecting if there's nothing inside? Let us go in.'

A low grumble started again as the crowd's suspicions rose. 'Open the door, open the door.'

Halil's voice drowned out the rest. 'What right do they have to lord it over us? We're only here temporarily. How do they assume the right to take all these decisions and arm people?'

A middle-aged man to the right of Erkan raised his voice. 'We elected the Mayor. Think we should have no ruler? We need government until help comes.'

Somewhat accustomed to the presence of weapons, the crowd seemed to relax now that things had moved to talking.

'Fine, but that wasn't under these conditions. Now we're drifting in the middle of the sea. What's with all these tough measures and pointless restrictions? We used to be part of the Republic of Turkey. What are we now, where are we?'

His interlocutor, one of Andalıç's top solicitors, yelled angrily. 'We're still part of the Republic of Turkey. Nothing's changed. And this is the soil of the motherland. We'll defend it until the last drop of our blood.'

Halil protested. 'So what are you defending the storage unit from? What are we, the enemy? These people are hungry. And food is hidden from them. Why is this food stashed away? Who benefits?'

'It's stored for the good of the public. For hard times. Think you know better than the administrators?'

'Is there a harder time than this?'

Hesitation had changed sides. The hawk eyes in the Care Home noticed the fingers relaxing on their triggers. The crowd took a couple of steps towards Halil.

'You're inciting the public to rebellion. You're weakening authority with your spurious allegations. You're turning your nose up at the elements representing our state. I'll take you down if you take one more step,' said the solicitor with the thinning head and sunken eyes.

There was only about ten or fifteen metres between them. The south-westerly swept the quick, deep breaths of the crowd.

Halil took a few more steps. 'Let the public share the food. Better have no authority than such people in charge. Open the door.'

Having detected the flagging will of the armed men, the demonstrators were now up in arms. Shouting, 'To the door! To the door!' they put all their force behind Halil. Thousands of voices rumbled through Andalıç, recognisable as the sound of the crowd. Riding this bow wave, equipped with a greater power than all the weapons in the world, and feeling the wind through his hair, Halil pressed on. He ignored the crackle of the loudspeakers. He opened up like floodgates for the rectitude pooling behind him. Elated by the will on show, he never heard the command, 'Fire!' Even though the footsteps behind him had fallen silent, he continued to walk. One single shot rang out when he was only a few metres away from the door. Then a few others at random. Stopped mid-movement as if he had slammed against a wall, Halil heard the sound of running as he fell. Felt the touch of two friendly hands grabbing him under the arms. His knees buckled under the unfamiliar searing, wet ache in his chest. His astonished eyes slipped up skywards. The last thing he saw was Muzaffer's wild eyes.

Jülide had been sheltering in a doorway in a side street as she waited for the scattering crowd to pass. Running towards the storage unit, she had to jump over the blood pouring from the head of a boy she knew from school. On the other side of the square, a man clutching his belly was screaming. She sank next to Muzaffer, whose face was smeared with blood as she closed Halil's eyes, then started rocking, still unable to release sobs.

With icy self-constraint Muzaffer said, 'Give me a hand, Jülide; let's not leave him here, not at their mercy. Let's take Halil away.' Jülide raised her head, hoping for help. She would have welcomed the approach even of Erkan, until she spotted the slack rifle he was holding clumsily. Just for one brief moment, she lamented Muzaffer's wasted tenacity above all. She grabbed Halil's legs with all her strength, as if she could lift him and take him away at once.

'Him ... was it you who...'

'Please let her go!' Erkan was trying to stop a middle-aged man who was aiming at them. 'Wait, Sulhi Abi. That's my betrothed.'

Jülide's venomous voice hissed in her throat. 'Whose betrothed? Whose?'

'Cut it out, Jülide. Cut it out. Not now. Let's carry Mr Halil,' said Erkan nervously.

A blood-curdling calm voice. Muzaffer's voice. 'Don't you dare lay a hand on him.' With Jülide's help, she shouldered Halil in a fireman's lift learnt a long time ago. 'Stay back Sulhi. Enough.' Ignoring the warm blood trickling over her waist and down her leg, she set off for the hospital with a strength unexpected from her petite frame.

Every once in a while, menacing footsteps came from dark streets now forbidden to humans. Eyes peering between curtains once they retreated saw nothing more than dark backs. There was no sound from inside other than the occasional whisper. The gardens were deserted. A conclusive clump of bullets sticking somewhere in the descending darkness. A damp chill seeping into houses from every gap, hole and crack, despite the warm wind. As the gibbous moon released its ominous silvery light, the doors of east-facing houses clawed their way out of the darkness. The doors became visible in sharp outline, vulnerable to knocks at any given moment. The windows shut tight. All breaths held and all ears pricked whenever the toilet door squeaked a little longer, the candle went out when it was carried a little faster, and a frog in the throat caused a loud cough. Constantly on tiptoe, trying to identify the south-westerly amongst the other sounds. Andalıç was shivering in the chill of its own fear in the warm wind. In the cool breath of its own gloom, its own defeat, and its own bewilderment.

Only the Care Home was ablaze with light. The noise of the generator spilled down the slopes, growing fainter as it did so. Filling the ears of the folks sitting in silence at home. Not a single human silhouette showed behind the illuminated windows of this enormous, this dazzling edifice, which looked like something from another world.

Once the street was clear of all footsteps, Jülide went into the garden with a bottle of paraffin and Muzaffer's bloodied clothing. Her face as serene as a sleepwalker, she picked up the rusty tin standing by the coal cellar. Dogs were howling in a distant neighbourhood. She dropped the clothes into the tin, poured the oil over it and struck a match. The sudden flare licked her face. Singed the ends of her hair, eyelashes and eyebrows. Ever rounder, the moon watched the garden where harsh shadows played on the walls. Pausing to think, she ran inside and returned grabbing the big, heavy dressmaking scissors. Muzaffer's sweat, Halil's blood and the essence of trees that had lived hundreds of years ago were all burning with a bluish flame. She snipped off one of the braids reaching down to her waist first, then the other. Threw them into the tin. The smell of burning hair spread into the whole garden. Neighbours' curtains twitched suspiciously.

An orange light played on her pale face. Her eyes looked purple. Against a wild backdrop of shadow play, she lifted her arms as if she would take flight, and then turned her palms up in a fluid move. Her long, slender, white hands filled with cold moonlight. The backs of her hands were burning bright scarlet. She lifted her gaze from the fire to the moon. Her eyes were now ice blue. She brought her chilled palms close enough to the fire to burn.

'Serene moon, mighty moon, who commands all the liquids in the world,' she murmured, 'Your cold cape on my back. Hot fire, mighty fire, who turns all things to ashes. Your apron before me.' She didn't know where these words came from. She was soaring on the insanity she had found within. A strange familiarity marked this thing she was doing. 'Muzaffer Abla's sweat, cold power; Mr Halil's blood. Hot power. Come to me.' Deeply breathing in the smoke, she felt her lungs burn, but didn't cough. 'I need power.' She felt something growing stronger inside. A fresh gust of wind hurled the smell of her burning hair over the town's streets. The dying fire was mostly embers now. Removing her slippers to stand in bare feet, she felt the sky and the soil fill her momentarily, the cold and the heat combining inside to rouse a dormant something. Shivered with pain and pleasure for a very brief, very long moment during which she forgot everything, then murmured, staring at the embers. 'If everything consists of nothing but strength, defeat is inevitable. Frailty also deserves authority.'

Just then she sensed another presence in the garden. Her ears twitched at the tiny clink coming from behind her, but she didn't turn her head. Something approached slowly and slunk into the shadow of the jasmine bush. Something big. Jülide failed to find any fear inside. She closed the lid over the tin. Her white face, blue shadows under her eyes, swung at the jasmine, where a few blooms still clung. A scared sigh came from behind the bush, then Rahmi's voice.

'Jülide, what the heck are you doing? Are you all right?'

Muzaffer was dozing on the sofa when they went in. Her weary breath rose and fell in the flickering light of the stub, which was all that remained of the candle. Rahmi didn't want to wake her at first, but then pulled himself together and nudged her gently. Muzaffer sprang up at once.

'What's the matter?'

'Muzaffer Abla, you need to hide.'

Jülide's face, now a daunting, calm mask, scanned the room, dismissing all emergencies.

'What on earth for?'

'There's a bloke. A gunman. He's going to kill you. He's been commissioned.'

Her sense of reality still shattered after the day's events, Muzaffer smiled at him.

'Zeliha told me.'

'Who's Zeliha?'

'The Commissioner's wife,' said Jülide with an alarming clarity in her voice, a response Rahmi found perfectly normal after the scene he had witnessed in the garden.

'Yes. She heard her husband talking to some bloke. From the crack in the door. He wasn't from around here. Wore a black suit. The Commissioner said, "Deal with it and I'll forget your attitude." The bloke looked like a nasty piece of work.'

Muzaffer was in a long-sleeved flannel nightgown, and had covered her hair with a white muslin kerchief after a bath. She glanced at her big watch. It was close to one.

'Have you seen Zeliha in your dream at this hour, or am I dreaming?'

'No, Muzaffer Abla. Our gardens adjoin. I've known her for a long time. She came over to warn me after her husband fell asleep.'

'Remarkable. I've never met her in my life. Why would she risk herself to save me?'

Looking at the woman who was only recognisable by her voice, her eyes squinting without the specs, her thin lips drawn over her teeth, sitting like an elderly auntie, Rahmi bowed his head. 'You want jam on it? She's done a kindness.'

Despite her grief, Muzaffer gave a knowing laugh, which brought a refreshing sense of familiarity into the room.

'Like we didn't know about your long-term love.'

Rahmi's crimson blush went unnoticed in the feeble light.

'We know what her husband doesn't. We're journalists, we are.'

'At least you're like your usual self, Muzaffer Abla. Wish this lass would look like herself, though.'

'No one's like themselves in such times.' Her sorrowful eyes slipped over Jülide on their way to the window… and stopped halfway.

'Hold up that candle to her, Rahmi.' The candlelight fell on Jülide's face. 'What have you done to your hair, lass?'

'That's what I was trying to tell you, Muzaffer Abla. In the garden…' He decided to keep what he had seen to himself. 'I once worked as an apprentice in a barber. I'll tidy it up if you like.'

Wrapping a bedsheet around Jülide's neck then and there, he tried to revive his childhood skills in candlelight. Dark blonde hair scattered over the floor like black insects. All that was heard was Rahmi's scissors. 'Wish I could trim my son's hair like this.'

'Find yourself a single woman and make one then.' Muzaffer's voice was regaining its customary edge.

'Don't say that, Muzaffer Abla. When you fall in love…'

Putting the final touches, he asked, 'How do you like it?' then drew back with the pleasant pride of an artisan. He caught sight of himself in the rusty mirror, along with Muzaffer sitting like a grandma on the sofa, watching this haircut as if she were at the theatre, and Jülide sitting with a strange mask on her face, as calm as though she had attained enlightenment. 'God give me strength! Muzaffer Abla, what the bloody hell are we doing here? You have to run away and hide. Maybe I should, too. Where do you hide in this island – with no room to swing a cat? What do you eat and drink? Everything's rationed. Are we going to wait for this bastard to come and kill us?'

Muzaffer gave him a look that suggested she might happily hand over her neck if there was a knock on the door and her executioner walked in.

'I know somewhere you can hide,' said Jülide, folding the sheet she had shaken out. 'Moon shadows are dark. Darker than the night itself. Let's go now. You go back home, Rahmi Abi. Come to me if you have to hide.'

20

A metallic morning ezan emanating from the loudspeakers blasted Andalıç awake from a fitful sleep. The exhaustion of fear cutting into their bodies. The soft south-westerly had dropped completely. Harder, damper, cooler beds turned out their sleepers. Breakfast was eaten listening to the silence of the streets, chewing mouths pausing to prick up ears at the faintest snap. A constant palpitation in hearts. Brighter in the sunlight streaming through the windows, untroubled by new incidents, the sense of security grew. The fixedness, immobility and demands of home life gently claimed the day. Standing at doors and windows and in gardens, people watched the prohibition on the streets. It was time to go out for bread, but the bakeries had yet to release their mouth-watering smells into the morning. The night-time patrols were nowhere to be seen. One or two doors opened tentatively. Clutching ration cards, heads of families tested the waters. They had barely taken a few steps when the loudspeakers crackled again.

THE CURFEW IS STILL IN FORCE. PLEASE GO HOME!

Anyone venturing out rushed back, gasping for breath, as if they had got away after a long chase. Eyes like saucers wandered over the dread dominating the interior. Hearts that had leapt up into mouths relaxed like weary fists. The throbbing in the streets briefly seemed to be drowning out the silence. Then the minutes grew longer and longer in an imperceptible threat. Next, the streets echoed with a horde of footsteps and fists pounding on doors. Someone was frogmarched away. Then silence again.

Muzaffer's door was the first to be pounded in the whole of Andalıç. Jülide, who had been listening to every single sound, wasn't in the least bit afraid. She opened the door, expressionless, marble white cheeks crossed by fine blue veins. Shoving her aside, six men crowded in. She stood at the door, waiting for the noisy scrambling to cease.

'Where's that bitch called Muzaffer?'

'I don't know.'

'Don't you live here?' asked the solicitor, the first person to fire in the square the day before.

'I'm a guest.'

'Then you'll know where she is.'

'She left last night without saying anything.'

'If you know where she is, and refusing to cooperate…' He would gladly crush Jülide's silence to dig out the bones of fear from underneath. 'Not enough room to swing a cat on the island, anyways. Where's she gone to hide?' His teeth gleamed cheese yellow under the crescent moustache. 'And we know how to make you talk if we can't find her, anyhow.' He turned his head, 'Erkan, this is your intended, right? You're to keep her in your sight. You're done for if she disappears.'

Suppressing his delight, Erkan yelled, 'Yes, Sir!'

He'd been staring at Jülide's hair since coming in, but held his tongue until the others left. 'Just as well he picked me. If he'd left someone else …'

Perched on the arm of the chair, Jülide had fixed her eyes on the Indian summer day in the garden. The only sound in the sitting room was the faint ticking of the battery clock counting the seconds. Erkan sat down on the sofa, nervously rubbing his hands. He made a move to get up and come closer to Jülide as soon as he had sat down, but her exclusion zone was so intense that he retreated back to the sofa. He stared again at her hedgehog hair framing the porcelain face. 'What happened to your hair? It was so nice. You look like a boy now.' The eyes, ice blue in this light, didn't deign to look at him, not even to halt him in his tracks.

'Why'd ya have it cut off?' He fidgeted, feeling awkward at doing all the talking. The sofa creaked. Jülide sat unmoving, still staring at the garden. She thought *I cut my hair off because that's where my fear lived,* pleased he'd never know why.

Unnerved by the tangible, chilly silence growing between them, Erkan launched into what was clearly a long-rehearsed speech. 'I know you're cross with me but I still love you very much. You're always on my mind. I'm always thinking of you.' He paused, blushing all the way up to his ears. Still ignored, he bowed his head and continued, 'I know I've got some traits you're not keen on. But I don't think I'm that bad. I may be a little possessive, but that's only natural. A man is jealous when it comes to his woman.' She recoiled and he thought he'd finally got through. 'You don't know, but all men are the same. They are jealous lovers. You'll get used to it. Enjoy it, even. Some women even like getting a beating by their husband.' Jülide scoffed. 'No, no, I'd never raise a hand against you. I was just saying.'

Cringing at his clumsy choice of example, Erkan played his last trump card. 'I love you. I want you to be my wife. Now your grandma's dead, you're stone broke. We can live with my parents until I do my national service. Then we'll have our own home and raise a family. I might even be transferred to a big team.'

Jülide turned a stony face towards him with abnormally cold eyes. 'No. I refuse. I don't love you. If you're my warden, then act like one. Keep an eye on me, that's all.' She went to the kitchen, leaving him to swelling anger and frustration, but she wasn't left alone for long.

'I said I love you. Doesn't this mean something?'

'No, it doesn't.'

'You used to love me.'

'Used to.'

The violence he was struggling to control was fast breaking away from the ethical decision centre of his brain: 'You can't refuse me.'

'How come?'

'Because… because… You're either mine, or belong to the earth. I won't let you go to anyone else.'

Jülide stared at his strength unfazed, at the clenched fists, swollen muscles and throbbing veins on his neck.

'I don't belong to anyone. I shall marry whomever I like. And if I so choose, I'll never marry at all.'

'No!' Amplified by the tiled walls, Erkan's howl exploded in the middle of the kitchen. 'You *will* be mine. You're mine, no two ways about it. I can't do without you. You *will* marry me.'

Grasping a slender wrist, he dragged her towards the bedroom. Jülide wondered how she could defend herself as she was knocked against the kitchen doorjamb and corridor walls. No point in expending her resistance at once by thrashing about, by engaging in a power game she was certain to lose.

Erkan flung her onto the bed. Her wrist was beginning to bruise. Instead of cowering, she had to present her body on a tray like a delicious dish. She listened to the bedhead slamming against the wall as her clothes were removed one by one. She had no energy to waste on modesty. She thought of weakness and power. Of how it was easier to destroy power than to resist it. Unashamed by her nakedness, her reclining pale beauty or fragile femininity, she pulled a pillow under her head. With absolute indifference, as though she had been doing this for years instead of for the first time ever, she spread her legs.

Flattered by this display of submission, Erkan's weight rose. He walked round the bed to first feast his eyes on the wonderful proportions and the skin covering them like the haze of fresh milk. Awed by the charms laid before him so unexpectedly, his hands hastened to his zip. To the spot where Jülide's steely ice blue eyes had been staring for seconds on end. He released his penis from the constraint of his trousers. Instantly recognising stiffness as the greatest weakness of this thing she'd seen for the first time, Jülide summoned all the soft things in the world. Summer breezes, placid lakes, the softness of air and water. The softness of feathers, of silk, cotton, satin, of everything that comforted, cuddled and indulged, and even the softness of certain gazes, words and colours… She commanded his erection to relax, to be confused, and to surrender: it worked. Erkan, who'd progressed from staring to gobbling her skin up like a greedy child, hesitated between her legs. His mouth and hands struggled for a while to perform the final move to claim his conquest, but he failed to rise above Jülide's icy stare and marble cold body. He was mortified. His passion had been doused by the shame of the inner voice screaming *Wrong! So wrong!* Shamed by his own masculinity and shamed by his humanity at the same time.

As soon as he had gathered his clothes and slunk away, Jülide blushed all the way to the slit between her legs. Her eyes melted into a soft green. All her power was spent, her body and mind enslaved by the softness of vulnerability. Pulling the bed cover over herself, she gently hugged the slenderness of her naked body. Silent tears finally fell onto the pillow, the tears held back all this time since her grandma died, Halil was shot, Muzaffer escaped, she was left all alone in this huge house, and had to open the door to a rabble all by herself. She got up and locked the door. On her way back, she caught sight of herself in the mirror: skinny waist, wrists and knees, narrow ribcage, breasts fresh out of childhood, mere buds, and her womanness concealed, barely discernible. She took pity on her own body as if it were a tapering candle, bending this way and that as it burned. She took pity on the femininity yet to settle on her organs, and on her childhood that had flown away unappreciated. She missed the father she'd barely known. Missed being protected, watched and fussed over. Not having to make spells to call upon the entire power of the world. Silent sobs punching her chest, tears streaming from reddened eyes down to her neck and chest, and an alien face framed by cropped hair… The image in the mirror was too much; she ran back to the bed and wept until the pillow was soaking wet. Her physical weakness spent, she got up and dressed. Her stomach was rumbling painfully. Looking out of the window, she spotted the pomegranate she should have picked when Halil and Muzaffer had pointed it out: the pomegranate that had miraculously survived the looting children was still hanging from one of the lower branches. It had cracked open right in the middle with an ostentatious fecundity, preparing to spread hundreds of seeds onto the ground.

Silently opening the window, she leapt down. Her hands were stained with the blood of the fruit as she worked the pomegranate's thick stem from the branch. She crouched below the open window, the pomegranate she'd divided down the crack in her sticky hands. First, she licked her fingers one by one. Then she began eating the sweet arils, crushing the hard seeds whole, making sure not to waste a single one. She didn't expect the pomegranate to change her entire life. Quite the opposite: she wanted everything to be like it once was, to awaken from a dream, see her grandma in bed, tell her about this nightmare, and bask in the solace of grandma's hands stroking her long hair. But minutes later, she was still crouching below the window with sticky hands and face, when the loudspeakers stated that it was now allowed to go out for bread.

At long last, the still air shrugs off its indecision as navy blue lines appear on the far north-eastern horizons of the colourless sea. Growing darker, recalling its colour, the wind will cross the country and the Aegean to reach the shores of Andalıç. Just when Andalıç was about to rub against the motherland's soil, it will push the island away, to the other side of the water. Dashing all hopes of return. But for now, silence and motionlessness still reign supreme. Andalıç, where every slope leads up to one single hilltop, which overlooks practically every street, now moves by command. Goes out on command, goes back in on command. Eats only as much as the amount that is deemed appropriate. Stomachs rumble. Rainwater is used drop by drop. All the same, what's pushing the island down into the sea, inch by inch, is not invisibility, hunger, being forgotten, or thirst. Something more ominous than the fear for life poisons the air, twitches in veins and wears hearts down. The shards of submission scratch the surface of pride. And invisible inflammation surrounds the conscience of the town. The north-easterly gives that wound a chill. Little by little. Cool.

Every house is transformed into an enforced prison and the taps are tightened on needs as well as desires; everyone has to take stock. Voices rise in homes, partisan and opponent. The perennial war between the virtues of restriction and those of liberty heat up the cooling air. Little grudges amass enmity.

ATTENTION, ATTENTION! ALL MEN BETWEEN FIFTEEN AND TWENTY-FIVE TO THE PRIMARY SCHOOL YARD. ALL MEN BETWEEN FIFTEEN AND TWENTY-FIVE TO THE PRIMARY SCHOOL YARD.

Mothers sniff as if they were holding a pin between their teeth. Their gums ache. They don't know where they're sending their children, or what for. Some of the boys are scared, others are curious. Some doors open and shut, following every command, others don't. Fewer than expected numbers gather at the schoolyard. There are people who've not sent their children.

ATTENTION, ATTENTION! ANYONE NOT SENDING THEIR CHILDREN WILL BE SEVERELY PUNISHED.

The words continue to crackle inside homes even after the loudspeakers have fallen silent. Every young man in Andalıç is now in the schoolyard. Some of the lycée teachers are telling them something, gesticulating wildly all the while. Making them take oaths. Then they are made to run in the yard. Orders are given. Obedience to orders is taught. They are told what to do when the enemy comes. There are huge flags everywhere. The boys are made to swear that they will never abandon Andalıç under any condition and defend it until their last drop of blood. Marching songs are sung.

Mothers wait horrified at home, all ears. Jumping at the screech of scrapping cats, the neighbour's carpet beating, coins trickling down to the stone floor, and a loud question unspoken. They would send their ears to the schoolyard if they could. Soothing whispers spread into town from the houses overlooking the school, from window to window, from door to door, crossing streets and walls. The boys are to train every day, wear uniform track suits, fight if the Greeks come, at the front, in front of us all. Some are proud, others are anguished. The boys' thumping steps echo, they march in step even on their way home, it's getting dark.

ATTENTION, ATTENTION! AS OF TOMORROW, CURFEW IS LIFTED BETWEEN EIGHT AM AND SIX PM.

Cemal was alone in the room when his eyes opened at the announcement. His fever was down, but he still had a headache and felt debilitated. Just then Saliha came in with an infusion of lime blossom.

'I don't know how he managed to find it, but Hakkı Baba put some brandy in. Says it's good for coughs.'

He inhaled deeply before sipping the hot drink, and the sharp vapour of the brandy permeated the farthest corners of his lungs. 'Oh! That's quite strong.'

Saliha laughed, not at the funny expression on his face, but because his fever was down, his nightmares gone, and he had regained consciousness.

'Remember the curfews? During the coup?'

'Uh-huh.' Saliha's eyes grew serious and stared at the floor.

'Halil Abi was at university at the time. We used to listen to the news, terrified. Some of his friends were imprisoned, tortured, but thankfully he was spared.'

The infusion carved a painful path in Cemal's sore throat as it went down to his stomach. He felt the warmth spreading into his chest and the infected places stung by the alcohol. 'Halil Abi will probably come visit me tomorrow when the curfew is lifted.'

Grabbing the empty water glass on the bedside table, Saliha hastened out. Cemal took laboured breaths in the suspicious void she had left behind. He finished his drink and placed the cup where the glass had been standing. Saliha returned before long, looking a little wary. Hakkı was with her.

'You'll have to go back home tomorrow,' said Cemal sadly.

Hakkı took the chair and Saliha sat at the foot of the bed. They had waited for Cemal to get a bit better before giving him the bad news, but the longer they left it, the harder it was going to get.

'When I turned seventy, I thought I'd seen everything there was to see in the world. But I was wrong. Life's a bitch.' As circuitous an introduction as any.

'A right bitch,' said Saliha.

'There's bad, and there's good, too. After Cevriye's death, I said to myself, I'm done. Then one day, my son turned up, after years of no word. He'd got married and was a dad. That's when he wanted to see me. Drove me to his place in his car. My daughter-in-law's charming. She must have been working on our lad. Anyway… they placed a tiny thing in my lap. Neslihan. My granddaughter.'

Like every story told to alleviate the terrors of the world, this optimism of this tale was also tinged with an ominous tone. Cemal's ears picked it up; and he started to wait for what Hakkı actually intended to say. As the latter came to the end of his flair for spinning it out, the pauses between sentences grew longer and longer… until the old man and Saliha exchanged helpless glances. Loath to drag out this mutual torment, Saliha rapidly explained the situation in a few sharp, broken words. After which Cemal took a great deal of convincing that the curfew was serious, and at any rate, he wasn't allowed to go out until he felt a bit better, so he absolutely had to stay in bed.

Next morning, the moment the curfew was lifted, they went to the cemetery, supporting Cemal under the arms throughout a journey stretched out by coughing fits and frequent rests on doorsteps. They walked along narrow, serpentine paths, reading dozens of familiar and strange names on the tombstones, reciting poems and prayers. A multitude of unnamed graves only marked with a board bearing a number stretched out in the newest section opened after the earthquake. Mounds waiting for their tombstones, for their sleepers to be identified. All identical.

'Which one?' asked Cemal, sitting on the marble surround of an older grave in a cold sweat. 'How will we know, which one?' The feeble fire in his eyes matched the insanity in his voice.

At a loss for what to do, they all stared at the numbers on the new graves. Headscarves were tied to some of the boards. Women's graves. 'Wish we'd gone to Yasemin Yenge first.' Saliha moved along the mounds in the hope of finding a clue. The third row, the fourth, all the same, absolute equality. Reaching the end of the fourth row, she spotted three new graves, practically out of sight at the bottom of the high perimeter wall, a little below where she was standing. Three forlorn new graves amongst the thorns and dry weeds, exiled even from the land of the dead.

Saliha, Cemal and Hakkı managed to get there, following the tracks of the digger, sinking into the damp earth from time to time. Three nameless graves, without even a number or a board.

Cemal sank to his knees with something that sounded like a moan. The warm tears spreading on his burning face were instantly cooled by the north-easterly. He peered at the graves, waiting for a sign from anywhere at all, even the invisible world. As he rose in despair, he spotted a branch of jasmine, which had rolled to the side of the grave at the right. The blossoms had turned brown. His throat filled with the sweet scent of the jasmine adorning Halil's garden gate in a thick arch. The jasmine that made you inhale deeply whenever you walked under it.

'Yasemin Yenge's been here,' he said to the gap between Hakkı and Saliha. 'Did she know? Did she know which one it was?' A question, whose torture was acute enough to cut through grief. The wildness in his eyes petrified. Holding her breath, worried and sad, Saliha watched his face freeze.

'How did she decide which one to place the flowers on?' The dry weeds rustled in the cold wind.

'How?'

A whisper in his ear from the cold, glaring wind.

'Which one, oh God, which one?'

Its seafront houses now sunk halfway, the island awakens to the day in absolute silence. Something is missing: a sound unnoticed by all and undetected by ear. The hum of a motor. One only heard – and indistinctly at that – by those living close to the coach station, one taken for granted due to its regularity. As the full moon darkened and stretched the shadows of the houses, the night concealed silent footsteps, blindfolded and covered the ears of the watchmen, and watched skilful hands at work. The storage unit's generator is now silent. Andalıç doesn't know, may never do. All it knows is that it's being dragged towards Greece on the north-easterly, as loudspeakers constantly remind them throughout the day. The children are training with makeshift weapons. Gunshots echo in the streets once a day from the schoolyard bang in the middle of the town. Targets are drawn on sheets of paper; the boy making the nearest hole to the ring in the centre becomes a candidate to bear arms.

DEAR RESIDENTS; AS YOU KNOW, OUR ANDALIÇ APPROACHES GREECE. NO MATTER WHAT IT TAKES, WE SHALL FIGHT TO PREVENT OUR ISLAND FROM JOINING GREEK LANDS. WE SHALL NOT ALLOW EVEN A SINGLE GREEK TO STEP ON THE ISLAND. NONE OF OUR RESIDENTS MAY LEAVE. ANDALIÇ WILL ALWAYS REMAIN TURKISH.

People beckoned to the mosques five times a day by the calls to prayer reverberating in the streets shiver in the damp chill peculiar to big buildings as much as the suspicious stares of familiar faces in their ranks. Faces that pop up the moment there is any chatter in a small group as the congregation disperses. Once welcome faces of acquaintances, relations and neighbours. Those whose ideas, parties they voted for, or voices rising angrily to drown everyone else out, were previously merely laughed at. But now they have this vast and terrifying new power. Powerful enough to stifle words, lower voices, change the direction of footsteps, and impose a self-assumed authority.

Foetid Friday sermons leave people speechless; all they can conjure up is glances sneaked at one another instead of words. It's so hard to figure out what and how much to say to whom, that it's better to stay silent.

An ear is always present somewhere near, even when condolences are murmured at funerals. Eyes counting the words one by one as prayers are murmured. Stares following steps taken in the streets cause feet to tangle. No one knows who the peepers behind curtains are, or what they're recording. Women who gossip with their neighbours at the door speak a little more softly each day. Everyone could be targeted by a watchful eye, a cocked ear, or a denouncing mouth. No longer able to baby their sons who train all day long, mothers gaze at them over the menacing distance that has come between them. Everyone entering or leaving the Care Home carries a halo of immunity. Entrapped, choking, the island sinks inch by inch under the weight of suspicion, fear, and dread. Nowhere to run. Out of touch with everywhere. Forgotten and invisible, Andalıç drifts in the most deserted part of the most crowded sea in the world, all hope of help lost.

Jülide blinked in the clear, cool and dazzling air. She had no wish to look at the building looming behind her in whose basement, in the middle of a labyrinth, surrounded by threats and the smell of damp, she had waited sleeplessly all night. Waited for the morning, for rescue, and above all, for a horrific end. There were no marks on her body, other than a bruise a little above her elbow and a split lip. The thin trickle of blood down to her chin might still have been there if she hadn't altered the course of the interrogation. In that dark place where morning never visited. With a few words about a hidden boat at the point where the red of blood trumped brutish paranoia, and the pure white innocence on her face had won her release.

She was in no mood to linger outside the Care Home, whose chilly breath licked her neck. The moment her eyes had adjusted to the light, she moved down the first slope that presented itself. Her cheeks trembling with her stomping steps, she reached the seafront. Touched the water. Stung her lip with her salty fingers. Then without a single glance at the hilltop, she walked along partly submerged roads all the way to her grandmother's grave. She was carrying a small bouquet of roses that had blossomed in the autumn rains. Even though she desperately needed someone to talk to, she realised she was unable to talk to a grave. She murmured what few prayers she knew and left. She knew the mirrored eyes of the Care Home were following her. Anyone she visited would get into trouble. She couldn't go to Rahmi or Saime.

She wandered in the rooms for a while when she got home. The huge house was empty and silent. A photograph of Muzaffer stood on the coffee table, young, hugging her father, wearing a floral frock, the same cropped hair. A Muzaffer barely a couple of years older than Jülide was now.

'You've gone hungry for two days,' she murmured, 'Oh, Muzaffer Abla, what am I to do? They only let me go so they can follow me. Because they knew I'd go to you. How can I bring you food?'

There was still a little of the previous day's rations left. Sitting at the kitchen table, she put her head in her hands. A few of the pomegranate's leaves were turning yellow. Taking pen and paper, she wrote a long letter. Went to the bedroom and tucked it under a pillow. Warming a little water on the cooker, she washed. Picking one of Muzaffer's clean flannel nighties, which looked a little strange on her, went to bed and fell into a deep sleep.

21

By the time the waning moon filled the streets of Andalıç with a gloomy light from its zenith, the townsfolk, who had retired indoors at six, were deep in sleep. They were rudely awakened by fists pounding on doors. Dazzling torches dived into homes. Their beams wandered over every nook and cranny. Went into the farthest corners of trunks. Riffled through drawers. Barks of 'Search!' cleaved the night. Young children were pressed over pounding hearts. Seeing their own sons in the two-men squads, some families were pierced to the quick. Andalıç was seen down to its most intimate corners. The eyes of the Care Home entered everyone's homes. Andalıç was turned over and left at the feet of the Care Home like a pair of dirty socks. The illusion of the inviolability of homes came to an end. The fact that anywhere could be entered at any moment rang out under the cold moon. The fact that you couldn't keep unwelcome people outside the door, that strange eyes could see the things kept from your nearest and dearest.

Steel was carried up the hilly streets: hunting rifles, heirloom Mausers, service pistols, officer's swords, unlicensed arms. Andalıç was disarmed. Sleep was banned. In the cold light of the moon seeping through the nets, people started ruminating. A sharp line was drawn between those who could get back to bed and sleep and those who couldn't. Supporters and objectors instinctively withdrew to either side of this boundary.

Saliha spotted the white envelope slipped under the door the moment she had come to the top of the stairs. As she was descending sleepily, her father suddenly came out of the sitting room, halted a few steps away from the letter, and, waving his ration card, stared at his daughter. He was about to turn and go out to the hall, when Saliha's urgent 'Dad?' stopped him. She grabbed the ration card without finishing her sentence.

'I'll go for the bread today. I couldn't sleep all night. I feel awful.'

Kadir gave her a suspicious look. 'Whatever brought this about now? You'd never go to get anything even if people begged you. Stay at home and prepare breakfast. I'll go for the bread.' He grabbed the card and was about to move out, but this time he was held back by the voice of his wife coming downstairs.

'Let her go, Kadir. She felt like it. Let her get a bit of fresh air. I'll prepare breakfast. And you can sit and rest.'

'Fine, I will sit, but for how much longer? No coffee house, no newspapers, no TV. I'm bored too.'

'You can go out after breakfast. Go to Sinan Bey's. I hear he's caught a bit of a cold.'

The moment her grumbling father turned back to the sitting room, Saliha grabbed the envelope. Her fingers felt something hard. She opened it in a hurry, expecting to see Cemal's handwriting, but it was an unfamiliar hand. And a key fell out. Stuffing them in her pocket, she shot out. As she sped off, her hand kept worrying the envelope in her pocket, fingers trying to become eyes. She cast a nervous look up at the Care Home. Didn't dare take the letter out.

On her return, she placed the loaf in the kitchen and ran up to her room. She started reading as soon as she had shut the door behind her. Still reading, she walked slowly towards her bed and sat down.

Dear Saime, my sweet friend. I wouldn't have written this letter if I could have thought of another solution. Muzaffer Abla's gone hungry for the past two days. But you know nothing about any of it. It was all one thing after another. We've not been able to meet. I need to talk so much. I'm very lonely here. The last few days felt like weeks.

I won't be able to give you much of an explanation. I was interrogated the other night. I guess my every move must be watched now. I am trembling in fear as I write this, in case it gets into the wrong hands. Not for myself so much as for Muzaffer Abla.

I've saved a bit of food. So you don't have to worry about that. Do you know the derelict house in the street below ours? It can't be seen from the Care Home. The door opens if you push it with your shoulder a little. The food is in the cupboard in the room at the right.

The key to our house is in the envelope. When you leave the derelict house, bear right; the second street on the right is also out of the Care Home's sight. There's a big mulberry tree at the end. Hide behind it as you cross the road. That will bring you to the street where our old house is. If you hide behind the houses on the left, you'll escape being spotted from above, but be very careful. Don't attract suspicion. It would probably be better for Cemal Abi to do this rather than you, actually. Saime; these blokes are really dangerous. I would never have asked you for something like this if Muzaffer Abla wasn't going to starve.

Go to our house. There's a big basin under the counter in the kitchen. Push it to one side. You'll see a door. Open it. A narrow tunnel leads to a cave. That's where Muzaffer Abla is. Give her the food and get away at once. I wish there was a way to keep you out of this.

I avoid going to anyone I know whenever I go out. Please speak to Cemal Abi and let him read this letter. I'll tell you everything when everything's better. We'll talk for ages. Take care.

Jülide

PS: If I find the food still in the derelict house tonight, I'll go myself, never mind the risk.

Watching Saime's innocent face throughout breakfast, Saliha was convinced it was the right decision to keep the letter to herself. She went out after absently clearing the table and helping with the washing up.

Hakkı opened the door at Cemal's house. Misinterpreting her preoccupation, he started explaining. 'He's in bed. Still the same. No matter what I said – it's no use. I've left him to it.'

Saliha checked the letter in her pocket again, tracing the rigid outline of the key. She glanced at the old man who had rushed to their help in these hard times, a second father to Cemal. A man full of advice. Then she spotted the already white rakı glass on the table. Carefully weighing up Hakkı's judgement, she pulled an empty hand out of her pocket.

Cemal was sitting on his mother's bed, blank gaze on the wall opposite. Glancing at the door, he gave his fiancée a smile. Patted the bed to show her where to sit. Saliha planted a timid, breeze-like kiss on his lips. At any other time, such a kiss would have elicited a reproachful look, but this time there was nothing in his eyes. Nothing positive or negative. It was the first time she felt his attention flagging since the start of their relationship. The first time she sought something she had never once thought of or even noticed its existence. Her expectant eyes failed to find the man she loved in his strange gaze.

'Cemal...'

'Yes, sweetie?'

That automatic, unemotional 'sweetie' hurt. But Cemal had already forgotten his fiancée was addressing him, and that he had replied. He kept staring at the blank wall.

'How do we find out which grave belongs to Halil Abi?' he murmured. Since he'd been saying precious little else of late, Saliha gave her automatic response.

'I don't know. Neither does Yasemin Yenge. Wouldn't it be better to give her a little bit of support instead of going to pieces like this, Cemal?'

He was refusing to get out of bed even though he had already got better. Not daring to ask anyone who could answer, his grief and hatred too weak to overcome his fear, repulsed by his own lack of courage to turn up at the door of the Care Home, he continued to lie in bed.

Saliha checked her pocket again.

'You know Muzaffer Hanım, Cemal?'

'Uh-huh.' He didn't turn his eyes to her. 'Which one do you think, Saliha?'

'I was telling you about Muzaffer Hanım...' She looked at the void which had settled into Cemal's body. 'Never mind.' Then, instead of thinking he was right, she felt angry for the first time. 'What good would it do anyway, Cemal? What's the point of knowing which grave it is? The poor chap's dead. He's dead.' Cemal slipped into the bed and pulled the blanket over his head.

Furious at her failure to reach him for days, Saliha stormed out. Just as she was reaching for her own doorbell, the loudspeakers crackled again.

ATTENTION, ATTENTION! FROM NOW ON IT IS FORBIDDEN FOR MORE THAN FOUR PEOPLE TO GATHER ON THE STREET.

Her finger briefly hovered over the bell. Turning her head, she looked up at the Care Home. Tried to read into the malicious intelligence behind the mirrored eyes. She felt constrained in a far tighter corner than the fences erected around her by her father, this town, and all kinds of men and institutions. It hurt, not being able to help Cemal, or not getting any help from him, but she couldn't dawdle for much longer under these mirrored stares. She set off on an aimless stroll. The key was sticking out of a hole it had pierced in the envelope. She pricked all her fingers one by one on the point. Scratched her cheek. The sour metal smell hit her nose. She felt sick. Leaning on a wall, she vomited and her retching attracted a pair of eyes from a house across the road. The sense of being followed was so strong, however, that one extra went unnoticed.

She raised her head, and recognised that this wall belonged to the derelict house, her destination. The door looked ramshackle. Maybe she could linger a little in this nook invisible from the hilltop. Or maybe, there was nowhere safe from eyes in Andalıç any more. Pushing the door, she went in, and shut it behind her straightaway. The sky was visible from the gaps in the partially collapsed ceiling. Broken floorboards, twisted frames, loosened floor tiles, the smell of rotting wood. Scared of making the floorboards creak, she entered the room at the right and made for the built-in cupboard by the door. She swapped the carrier bag for the letter and hastened out of this space inhabited by strange sounds and smells. Hugging the walls, she followed the route that had been set out for her The mirror glinted behind the mulberry, which still had practically all its leaves, and she crossed the road. Her attention focused on the hilltop failed to notice the silent footsteps behind her. The building she entered was noted by the eyes at the corner of the stone house, at the point she had crossed the street.

Listening to the silence outside, Saliha pushed the basin to the side and opened the door. Crawled down the narrow passage. She emerged into a somewhat larger space at the end and blinked, realising she had come unprepared. She was afraid to take a step without knowing what waited ahead.

'Muzaffer Hanım,' she whispered. He voice echoed in the cavern. There was no answer.

'Muzaffer Hanım, don't worry; it's me, Saliha,' she said, a little louder. 'Jülide sent me. I've brought you some food.' The movement she heard was difficult to locate in the pitch darkness.

'Why didn't she come herself?'

'I've not spoken to her either. She sent my sister a letter. Says she's being followed. She was trying to avoid putting you at risk.'

The startling touch of a cold hand on her arm. The hand followed the arm down to grab the bag.

'Don't you have a torch or something?'

'No. Sorry; I came unprepared. It was a last-minute decision.'

It smelt of damp soil and stone. She heard the rustle of the bag and then a spit. 'Fuck! It was a candle!' A dry cackle echoed on the walls. Scared, they both held their breaths for a moment. The manifold rattle of a match falling out of the box. A match scratched into flame, touched the wick of the bitten candle, and the cave relinquished its black void, extending broader and higher.

'So big!'

'Eah, i' i'...' Muzaffer's reply came over the morsel she was chewing. After struggling to swallow, she glanced into the bag and her eyes shone. 'Clever girl! Even put some cigarettes in. Change of clothes. There is water here; it seeps down the walls.'

'I had no idea there were caves like this under Andalıç.'

'There were entrances to these caves when I was a child; then one of the kids who went in got stuck and died, and all the entrances were blocked. The one in Jülide's house must have been overlooked. Probably because it was inside a house.'

Taking the candle, Saliha was moving along the walls. 'I can't stay for long. I could come again in a couple of days if you need anything.' She added, without much conviction, 'And who knows, help might come by then.'

Chewing in a hurry, Muzaffer swallowed. 'How are things outside?'

'Bad.'

Just then something like a scream came from somewhere in the distance. They both pricked up their ears, but there was nothing more.

'Then there's this. These sounds. Imagining how and who's making them. I may come out tonight. Come what may. I'm not going to hide here for ever. You can only be afraid for your life for so long. Let them do what they will.'

Saliha looked at the distant dark corners of the cave. They might well lead to an absolute infinity, to where those screams came from. She shivered. 'I don't know. I suspect you're better off here until you find somewhere new to hide.' She felt she was suffocating in air imprisoned in the cave for thousands of years. 'I'd better go now; otherwise I'll be arousing suspicion.'

Muzaffer wasn't yet ready to let her go, though; she was in no hurry to retire back into her dark, mouldy solitude. 'Hiding in caves! The one bloody thing I'd never got up to.' The breach in her self-respect gave her voice a hollow ring. 'Once, where I was in Bulgaria ...' She paused to listen. 'Did you hear it? Coming from the passage.'

They leapt up to their feet, grabbed the candle and ran to the other end of the cave. 'I'd left the door open,' whispered Saliha, gasping.

'There's an alcove that way. We can hide there. Oh, fuck, the candle's gone out.'

Feeling their way with their feet, they moved slowly in the pitch dark. A faint light behind them brought their hearts to their mouths as they flung themselves into the alcove. Saliha moaned, gritting her teeth. 'I've twisted my ankle. You carry on.'

Being so petite, Muzaffer slipped easily under her arm. She could feel Saliha's heart beating on her shoulder. 'Through thick and thin; c'mon.'

The light growing brighter, running feet, shouts, the *zing!* of the trap falling. 'Come out. You can't hide. Give yourselves up.'

They were moving, grabbing the walls of a narrowing corridor. 'Will you look at this! A stage play in this tiny space. Not that it would make any difference if it was bigger.'

The growing threat behind them, the narrowing rocky tunnel – like a funnel.

'There's no way through,' said Saliha, her voice trembling.

Patting the rough surface of the porous rocks, they were looking for an opening.

'There's a narrow crack here, but only wide enough for my arm.' Muzaffer was trying to squeeze her whole body through the crack. 'It opens out on the other side. Dammit!'

Averting her eyes from the approach of the dazzling torches, Saliha saw Muzaffer huddling into that crack. 'They're here. We're caught.'

Coming out in the bright, fresh air from the iron door of Jülide's small house, Saliha felt like she was choking. 'What's with the handcuffs and everything? What have we done? Have you lost your minds?'

Her wrists encircled by the cold metal were behind her back. She looked at the sullen, silent men. One of the faces seemed to ring a bell from her neighbourhood. Then her gaze was fixed on a very familiar face. Cemile's big teeth showed as she gloated. She came over, faking surprise and sadness.

'Aa! Saliha! I came over when I saw the crowd. Is that you?' She turned to a man in police uniform. 'Constable. I know this lady. My big brother's fiancée. Let her go for his sake. Abdurrahman Bey will reward you.'

The fury in Saliha's glare hissed in Muzaffer's voice. 'So now it's Abdurrahman Bey's mistress that decides who to arrest and who to release, is it?'

Swinging her head playfully to the side, Cemile raised a cheeky nose in the air. 'Huh! Wasted kindness. Suit yourselves.'

There was a dark relish in the look she gave Muzaffer. 'You must be that journalist. Oh, dear! Saliha got mixed up with some real bad shit.'

'Of course. It would never have happened if she'd become the mistress of an influential bloke, though, would it?'

Sneering, Cemile looked them both top to toe. 'Ohmygod, like you two could become mistresses if you wanted! One's a tomboy, the other's a snowman.'

Relaxing at having succeeded in their mission and back out in the sunlight after the pursuit – whose reason or purpose was unknown – in the dark cave, the policemen were taking it easy.

'Just you wait. Cemal's sure to find out what you've done.'

'But what have I done, my sweet sister-in-law? I saw you in the street as I was passing and stopped.'

An utterly unconvincing role, acted with amateur enthusiasm. The policemen, grinning as they watched Cemile, seemed to have forgotten why they were there.

Saliha's revulsion got the better of her fear. 'Can we go now, constable?'

'That's for us to decide,' glowered one of the men. In a toadyish tone, his words unctuous, he turned to Cemile. 'And Madam's permission.'

'Oh, constable! It would have been great if you could have let my sister-in-law go. How am I gonna tell my big brother now?'

Her eyes flashed with a spiteful look at Saliha. 'I'd better go at once so he'll hear it from me. And I can console him, too.'

Hakkı had originally arrived in Andalıç to remember the past, with the suit on his back, pyjamas and a set of clean underwear and a wedding present in his bag. That temporary visit had gone on and on. Now in a tracksuit procured somehow, staying with someone young enough to be his son, someone he didn't know all that well, but grew to like, he was trying to fit in with the rhythm of an unfamiliar town. To be fair, the town was equally unfamiliar with this new rhythm. A lifetime of witnessing how so much started out well and got worse, and there was always something even worse than what was much mistaken for the worst, he had learnt to stop and take stock when he hit bottom, to be patient and to care. And now he was caring for Cemal. Kind Cemal. Gentle Cemal. Cemal, whose violence was spent inside. Watching the healthy body in the sick bed, the weak mind in the strong body. Well acquainted with weakness and how painful it was, he had little desire to indulge this pathetic sight. He went out for long walks whenever he wasn't drowning himself in rakı.

The call to prayer was still broadcast from the loudspeakers since the revolt, but no one was forced to attend mosque. All the same, Hakkı, who had never stood to prayer other than at funerals, and that only by copying those around him, got ready to go to Friday prayers. He put on his beige suit, now a little too thin for the advancing autumn air and tidied up his tie and the thin handfuls of white hair in the small mirror in the toilet. He went into the sitting room, which he had been using as his bedroom since Cemal had fallen ill, then swung back for a look, hoping against hope, through the door he'd just walked past. Cemal was still staring at the white wall opposite, sitting in bed. The increasingly introverted and withdrawn gaze turned towards Hakkı. Like a man dodging a stone aimed at his head, he shot into the sitting room to avoid the question 'Which one?'

'Never mind which one! A strapping man's down. What does it matter which hole he lies in!'

He struggled with the shoehorn as he put his feet into the perforated beige shoes by the door. He stood up, his face now purple, and tidied up his dishevelled hair once again. Checked his tie, using three fingers. Thinking he heard a sound from inside, he stopped and pricked up his ears.

'Instead of lying there, go find whoever's buried him, and ask! Oh, child! Oh, child!'

He opened the door as he murmured the last word. And drew back a step the moment he did.

'Who's this child, then, Uncle Hakkı?' Cemile had slipped in through the gap.

'What the heck are you doing here, girl? Cemal doesn't want to see you. What's the point of insisting?'

Taking in the poor, modest room of the house she had entered for the first time, Cemile turned to the old man with a serious face. 'I have important news for my big brother.'

'Cemal's sick. He's in bed. Do it some other time.'

Cemile was staring at Cemal's mother's photo on the wall. There didn't seem to be any mementos of her father. She thought of the framed, enlarged passport photo in her mother's home. The absence of that shared father offered an unexpected sense of relief. She stared at her blood-red fingernails for a while.

'No, uncle. It's very urgent. I must tell him at once. About his fiancée.'

'What about his fiancée? Poor girl was here just a few hours ago. Wore herself out, looking after him.'

Hakkı made a move to remove his shoes, but she waved at him in a hurry. 'No, no. You go wherever you were going. I saw Saliha on the way, see, and she gave me a message for my brother. Something that concerns women. Best I only tell my big brother. It won't take a couple of minutes even. I'll leave at once. And I'll pull the door shut behind me. Don't worry.'

Unconvinced as he was, Hakkı glanced at the shoes that had been such an effort to put on.

'I'm not desperate to get kicked out, don't worry.'

The old man was still hesitating at the half open door.

'Ohmygod, uncle! Anyone would think I was gonna eat a grown man. Go, wherever you're going.'

'OK,' said Hakkı willy-nilly, 'But the lad's unwell, keep it short. If it's anything that's going to upset him, or wind him up, best not to tell him now. He's still not himself since...'

'OK, OK, don't you worry. I'm not his enemy, anyway. I'm good to my big brother.'

After Cemile had shut the door, Hakkı stood on the spot for a while, regretting having left her inside. He did think of letting himself back in with the key, but then he changed his mind. Shaking his head, he started an indecisive walk.

'Of course, he's a grown man. She's not going to eat him. And anyway, who are you? His father? What a father. Who knows though, he might come to his senses if he loses his rag.'

Expecting to be ejected with insults, however feeble the voice, Cemile stood baffled in the room where she was met with total silence and blank looks. Cemal's long fingers kept rising and falling on the nap of the light brown blanket. He was sitting upright, resting on two pillows tucked behind him. The bed looked as if it hadn't been slept in. Cemile flinched when he suddenly swung round and asked, 'Which one?'

Cemal's eyes went back to the blank wall.

'Don't you know either? But you must. You... Which one?'

'What?'

'The grave. Which one?'

'What grave?'

'Halil Abi's.' He stopped, screwing his face as though he had bitten his own tongue.

'I don't know.' Cemile stared at his dim eyes, drawn face, and skin as dull as if it had been sprinkled with ashes. 'How the hell would I know?'

'But you... you... Which one?'

Unable to get the answer he sought, Cemal squinted as those matt eyes slowly turned towards her... before fixing back on the wall again. Far from temper, anger or hate. As far as he was from enthusiasm, joy or love. Blank, just like the wall he was looking at. Detached from the world, left alone with himself. All connections with his emotions severed. He was nothing more than a third pillow on the bed.

'You really are sick; but what kind of sickness…' Cemile hesitated a little before pressing a hand on his forehead. 'No fever.' No reaction. She pressed her lips this time. Then gazed at his eyes inquisitively. 'Actually… your fire's proper gone out. Well, lie down with dogs and you get fleas. That cold fish…'

She stopped, scared when Cemal turned his head. She perched on the edge of the bed. Tentatively picked up the long fingers, but Cemal only gave his hand a disinterested look, as if he was looking at a stray cat, and nailed his eyes to the wall again. 'Which one?'

'Cemal!' She shouted, as if talking to a deaf man. 'HOW-ARE-YOU?' But no amount of shouting attracted his attention. 'Don't you understand anything? Have you lost your bloody mind? What's the matter with you? Are you not with it?'

'You know… you…'

'Don't you recognise me? I'm Cemile. Cemile.' This inertia, this silence: it was worse than anger. She missed the scolding, the disdain, and being sent packing. 'You don't get anything. Like I'm not even here.' She stared vacantly for a while at the free zone granted her by the disconnect between the ears and the brain. 'I'm head over heels in love with you, you know?' She stopped. Still no reaction. 'You don't know. You can't know. I fell for you when I first saw you at the pavyon. Before I knew who you were. Like, what difference would it make if I knew, anyway. We're half siblings, half. Doesn't everyone marry a relative in this country? Aunt's daughter, uncle's daughter: are they less close?' She was softly caressing Cemal's fingers. 'Why the bloody hell would I come to this godforsaken village if I wasn't in love!' The warmth in her voice was unrecognisable as she opened up in a way she had never done before anyone, least of all herself. Peering at Cemal's face, she fidgeted. 'I fell for this Zaim the same way. I was seventeen. He took me to bed on our second date. That's me, see, it's all or nothing.' She glanced at the old floral frock visible through the half open door of the wardrobe. 'Dad only raised his hands against me once. When he saw me on the street with Zaim. He beat me black and blue in the middle of the street. That buster took to his heels the moment he spotted my dad. No good will ever come of the bloke who leaves his woman alone and runs away in times of danger.' The harsh autumn sun hit the foot of the bed. She got up and drew the curtains. She couldn't bear the light. 'So what did I do? Left my dad and ran away with that brute.' The room looked even more desolate with Cemal's blank eyes focused on the wall. 'But women can't desire you, right? Only you can desire them. The woman who wants you is worse than a piece of shit. And you get what you want so long as you can pay, right?' She gave a despondent sigh. Cemal's fingers were still rising and falling on the blanket. 'I never thought I'd see you in bed like this. You, in bed. The two of us alone.' She giggled. 'You'd be married now, but for the earthquake.' Cemal suddenly turned to her with a squint. She cringed when his hand rose, but that hand reached out for the glass on the bedside table. The eyes went blank again after he had drunk the water.

'How I've been dreaming of being in bed with you... When that hairy beast mounts me. I've seen worse, of course. And he improves his record every time,' she giggled again. 'I really wanted you to see me naked too.' Those words offered an exciting possibility; she assessed his state once again. Avoiding sudden moves, she went over to the wall and waited bravely, as if she was about to face a firing squad. There was no change in Cemal, so she began to undress. She stood stark naked, but he kept staring at a point somewhere above her belly button. She shivered in the chill of the stone house. Rushed under the blanket. 'Here we are, in the same bed. Don't you dare come back, wherever you've gone.' She slipped her hand under his vest. 'Your skin's lovely. Lovely. Oh, but...' She put her head under the blanket; disenchantment showed on her face when she pulled it out. 'Oh, but you've gone so far away! That's too much! I thought these things were automatic with you lot.' She glued her lips on Cemal's, tried in vain, and moved to his ears to whisper, 'Saliha... Saliha...' She giggled. 'See? That worked a treat! It's called experience, mate! Shame, you may never see her again. The way she went, with handcuffs on her wrists, enough to make even me a little sad. You never know what they'll do to her in there. They'd already had it in for that bitch called Muzaffer. If I knew the two were connected... I heard someone who died in their hands recently was slipped into the sea, and no one any the wiser. Not even bothering to dig a grave… ah! Ah! What's the matter now?' Handcuffs of flesh gripping her wrist tugged it out. Looking at his eyes, she tried to sit up and get away, but her wrist was imprisoned inside that vice-like hand even if her body was thrashing about out of the bed.

'Aaaah! It hurts! Let me gooo! Let me go, it huuurts!'

'Where's Saliha?'

'The police took her away.'

'Where?'

'Where else, up there.'

Cemal swept out of bed and set off, the wrist forgotten in his grip. He was thundering around the house like an ungainly waggon, dragging Cemile behind, who occasionally slammed into him. Energised by the sudden rush of comprehension, he was asking questions, receiving answers correct along with lies, recognising the lies instantly from their tone, and squeezing the truth out of Cemile's wrist. Down to the last drop. Down to that last point where a jealous woman would have to confess her jealous crime. He crossed the small house several times without letting her go, but opening the doors of his mind. Once the final door was open and he had reconnected with the world fully, he opened his hand in disgust.

'You're naked.' He averted his eyes angrily. 'Go get dressed. Now. Nooow!'

He sat down on the untidy sofa Hakkı had been sleeping in. Got up again and went to the window. Like a cornered animal, he found a desperate strength inside. A strength he knew would never be enough for anything, yet that tensed up all his muscles, rippled his mind and shattered his indolence.

'Get a move on!'

Cemile passed by, staying as far as possible, never taking her eyes off her half-brother, her back against the wall. He swung open the door and rushed outside. The devilish glint in Cemal's eyes was identical to the one in her brute, just before he had stabbed her twice. She never glanced one last time at Cemal, who looked too lost in thought to threaten her. She broke into a run, barefoot over the cobblestones, the memory of the old ache in her side.

22

Marching tunes ring out all day long as Andalıç creeps towards Greece on the north-easterly. The moment ships were detected on the horizon, every flag in the town came out to hang – was made to hang. Flags fly from every home, every pole, every tree, every official building: everywhere one could hang a flag. The gigantic flag virtually covering the façade of the Care Home now lifts away in the wind, now dips into the indentations of the windows. The two columns of windows flanking the flag continue to observe Andalıç. From the other windows, the town looks like a red mirage. The higher the volume of the marches and number of the flags, and the fiercer the speeches and sermons, the less the fervour of the original defenders of order on the island; stomachs rumbling, they gaze at the barely visible ships in the distance; their thoughts no longer tumbling out of their lips as if this were the most natural thing in the world, no: caught in some thorny part of their minds, they writhe; as they writhe and dawdle, they notice what they had missed earlier. The longer the marching tune broadcasts, the fewer the feet and fingers keeping time. Since the deaths outside the storage unit, the subsequent arrests, the words pronounced by the increasingly graver faces of the boys in weapons training, and the elegies of the women pressing their handkerchiefs to their eyes and beating their own knees, even the most passionate supporters of the Mayor, the Commissioner and the spineless District Governor appear more subdued.

The boundary bisecting public opinion is shifting. The land of the despised, of those shoved and terrorised into shrinking into themselves is slowly growing. The indicator of solid rectitude given by common sense slides towards them. Smaller, ever smaller grows the other land, reduced to guns, loudspeakers and guards.

The town, which has sunk into a deep silence as it takes stock, regains its voice in whispers blown only into trusted ears, which may not even include one's nearest and dearest. A fine web, which excludes those who carry news to the top, and their informers, grows and its sticky threads joins one by one: a raised eyebrow, a creased forehead, a squinting eye, a twisting mouth, a nod. Its head pushed under water, Andalıç instinctively tries to emerge for a breath, but does so without fighting, but by pretending to be dead. Houses raided at night are found to be unoccupied, wanted men suddenly disappear, and in suspect mouths' questions never get a truthful answer.

Timid ideas, news and solutions are carried from one end of that fine web to the other. The town is making secret plans. Plans concealed from the eyes that can breach bedrooms, drawers and cupboards, and ears that materialise close by. Plans unrecognised as such. Just thought and wished for. Visitors never before entertained are invited in, momentary hints flash in the midst of small talk, increasingly weaker teas are sipped as the bottoms of the caddies became visible, and secret information dives in one mind and emerges in the other during long silences. The town speaks sparingly, weighing every word by the gramme. Expressing several ideas with a single word. Shadows passing by windows, patters on the landing, and footsteps light or heavy, tighten and stretch the springs of the jaws.

'My fiancée's been arrested. Saliha Akgün has been arrested. Along with journalist Muzaffer. Muammer Süren's been killed, and his body thrown into the sea.'

The town listens to these words Cemal yells not into a well, but into every street he covers; it listens, scared lest that slender web is shattered by such brutality.

Alerted to Muzaffer and Saliha's arrest by the same web, Jülide had got away five minutes before her front door was broken down; she keeps hearing Cemal's yells as she goes into homes from the front and leaves by the rear, hides in the jasmine and trumpet vine bushes in the gardens, and in the streets where she crouches at the bottom of walls.

'Don't just sit there! Do something! Rescue them in the name of humanity!'

Angry faces appearing in windows, spiteful hands and arms waving, and brutal voices overpowering even the sound of marches chase Cemal from street to street. 'Bugger off! They must have done something to get arrested. Look at us: do we get into trouble? Nothing happens to decent, honest folk. Go away; stop disturbing the peace. Don't go causing trouble.'

In the afternoon, as the sun heats up, the north-easterly spreads an awful stench into the streets. It sneaks in through the narrowest holes and cracks despite the windows and doors shut up one by one, becoming increasingly unbearable as it settles. Folks looking for the source spot the blood-red stream flowing downhill to the town centre from the cold storage unit. This scarlet moat surrounding nearly half the town sends up the hills that ghastly smell of rot. The stink of tonnes of rotting meat, fresh fruit and vegetables: waste, bloody-mindedness, tyranny and murder. Nobody in Andalıç can miss it.

'They have no right!'

Cemal's pathetic yells and wild eyes, combined with the stink, strengthen that fine web. That the storage unit really was stuffed to the beams is whispered in the homes Jülide passes through after accepting a sip of water. That it would have been kept from everyone if the generator hadn't broken down. That those unnamed graves were the result of a power grab. Andalıç talks in whispers, signs, in thoughts that pop into every mind at once.

The town's eyes follow that dark stranger tailing Cemal like a black shadow. Look at the bulge on his waist that he pats. See a very young, very fair short-haired girl trying to catch up with them even as she enters through the doors that open before her one after the other, and, staring into everyone's eyes, leaves words in ears without moving her lips. Transferred from one to the other, plump women's arms and heads covered with fine white muslin, and cracked, fatherly men's hands make sure Jülide can stay the course on her hunt. Carefully saved hard-boiled sweets are given to her mouth, her hands are sprinkled with eau de cologne, and morsels kept for a rainy day pass through her slender throat. Jülide is borne on the conscience of Andalıç. She may not know anyone, but everyone knows her story.

As the sun descends, Cemal ascends, covering the length of all the town's streets running parallel to the sea. He approaches the Care Home step by step, having failed to enlist anyone other than Zaim. The shooing voices may now be too faint to drown out the thundering marches, but he is alone in the streets that clear out the moment he enters them, as if he carried an infectious disease. His shoulders sag. He has no accompaniment other than his hunched shadow lengthening on west-facing walls. And Zaim, who gets closer by yet another step every passing minute.

Cemal is walking, his mind on Saliha's hair, eyes and arms. A painful panic inside. Scenes appear before his eyes. The most unbearable scenes. Her fingers growing thinner as she lost weight, the way she constantly pushed up the loose engagement ring. The way she blew her now-much-longer fringe as she chopped onions and the tears trickling down her cheeks. He feels awful. Grabs the power pole. With no idea where Saliha is or what she's going through, whether she is alive or dead, he climbs up towards the Care Home, beseeching a god he never prays to. Zaim gets closer by one more step every time Cemal takes these painful breaks. He's in no hurry. Jülide on Zaim's tail. Andalıç's dogs enticed by the sweet, inviting scent she exudes. Hungry and exhausted dogs that have somehow managed to cheat death and whose numbers rise street by street. Some with their heads hanging down between protruding shoulder blades, just like Cemal.

The darkening sun sinks down to the horizon. The shores of Greece, now much more easily discernible, stretch behind like a range in pulsating navy. In shadowed Andalıç streets, upstairs windows mirror the sun's orange blaze. The island bursts into flashes from one end to the other, like a firework display. As the reddening sun goes beyond the horizon, dusk rises from the waters, capturing houses one after the other as it climbs the hill. For one brief moment, the Care Home of scarlet windows, pink star and crescent on a bleeding red field, and stained walls, grabs the last light of the earth.

On hearing footsteps behind him, Cemal pulls his gaze away from this glittering light show, and turns back at the bottom of the Care Home's wall. All of a sudden, the marches fall silent, leaving behind only the gentle flapping of the flag in the dropping north-easterly. Cemal spots Zaim some ten or fifteen metres below. The man has already donned the darkness of the night. Still wearing his sunshades. The high retaining wall stretches on one side of the road. Small clumps of dried weeds sprout from the hollows. A distant scream reaches Cemal's ears, like decaying rings of a ship's wake; incapable of activating the auditory sense, all it does is trigger an unpleasant unease. One connected to Zaim, approaching in deliberate steps to reduce his range.

Zaim's hand flicks away the right flap of his black pinstriped jacket and goes to his waist. A click echoes in the street. Experience braces Andalıç's conscience for another wound. Cemal's despair, heartbreak and loss wobble inside, a warm movement in the suddenly cooling autumn evening. He wants to look into the eyes behind the mirrored windows above before dying. Raising his head, he stares at the grey pile of concrete now that the sun has gone. He sees Zaim pull out a gun and point it at him. Zaim hesitates briefly at Cemal's stillness; replacing the gun, he brings out a flick knife from under a trouser hem.

Cemal waits. Waits with the consuming pain of all that he failed to do in life: failed to find his father, failed to stand beside Halil, and failed to rescue Saliha. Waits, raging against his fate for that last one in particular. He notices Zaim remove the sunshades as he approaches. Then a few steps behind these glowing blue-green eyes, a slender white face and a pair of eyes in an identical colour. Staring at those eyes, Cemal misses Zaim's hand holding the knife stretch behind. There are more dogs than he had ever seen behind that slim white silhouette. Standing in total silence. Without letting Zaim sense their presence. The hand holding a glint of steel makes a move towards Cemal and is captured in the air by fangs. Jülide's feather-light hands pull Cemal away from the sound of growling as dozens of jaws lock on Zaim's body. He manages barely a second's scream, just before his throat is ripped out. In the descending twilight, his blood is a black spill over the stones. As the evening ezan rings out, Cemal vanishes from the earth before he knows what's happening.

Having found himself alive but underground, just when he was getting ready to die, Cemal was gently scratching his ankle as he listened to the sounds of the cave he had been pulled into. A slippery sensation climbed up to his hip. He shivered. And relaxed once it stopped; thinking he must have been imagining it. After all that terror, roads he'd covered in despair, frustration, and fear for his life, he was sitting silently in the dark.

'I didn't recognise you with short hair.' He bit his own fist. 'But oh, I have to go. I have to do something. I can't just sit here. I should've gone up first off anyway. I made a mistake. I thought we could save everyone.'

Jülide's face sensed the slow motion of the air in the cave. She listened to the rocks and the rotting, dead soil accumulated underfoot, and launched yet another premonition that visited her. 'Saliha Abla's alive. Don't worry, nothing will happen tonight. At any rate, you couldn't have done anything if you'd gone up to the Care Home on your own.'

'How do you know? How can you be sure?' He paused to listen. 'Oh, those dogs… I mean those dogs… how…'

'I don't know.' Putting her hand in her pocket, she drew out a small torch, no doubt picked up on an impulse in one of those town homes. She pressed the button. The cave was illuminated. 'Cemal Abi, let's go in deeper. They may find us here.'

'No. I have to get out.' He paused and scanned the walls around him in a daze. 'So these caves were real! I always thought it was just rumours.'

Jülide looked at him with eyes transformed into lucid pools in the upward beam. 'Come on.' They set off, occasionally crawling in the tunnels that narrowed before widening up again. A cramped passage led to a large hall now illuminated by the torch. There was a small puddle in the middle pierced by stalactites hanging down from the ceiling. Hourglass pillars, more like, slender middles connecting stalactites to stalagmites, glistening like gold in the light.

'The dogs were…' He stared at Jülide for a second before she switched off the light. 'I mean, how did you…'

'Like I said, I don't know. I don't know how it happened. Everything's so confused today.' A sob suppressed in the darkness echoed on the walls. 'It's like, the more powerless I feel, the more desperate, the more…' Feeling a large hand stroking her hair, she wept in silence for a little longer.

'Turn on the torch so we can find somewhere to sit.'

After wandering around the cavernous hall, the beam settled on a ledge set a little higher, where two tunnels opened. They climbed up and sat down on the ledge. There was an opening overhead, like a chimney.

'Can't they find us here?'

'I know all the routes. Even if they came here, they couldn't catch us. We can get away.' Jülide held up the weak light at the high ceiling and the clear puddle.

'I used to call it a palace. Used to come here to talk to my mother. Because it's underground. When you talk to yourself in a cave, it's like someone replies.' She pointed the beam at the clusters of rock on the floor. 'I thought this place would collapse when the Care Home was being built. Huge blocks kept falling from the ceiling.'

'You mean the Care Home is above us?'

'Uh-huh.'

'So it's these skinny pillars holding that enormous building?'

'Don't know.'

The torch wandered over the cracks in the thinner sections of the stalactites.

'Like they'd snap if you pushed.'

'So long as it doesn't come down over our heads.'

They paused. Jülide's head dropped to Cemal's shoulder. She was exhausted. Once again, Cemal was left alone with his mind torturing itself. A dreadful worry made it impossible to wait patiently; he imagined Saliha being tortured, or even amongst the disappeared. He would never have been able to keep still, keep seated, except for Jülide's head on his shoulder.

Saliha's face, gaze, hand taking a glass to his lips when he was sick, her voice.

'How are you?'

Cemal jumped at her voice.

'Are you all right?'

'Saliha!' His yell woke Jülide up, making her jump too.

'Oh, God, I must be losing my mind. I heard her voice.'

He was on his feet, having leapt up without thinking, his impatience and panic whipped up. Jülide hushed him. This time they heard another voice.

'There's not a frost gets a bitter aubergine, child. We've seen far worse in our time!'

'Muzaffer Abla!' whispered Jülide, delighted. They raised their heads to the chimney.

'How are you?'

'I'm fine. Well, not really; but they didn't rough me up too much. Weird how you can get hungry even at such a time, eh?' Cemal noticed his own stomach rumbling.

'What did they ask you? They kept saying to me, who do you know? What have you been planning? What are you gonna do?'

Unable to check himself as he listened to her, Cemal yelled at the top of his lungs. 'Salihaaa!' There was no reply, even though the final syllable kept echoing. Clearly his voice wasn't carried in the same way.

'Always the same thing. Always the same. Like, who's scared of them now! You were hit in the face.'

'Yes. Is it bruised?'

Tormented in his despair and anger, Cemal couldn't hold back. 'Sons of bitches!'

'But you look like you had a worse time.' Jülide's sad sigh caught on the tail of this sentence as it rang in the void.

'Not as bad as I'd feared. Not as bad as I'd heard.'

A silence followed, one that both Jülide and Cemal willed to end. Then Saliha's voice was heard again.

'My folks must be worried sick.' Pause. *'Cemal would have been too; the old Cemal, that is. He's probably still in bed, staring blankly at that wall. Poor fellow.'*

Something hot poured into Cemal, something like shame, like a revolt. He whispered in a barely audible voice. 'She thinks I could stay in bed when something like this happens to her. I'd have leapt out of my grave if I was dead.'

They could have been listening to two ghosts across an inaccessible divide. There was nothing they could have done, even if this anxious conversation were to be hacked by terrified screams. They could never make themselves heard, not even for one last time.

'What do you think they'll do to us?'

A bitter laugh from Muzaffer. *'Whatever the bloody hell they like. We're at their mercy now. That's what really hurts, anyway.'* A low moan. *'Whatever; ignore me. Go on, sleep a little. You won't feel your hunger. Not to mention, there's no telling when we can sleep again.'*

Saliha spoke for the last time. *'I hope help will come now. I hope we'll be rescued tomorrow. Good night.'*

'Good night, my darling,' said Cemal. The tracks of two tears coming down his cheeks were burning his neck. 'At least you're alive.'

'They're both alive, Cemal Abi. They'll both be rescued tomorrow.' Jülide's strangely convincing declaration was carved into the darkness.

'How do you know?'

'I just do. Something's going to happen. Something's going to happen tomorrow.'

Townsfolk whose windows faced the storage unit got no sleep that night, what with the lorry headlights, the noise of diggers and dumpers, and the traffic between the store and the sea. Evidently the diesel hoarded during the rubble operation earlier was readily available this time. The noise of the monstrous vehicles, which had been lying idle for weeks, reached the farthest homes. Their growling accompanied gunshots as the dogs were hunted. Every dog in Andalıç was shot on the spot that night. It was dawn by the time street sprinklers used seawater to wash off their blood and the blood pouring from the storage unit. Freshly purified, Andalıç was running west with a bloody trail in its wake when the sun caught it. But this time, the island wasn't alone in the sea. A massive freighter nearby was sniffing like a curious cat. The sleepless townsfolk jumped out of bed at the protracted blast of the ship's horn. The curfew did not stretch to their windows. They looked at the unladen black freighter, rust-coloured waterline riding high, and the moment they did, all those prohibitions were forgotten. A colossal ship that could take five hundred, maybe even a thousand. The Greek coast, which had been visible for a while, and had moved even closer since last night. Boarding the ship and going back home. That evening. Sending news home via the ship. Other ships. Acquaintances, relations, friends, food, piped water, work, order, salvation, prohibition-free streets, fearless conversations. All of Andalıç was on the streets in thin pyjamas. Some women had rushed out without their kerchiefs, never mind how much older they looked with the mark of salt-and-pepper neglect.

They watched the approach of the tender. Since the island was drifting, the skiff remained always just a stroke behind, and impatience grew. The island, which had eluded all help, wandering in the most deserted part of the crowded sea, confounded expectations, hopes and thoughts as it turned now east, now west, and forced upon its inhabitants a dull despair and the cruel permanence of a temporary existence, seemed to be on the verge of evading this possibility too, the possibility nearly forgotten after weeks of waiting. It was going to foster the terror, which would be recognised for what it was only after having swelled into such a colossus, having seeped undetected into the normal, the everyday, and the ordinary drop by drop. It has been approved instinctively, or accepted even if not approved, and thus thrived; it would reveal to these wretches who regarded themselves as its owners their own ugliness in all its nakedness, and wait for them to die in shock and remorse. A living thing, an angel of wrath; a treacherous bit of land torn away from the umbilical that had defined its identity, wandered idly in the seas, and hurled its folk into the lap of its greatest enemy. A place where one opened one's eyes to this world in a tiny room in one of those houses, a place one loved and was devoted to. Land. A place dictates made impossible to love.

The townsfolk gathered at the seafront, waiting in the yellow haze slicing through the horizon, wanting to forget how silently they had obeyed those regulations themselves. The town was in the shade.

The men disembarking from the tender were led up to the Care Home. Nothing more than a dark box, now that the sun had risen to the same height, it lit up from the inside with a yellow light. The townsfolk waiting with their eyes on the hill instead of the ship now thought they could see tiny human silhouettes behind the windows. It wasn't long before the sailors went downhill and boarded the tender with glum faces. As soon as the tender had been hauled up, the freighter's engines burst into life. The north-easterly that was beginning to crinkle the surface of the sea unfurled the blue and white flag. The ship went away.

ATTENTION, ATTENTION! THE DECISION NOT TO ABANDON ANDALIÇ, NO MATTER WHAT IT COSTS, HAS BEEN CONVEYED TO THE SAILORS. ANDALIÇ IS OURS AND WILL REMAIN OURS. WE SHALL NOT ALLOW A SINGLE HANDFUL OF OUR SOIL TO FALL INTO GREEK HANDS.

The streets of Andalıç rang out with marching tunes immediately after the announcement. As some people made for home, others remained glued to the seafront. The marches paused for a moment.

ATTENTION, ATTENTION! IT IS FORBIDDEN TO GATHER IN GROUPS OF MORE THAN FOUR!

Thinning out a little, the crowd moved away in groups of four. People stood a few steps apart in the street as they continued to wait in silence. Groups of four, some on their feet, others sitting on doorsteps, and some squatting on the ground, continued to wait, listening to the by now memorised marching tunes blaring out at full volume, without saying much, just nurturing an emotion with tiny gestures and brief sentences. So cornered was Andalıç, so denied a last way out, a final hope for rescue, that there was nothing for it but to show its teeth and attack its hunter. Do or die. Break through the siege or die. Armed men patrolling amongst the groups of four were met with defiant stares. Most were policemen from outside, appointed here, with no relations or friends in the town. They had shot before and they would do so again. The solicitor now appeared in one of the windows in line with the star on the flag. The marches paused again.

THERE WILL BE NO DISTRIBUTION OF BREAD OR PROVISIONS UNTIL EVERYONE HAS GONE HOME. THE ADMINISTRATION IS EMPOWERED TO TAKE THE BEST DECISION FOR OUR MOTHERLAND AND YOU. DISSENTERS WILL BE PUNISHED AS TRAITORS.

The groups of four lingered for a little longer until the impatience in the policemen's weapon-holding hands grew, and then they dispersed as if intimidated into submission. The crowd melted. Everyone retired home with their convictions, fears and courage, with a willpower they had not known for some time. This time, the marches didn't stop even after the evening call to prayer.

23

Jülide and Cemal emerged into the cool, fresh air in the darkest night of autumn after a whole day in the cave listening to Saliha and Muzaffer; the water they drank to suppress the rumbling of their stomachs stuck in their throats, knowing their loved ones would be denied even a sip. Patrolling footsteps echoed in streets beginning to fill with a desperate resolve. Most of the windows in Andalıç were dark with an unplanned, sensed preparation. Attributing it to sleep, the captors of the streets relaxed. But Andalıç had not slept well for a week. It sat in apprehensive darkness after prudently blowing out the gas lamp or the candle. Lightless, soundless nights; lonely, helpless nights when thoughts disrupted by the footsteps outside swelled with an anger that would only be visible when it exploded. Nights when approbation, tolerance, forced endurance, and patience grew thin, stretched by the weight hanging on the end, grew ever thinner into a single strand. The town, which had woven that extremely delicate, extremely fragile cobweb materialising unconsciously in conversations and plans, now anticipated this inevitable break. The languid night rippled like a still lake when Jülide and Cemal stepped into it, a fleeting ripple detected straightaway by the threads of that web. Wakeful people silently came to the windows.

'The dogs are gone,' said Jülide.

Cemal turned to her anxiously. 'You're so white, it's like you're radiating light. We'll be spotted at once.' Something black floated over them from the window above where they'd stopped to listen to the night. A long sleeve, long evening dress, too precious to throw away, preserved in a trunk for years, smelling of mothballs, moth holes for Jülide's skin to sparkle like stars. Cemal laughed at Jülide slipping into the dress of a woman who might well have become dust long since.

'Which means I need a tuxedo now.'

Their smiles altered the town's fear. A nervous desire to act replaced the indolence fostered by the instinct to flee.

Jülide and Cemal advanced, following the lights flashing on and off in windows. They didn't meet a single patrol. People looking out of the windows saw a white face floating in the air, towing a very tall shadow. Rahmi's door opened before them by itself. Without knocking. Rahmi had already put on his shoes. Down the narrow path flanked by spruce trees and wild rose and lavender bushes they went to the gate between two gardens. Rahmi dribbled a little lubricating oil over the old hinges. The gate swung open without complaint.

They sidled up to the large stone house that made a grim spectre with glowing whitewashed walls. A patter on the street drew the guards outside. Rahmi silently unlocked the door with a key he pulled out of his pocket and they all stepped in at once. Two simple villagers accompanying a princess of the darkness. They tiptoed all the way to the bedroom door. Rolling his jumper up, Rahmi untied the rope on his waist. All that could be heard in the house was the breath of sleep. Cemal pushed Jülide aside and slowly opened the door. He switched on the torch as Rahmi had followed him in. The beam found the bed. Feeling he couldn't face this scene, Rahmi had turned his head away. He heard Cemal's whisper.

'He's not here. It's only his wife.'

Zeliha's eyes were shut, but her eyelashes were moving. She parted her lips, getting ready to scream, triumphed over her fear and opened her eyes, but she couldn't see anything in the dazzling light. 'It's me, don't be scared,' said Rahmi. 'It was very short notice, otherwise I'd have given you a heads-up.'

She drew her hands away and the relief spreading on her face gleamed in the light. A skirt swished to the rear. 'Switch off the torch.'

Rahmi sat on the bed and held Zeliha's hand. 'We weren't going to do anything bad. Just tie him up and take him hostage. So they'd release those inside.'

'He didn't come home tonight. Some nights he doesn't.' Zeliha looked at Cemal, whom she knew by sight. 'You'll have a better idea where he is.'

The soft tap on the door made them all jump. Zeliha's blood draining from her face was all but audible amongst the heartbeats pounding in the room. 'It can't be Abdurrahman. He has a key. Wait here. Let me go see.'

The three people slinking into invisibility in the pitch-dark corners of the room pricked up their ears for the conversation outside the front door. But all they could hear until Zeliha's return was their loud heartbeats. Only one set of footsteps came back to the bedroom after the door was shut. 'They heard a noise outside and came to check if everything's all right.' She waited until her voice steadied. 'Are you out of your minds? How are you going to get out of here? D'you think they'd even let you in to see him? Do you have a deathwish or something?'

They sat in silence, waiting for the guards to settle and their attention to wander. There was the sound of movement in the pitch dark. 'No,' whispered Rahmi, 'You can't come.'

'Nah – I'm coming. Something's wrong. It was the girl's birthday today. He said he'd come in the evening. Then he told me when he came home at noon. Something happened. He'd argued with the Mayor. The bloke said to the people from the ship this morning, both countries are aware, we're getting help all the time, and our fella was angry because he'd refused help.' She fell silent for a moment. 'He should have come this evening.'

A racket outside, the threat of the darkness: they all held their breaths until the yowls of cats that followed straight after.

'He'd clashed with the District Governor, too. Because of the food in the store. Strange thing, the District Governor's gone missing, too. The generator broke down, and everything went rotten. What a waste.' The sound of a zip. 'I'm ready. He was ranting and raving at Abdurrahman. Not that my old man's likely to take it sitting down. Like they could take on the Commissioner!'

'Let them kill each other. The world would be shot of two pieces of filth. Like yours was as pure as driven snow. Who gave the order to shoot? The Mayor?' The deep wound underlying Rahmi's hatred caused a restless silence in the room. 'You're coming because you're worried about your husband, is that it?'

Zeliha's guilty silence had to be a habit, as neither of the strangers in the room thought it unusual. But it wasn't long before her voice rose in indignation. 'Who was it who told me to catch my husband with his mistress and divorce him?'

Following the lights that showed the way in perfect timing, they crossed dark streets and gardens redolent of dampened dry weeds as they approached Cemile's house. Jülide was totally invisible with one of Zeliha's black shawls on her head. They sat down in a corner to watch the house. There were no guards. Waited. Nobody came or went out. Jülide, now nothing more than a black motion in the blackness, left in silent steps. She walked around the house, and with a faint grating sound, a window with a loose latch opened under her gentle hand. They followed her into an empty room, stepping on a large stone and pulling themselves up. Rahmi slowly went out of the open door, mindful of the potential of creaking floorboards. Once he was convinced the coast was clear, he beckoned the others to the security of the stone floor.

It was deadly silent. They waited undecided in the darkness pierced by the torches of a passing patrol.

The two doors opening to the front of the hall had to lead to the kitchen and the sitting room. The closed door they were facing was the only one other than the room they had just left and the bathroom. Listening to the disappearing footsteps, they blinked into a decision, which slowly took shape in the dark.

Once the absolute silence alerted them to the night's will, Rahmi turned the handle gingerly. He let go of it briefly to wipe his sweaty hand on his trousers when the door swung open with a tremendous squeak and slammed against the wall. All four stood nailed to the spot, waiting for the calamity that was sure to come, but there still was no sound nor breath inside the house.

'Guess they're not at home,' whispered Zeliha.

They waited until the lumbering growl of a low-flying cargo plane had passed. Wrapping the torch in his shirt, Cemal held his finger on the button for a second and released it. The subdued reddish beam fell on the two bodies lying on top of each other in the bed.

'So out of it that they didn't even hear the door!' said Zeliha, her voice louder this time.

Seeing that the dark curtains were drawn, Cemal shut the door behind them and switched the torch on again without shading it. Abdurrahman lay on top of Cemile. Their shadows on the wall were moving. As Rahmi ran to the bed, rope in hand, Zeliha couldn't stop herself from shouting, 'Shame on you, you bastard!'

Jülide gently drew her back by the arm. 'Hold on, abla. Wait a minute.'

Rahmi tugged away the quilt, revealing Abdurrahman's naked back and a dark stain, which didn't look at all like a shadow. Cemile's half open eyes sparkled like glass right under his shoulder. The man and woman had been frozen in the middle of this intimate pose, intertwined limbs turned to stone. There were two holes in the Commissioner's back, one at the right and the other at the left. The boundary line between the bonded bodies was bright red. Rahmi covered them with the quilt straightaway. Zeliha, who had come here to catch her husband in the act and watch him get tied up and kidnapped, began to weep. 'They've killed him! So he did what he said, hope he dies! Oh my babies, they're fatherless now…'

His anger flaring again, Rahmi gave her shoulders a rough shake. 'Cut it out, hush! Whose father…' Remembering the dead behind him, he shut up.

This stage of the mission had sorted itself out. The Commissioner was out of action. The news reached all the sleepless folk at once. Something had altered in the consistency of the night; and action was now much easier. The black air between the houses quickened in a conductivity which sharpened all the senses. First, Cemile's front door opened the moment the patrol came by; making them stare, mesmerised by a white face floating in the air, then Cemal and Rahmi grabbed them, tied them up and gagged them. The doors of all Andalıç houses where unspecified preparations had been ongoing opened as one. Hands and feet endowed with extraordinary skill and speed captured the patrols in absolute silence, trussed them up and tossed them into nooks and crannies. Torches were seized before they hit the ground. Lights advanced down dark streets, turning to random doors and windows, moving from hand to hand. Of those who brought the menacing patrols to an end, some undertook to maintain a semblance of normality; others started climbing the hills in orderly rows like armies of ants.

When they reached the Care Home, every window was ablaze with light. Those inside could not see out because the windowpanes were like mirrors. Some were dozing at tables, others wandering sleepily, drinking tea to stay awake. Silent feet picked up the ten or fifteen men dispersed around the enormous building, one by one, like picking over a tray of rice. Not a single whisper was heard in Andalıç from the start to the end of this wordless operation.

There no longer was any obstacle to grabbing keys, descending down narrow staircases to the labyrinths in the basement, and one by one unlocking all those who had been missed so much, fretted over so much. A sip of water and a sugar cube for parched mouths, and drained bodies were carried up to the surface one by one.

On reaching the brightly-lit, long corridors stinking of urine, Cemal had no idea which way to go. So many doors to unlock after all that wait, all that going to the edge: it turned his stomach. He entered the strangely empty, windowless rooms in turn. Turning right or left at the end of every corridor, he felt as though he had come back to the same spot. It was all too much; his knees were shaking with it: this pointless snag when he thought he had reached that great joy, the scenes he faced in some cells, and the shrieks of people whose relatives had not survived.

'Saliha! Saliha!'

Every time his fingers left the cold touch of the grey metal doors, better suited to an asylum than a Care Home, he held his breath expectantly before letting it go in disappointment. Thronging footsteps, people coming from all directions, banging into his shoulders, the cells that seemed to just go on and on, shrieks of joy, grief-stricken moans, human ruins, those endless roaring questions turning in the mind… The strip lights overhead, the inability to recall which side of the fork he had come from on slamming into a wall at the end of a corridor and pivoting on his heels. His scream that is now nothing more than a murmur, ringing loudly only in his head.

'Saliha! Saliha!'

Pupils enlarged, sweat beading on his forehead, he paused in the middle of one of the increasingly quieter corridors. He saw the ceiling come down and the floor rise up to the ceiling. He put out a hand to find something to hold on to. His hand closed over the void. It went dark.

'Saliha! Saliha!'

'Yes?'

He opened his eyes. Saliha's head was encircled by the stars of Corona Borealis, shining twice as brightly in the dark night.

'You're here.'

'Yes.'

'We're outside.'

'Yes. You're very heavy. You'd fainted; we carried you out.'

Cemal breathed in the fresh scent of the cool earth under his head.

'I'm sorry.'

'Why?'

'For fainting.'

Laughing for the first time in days, Saliha dawdled in the smile, in this nostalgic reunion.

'Why apologise for something like that? You came; that's enough.'

'How could I not, though, Saliha? How could I not?'

Saliha stretched out beside him on the cool ground. Rested her nose against his neck.

'You were sick, Cemal. You were unwell. You weren't really yourself.'

'But I...'

'Never mind that now. Let's watch the stars. Without speaking. We can talk later.'

They kept watching until the sky grew lighter from one edge and the stars vanished in ones and twos. 'These are the only nice things in the world. The sky, the sea, trees. Things that don't talk.'

Saliha rose on an elbow and traced Cemal's eyebrows, cheekbones and lips with a finger. They looked at the horizon turning red in the east. A few faint cracks were heard in the silence. Turning back for a look, they saw one big crack widening in the scarlet light hitting the Care Home.

'You know it's hollow underneath? There's a cave below it. I heard your voice there.'

Just then, one of the lights in the Care Home came back on. A grey-haired man sat at a desk in a spacious room and tugged the mike towards himself. Put his specs on. Re-read the sheet of paper in his hands. The whine when he switched on the mike surrounded the whole of Andalıç. The vibration animated the cracks in the walls. The Mayor glanced around in fear. Leapt up to his feet, still clutching the sheet of paper, and made a move for the door. But the building was already disintegrating and collapsing. Like a colossal ship, it sank into its own dust with a thunderous crash.

Saliha and Cemal shot up and ran from the dust spreading everywhere. Once they had got far enough away, they stopped to look back, still panting.

'It looked so solid too! Like it would never collapse.'

'So it stood on hollow ground. We never knew, but it was hollow.'

'Yes. Yes. Amazing how it stood for so long. Did you see the Mayor at the last moment? That last moment...'

'So there is something called divine justice after all.'

'Now someone will come and rescue us. We'll go somewhere. We'll have a home together and start everything from scratch.'

Cemal gave her an ecstatic embrace. 'At long last. At long last.'

Saliha looked vacantly at the dusty stone pines to the rear. 'Like nothing had happened. From scratch... just like... just like...' A teeny, sad smile hung on the breath she exhaled.

The sun began to warm Andalıç's back once again. The north-easterly outlined the horizon on the sea. The bright blue dome of the sky rose over the ultramarine Aegean. Ships and helicopters approached the forgotten island to draw its inhabitants back into normal life.

All that remained in the festering wound was a tiny thorn.

The Author

Born 1970 in Bursa, ASLI BİÇEN holds an Honours degree in English Language and Literature from Boğaziçi University. Quite possibly Turkey's most acclaimed literary translator of English language fiction, as well as being a founder member of the Book Translators' Association, she has translated Dickens, Faulkner, Durrell, Rushdie, Fowles, Barnes, Berger, and Barth, to name but a few. She has published three novels to date; *Snapping Point* (*İnceldiği Yerden*, 2008) is her second. *Tehdit Mektupları*, 2011 (*Threatening Letters*) and *Elime Tutun*, 2005 (*Take My Hand*) are not as yet translated.

An enthusiastic gardener, Biçen is frequently found sourcing unusual perennials.

The Translator

Born in Izmir and a graduate of Robert College, Istanbul, FEYZA HOWELL holds a UK Honours degree in Graphic Design. Throughout a life in design, advertising, TV production, marketing, product management, and international business development, she has always drawn, written and translated. *Snapping Point* is her second translation for Istros Books; *The Highly Unreliable Account of the History of a Madhouse* by Ayfer Tunç was published in 2020.

Howell's backlist includes *Fiasco* by Coşkun Büktel (Nettleberry, 2008), *Madam Atatürk* by İpek Çalışlar (Saqi, 2013), *Unto the Tulip Gardens: My Shadow* by Gül İrepoğlu (Anthem, 2016), *Kurt Seyt & Shura* by Nermin Bezmen (CreateSpace, 2017), and *Forget Me Not* by Aslı Eti (Balboa, 2018). She lives in Berkshire, and swims, dances, and plays tennis for relaxation.

First publisahed in 2021 by
Istros Books
London, United Kingdom www.istrosbooks.com

First published as *İnceldiği Yerden* (Metis, 2008)

Cover design and typesetting: Davor Pukljak | www.frontispis.hr

ISBN: 978-1-912545-95-7

The publication of this book has been funded with the support of the TEDA programme of the Ministry of Culture and Tourism of Turkey.